Praise for Ann Charles'

DANCE OF THE WINNEBAGOS

"Ann Charles delivers laugh-out-loud dialogue, unforgettable characters, and pulse-pounding suspense."
~**Vicki Lewis Thompson**, NYT Bestselling Author

"Don't pick up one of Ann Charles' mystery romances if you have other pressing engagements. Ms. Charles writes with an engaging style that is demonstrably impossible to set down. Quirky characters, plenty of menace and skullduggery in abandoned old mines, and loads of good, clean sex hustles this story briskly on its way. Four stars and a passel of happy hoots for *Dance of the Winnebagos*."
~**John Klawitter**, Author of the prizewinning Hollywood Havoc action thriller novels

"Ann Charles crafts another hilarious romp of a mystery with quirky characters and laugh-out-loud dialogue."
~**Amber Scott**, Author of *Soul Search* and *Fierce Dawn*

"Hang on to your hats, Deadwood fans, because you're gonna love the Jackrabbit Junction series, too! If you love mystery with a little romance and a lot of humor, you're in for a wild ride with *Dance of the Winnebagos*."
~**Jacquie Rogers**, Author of *Much Ado About Marshals*

"The quips come fast and furious and the plot twists with more alacrity than a jackrabbit on the run from a coyote in this fast-paced humorous mystery/thriller/romance."
~**Susan Schreyer**, Author of *Death By A Dark Horse*

"... two thumbs up and a standing ovation for laughs, sighs, thrills, and an excellently crafted mystery."
~**Maxwell Cynn**, Thrillers Rock Twitter Reviews and Author of *The Collective*

What Authors and Reviewers are saying about
Ann Charles' 1st book in the Deadwood Mystery Series

N̶early Departed in Deadwood

"Full of thrills and chills, a fun rollercoaster ride of a book!"
~**Susan Andersen**, NYT Bestselling Author of *Burning Up*

"Smooth, solid and very entertaining, *Nearly Departed in Deadwood* smartly blends all the elements of a great read and guarantees to be a page-turner!"
~**Jane Porter**, award-winning Author of *She's Gone Country* and
Flirting with Forty

"Violet Parker follows a path blazed by Stephanie Plum (the heroine in Janet Evanovich's best-selling series), but she is no copycat. Violet is sexy and smart. Charles' mystery *Nearly Departed in Deadwood* is out of this world."
~**Sarah M. Anderson**, Reviewer for Romance Novel News

"I found myself laughing loudly at Violet's thoughts. Her sarcastic sense of humor is refreshing an unlike any of the books I've read within the last year. Ann's storytelling capabilities are tremendous." ***** FIVE STARS!
~**ParaYourNormal** Book Reviews

"Winner of the Daphne du Maurier award for Excellence in Mystery and Suspense, Ann Charles's debut novel, *Nearly Departed in Deadwood* will keep you glued to your chair even if you have to go to the bathroom."
~**Norman W. Wilson PhD**, Reviewer for Novelspot Book
Reviews

For more reviews, check out Ann's Deadwood website, as well as the reader reviews for her books on Amazon, Barnes & Noble, and Smashwords.

Dear Reader,

For once in my life, I'm going to keep something short and sweet—this note to you. My editor will be amazed.

I am often asked how I came up with the title of this book, DANCE OF THE WINNEBAGOS.

Once upon a time, I was playing hangman at work with one of my coworkers, who is also a very talented artist (that has nothing to do with this story, but she really is amazing and I like to crow about her, even when not mentioning her name). It was her turn to come up with a word, and she added a lot of spaces on the white board. After I landed two consonants and a vowel, the board looked like this:

T _ E _ _ _ N _ _ _ T _ E _ _ _ _ E _ _ _ _ _ E _

I was feeling pretty ambitious that day. I took one look at this puzzle and yelled, "The Dance of the Winnebagos!" (I know, the letters don't match up—I've never done well in spelling bees.)

My coworker laughed, hung my poor stick man, and then wondered what in the heck The Dance of the Winnebagos was.

I said, "I don't know, but it would make a great book title, don't you think?"

This game of hangman kick-started my brain. A weekend of plotstorming with my critique group fleshed out the story even more. Before I knew it, I had a fun cast, an intriguing mystery, and a book that practically wrote itself.

After I finished it, this book caught the interest of my agent. It was also a finalist in the Pacific Northwest Writers Association Literary Contest. But being that it's a mix of genres (my usual style), my agent and I couldn't find a home for it with a publishing house. Now, years later, it will finally have its chance in the spotlight, and I can't wait to share Claire's story with you.

I picked Arizona as the setting, because I lived there for a year and loved every minute of it. I picked a beagle to share the limelight with Claire, because I'm a fan of Snoopy.

For those of you who have read my Deadwood Mystery series, you may remember that Claire Morgan is Violet Parker's childhood neighbor, as well as Natalie's cousin. Harley Ford is Natalie's grandfather, too.

And now, this short note has become a little long, so I'll wrap it up with a tip of my cowboy hat.

Welcome to Jackrabbit Junction!

Ann Charles

www.anncharles.com

DANCE OF THE WINNEBAGOS

ANN CHARLES

ILLUSTRATED BY C.S. KUNKLE

DANCE OF THE WINNEBAGOS

Cover Art by C.S. Kunkle
Cover Design by Sharon Benton
Editing by Mimi the "Grammar Chick"

Printed in the United States of America
First Printing, 2011

ISBN: 978-1-940364-07-0

This book is for my dear ol' dad, who is my inspiration for Harley (aka Gramps).

A bit crusty, a little ornery, and a general smartass at almost every turn; fun-loving, wise-cracking, and always candy-carrying.

You let me "clean" your shop, "organize" your tools, and "serve" you mud pies. You let me drive you around the farm when I was twelve, race combines against you up and down the lane when I was sixteen, and race school buses with you in the wheat field when I was thirty-five.

You have always been there for me.

Your determination to succeed in life taught me to never give up on my dreams.

P.S. You were right about so many things, including Jolly Ranchers filtering out the pollutants.

Also by Ann Charles

Deadwood Mystery Series
Nearly Departed in Deadwood (Book 1)
Optical Delusions in Deadwood (Book 2)
Dead Case in Deadwood (Book 3)
Better Off Dead in Deadwood (Book 4)
An Ex to Grind in Deadwood (Book 5)
Meanwhile, Back in Deadwood (Book 6)

Short Stories from the Deadwood Mystery Series
Deadwood Shorts: Seeing Trouble
Deadwood Shorts: Boot Points

Jackrabbit Junction Mystery Series
Dance of the Winnebagos (Book 1)
Jackrabbit Junction Jitters (Book 2)
The Great Jackalope Stampede (Book 3)

Goldwash Mystery Series (a future series)
The Old Man's Back in Town (Short Story)

Dig Site Mystery Series
Look What the Wind Blew In (Book 1)
(Starring Quint Parker, the brother of Violet Parker from the
Deadwood Mystery Series)

Coming Next from Ann Charles

Jackrabbit Junction Mystery Series
The Rowdy Coyote Rumble (Book 4)

Deadwood Mystery Series
Title TBA (Book 7)

Acknowledgments

Each time I sit down to write my "thanks" to all involved in creating one of my books, I'm amazed at how many people there are to include. For me, writing has never been a solo endeavor. With each book, I add more readers and editors and helpers, who all play a role in making my stories sparkle. Let's see if I can fit all who helped me with DANCE OF THE WINNEBAGOS in the next couple of pages.

I always like to start with my husband, not because he keeps me and the kids fed and groomed, but because he helps me brainstorm, makes sure my male characters sound like real men, and picks me up and dusts me off every time I fall or get knocked down—which is often, since I'm a bit klutzy and should be banned from using sharp and/or pointy utensils.

Thanks to Mimi, aka the Grammar Chick, for your excellent editing help and for making me laugh every time we talk. Nobody can throw a peach like you, woman!

Thanks to my brother, Charles Kunkle, for hitting me in the head with a piece of gravel when we were kids. You knocked something loose, and I think all of the rattling around going on in my head makes my stories even funnier. Your awesome drawings of monsters will always inspire more stories.

As usual, a big thanks to Margo Taylor for all of your help in talking up my books, and to Dave Taylor for driving Margo here, there, and everywhere when needed. I also want to thank Judy and Frank Routt for your willingness to canvas Northwest Ohio and crow about my book to one and all there.

As always, I need to take a moment to thank all of those who have helped me over the years with critiques and read-throughs.

Thank you to the following for reading this book time and again and giving me the feedback I needed to make it shine: Wendy Delaney, Beth Harris, Jacquie Rogers, Sherry Walker, Marcia Britton, Mary Ida Kunkle, Amber Scott, Paul Franklin (for edits and research help), Joby Gildersleeve, Wendy Gildersleeve, Jody Sherin, Renelle Wilson, Marguerite Phipps, Denise Garlington, Stephanie Kunkle, Thea Taylor, Sharon Benton (the amazingly talented artist/hangman player), Susan Schreyer, Margo Taylor, Brad Taylor, Gigi Murfitt, Cheryl Foutz, Carol Cabrian, Sue Stone-Douglas, Cammie Hall, and Devon Chadderton.

Thanks to Kathy Thomas for all of those lunchtime walks when we brainstormed what happened next to Claire.

Thanks to all of my wonderful co-workers, from Washington to Colorado to Florida, who talk me up to family, friends, and anyone willing to listen. I couldn't ask for a more marvelous support group who cheer with me when things go well and laugh with me whenever I put my foot in my mouth. You guys are the best!

Thanks to the magnificent reviewers who offered their time to read and comment about this book; and to the amazing authors who gave me incredible quotes.

Thanks to the Deranged crew: Jacquie Rogers, Wendy Delaney, and Sherry Walker for over a decade of putting up with me.

Thanks to the columnists and crew at 1st Turning Point for years of teaching and sharing.

Thanks to Gerri Russell and Joleen James for bemoaning and cheering with me every week when we talk goals.

Thanks to the lovely and funny Amber Scott for making me laugh loudly and often, and for sharing war stories and advice every step of the way! Buy yourself another song from me.

Thanks to my friends and fans for your constant support and tireless help in telling the world about my quirky books. You all make me feel like the luckiest girl around!

Thanks to Lee Lofland for your help with bone details.

Thanks to Vickie Haskell for the tons of shipping help and sharing dirty jokes while doing it.

Thanks to Arlene Psomas for all of the bouquets of flowers and words of encouragement along the way.

Thanks to Dale Kunkle for teaching me how to play Euchre and chewing me out in your loving way when I threw the wrong card.

Thanks to my siblings and step-siblings, and all of your wonderful and supportive spouses, for being there for me year after year as I struggled to reach this point in my career. You never gave up either.

And finally, as always, thanks to Clint Taylor, for being a worse driver than I was back when we were just learning. Only you could have run over that gas can in an otherwise empty pasture. So many great memories!

DANCE OF THE WINNEBAGOS

Chapter One

If Claire Morgan had known she'd be chaperoning a senior citizen sock hop, she wouldn't have given up smoking. Yet here she was, stuck in Jackrabbit Junction, Arizona, with an ornery old man, his smartass dog, and a parade of blue-haired babes.

"Gramps, your dog found a bone!" Claire yelled, staring at the foot-long bone clenched in the jaws of her grandfather's beagle.

Harley Ford stepped out from behind a half-dead cottonwood tree, zipping up his faded Levi's. "Damned prostate. I have faucets that leak more." He shuffled towards Claire. "What'd you say?"

Claire wrinkled her nose. After traveling together for three days in his well-used Winnebago Chieftain, she'd learned everything about him from the pattern of his snoring to the number of prunes he needed to maintain regularity. He'd left his modesty in Colorado, and she'd lost most of her sanity long before they had crossed the Arizona state line and pulled into the Dancing Winnebagos R.V. Park.

"I said Henry found a bone." She squatted next to Henry and examined the broken end of the white fragment hanging from his black lips. "It's pretty chewed up already."

Gramps stood behind Henry. "Is it made of gold?"

What kind of a question was that? "Of course not."

"Then why get your knickers all bunched up over it?"

Ignoring his sarcasm, Claire tried to wrestle the bone from the dog's teeth. Henry growled and dug his back paws into the sand. He yanked the slobber-covered bone free of her grip, ran several feet away, plunked down next to a prickly pear cactus, and watched her with the shaft still locked in his jaws. She wasn't sure who was harder to live with, Gramps or his spoiled dog.

Gramps snorted. "As soon as you're done playing with the dog, can we get the hell out of here?"

"What's your hurry? Got a hot date tonight?"

"That's none of your business."

Grinning, Claire stood and wiped Henry's slobber onto her jean shorts. "I wouldn't be here with you if it wasn't my business."

"I told you I don't need a chaperone."

"And I told you that Mom put the squeeze on me. She's expecting a call tonight with the first of my weekly reports on your love life."

Just the thought of hearing her mother's voice made Claire's fingers itch to hold a cigarette. Instead, she dug a stick of cinnamon-flavored gum from her pocket. Three weeks now without a single cigarette. God, she missed nicotine. Even more than sex.

"If I wanted my private life spilled to your mother, I'd write a story for the *National Enquirer*." Gramps crossed his arms over his chest. "The nosey busybody."

Henry trotted past Claire, obviously teasing her. She lunged for the bone, but the dog sidestepped her and bounded away. "Would you tell your damned dog to sit still for a second?"

Gramps smirked. "It's more fun to watch you chase him."

Claire took a deep breath, inhaling the sweet smell of sun-baked greasewood trees. She wouldn't kill the little bastard. Not for a bone.

"With your cheeks rosy like that," Gramps said, "you remind me of your grandma when she was your age."

A warm breeze rustled the leaves of the cottonwood overhead. Claire's mind flashed to an old black and white picture hanging on Gramps's wall back in Nemo, South Dakota. A young version of her grandma stood in the shade of the same tree, only its canopy had been full then.

"She sure loved this spot," Claire said, remembering Gramps and her trip six years earlier to this corner of the state on a chilly fall day. Her throat ached at the memory of him sprinkling her grandma's ashes around the base of the tree.

"She called it her own little Utopia." Gramps's tone was scratchy around the edges. "She'd drag me here for a picnic every damned day while we were staying at the R.V. park."

The man hated eating off a blanket. *Ah, true love.* Claire smiled. Some people found it; others ran screaming from it.

She fell into step behind him as he hiked back toward the car.

"Your grandmother had a way of making life interesting." He looked at Claire over his shoulder. "She could turn a funeral into a carnival. I doubt I'll find another like her, but a man needs a woman. Especially an old man." He whistled for Henry.

"I understand, Gramps. But did you and your Army buddies have to round up a harem to find one?" Why couldn't he just get another dog?

"It's nice to have choices."

"Yeah, but there are better, less flea-market-like ways to meet women." She never should've shown him how to use the Internet. He'd become the king of the senior-set chat rooms.

Henry trotted up to Gramps and dropped the bone in

his outstretched palm. She could've sworn the dog snickered at her before dashing ahead.

"Just keep out of my way and we'll get along fine for the next month." Gramps wiped the slobber-covered bone on his pants before handing it to Claire. "And remember the rules."

"I know." She gripped the bone. As the trail widened, she upped her pace until she walked next to him. "Rule number one: When you have a lady friend over, I should make myself scarce for a half-hour—"

"An hour," he blurted, then glanced at her. "My equipment is a bit rusty these days. Getting the gears all greased takes—"

"Ahhh!" She waved the bone in front of her. "Stop before I lose my Twinkies."

"Fine, smartass. Just make sure you stay lost until I give you the sign that the coast is clear."

She nodded as her gaze locked on the bone. Her footsteps slowed. "This kind of looks like a femur." The marrow was long gone. She measured the thickness with her finger.

Gramps stopped. "Child, it's hot, I'm thirsty, and there's a six-pack waiting in the fridge. Quit playing CSI."

She ran her fingertips along the length of the bone. Its smooth hardness was cracked and bleached from the sun. The other end was broken and rough with the gnaw marks she'd noticed earlier.

"Claire, are you listening? Because heatstroke is knocking."

"Look at the diameter. It's as thick as Mr. Bones's femur," she said, remembering the male skeleton from her Human Anatomy 101 class.

"Sweetheart, I know you've taken more college classes in the last decade than most people take in a lifetime, but you're making something out of nothing. It's just an old bone."

"No." Her heart galloped. "This isn't just any old bone." She thrust it in front of Gramps's pale blue eyes. "It's a human leg bone."

Chapter Two

Saturday, April 10th

W ell, well, well, look who we have here," Sophy Wheeler-Martino said, cranking up her southern drawl. "Richard Rensburg, just the man I hoped to see this morning."

She leaned her hip against the booth table in Wheeler's Diner where the two-month-new vice president of the Cactus Creek Bank sat. Sophy had wanted a moment alone with him, and with the breakfast rush over that moment had come.

Pots clanged in the kitchen as the first shift cook cleaned up the breakfast-prep mess. Charley Pride sang, "Kiss an Angel Good Morning," from the boom box sitting next to the cash register. The smell of grease filled the air, just as it had every morning for the past forty years that Sophy had wiped down the lunch counter.

Plucking her compact from her apron pocket, she flipped it open and added a fresh coat of glossy Cherry Burst lipstick to her full lips. Not a single wrinkle. The Botox therapy had erased years of hard time under the Arizona sunshine.

She winked at Rensburg over her mirror. "When was the last time you did more than just speak big, fancy banking words with that tongue, sugar?"

Rensburg stared as she added a second coat to her upper lip, his steaming cup of coffee halfway to his mouth.

A blush spread from his neck to his silver sideburns.

Men were so easy to play. She snapped her compact shut and dropped it and the lipstick into her pocket.

"You're a big man in the county now." Bending over the Formica table, she graced Mr. Vice President with an R-rated view of her 36 double D's. "And I sure do like *big* men."

Coffee sloshed over the edge of his cup. "Uh, Ms. Mart—"

"Call me Sophy, darlin'." The booth's vinyl seat creaked as she slid next to him. She reached under the table and walked her fingertips up his inseam. "And I'll call you ... Dick."

She watched him blink rapidly, his mouth opening and closing.

Easy, easy, easy.

"Now," she whispered, her lips nearly brushing his ear. "Did I hear you say something on your phone about foreclosing on Ruby Martino's loans?" She pressed her breasts against him.

His breathing grew more ragged the further north her hand traveled. "You know that's private—"

She dragged her fingernails across his zipper.

"—business." He slopped more coffee onto the table.

"Is it true?" She pressed harder.

"Uh ..." Wheezing, he shifted so that the bulge in his polyester-blend pants rubbed against her hand. "Yes, it's true."

She rubbed back. "And what was that you said about her nephew?"

"He's coming to ... to determine the value of her ..." He closed his eyes and gulped. "Her mines."

Damn! The last thing she needed right now was someone nosing around inside those mines. "When?"

"Today."

"For how long?"

He leaned his head back against the sun-faded orange cushion. "Three weeks."

"Why? Is the bank going to take them away, too?"

"No." Sweat beaded his upper lip. "The mining company wants the copper in them."

So, Ruby was going to sell the mines in order to pay her debts. Sophy gritted her teeth. Time was running short.

The bells on the diner's glass door jingled. Sophy glanced up as three members of the Company's third-shift mining crew trickled in for their "usuals." She gave the vice president's crotch a final squeeze and slipped out of the booth.

The banker's eyelids snapped open. He frowned. "But—"

She hiked her short skirt even higher and flashed him a complimentary glimpse of her black garter snaps and straps. "Thanks for the dirt, darlin'." She caught a whiff of pine-scented aftershave as she kissed his smooth cheek. "Give Judy and the kids my love."

With a wiggle of her hips, Sophy strutted toward the three miners leering at her from the corner booth. Come hell, high water, or some meddling nephew, she was going to find that damned loot.

———⟡———

"Damn it, Gramps!" Claire shoved open the Winnebago's screen door and stormed out into warm, mid-morning sunshine. "Why'd you shut off my alarm?"

Harley, wearing a pair of green Bermuda shorts and a yellow shirt, leaned against Mabel, the 1949 cobalt blue Mercury he had hauled from South Dakota. He frowned as Claire approached. "I thought you could use your beauty sleep. Look at you." He pointed at the tear in the knee of her jeans. "This is no way for a respectable young lady to dress." He yanked her red Mighty Mouse baseball cap off her head.

"I'm not here to impress anyone." She lunged for the hat, but he held it out of reach. Despite the frustration bubbling inside her, she giggled at the mirth dancing in his eyes. "Give me that. You're going to make me late for work on my first day."

A wolf-whistle sounded from behind her.

Claire whirled around. Manuel Carrera, one of Gramps's Army vet buddies, lounged in a lawn chair in the shade of Gramps's Winnebago. The other two Army cronies, Chester and Art, must not have rolled into the R.V. park yet.

"Well." Claire grinned. "Look what the coyotes left on our doorstep last night." She hadn't seen Manny in years. His hair had more salt than pepper in it now, but he still looked like an older version of Jimmy Smits.

Manny pushed to his feet and sauntered toward her, his machismo thicker than the aroma of Old Spice that burned the back of her throat when he hugged her. "*Buenos dias*, my love bunny," he said in a soft Mexican accent, squeezing her against his side.

Claire glanced down to make sure she'd closed the top button of her shirt. Harmless as a newborn puppy, Manny lived for two things: women and sex.

"Keep your hands off my granddaughter, Carrera," Gramps warned jokingly, playing the age-old game he and Carrera had started decades ago. He pulled a new cigar from his shirt pocket.

"How old are you now, Manny?"

"Sixty-nine." He waggled his eyebrows at her.

"Oh, dear God." She elbowed him lightly in the chest. "Manny, you're hopeless."

"Hopelessly in love with you, *mi amor*."

Something over Claire's shoulder suddenly caught Manny's eye. He let out another wolf-whistle. Claire turned to see what had distracted him and nearly had her retinas fried. Who in the hell wore a rhinestone-studded running bra in the desert? The thing glittered like a disco ball on the surface of the sun.

With copper red hair and Hollywood sunglasses, the woman waved at Claire's grandpa as she strutted along the campground drive. "Hi, Harley." Even her fingernails sparkled. Purple hot pants molded her very full bottom.

Claire shot Gramps a glare. "That's why you shut off my alarm."

Gramps had the decency to blush. "What? How was I supposed to know she'd be out exercising this morning?"

Claire snatched her cap from him. "She looks like trouble."

"*Ay yi yi!*" Manny moved up next to them and leaned against the car, his gaze still glued to the woman's extra-voluptuous backside. "I can't wait to see where else she sparkles."

Listening to Manny's comments for the next month was going to warp her mind. Claire shoved the cap down on her head. "How many women did you guys line up to meet you here?"

Gramps shrugged, chewing the end off his cigar and spitting it on the ground next to him. "Enough to be picky."

"Geez-Louise, I've landed in the middle of a senior citizen orgy." She rooted in her shirt pocket, needing a cigarette, and pulled out a squished York Peppermint Pattie.

"At least you're not sitting in another useless college class." Gramps grabbed the pack of matches sitting on Mabel's dashboard. "Maybe you'll actually learn something here."

"Hey," Claire mumbled through the chocolate and

peppermint goo in her mouth. "An education is—"

Something bumped against her kneecap. She looked down to find Henry staring at her with his tail wagging and the femur he'd found yesterday hanging out of his mouth. "What's he doing with my bone?"

"He found it," Gramps said.

"Oh, really? In the cupboard over the fridge?"

Gramps squinted as he lit his cigar. "He's a beagle," he said out of the side of his mouth. "They're good hunters."

"I don't think he should be playing with that bone." Claire reached for the femur. Henry zipped just out of her reach. *Damned dog!* She glanced at her watch. Shit, she was officially late.

"Why not? Dogs are born to play with bones."

"I told you last night, that's not just any old bone. Besides, I want to take a closer look at it when I have more time. That might be important evidence in some murder case."

Gramps rolled his eyes. "Girl, when are you gonna learn? Don't go looking for trouble. It'll find you soon enough. It always does."

"Thanks for your vote of confidence," she said with a grin, standing on her tiptoes to kiss his scruffy jaw. "I have to go. Don't let Henry eat that bone." She punched Manny lightly on the bicep. "And don't let Manny talk you into skinny dipping again."

"We don't do that, anymore," Manny said seriously, and then ruined it by winking. "At least not in the daylight."

Good. That would be one less trip to the county jail this spring.

With a salute goodbye, Claire did her best impression of jogging all the way to Ruby's General Store.

The screen door squeaked shut as she stumbled inside, her breath coming in short bursts. The knife-like stitch under her ribs reminded her that surfing channels with a remote control was not really a cardiovascular workout.

She skidded to a stop at the sight of a hammer and pipe wrench lying on the counter next to the cash register. "Ruby?"

"Shitfire!" A woman's voice, laced with a southern drawl, came from the doorway in the back corner of the room.

Claire slipped down an aisle shelved with potato chips. She rounded a life-size cardboard display of Elvis holding a can of Diet Coke and stopped in the doorway. The R.V. park's owner, Ruby Martino, sat on the floor with her back against the toilet. Her curly, reddish blonde hair was tied back in a ponytail, which emphasized her slender, freckle-dotted neck.

"Rough night on the town?" Claire asked her new boss, grinning.

"I wish." Ruby's green eyes flashed. She threw a pair of vice grips across the yellowed linoleum. "Damned sink!

This place is fixin' to crash down around my ears. Soon there won't be anything left for the bank to take."

Claire's grin wilted. What did Ruby mean about the bank? Claire opened her mouth to ask, then closed it. It wasn't really any of her business. In a month, she and Gramps would be driving back home.

She lifted her gaze to the sink where a rust stain ran from the faucet to the drain. "Looks like you have a leaky faucet."

"That's dripped for years," Ruby said with a dismissive wave. "But the drain plugged up last week. I figured I'd fix both in one swoop. But these damned nuts won't budge."

Those *damned nuts* looked stripped. "Mind if I have a try?" Thanks to Gramps's contractor business, Claire and her cousins had tinkered with plumbing since their teens.

"Be my guest, honey." Ruby handed Claire the flashlight and moved out of the way.

Squatting in front of the sink, Claire shined the light under the basin. "Your bolts are rusty."

Ruby groaned. "Story of my life."

"You need a plumber."

"Can't afford one. They won't take minimum wage."

Claire ignored the warning bells ringing in her head. Ruby's problems weren't hers. "Tell you what." She wiggled further under the sink. "Bring me your toolbox and that pipe wrench I saw on the counter, and I'll see what I can do here."

An hour later, Claire walked out of the bathroom wiping her hands on her jeans. She paused next to Elvis, catching the faint sound of Ruby's voice over the buzz of the florescent lights overhead. A green curtain hung in an archway behind the counter. The wood floor creaked under Claire's feet as she inched up to the curtain. She hesitated, her nose brushing the cloth. The smell of stale dust and varnished wood clung to the material. "Ruby?"

"Come on back, Claire," Ruby called.

Claire pushed through the curtain and stopped dead. She'd stepped back in time to 1977. Orange shag carpet covered the floor from one lemon yellow cinderblock wall to the next. A pea green couch sat below a photo of a ten-point buck; two brown bean bag chairs cluttered the far corner next to a glass-front cabinet stuffed to the gullet with antique beer cans.

Ruby, with the phone to her ear, stood at a long walnut bar with a brass foot rail. Four barstools with purple velvet-covered seats framed the bar. Beer steins lined the wall behind it.

"I know all about the deadline, Mr. Rensburg," Ruby said, each word terse, her shoulders rigid. "You'll have your damned money by the end of the month!" She slammed the receiver down.

Claire cleared her throat. "I unclogged the drain." She waded through the thick shag toward the bar, pretending she hadn't overheard the end of Ruby's conversation. "And installed the new faucet."

Ruby glared at the telephone, her forehead furrowed.

"Are you okay?" Claire asked against her better judgment.

"No. Yes." Ruby took a deep breath. "I'm fine. It's just that ever since Joe died ..." She looked at Claire and hesitated.

Yesterday, when Claire had applied for the job, she'd learned that Ruby's husband, Joe Martino, had died last year from a stroke. Ruby hadn't offered any more details, and Claire hadn't asked.

Ruby shook her head. "Never mind."

"It must be tough running the R.V. park on your own."

Ruby narrowed her eyes at Claire for several seconds, then nodded. "It would be much easier if Joe hadn't left me with a heap of bills and just a handful of money to pay them."

That explained Ruby's comment about the bank.

"But if I can sell those mines and the surrounding valley that he left me," Ruby continued, "I might be able to save this place."

"You mean the two mines up on the hill out back?"

"Yep, and the two on the other side of the hill just off County Road 588."

Claire almost choked on her tongue. Her grandma's desert grave was on the other side of the hill just off County Road 588. "Do you have someone interested in buying them?"

"The mining company up the road." Ruby slipped behind the bar and pulled a can of Coke from a mini-fridge. "If you guys came through Tucson, you passed their flagship mine after you left the Interstate."

Claire had seen it all right. It was hard to miss the gaping open-pit mine as long as three football fields and almost as wide. Twenty years ago, when she'd come here as a teenager, there'd been a hill there, covered with black-eyed Susans and red skyrocket flowers.

The gears in Claire's mind spun. If that company bought the mines, it would gut the hillside, including her grandma's sacred valley below. She'd seen the same thing done in the Black Hills.

Personal stance aside, didn't Ruby realize how much this would affect her long-term income? Who would want to camp next to the boom of regular blasting and the constant rumble of those huge quarry trucks?

"Where'd you learn how to fix sinks?" Ruby cracked open the soda pop.

"I, uh ... I worked for my grandpa during the summers. He was a contractor before he retired." Claire hid her alarm behind a smile as she grabbed the can of pop Ruby offered. "He taught me and my cousins all kinds of things about plumbing and carpentry." She sipped the ice-cold cola.

Ruby's eyes lit up. "How do you feel about working outside instead of behind the counter? I could use help fixin' this place up for the spring bird watching season."

"Sure," Claire said without hesitation. Working outside would give her time alone—time to figure out how Ruby could pay off her debts without selling the mines and surrounding valley. Maybe, just maybe, she could come up with a way to stop that mining company from staking its claim on her grandma's burial ground.

⊷⊷⊷ ✦ ⊶⊶⊶

"Who the hell is that?" Mac Garner tapped the brakes and slowed his pickup to a crawl. He stared through the front windshield. The drone of Paul Harvey's voice from the speakers faded.

Twenty feet in front of him, a woman pranced over the bridge that led into the Dancing Winnebagos R.V. Park. With long, black hair and an ass hard enough to make quarters bounce, she was decked out in stiletto heels, a silver miniskirt, and a hot pink bustier.

Mac inched up behind her. The right side of his front bumper drew level with her hips as she reached the other side of the bridge and stepped onto the shoulder. He rolled down the passenger side window, craning his neck to see if her front was as curvy as her back. His gaze landed on the white Persian cat she hugged between her full, bouncing breasts; Dolly Parton had nothing on this lady.

The cat glared at him, a piece of sagebrush tangled in the red bow ringing its neck.

"Howdy! Wanna ride?" he asked, shoving his field books, hard hat, and work gloves behind the pickup seat to make room for her. He'd been doing a lot of solo fieldwork down by Rio Rico for the last few months. Sharing the cab with a pair of shapely legs would be a treat.

"No, thanks, sweetheart." Her voice crackled, like a poorly tuned AM radio.

Mac glanced up at her face for the first time and barely bit back a horror-filled shout. Deep wrinkles criss-crossed her forehead and cheeks, and furrowed her bright pink lips. The woman had at least thirty years on him.

His smile flash-frozen on his lips, he rolled up the window, hit the gas, and didn't look back until he'd skidded to a stop in front of his Aunt Ruby's General Store. Only then did he peek in his rearview mirror and watch as the lady sashayed out of view around the side of the store.

Shoving open his door, he scrambled out and took the front porch steps two at a time. "Ruby!" He marched past the cash register and peered down each of the four aisles. "Ruby, where are you?"

"In the rec room," his aunt hollered.

Mac pushed through the curtain. "You'll never guess what I—"

He stopped at the sight of a brunette sitting on a barstool in front of Ruby's bar. As he stared at her, she pulled her red cap low over her brows. Mighty Mouse smiled back at him. Mac's eyes narrowed. Ruby didn't usually invite customers into her favorite hangout.

"Hi, honey," his aunt said, drawing his gaze away from the other woman to where Ruby stood behind the bar. "How about a cold one?"

"No, thanks." He shot Ruby a what-the-hell look.

"Suit yourself." Ruby nodded toward her guest. "Mac, say hello to Claire. She's my new handywoman."

Handywoman? Mac crooked his head a little, trying to see under the red brim of her cap. She looked about thirty. "Nice to meet you."

Claire's dark eyes looked him up and down. "Same here." She slid off the stool and set her pop can on the bar.

"Thanks for the drink, Ruby. I'll get started on the fence out back." Her voice sounded soft, musical, with a hint of breathiness. Her blue jeans rode low on a pair of nicely curved hips; the strip of fair skin peeking out above her waistband looked smooth to the touch.

With a nod his way, she walked past him and breezed through the curtain. The subtle scent of watermelon trailed in her wake.

Mac sidled up to the bar and picked up the Coke can, still warm from Claire's touch. "Where'd you dig her up?"

"She's fixin' to stay for a month and needed a job."

"Did you check out her background?"

"Nope, and I don't plan to. Her grandfather's been visiting every spring since before I took over the park."

"That doesn't clear her from a history of chain gangs."

"She's as trustworthy as the next person." Ruby leaned her elbows on the bar, her forehead wrinkling. "Are you feelin' okay?"

"Sure." *Hell, no!*

He was supposed to be on his way to China to see the one wonder of the world that had always captivated him—the Great Wall. Instead, here he sat in Jackrabbit Junction, Arizona, with the task of determining the value of his aunt's mines in three short weeks. If it had been anyone else needing his help, he'd have recommended a bankruptcy attorney.

Not that his aunt had asked for help. She'd sooner cut off her left thumb.

Doubt darkened Ruby's eyes. Mac switched subjects. "What's the story on the dame who looks like *Miami Vice* from the back and the *Golden Girls* from the front?"

"Which one?"

He did a double-take.

Ruby grinned. "I've had strange-looking women of all shapes and sizes pouring in here every day for the last week."

"And you just up and hired one of them as a handyman?"

"*Handywoman.*" She patted his forearm. "Don't fret, you'll have your old job back before you know it."

"It's not my old job I'm worried about."

Her blush confirmed she'd caught his meaning. "There's nothing to worry about here." Ruby broke eye contact and brushed some nonexistent crumbs off the bar. "I appreciate you taking time off work to come all the way out here, but like I told you on the phone, I have it all under control."

Receiving daily calls from bill collectors was not Mac's idea of "under control." But if Ruby ever found out he'd canceled his vacation to come help her, she'd knock him over the head with a frying pan.

The air conditioner on the wall across the room rattled to life. When the rattling didn't stop, he glanced over. "Is that thing giving you trouble again?"

"Of course. It gets all uppity every time the temperature reaches eighty degrees." Ruby marched over to the duct-taped unit and flat-handed it near the vent. The clattering stopped. "That'll teach it."

Mac grinned. "You should ask your new *handywoman* to fix it."

She turned to him, hands on hips. "Maybe I will. And maybe I'll have her show you a thing or two while she's at it."

The spark in her eyes made him chuckle. After a year of hard times for his aunt, it was good to see a glimpse of her old, feisty self. "Where's Jess?" Without his fifteen year-old cousin jabbering about her latest heartthrob, the place was funeral-parlor quiet.

"Babysitting. She'll be ba—" The store's screen door squeaked. "A customer." Ruby headed toward the curtain.

"Listen, I'm glad to have you here for the next few weeks, but I'm sorry you had to come to my rescue." She stopped long enough to drop a kiss on his cheek.

Mac crushed the Coke can in his hand. If he couldn't help her sell those mines for a good price, he'd be sorry, too.

Chapter Three

Holy crap! What crawled in here and died?" Claire plugged her nose to keep from gagging as she tiptoed into the shadow-filled tool shed.

Overhead, the tin roof clicked and clinked as the metal expanded from the heat of the mid-afternoon sun. The floor boards creaked under her shoes. Daylight peeked through the cobwebs clinging to the dirty window, outlining a workbench buried under a mound of rags. The previous handyman must not have subscribed to *Good Housekeeping*.

Searching for the drill Ruby had mentioned, Claire stepped over a weed-whacker with its nylon thread guts spilling out, then skirted a generator with a dented gas tank. She waded toward the workbench, lifted a handful of rags, and gasped.

A dead rat lay belly-up on top of the remaining rag pile. As she grimaced, its stomach hiccupped and boiled. The wet, sticky sound of something crawling through slime held her captive, then two maggots wiggled out from between the rat's gaping jaws.

"Ugh," she groaned and gulped, dropping all but one of the rags. She pinched her nostrils tighter. Shielding her hand with the cloth, she reached for the long, hairless tail.

A scream rang out right behind her.

Claire nearly rocketed out of her tennis shoes. She whirled around to see a teenage girl with red curly hair and a freckle-covered nose standing two feet away. The girl's gaze was locked on the rat.

Who in the ... Her thought was cut off by another piercing scream. Ears ringing, Claire grabbed the girl's arm and dragged her out of the tool shed into the bright sunlight. Only then did she notice the plastic tumbler filled with an opaque liquid in the kid's hand.

"Take a deep breath," Claire told the girl, whose face had turned a ghoulish shade of gray.

"Did you see that ... that," the girl crinkled her little, upturned nose, "thing?"

"It's just a dead rat." After several frog dissections in *Ecology—Introductory Biology*, dead animals had dropped several levels on Claire's *Disgusting Shit* scale. But maggots still reigned at the top.

"Here." The girl shoved the tumbler toward Claire. "Ruby told me to give this to you."

"What is it?" Claire asked as she took the cool, sweaty cup. She didn't trust strangers offering drinks, especially teenagers. Besides, Gramps and Manny were not above practical jokes.

"Lemonade." The redhead shot a dismayed look at the tool shed while brushing her hands on her pink cotton shirt.

Claire sniffed the liquid. It smelled like lemonade. She took a sip, tasting sweetened citrus, then gulped down half of it.

Hands in the pockets of her hip-hugger shorts, the girl squinted up at Claire. "Were you actually going to pick that thing up?"

Claire wiped her mouth with the back of her wrist. "Maybe."

"Are you some kind of freak who plays with dead animals?"

While most of Claire's family considered her to be a few cherries short of a fruitcake, that didn't mean she had to take any crap from this kid. She glared at the girl. "Who are you?"

"I'm Ruby's kid."

That explained the hair and freckles. "You have a name?"

"Jessica, but my friends and family call me Jess." She batted her eyelashes and offered Claire a want-to-be-my-friend-too smile.

Claire stepped back. The last thing she needed was Ruby's kid shadowing her. She was having enough trouble keeping her nose out of Ruby's business as it was.

"Thanks for the lemonade, *Jessica*." She handed back the tumbler. The hunt for the drill could wait. With a dismissive nod, she strode toward the fence she'd been working on all morning. If she was lucky, Ruby's daughter would take the hint and go home.

Jessica jogged up beside her. "What are you doing?"

Claire didn't slow her pace. "Working."

"Did you come with one of those crazy old ladies?"

"Nope."

"With one of the old dudes?"

"Yep." Claire grabbed several nails from the pouch of her tool belt and bent over a cedar plank that straddled two sawhorses.

"Do you know the old dude with the tight car?"

Tight? Did that mean cool? Either way, Gramps was the only one with a car. "He's my grandpa."

"Sweet! Does he ever let you drive it?"

Claire nodded. She positioned a nail's tip against the wood.

"You think he'd let me drive it?"

Sure, when Tyrannosaurus Rex roamed the Earth again. "Probably not."

"Bummer. Ruby never lets me drive her truck, either. She never lets me do anything fun."

Claire paused, the hammer raised. She'd have to be deaf to miss the undercurrent of animosity toward Ruby in

Jessica's voice, not to mention the fact that she kept calling her mom by her given name. *Stay out of it*, a voice in Claire's head warned.

"Where's your grandma?" Jessica asked.

"Dead." That sounded a bit too harsh even to Claire's ears. Maybe she should tone it down.

"Mine is, too." The girl sounded excited, as if she and Claire shared the same birthday.

Claire sighed and pounded the nail until the head sat flush on the wood. Jessica wasn't taking the hint. "Shouldn't you be helping your mom with something?"

"Nah. I get on her nerves too much. How old are you?"

"Old enough."

"With those bags under your eyes, I'd guess forty."

Claire drilled Jessica with a skin-shriveling glare, but the girl was too busy picking the pink polish off her thumbnail to notice. The reason Claire had "those bags" under her eyes was from tossing and turning on two inches of foam covering a rock-hard table.

"Do you have a boyfriend?" Jessica asked.

Criminy! Did this girl ever stop asking questions? Claire crossed her arms over her chest. "Don't you have any friends to visit?"

"Nope."

"School pals?"

"I'm not going to school right now."

"Why not?"

"I got kicked out. Ruby keeps trying to ship me off to private school, but nobody will take me, so she's stuck with me."

That sounded downright fishy. "Why don't you go to school around here?"

Jessica shrugged. "Ruby doesn't think the school is good enough, so she's home-schooling me for the rest of the year."

No wonder Ruby needed help around the place. Jessica didn't stop talking long enough to let a person think, let alone do any work.

"My dad lives in Ohio, up by Lake Erie."

Claire raised an eyebrow. So, Jessica wasn't Joe's kid.

"I haven't been there yet, but when he hears that I've been kicked out of school and Ruby doesn't want me around, he'll send for me. I just know it."

Gramps was right, Claire thought. Trouble had found her soon enough, this time in the form of a lonely teenage girl. But Claire wasn't in the mood for drama today. "Well, good luck with all that, Jessica." If Jessica didn't pick up on that dismissal, her head had to be full of marshmallows. Claire placed another nail against the cedar plank.

"You can call me Jess."

Warning bells clanged in Claire's skull. She'd just leaped from stranger to friend in record speed. "It's been nice chatting with you, Jess." She tried again to dismiss the girl.

"Ruby says Dad doesn't want me around and I have to learn to accept that, but I think he's just busy with work."

Claire stared down at the grooves in the weathered-gray wood. The poor kid.

"When I'm eighteen, and Ruby doesn't have control over me, I'm going to go stay with him for good."

With a sigh, Claire set down the hammer and nails and looked at Jessica. The girl stared back, a determined glint in her eyes.

"When was the last time you talked to your dad?" Claire asked, lifting her hat and rubbing her forehead to see if she could feel the word *SUCKER* etched in her skin.

She hated it when Gramps was right.

Later that evening, Claire sat at the table in Gramps's R.V. The five cards she was holding made up the shittiest hand she'd had all night. "What do you mean Art's dead?" she asked, waving cigar smoke out of her face. She dropped her cards facedown on the orange tabletop and frowned at Gramps, who sat diagonally across from her.

Gramps plucked his cigar from his mouth. "I mean he's pushing up daisies." He log-rolled his ashes into the ashtray.

"He kicked the bucket," Manny mumbled around the cigar he was lighting.

"Cashed in his chips," added Chester Thomas, who sat on the bench seat next to her. He gulped down some beer and let out a window-rattling belch.

Claire cringed. Another one of Gramps's old Army buddies, Chester had shown up for the boys' *Flesh Fiesta* earlier that afternoon, parking his decrepit Winnebago Brave next to Gramps's Chieftain. He'd been married four times, but never long enough to celebrate a one-year anniversary.

"Okay, I get it. He's dead." Claire said, wondering why in God's name she'd ever agreed to sit in as Gramps's partner for a few hands of Bid Euchre.

For the last hour, she'd been squished next to Chester, who kept noisily decompressing after eating a whole bowl of *chili con carne* for supper. All the while, Gramps repeatedly snapped at her for playing the wrong damned cards, and Manny told raunchy love stories from his glory days in the service. Thumbscrews would have been less agonizing.

"What I want to know is *when* did he die?" She glared at Gramps. "And how come you never told me about it?" She hadn't seen Art in years, but it seemed like just yesterday he was telling her about his daughter's acclaimed peanut butter pie.

"Eight months ago," Gramps answered, throwing a Jack of hearts on the table to lead the round, "and you never asked."

"After his wife died," Chester said, tossing a ten of hearts on top of Gramps's card, "he just kind of withered up inside and out. When we were here last year, he couldn't even focus on the game enough to remember what suit was trump thirty seconds after he'd called it."

Gramps shook his head. "I knew he was a goner when he mentioned selling his collection of Wonder Woman comic books. He'd saved those from when he was still wet behind the ears." He frowned as Claire laid an Ace of hearts over Chester's card. "Now what'd you go and throw that out there for?"

Claire ignored him. She would be hoarse by now if she defended every card she'd played all evening.

"Ah, Wonder Woman." Manny shuffled the cards around in his hand. "I'd like to have been the man who polished her brass b—"

"Manny!" Claire kicked him in the shin. "There's a lady present, remember?" She picked up her own cigar and took a few puffs, savoring the flavor of tobacco mixed with a hint of spice.

"What? I was going to say her brass *buckle*." Manny laid down the King of hearts. "I thought you quit smoking. Weren't you wearing one of those nicotine patches earlier?"

Claire blew out a smoke ring. "Cigars don't count."

Besides, the patches did something to her brain that made her feel extra anxious, so she only wore them when the cravings really had her climbing walls.

"Art's heartache is all the more reason to find a woman to keep my bed warm every night," Chester said as he watched Gramps collect the cards piled on the table.

"You know there's more to being married than just having someone around to warm your bed," Claire said, setting her cigar down in an ashtray with *Viva Las Vegas* scrawled across the bottom. These guys didn't seem to understand how dangerous marrying one of those Internet babes could be, especially without checking out more than just their backsides.

"What do you know about it?" Gramps asked. "You run like hell every time a guy asks you for a second date."

Claire ignored his smug tone. "I've read a lot of books on the subject of relationships."

"And I'm sure you've taken several classes on it, too."

"As a matter of fact—"

Chester let out another earth-rumbling belch. "I'd like a woman who's still flexible," he said. "One who can bend like a pretzel. With my trick hip, I need someone who can do the work for me in the sack."

Claire shuddered.

"Who cares if she can bend?" Manny leaned back into the plaid seat cushion, his eyes sparkling. "I want a woman with hips you can grab onto and ride into the sunset." He sipped his beer. "Of course, she'll also need a great set of *chi-chis*."

"Did you guys forget that I'm sitting here?" Claire asked.

"A firm set of hooters is nice." Gramps piped in. "But I need someone who can make me happy in and out of the bedroom. There's nothing worse than a woman who only wants to talk about how many shoes she has in the closet."

Manny grunted in agreement.

"You got that right, Harley," Chester said. "Speaking of shoes, I saw a sweet piece of meat walking out of the laundry this afternoon in nothing but a short robe and a pair of cowboy boots."

Claire rolled her eyes. Chester's love for women in boots was no secret. He had a big red bumper sticker that read, *Free Rides to Women Wearing Spurs*, on the front of his

Brave. "Women are not pieces of meat."

"She's right."

"Thanks, Gramps."

"They're made of sugar and spice and everything nice." He winked at Claire as he dealt another round of cards.

"I'd like to try a spoonful of your sugar, *Bonita*," Manny said, making a growling noise in the back of his throat.

"Stay away from my granddaughter, Carrera," Gramps ordered without looking up from his cards.

"Piece of meat or not," Chester continued, "that cowgirl is coming over later tonight. I'm gonna put on some Sinatra, pour some wine down her throat, and then introduce her to Chester Junior and see where we end up."

Much more of this talk and Claire knew where she'd end up—with her head hanging over the toilet bowl.

Gramps glanced at his watch. "Shit." He shot Claire a frown. "You gotta go."

"I do?" She blinked. "Where am I going?"

"Anywhere but here." Gramps scrambled to his feet. "You guys hit the road, too," he told Manny and Chester. "She's gonna be here soon."

She? Claire crossed her arms over her chest. "Who is *she?*"

"None of your business. This is our first date. The rules say you don't get to see her until the third—and then only from a distance."

"Fine." Claire scooted across the cushion. A walk under the stars in the cool night air might numb her brain enough to stop all thoughts about old men having sex. "I'll be back in an hour and a half."

"Make it three."

"What?" She stopped at the edge of the seat. "You said—"

"I know what I said, but this is different. I need time to show her how romantic I can be."

"It's already eight o'clock."

"You're right." Gramps brushed the crumbs from the table onto the floor. "Make it midnight."

"Is that when she turns back into a pumpkin?"

"Very funny, young lady. Now out." He pointed at the door. "And take Henry with you."

She glanced over to where Henry lay on the olive green couch. The beagle looked up when he heard his name. "I'm not taking your dog. He doesn't like me."

"He does, too. He's just not good at showing his feelings." Gramps yanked Henry's leash from the peg next to the door and threw it at her. "I don't need him here watching. It'll give me stage fright."

"What am I supposed to do until midnight? Count stars?"

Manny popped his head back in the doorway. "You can come over to my trailer. I can keep you occupied for four hours, and I don't care if the dog watches."

Jeez! The guy must shoot Viagra straight into his bloodstream. She threw a pleading look at her grandfather.

"I don't care what you do, as long as you aren't here with me."

"Whatever!" Claire grabbed her jean jacket. "But I'm taking your car." She swiped the keys to Mabel from the counter. "And the bone." She snatched it out of Henry's dish before the dog could lock his teeth onto it again.

Henry growled.

She flashed him a victory grin, then hooked the leash onto his collar.

"I'll be back at midnight, and no later." With Henry leading the way, she stepped outside. "Call it what you want—smoker's lounge or love shack—but that R.V. is my bedroom, and I need my sleep."

"Fine! But if the Winnebago's rocking, don't come in without knocking." Gramps slammed the door in her face.

Mac opened the door of his pickup and tossed his hard hat and gloves onto the bench seat. The dome light glowed, making the cab seem bright compared to the pitch-black mine he'd just left. An owl hooted in the darkness. Nearby, greasewood and mesquite trees rattled as a cool breeze rushed past him, the air swept clean by the desert wind.

Staring at the Big Dipper, he pondered how he was going to figure out the value of four mines while short on time and help. Hell, he hadn't even dabbled in this kind of work for years. Good thing he had friends in the right places. Tomorrow, he'd call Steve Zimmerman, his old college roommate, and see if he could finagle some sample testing time at the Phoenix-based lab where Steve worked.

Mac unbuckled his pack and tossed it on the seat. He cast one last look up at the hillside. The night camouflaged the gaping mouth of Ruby's Rattlesnake Ridge Mine, carved beneath 150 feet of Pre-Cambrian metamorphic rock.

These mines were going to be his home away from home for the next three weeks. The day Ruby handed them over to the mining company and got the damned bank off her back couldn't come soon enough. Money had been tight for her for too long. He was a bit surprised she could afford to hire some help. Although how much help her new handywoman would be was yet to be seen.

Even if Claire did have a sweet ...

All of his thoughts screeched to a stop at the sound of something crashing toward him through the brush.

Chapter Four

Grabbing a flashlight from his dashboard, Mac jerked around in time to see a small, white and tan body bulleting toward him. It slammed into his thighs at full speed, knocking him back into the crease between the door and the cab. His head thumped against the doorjamb.

"Henry!" a familiar female voice yelled. "Get off him!"

What was *she* doing out here?

Mac trapped the squirming body against him and pushed upright. The wriggling beagle covered his jaw and neck with licks, smothering him with dog breath.

"You lousy mutt!" Ruby's handywoman said, gasping as she slid to a stop in front of him. The pale light spilling from his pickup cab cast a soft glow on her high cheekbones and shoulder-length, dark hair. She clutched her side and huffed as if she'd just sprinted a mile. "I'm sorry," she said as she took the beagle from him.

"It's okay." He wiped at his face with his shirt. "No harm done."

She smelled like watermelon again.

"He refuses to take a leak while being watched," she said while trying to hold on to the wriggling dog. "As soon as I turned my head to give him some privacy, he slipped out of his collar and shot off across the creek like Speedy Gonzales."

Mac searched her face. Was she kidding?

The beagle bared its teeth and growled up at her. She wrinkled her upper lip and growled back.

Curbing a smile, Mac glanced away. The dog wasn't the only one with a quirk.

As he brushed the sand off the front of his shirt, she withdrew a collar, still attached to a leash, from her pocket. Clutching the dog to her chest, she struggled to slip the collar over its head. Nailing Jello to a wall would have been easier.

"Uhh, Claire ..." He reached awkwardly toward the dog. "You want some help?"

At her nod, Mac stepped closer and took the collar. "You hold his head and I'll slip it on." His knuckles rubbed down the front of her jean jacket as he slid the nylon over the beagle's head. "Sorry 'bout that," he muttered as he tightened the collar a notch, feeling like a teenager pinning a corsage on his prom date's dress.

She let out a husky chuckle, her eyes flirting. "Next time buy me dinner first."

With his cheeks warm, Mac retreated to safety—his pickup. He crossed his arms, leaned against the bed, and tried to act like he hadn't just felt her up.

As Claire put the dog on the ground, a coyote howled off to the south. Judging from the decibel level, Mac guessed it was in the next valley over. Claire peered into the shadows around them, appearing more wary than fearful.

"What are you doing out here?" Mac asked.

"Walking Henry." She didn't meet his eyes.

"Who?"

"Henry Ford, my grandfather's dog."

Mac grinned. "That's his name?"

"Yep. Gramps's last name is Ford, so he named the dog 'Henry' after one of his idols."

Seemingly oblivious to being the topic of discussion, Henry waddled over to a barrel cactus at the shadow's edge and began sniffing its base.

Mac lifted an eyebrow, turning back to Claire. "You're

walking your grandfather's dog at ten-thirty at night?"

She shrugged. "He's allergic to the sun."

Sure he was. "Is that the story you're sticking with?"

That brought her gaze up to his in a flash. She stared at him, as if she was weighing something behind her dark eyes. Then she smiled. "You win. My grandfather kicked Henry and me out of the Winnebago for a few hours. He's entertaining a lady friend."

Mac was having problems taking his eyes off her mouth. She had a nice smile, the kind that radiates a glow on moonless nights. "That still doesn't explain what you're doing out here in the middle of nowhere."

"I could ask you the same thing."

He frowned, not used to having his actions questioned. "I was working."

"At ten-thirty at night?"

She had spunk. He liked that in a woman—along with curves. And boy, did she have curves. "How was your first day on the job?"

"Not bad. I made a new friend."

"Really?" He wondered if she was referring to the lady with the purple afro, florescent blue eye shadow, and ruby spandex pants who'd checked into the campground earlier in the afternoon. She couldn't have been a day under seventy-five.

Claire nodded. "She's fifteen going on twenty, filled to the brim with rebellion and hormones, and determined to teach me how to make my lips irresistible to every man in this county."

They were nice lips. Full, kind of heart-shaped, pinkish in the glow cast from the pickup's dome light. But not irresistible. His gaze moved back to her eyes. "Sounds like you met my cousin, Jess."

"I think she's attached herself to me." She opened her jacket and pointed to her ribs. Her hand bumped what looked like a white stick jutting out from the waistband of her pants and knocked it to the ground between them.

Mac snatched it up before she could. "What's this?"

"Nothing." She grabbed for it, but he held it just out of reach.

"Then why do you want it back so badly?"

"I don't. It's just a stick—of sorts. I picked it up back by the stream. Henry likes to play fetch."

Judging from the texture and weight, it wasn't a stick, but a bone. But why was she carrying a bone around under her coat? "If it's just a stick, why do you care if I look at it?"

"You promise not to laugh?"

Now he really wanted to know. He nodded.

"It's a human leg bone."

He lifted an eyebrow and grinned. "Is it Santa Anna's?" he asked, referring to the infamous Mexican general who'd lost his leg during the Pastry War with the French.

"No, wise guy. Santa Anna lost his right leg *below* the knee. This is a femur."

She knew her Mexican-American history. Impressive for a non-local.

Mac ran his fingers over the hard surface. It looked like hundreds of other bones he'd seen scattered throughout the desert. "So it is." He handed it back to her.

Claire slipped it inside her coat. "Henry found it yesterday while Gramps and I were ... um ... out here hiking."

Mac doubted she was just *hiking*. It was more likely she'd ignored the No Trespassing sign and slipped into the mine to explore. A gaping hole in a hillside usually lured teenagers and tourists like a Vegas neon sign. That might explain the cigarette butt with red-lipstick smeared on it that he'd found earlier in the mine.

"Do you have any idea whose bone it is?" Claire asked. "Has anyone from around here disappeared in the last ten or twenty years? Have you seen any other bones in this area?"

Mac chuckled and shook his head, leaning back against his pickup.

She continued without taking a breath. "Henry dug this up from somewhere around here. He was only gone—"

"Do you realize what state you're standing in?" He said, cutting her off. The woman needed to breathe before she keeled over.

Her brow wrinkled. "Of course I do."

"Do you have any idea of the history of this area?"

"I took a class on Southwest U.S. history a few years ago. Why?"

"Because you're standing on land that used to be Apache territory. I'm not sure what exactly they taught in your class, but Apaches didn't like strangers on their land."

She crossed her arms over her chest. "I've read more Louis L'Amour westerns than you have fingers and toes. He made it crystal clear what Apaches were like. What's your point?"

She read westerns? He'd grown up reading them. Miss Claire Handywoman was growing more interesting by the moment. "These hills are littered with bones. You could be holding the femur of some foolhardy pioneer shortcutting across Apache land on his way to Sutter's mine in California. Or some outlaw riding through these hills to outrun a U.S. Marshal. It could even belong to some Spanish monk who came to civilize the natives and search for Coronado's gold."

He paused to see if she understood what he was trying to tell her. She stared back with her lips pursed and her chin lifted.

"My point is," Mac continued, "if you think you're on the way to solving some great mystery, you're wasting your time. There are just too many bodies buried in this land."

"Yes, but—"

"If you want to keep digging around here for more bones," Mac could tell she wasn't going to listen to reason, "that's your choice. But don't count on the local sheriff to help you out. He won't blink twice at old bones—unless you find a complete skeleton."

Mac climbed into his pickup. "And I don't have time to play Sherlock Holmes with you." He had enough on his hands with Ruby's dilemma. Without another word, he shut the door.

Claire rapped on his window and mimed rolling it down. He lowered it halfway.

"I didn't plan to ask for your help, or the local sheriff. He'd probably confiscate the bone and I'd never see it again. I just wondered if—" Her body jerked to the right suddenly. "Damn it!"

"What's wrong?" He rolled the window all the way down and leaned out to see.

"Henry just pulled the leash out of my hands. I gotta go." She patted the door twice and raced off into the darkness.

Mac stared after her. He fought the urge to help track down the dog. Common sense told him to stay put. Claire might not actually be loony, like the oddballs waltzing around Ruby's campground, but her brain was definitely frayed around the edges.

He turned the ignition key. The starter cranked, but the engine didn't catch. He frowned at the gas gauge. Half a tank. He turned the key again. The starter ground, but the engine still wouldn't fire. His gut tensed. Something wasn't right.

He popped the hood and stepped outside. As he lifted the hood, the light under it flickered on.

Someone had sliced all of the sparkplug wires.

"Fuck me."

Sophy blew out a lungful of smoke. The valley spilled out below her, dark as a midnight blue sea in the moonless night. Coyotes howled their lonely love songs while an owl hooted in sympathy. A cool breeze ferried their tunes across the desert floor.

If only her ex-husband were alive to see her now. Like Joe Martino, her youth might be dead, but she wasn't about to wither and fade away in this wasteland. Her time among the bright lights and high-rollers was on the horizon, only forty years later than Joe had promised her.

She stubbed out the cigarette on the sole of her boot and pocketed the butt. Her heels clunked on the planks of pine spanning the rubble-filled floor as she walked through the mouth of Socrates Pit toward the black throat of the mine.

No matter how much time she spent in these holes, the smell of damp dirt and the faint stink of mule shit combined with the thousands of tons of rock sitting over her head made her skin crawl.

Safely out of sight, she turned on a flashlight and ducked beneath several ceiling beams that had sagged from the weight of the mountain bearing down on them for more than a century. In the main tunnel that led to the chamber she'd spent the last month excavating, she heard a clacking noise behind her.

She stopped, her breath whisper quiet. The sound of panting reached her ears. Claws clattered on the stone floor, drawing closer.

Whirling, she swung the flashlight beam wildly. A pair of eyes glowed in the shadows. Her gut clenched.

A loud, high-pitched bark echoed through the tunnel.

She gasped. "Holy Mary Mother of Pearl!" Her heart

galloped like a wild mustang. It was just a dog, a beagle from the looks of it. But what was it doing out here in the middle of nowhere?

The dog took a few steps toward her and barked again. Then it dropped onto its ass and sat staring at her with its beady black eyes.

She snickered at it. "Look at you. I've seen bigger housecats."

The beagle cocked its head to the side.

"Go home." Sophy turned away and headed deeper into the mine. She stopped again at the sound of toenails clicking on the stone floor behind her. She didn't need a dog following her, knocking her tools around, digging where she'd already dug. She pointed toward the exit. "Get outta here, ya mutt."

The dog dropped onto its haunches and stared at her.

She picked up a dime-sized rock and threw it at the beagle. It leaped aside at the last moment and the stone missed its mark. The dog glared at her for a split second, then lunged, skidding to a stop about ten feet from her. It rattled out a string of yaps, its whole body shaking with effort.

Panic tightening her chest, Sophy glanced up. How stable were the ceiling beams in this section of the mine?

The barking stopped.

Sophy's ears rang. The damned dog had to go. "Shoo!" She rushed the mutt, waving her arms at it. "Get on out of here, you little varmint."

With a yip, the dog raced back toward the entrance, barking over its shoulder every few feet. When it reached the planks leading out of the mine, it turned and squared its body, growling at her.

"Go home, ya little shit!" Sophy picked up another rock and threw it. The dog yelped as the stone struck with a muffled thump. She scooped up more.

"Henry!"

Sophy froze, rocks clutched in her fingers.

The female voice had been faint, but loud enough to be heard over the racket the dog was making. She raced to the entrance, skirting the growling mutt, and peeked out over the tailings, searching the valley floor for a beam of light in the darkness.

Not fifty feet below, off to the left of the trail leading up to the mine, she caught the pale glow of a flashlight bouncing through the brush.

Oh, Jesus! Someone was coming.

She had to get rid of the dog. His barks were like goddamned air horns. "Here doggy, doggy," she whispered, pulling a package of beef jerky—her supper—from her pocket.

⟶ ⊹ ◆ ⊱ ⟵

"Henry!" Claire yelled again as she stood at the bottom of a huge pile of gravel and rock. She pressed against the stitch in her side and tried to catch her breath.

The damned dog was barking somewhere above her on the hillside, but she couldn't see further than three feet away, and her flashlight was growing dimmer by the minute. She smacked the light against her hand. It brightened, then faded.

Henry's barking grew frenzied. Claire's heart beat in triple time as she strained to hear why. A loud "yip" echoed down through the valley. Silence followed.

"Henry?" she called, hesitantly. She directed the weak flashlight beam up the hillside and scrambled around the pile of rocks toward a stand of mesquites. Her light died before she'd made it ten steps.

"Crap." She whacked the light against her leg, but nothing happened. "Just great." She wondered if the other flashlight she'd seen in Mabel's trunk had fresher batteries.

She looked up at the stars cluttering the night sky. Without the moon's light, she'd have to wait until her eyes adjusted before taking another step.

Nibbling on her knuckle, Claire filled the seconds worrying about Henry. Damn him for running off like that. Gramps was going to chew her ass royally if anything happened to his dog.

Heading back for the other flashlight was probably the wise choice, but what if she couldn't find her way back to this spot? If Henry was hurt, she might have only a short time to find him before he ended up being the entrée for a coyote buffet.

Wait! Her lighter. She reached for it, then stopped midway. *Frickity frack!* Why in the hell had she decided to quit smoking?

Stuffing her hands in her pockets, she heaved a sigh. She'd eat a cricket for a cigarette right about now.

She sniffed, then sniffed again. Was that cigarette smoke? Damn, not two minutes alone in the dark and she was already hallucinating.

A coyote howled off to her left, this one closer than the one she'd heard earlier. She held her breath, straining to hear more. The sound of more coyotes yipping and laughing in their eerie, human-like tones echoed through the valley.

Claire peered up the steep slope. Henry was up there somewhere and she needed to find him quick. She wished to God he'd let out another bark. "Henry?" she yelled again.

Silence.

That stupid dog was going to get them both killed. She started up the steep slope on all fours. A rustling sound in the brush behind her stopped her short.

Twigs snapped.

Something was coming for her.

Something big.

Heart pounding in her ears, Claire pulled out the bone that had landed her in this whole sorry mess and wielded it like Excalibur.

She waited, teeth gritted, ready for battle.

Chapter Five

Is that a bone in your hand?" Mac asked, stepping out through the brush, flashlight in hand.

Claire squinted, shielding her eyes from the bright light.

"Or are you just happy to see me?"

"Jeez, Mac!" She plopped down before her knees gave out. The gravel dug into her ass. "We need to quit meeting like this."

"Where's the dog?"

"Up there somewhere." She pointed up the hillside with the bone. "I heard him barking like a cornered seal about five minutes ago." Although Henry had been too quiet for comfort since then.

"The coyotes are just over there." He motioned with the light toward the opposite side of the valley. "If you don't find him soon, you'd better hope he's half greyhound."

Claire rose to her feet, absently rubbing her backside as she stared at Mac. "What are you doing here?"

"I need a lift. Someone sliced the wires to my sparkplugs."

No shit. "Who'd you piss off?"

"It was probably just some kids out messing around on a Saturday night." He shrugged it off.

"Does that happen a lot in your line of work?"

"Let's just say my insurance agent sends me a personalized Christmas card every year."

What in the world did this man do for a living? More

importantly, "What were you doing out here tonight?"

He took his time answering. "Like I said before, working."

"Are you trying to be mysterious on purpose, Mac, or is it just part of your charm?"

"Neither." He shined the light up the hillside. "We'd better find your dog before the coyotes do." As if on cue, several high-pitched yips and then one long howl echoed through the valley.

"Smooth segue." She knew a polite "it's none of your business" when she came across one. She stuffed the bone back in her waistband and waved for him to go first. "You lead, I'll follow."

Five minutes later, Mac paused on the deer trail they'd found a short distance up the slope and waited for her to close the fifteen feet separating them. "You gonna make it?" he asked.

Claire shot him a warning glare, then huffed on up to him.

Five minutes after that, Claire fell. Mac slid back down ten feet of gravel tailings—a shortcut—to take a look at the scrape on her palm. "I told you to watch out for those broken boards. You're lucky you didn't break your ankle."

He shined the light on her open hand, grimacing at the scrape. His touch was surprisingly gentle for as rough as the pads on his hands felt. She inhaled sharply as he prodded around the scratch, and noticed how earthy he smelled—like a breath of warm, desert air.

He pulled a handkerchief out of his back pocket and wrapped it around her hand. "It looks like you'll live. Now quit wasting your energy telling me where and how I can shove it and pay attention to where you're stepping." He hiked back up the tailings.

Claire flipped him off behind his back before following.

Ten minutes later, Mac crested the top with Claire right behind him—clutching onto his belt. He'd pulled her along the last half of the climb like a ship dragging anchor.

"Dang, woman," Mac said as he grabbed her hand and hauled her to the solid rock lip jutting out from the mine. "I think you've severed my spleen."

Claire collapsed onto the ground. She looked up from where she lay, sprawled at his feet. "A gentleman," she said between gulps of air, "would never make such a comment to a lady."

Mac squatted next to her. He brushed her hair out of her face. "A lady would never curse Mother Nature, the North Star, and all four-legged animals in English, Spanish, and ... what was that third language you swore so eloquently in?"

"Canadian."

A grin spread across Mac's face. The shadows from the glow of the flashlight gave him a craggy, rugged look, and in her oxygen-deprived state, Claire found him kind of hot. Too bad he seemed to be cinched up on the inside tighter than a corset.

She'd once had a boyfriend who'd dusted three times a week, showered twice a day, made sure the food on his plate never mixed, and used a protractor to line his ties up straight. Rather than kill him in his sleep, she'd walked out on him and moved back in with her mom for two months.

Make those two torture-filled months with the woman who bore her, pointing out all of the ways Claire was living her life wrong. Needless to say, she'd learned her lesson about uptight men.

Mac stood. The bastard wasn't even breathing hard. "How about you just lie there while I go inside the mine and look around for any sign of your dog?"

Gulping cool air she hoped would douse her flaming lungs, she stared up at the black sky full of glittering rhinestones. "Okay. I'll hold down the fort out here and fend off any ravenous coyotes that come our way."

"You do that," he said with a chuckle. "Just don't go dying on me while I'm in there."

—✦ ✦ ✦—

Sophy clamped her hand tight around the dog's muzzle and squeezed his wiggling body against her chest. She slipped deeper into the dark tunnel, using the damp, jagged rock wall as a guide. Turning on her light would give her away.

"Henry," a man called out in low, hushed voice. He was either nervous or knew better than to shout in an old mine.

The varmint in her arms stilled.

"Henry?" Footsteps thudded on the stone floor behind her.

Sophy grimaced as the dog wiggled against her stomach, slicing her with his toenails. If "Henry" didn't want to end up roasting on a stick on the other side of the Mexican border, he'd better calm his little ass down.

She tore open the last of her supper with her teeth. The smell of teriyaki-marinated beef made her mouth water. It'd been over five hours since she'd eaten that last piece of key lime pie back at the diner.

Henry stopped thrashing about. She heard him sniff several times.

"Henry?" The man's voice was closer now—too close.

Inching several more feet along the wall, she turned into a side tunnel. Seconds later, a flash of light bounced off the walls at the junction to the main tunnel. Sophy tightened her grip on the dog, in case he got any ideas. Where was the woman who'd been calling for the dog? There must be two looky-loos out searching.

Henry rubbed the end of his muzzle against the jerky. Food apparently ranked higher in priority than being saved.

"Henry!" The guy's voice was so close she expected him to round the corner and nail her with the light at any moment. She could hear him breathing, slow and steady. Sinking against the wall, she ignored the sharp stone digging into her upper vertebrae. If she could only get to her pack and the 8-inch-blade combat knife inside of it.

The light at the mouth of the tunnel grew brighter.

Then the footsteps stopped. The light dimmed a bit. "What's this?"

What's what? She'd tried to be careful over the last few months and not leave any traces of her trips in and out of the mine. Nobody needed to know she'd been digging around in Socrates Pit.

"I'll be damned." The light dimmed even more, followed by the sound of his footsteps fading. He was heading back toward the entrance.

Sophy frowned in the growing darkness. Slowly, she loosened her hold on Henry's muzzle.

The dog chomped on the jerky like it might run away at any moment. With the mine silent and black again, she took several deep breaths. Henry gulped down the last of her supper, then cleaned her fingers with his leathery tongue.

Now that she'd fed the dog—twice, she was in a bit of a pickle. Not only did Henry know how to find Socrates Pit, he'd probably associate it with food. She had a feeling he might stick to this area like flies on shit if she let him loose. Or, worse yet, lead his owner back here. She didn't need any visitors. There was no way in hell she'd share any of the loot when she found it.

"The question is," she whispered, pulling the flashlight from her utility belt, "what am I going to do about you?" She directed the beam on the dog. Only one answer came to mind.

Henry stopped licking his chops and whimpered.

⇢ ◆ ⇠

"You are sexy as hell," Mac said to the 1949 Mercury beauty as he caressed her sleek curves with his palm while circling her. He licked his lips, entranced by the feel of her buffed, smooth surface.

"Yep. Mabel's a guaranteed testosterone rocket," Claire told him, leaning against the driver's side door of the chopped top, two-door car with painted flames shooting up the hood and sides.

Mac shined his flashlight inside the passenger side window. Flawless, diamond-patterned, white leather seats and door panels; cherry red carpet; chromed dial casings; manual three-speed transmission on the floor; and a custom flame design on the dashboard.

This car was a dream.

"Mabel?" he asked.

"That's her name."

"You named your car Mabel?" Mac stepped back and ran his light along the length of the Merc. Player spoke wheels in front, skirts on back, shaved door handles, and side pipes.

This car was a *wet* dream.

"No, Gramps named *his* car Mabel—my grandma's middle name."

He walked around the front of Mabel and admired her huge chrome grill.

"We should have poked around that mine some more," Claire said.

Her miffed tone was back. Oh, joy. He'd been subjected to it all the way back down the hillside and across the valley floor.

"Henry still has to be in the area. For crissake, his legs

can't be more than six inches long. How far can a short-legged dog run?"

"Apparently a lot farther than a certain long-legged woman can," Mac answered without looking up from the grill's teeth.

"Good looks and a comedian, too." Her sarcasm made him smile. Her compliment didn't go unnoticed, either. "I wouldn't quit your day job, though, whatever it may be, Mr. Mysterious."

"Building walls." Mac slipped around to the driver's side, noticing the high gloss on the front quarter panel. "She must have several coats of paint to make her this smooth."

"Twenty-five coats, hand rubbed," she answered as if every car coming out of Detroit received the same treatment. "What do you mean building walls?"

"That's what I do for a living."

"In houses?"

"No. Retaining walls. I'm a geotechnician for a private engineering company in Tucson, but we do a lot of state work."

"So you build those walls along freeways?"

"That's one example. We also work on maintaining and replacing the hundreds of miles of aqueducts and tunnels, and thousands of miles of canals coming from the Colorado River."

"Do you do the design work or the actual hands-on work?"

"Both."

"Then what are you doing out here?"

Mac looked up at her. The flashlight reflected off the side of the car and cast her in a dim glow. She had a cute nose, with a little uplift at the tip, placed perfectly on her face. If only she'd stop trying to shove it into his business. "Stuff."

"Stuff?"

"Yep. Just some stuff." He flashed her a drop-it smile.

She placed her hands on her hips, her grin cocky. "So we're back to that again, are we?"

"Back to what?"

"You brushing me off."

"I guess so."

"Well, I wouldn't want you to vary from your routine."

He ignored her comment. "Listen, it's late. I'm tired. You're tired. Can we head back to Ruby's now?"

"Sure, on one condition."

Mac narrowed his eyes. This couldn't be good.

"You agree to come with me tomorrow and search for Henry."

He didn't have time to go trekking through the valley, scouring creosote bushes for a missing dog. The clock was ticking on Ruby's deal, and he was too short on time already. "I really can't—"

"Come on. I don't know my ass from a hole in the ground out here. You're the only one who can show me where the mine is that we climbed up to tonight. I need your help."

He wasn't the only one. Ruby knew how to get up to Socrates Pit, as did Jess. But Ruby couldn't leave the store for any length of time during the day, and Jess was supposed to spend her spare time working on the homework Ruby assigned to her each day.

There was also his pickup to consider. First thing in the morning, he'd have to drag Ruby and her truck with him to tow his pickup back to the R.V. park. Since he didn't carry around spare spark plug wires, he'd have to drive Ruby's truck to Yuccaville and see if the Roadrunner Auto Parts store carried what he needed.

Sometime between it all, he wanted to do some research on the old coin he'd found tonight up in Socrates Pit. It had to be rare. How much was an 1879 twenty-dollar gold piece worth nowadays? Ruby could use all the help she could get paying off her creditors.

He opened his mouth to offer to show her the mine's location on the map in Ruby's rec room, but then he noticed the worry lines criss-crossing Claire's forehead. He sighed, cursing silently. "I'm busy until after lunch."

"Me, too. I have to work for Ruby until two." She pulled a key ring with a black plastic remote dangling from it out of her jacket pocket and pushed a button. Something clunked inside the Mercury and the doors popped open. "Let's get out of here."

Feeling like a kid about to take a ride in his dad's new car, Mac knocked the dust from his shoes before climbing in next to Claire. She turned the key. The V-8 rumbled to life. She whipped the car around and they bounced out onto the asphalt.

A comfortable silence settled around him as they cruised toward the campground. Mac ran his hand over the leather-covered dashboard. The raised imprint of the flame design under his fingertips was soft as a lambskin jacket.

The car smelled of sun-baked leather and bananas, no doubt due to the banana-shaped air freshener hanging from the rear view mirror. What he wouldn't do to take her out on the open road, crank her wide open, and bury the needle on the speedometer.

"Gramps is going to kill me when I tell him I lost Henry," Claire interrupted his Route 66 fantasy.

"You didn't lose him. The dog ran off."

"Make sure you tell him that at my trial. Maybe he'll consider using a firing squad instead of the noose. It'd be much better to die quickly, don't you think?"

"It's just a dog. Surely you're more important than Henry."

"One would like to think that, but Henry does things for Gramps that I won't."

Mac stared across the car at the woman. He was afraid to ask, but did, anyway. "Like what?"

"Well, he cleans the fried chicken grease off Gramps's fingers."

That wasn't so bad.

"He licks the corns on Gramps's feet to keep them from growing too thick." She flashed a smile. "Henry has a pretty rough tongue."

Mac grimaced. That same tongue had been licking his face a short time ago.

"He chases his tail on command, which entertains Gramps and his cronies for hours on end."

"Okay, but you are—"

"Oh, and he eats bugs, lots of them. Especially those big, fat, black flies. They're his absolute favorite—after sour cream and onion potato chips, of course."

"—his granddaughter," Mac finished, happy to see the bridge to the campground in the headlights. "I'm sure he'll understand it's not your fault when you explain the circumstances."

"You don't know Gramps." Her voice sounded tired. The park's gravel drive crunched under the tires as she slowed to a stop in front of Ruby's place.

Mac gazed at Claire in the soft green glow of the dash lights, liking what he saw too much for his own good. He needed to focus on dirt and rocks for the next three weeks, not Claire's backside, even if it did look extremely touchable in her jeans.

"I'll meet you here in front of the store tomorrow at two-thirty," she said, her smile back in place.

Mac nodded. That would give him time to swing by the county library to see what he could dig up about the initial owners of the mines, and maybe find a book on old coins, too. "Good luck with your grandpa."

He stepped out of the car.

As the red taillights disappeared around the bend, he mentally shook himself. Soft curves aside, Claire was trouble. A couple of hours with the woman and she'd already managed to completely rearrange his plans for tomorrow.

He'd give her one day to track her dog. After that, she'd have to find someone else with whom to play search and rescue.

⇥ ✦ ⇤

Claire snuck inside the Winnebago and closed the door behind her with a quiet click.

A strange smell, like a mixture of lilies and stinky shoes, greeted her. She didn't want to decipher from where the smell came. Some things were better left a mystery.

She tiptoed toward Gramps's bedroom. For the first time since they'd left home, she found comfort in his chainsaw-like snoring.

Glancing at the couch, she wished by some miracle she'd see Henry snoozing on the cushions. But the couch was empty, and she was in deep shit.

If Lady Luck was on her side, Henry would find his way back to the campground and be scratching at the door when her alarm went off at five-thirty. And Gramps would never know any different.

Yeah, right. And Tinker Bell would fly out her butt, too.

Either way, now was not the time to bring up the missing dog. After all, Gramps probably needed his sleep after spending the evening romancing a woman.

Claire crept over to the couch. Since Henry wasn't going to be sleeping on it tonight, she might as well be comfortable. She grabbed a soft quilt her grandmother had made, draped it over the beagle fur-covered cushions, and tossed her pillow at one end.

As she slipped into her pajamas and settled under the covers, Mac seeped into her thoughts. What had he been doing out in the desert so late on a Saturday night? She'd have to ask Ruby.

Closing her eyes, she remembered the feel of his hands around her waist as he'd helped her climb up to the mine. He must have felt the roll of fat she'd acquired over the last month, binging away her problems with chocolate and caramel.

That was it. As of tomorrow, she'd start exercising and eating healthier. She'd keel over dead from an overdose of shame and humiliation if Mac ever saw her naked.

Her eyelids snapped open.

Who said anything about getting naked?

Chapter Six

Sunday, April 11th

"Where's my damned dog?" Gramps hollered.

Claire jerked awake. She sprung from the couch and stubbed her bare toe on the side of Gramps's boot. "Son of a—arrggghhhh!" She circled, limping, blinking away sleep.

"Claire, where's Henry?" Gramps watched her with a scowl.

"He's uh ..." A glance at the alarm clock made her grimace. *Shit!* She was late—fifteen minutes late. She'd forgotten to set the alarm last night. Running her hand through her bangs, she looked around for her Mighty Mouse cap. "He kind of umm ..." She scooped up her jeans from the floor and snagged her faded yellow *Cheerios* T-shirt from the stack of clean clothes piled on top of the television, then backed toward the bathroom doorway.

"Claire!" His face was the same color as the string of red pepper lights hanging from Manny's awning. He stepped toward her.

"He's kind of lost." She ducked into the bathroom and locked the vinyl accordion door behind her.

"Claire Alice Morgan!" Gramps pounded on the flimsy barrier. "Get your butt out here this instant and explain yourself!"

"I can't," she yelled, yanking on her jeans. "I'm changing right now." She tore off her Oscar the Grouch pajama top and pulled her T-shirt over her head; squirted a dab of toothpaste on her toothbrush and scrubbed her teeth long enough to taste the mint-flavored gel on her tongue.

With nothing left to keep her, she took a deep breath and braced for the storm.

She slid open the door. "Listen," she pleaded, staring into Gramps's icy blue glare. "It sounds worse than it actually is. He ran off and my flashlight died, so I lost him in the dark." No need to bring up the coyotes at this point. Nor Mac. Both would only lead to more questions. "But I promise, as soon as I get off work this afternoon, I'll go straight out to that mine and find him."

Gramps's bushy brows furrowed deeper. "What mine?"

Time was ticking and she was twenty minutes late already. Ruby was going to be sorry she ever hired her worthless ass.

"I don't have time to explain right now. Just trust me—I'll find him." Standing on her tiptoes, Claire dropped a peck on his stubble-roughened cheek, then slipped past him and grabbed her cap on the way out the door.

"*You* will find him?" Gramps followed her outside into the early morning sunshine. "The last time you said those words to me, you brought home a skunk. We had to burn the couch, rip up the carpet, and bathe the dog in V-8 juice for a week to get rid of the stench."

Claire shoved her cap over her uncombed hair and lifted her chin. "That's not fair. I was eight. Besides, you were the one who painted the white stripe on Blacky for shits and giggles."

Gramps's lips twitched. "Yes, well," the irritation had seeped from his tone, "just make sure it's my dog you bring home this time."

He stared off toward the stand of cottonwood trees sheltering Jackrabbit Creek, which meandered around the park's western and southern border. Deep, straight grooves ran down his cheeks where crescent moons usually dwelt. "The ol' boy doesn't like to miss a meal, let alone two."

"I know." The dog's pitiful howls of hunger were hard to forget. "He'll show up. Don't worry." She'd worry enough for the two of them.

With a goodbye salute, she half-jogged, half-skipped toward Ruby's store. Minutes later, huffing, she climbed the steps and reached for the screen door handle. The door flew open before she touched it, and Jess burst out, a huge grin plastered on her face.

"Hi, Claire," she sang and leaped to the ground, missing the porch steps completely, then raced across the drive to Ruby's old, blue Ford truck.

Claire caught the door before it shut, backing into the doorway as she watched Jess climb into the driver's side of the pickup and pretend to steer. "Where is she going?" she wondered aloud.

She turned around to go inside and stopped short at the sight of Mac's Adam's apple.

"With me."

She looked up. His honey-brown hair was damp and curly on the ends. His hazel eyes stared back from behind wire-rimmed glasses resting on his straight nose. "Morning, Mac." The glasses gave him a sophisticated look that left her a bit winded.

"Claire," he said, nodding, then grabbed her shoulders and gently shifted her to the side so he could step past her. The scent of warm sage baking under the midday sun clung to his skin.

She stared after him as he strode across the packed-dirt and gravel-strewn drive. His Levi jeans hugged his long legs. She whistled under her breath. *Nice butt.*

Mac waited for Jess to slide to the passenger side before he crawled in and started the truck. He held Claire's stare for several seconds through the front windshield.

Jess bounced and waved as they rolled toward the bridge leading out of the park. Claire waved back, wondering if someone had slipped Mexican jumping beans into Jess's shorts this morning.

Turning away from the cloud of exhaust and dust, Claire stepped inside the florescent-lit store. Ruby stood behind the counter, her hip resting against the cash register drawer as she spooned what looked like strawberry yogurt into her mouth from a small plastic cup.

She smiled as Claire approached. "Mornin'."

"I'm sorry I'm la—" Claire started, but Ruby waved Claire off with the spoon.

"Mac told me your grandpa's dog ran away last night. Do you want to take some time this morning to go look for him?"

Claire shook her head. "Henry won't come to me unless he thinks he's dying of starvation, so I might as well wait until he's good and hungry before heading out."

She reached over the counter and grabbed her tool belt from the shelf. "Where are those two heading?" She tried to sound indifferent as she swung the belt around her hips.

"To tow Mac's truck back here. I'd have gone with him, but I have company coming soon, so Jess is going to steer it home."

"You're expecting company this early in the morning?"

Ruby nodded. "Some bean counter from the mining company is coming to answer my questions about their offer for the mines."

Claire halted in the midst of buckling and stared at Ruby. "Do you think they'll use the open-pit mining method like they did down the road?" She already knew the answer to that question, along with what would happen to her grandma's grave if the land sold. But did Ruby?

Ruby tossed her spoon on the counter and set the

yogurt down. "Of course. That's what they do nowadays. It's easier to gut the landscape than tunnel beneath it."

"So why sell the mines to them?"

"I need the money more than the land."

"Couldn't you get a debt consolidation loan instead?"

Ruby grunted. "That's how I got in this fix in the first place. If I don't pay off my loan with the bank by the end of the month, they'll take this store and the R.V. park."

Frowning, Claire finished buckling the tool belt. "There has to be some other way." She couldn't let her grandma's resting place be obliterated.

"Honey, if you find the tree that money is growin' on these days, I'll come running with a suitcase."

"How much money are we talking? The cost of a house?"

"Twice that."

Okay, that made it a bit tougher than just taking out another loan somewhere else. "There has to be some way to save this place without sacrificing the mines." And the ash-sprinkled valley below them.

"Well, until you or someone else comes up with a better idea, I'm going with the mining company's solution."

Claire kneaded her hands, her thoughts on the mine Mac and she had climbed up to last night. "Mac says he works in Tucson."

Ruby turned the key on the side of the cash register. "He sure does. Has ever since he graduated from college."

"Is he just here for the weekend?"

"Nope. He'll be staying for a few weeks."

"On vacation?" Claire watched Ruby break open a roll of quarters and dump the coins into the cash drawer.

Ruby shook her head. "This is probably one of the last places Mac would go on vacation. He's much more into geological-oriented trips and that kind of scientific hoopla."

"So what's he doing here, then?" Mac had refused to

spill last night. Claire hoped Ruby wouldn't be so tight-lipped.

"Making sure I sell those mines for the right price."

"What can I get ya, sugar?"

Mac looked up from *A Guidebook of United States Coins*, his eyes honing in on the waitress's red fingernails. He noticed one of them was broken as she tapped the tip of a silver pen against the pale green order pad in her hand.

Dolly Parton sang "Here You Come Again" from a radio that looked like it hadn't seen the sticky side of a price tag since the early eighties. The smell of greasy burgers hung thick in the air.

It was a far cry from his Aunt Ruby's kitchen, but Mac didn't need to run up her grocery bill. Besides, he must have passed by this diner a hundred times over the last decade. It was about time he gave it a try.

"I'll have a cheeseburger and fries."

The waitress hesitated, her pen hovering over the pad.

Mac glanced up. What was it with older women wearing so much makeup? Between the glittery eye shadow on the women strutting around Ruby's place and the waitress's fire-engine red lips, he was starting to feel like he'd stepped onto the set of an old *Laugh-In* episode.

"Anything to drink?" she asked, her voice deeper than it had been before. It reminded him of Kathleen Turner's— low, sultry, the kind that made men listen up.

"Iced tea."

She must have been quite a bombshell in her day. As she walked away, hips practically knocking the pictures off the walls, her short candy-striped skirt flashed glimpses of the tops of her stockings.

Mac grimaced. Apparently Jackrabbit Junction was the

site of this year's Playboy Bunny reunion, sponsored by AARP.

He turned back to the page he'd been reading. According to the book, in 1933, President Roosevelt sent out an Executive Order requiring Americans to turn in their gold U.S. coins.

Unfortunately, the myth that millions of these coins were melted down or refined into bullion bars wasn't true. The government gave foreigners the gold coins instead of fine gold bullion because the coins contained only .9675 ounces of gold instead of the .999 in the bullion.

In the grand scheme of things, of the 100 million twenty-dollar gold Liberty coins turned out between 1850 and 1907, tens of millions most likely still existed, with the majority of them sitting in European bank vaults.

If gold rallied, European banks could sell massive quantities of the coins, and the rare gold Liberty coin he'd found in Socrates Pit wouldn't be so rare.

Figuring out how much Ruby could get for the coin was another matter. Depending on the coin's wear, it could be worth anywhere from $300 up to $1000.

Mac closed the book. So much for buying Ruby more time by placating the bank with a few thousand dollars.

He pulled the coin from his pants pocket, careful to keep it hidden from the rest of the patrons. A ray of sunlight shined through the faded orange curtains, glinting off the unmarred gold surface, lightly hazed from oxidation. Its lack of scores and scuffs had him scratching his head.

He'd found it in a crack between the mine's wall and floor, hiding partway under a small rock. Sure, it had been protected from the elements, but how could a coin lie in a mine for over a hundred years and still be as shiny as a one-year-old penny?

Slipping the coin back in his pocket, he spread out the copies he'd made of the mining claims for Socrates Pit.

"Here you go, darlin'." The waitress placed his tea on the table.

"Thanks," he said, eyes focused on one of the copies.

"I haven't seen you in here before. You just passing through?" Her soft drawl was typical for this corner of Arizona.

"No, I'm visiting my aunt."

"She live close by?"

"She owns the R.V. park just up the road."

Her swift intake of breath surprised him. He looked up and raised his brows at her narrow-eyed glare. Then, in a blink, it was gone, and her lips were again pursed in that flirty, pouting look some women thought all men found sexy.

"I'll be back with your food in a quick shake," she said and wagged her tail across the room to a table full of suits—an after-church gossip session raged among them.

Mac shook his head. Women were fickle creatures, a commodity he could live without—except for the sex. Too bad they rarely climbed into bed without some kind of promise for the future first. That's what had gotten him in trouble with the last one. He'd vowed to keep them out of his bed after that disaster. Hotel rooms worked just fine.

Claire's face popped into his head, followed by her perfectly snug Cheerios T-shirt.

Ruby had given him a conspiratorial smile and wink over breakfast when he'd asked what Claire's last name was. Jess had seemed oblivious during most of the meal, thank God, singing some pop song under her breath.

But during the five miles to his pickup, his cousin had talked non-stop about the handywoman. He doubted much of it was true. The part about Claire picking up a maggot-filled rat with her bare hands in particular. Jess had a tendency to fictionalize people, like she did her father, in order to make life more entertaining.

"Burger and fries." The waitress shoved a plate of food under his nose. The hamburger bun was coated with a sheen of grease. "Can I grab anything else for ya?"

Mac's mouth watered. He shook his head.

"We have lemon meringue and cherry pie for dessert today. Give me a holler if you change your mind."

After dumping ketchup on his cheeseburger, he plowed into the hot fries. Nothing tasted as good as fried potatoes. He scanned the mining claim as he ate, his eyes on the paper, but his mind on his pickup.

Roadrunner Auto Parts was closed Sundays, so he was stuck using Ruby's old Ford until Tuesday, since the parts he needed would most likely have to be shipped. Unless he drove into Tucson today and picked up the parts.

But even if he were to leave straight from the diner, he wouldn't be home until close to six, which meant he'd have to back out of his agreement to help Claire find her dog.

He bit into the cheeseburger and contemplated the idea.

Providing Ruby didn't need her truck over the next couple of days, he could probably get by using it to drive to the mines. But there was no way her old Ford could make it through the creek on the old road up to Socrates Pit or Two Jakes mines. The truck was two-wheel drive with barely twelve inches of clearance. He'd have to carry his equipment from the main road up to the mines and back.

Patsy Cline wailed on the radio about being crazy for feeling so lonely as he swallowed the last bite of his burger.

Driving to Tucson would undoubtedly be more productive than scouring the desert with Claire. But much less entertaining.

He gathered his stuff and stepped up to the cash register. The waitress wore her sultry smile as she punched a few keys on the register.

Mac threw down a ten. "You haven't seen a beagle

running around outside here today, have you?" he asked, watching her count back his change. "His back is about as tall as my shin, and his right eye and left ear have black around them."

"Can't say I have," she answered, looking him in the eye.

Damn. He dropped a tip on the table on the way out. As he stood under the noon sun, he stared down the road leading toward Tucson. He could be there in about two hours.

He climbed into the old Ford, fired it up, and headed back to the R.V. park.

⟶ ✦ ⟵

Sophy watched through the finger-smudged diner windows as Ruby's nephew sped away. The knot in her gut confirmed her worst fears—the door out of Jackrabbit Junction was on the verge of slamming shut.

She scooped up the tip he'd left and stuffed it in her bra, the crisp bills tickling her skin. The fact that Ruby's nephew was the man who'd been looking for the dog last night made her upper lip sweat.

Pulling a pack of Pall Malls out of her apron pocket, she pushed through the diner's front door and slipped around to the back of the restaurant. The roar of a passing semi drowned out the click of her lighter snapping shut.

The dog was safely tucked away for however long she needed him out of her hair. Although his nonstop baying had her contemplating shooting the mutt. Damn her weakness for four-legged creatures.

She took a long drag from her cigarette. So, if Ruby's nephew had been the guy in the mine, who was the woman who'd been hollering for the dog? It hadn't been Ruby.

The back door swung half open. "Sophy," her line

cook called. He jerked in surprise when she came around from behind the door. "Oh, there you are. The dude in the pink shirt wants his bill."

"I'll be right in." She exhaled a stream of smoke.

As she stubbed out her cigarette and flicked it in the general direction of the garbage dumpster, she thought about the copies of mining claims Ruby's nephew had been looking at Socrates Pit had been among them; where Joe had stashed the loot.

She had to find a way to keep Ruby's nephew out of that mine.

"Where ya going?" Jess asked.

Claire paused on the top step of Ruby's porch. Jess lounged in a plastic lawn chair with her feet propped up on the porch railing and a bottle of Mountain Dew in her hand.

"To grab some lunch." Claire stepped to the ground, the gravel crunching under her tennis shoes. She'd been in such a rush this morning, not to mention distracted by a certain old man complaining about his missing dog, that she'd forgotten to eat breakfast, let alone grab some cash for lunch.

She heard footsteps running toward her from behind. "Can I come with you?"

"Don't you have schoolwork to do?"

"Nah. I'm at recess." Jess matched her pace.

"High schoolers don't have recess."

"Well, Ruby says I need to run around the park for a bit each day to get rid of some of my energy. She calls it recess."

"You have a cool mom." Claire's mom probably wouldn't have even given her a bathroom break—the dictator. She would've said it was important to learn how to control one's bodily functions.

"I think I just get on her nerves. That's why she wants to ship me off to school." Jess let out a dramatically pathetic sigh. "I don't know why she even bothered having me."

Ah, the drama of adolescence. Behind her sunglasses, Claire rolled her eyes. "Probably just to have someone to torture."

"Probably." The flippant tone in Jess's voice signaled the end of that particular conversation. "I hope Mac comes home soon. He promised to show me how to parallel park."

Claire gritted her teeth at the sound of Mac's name. If she didn't need his help finding Henry, she'd hogtie him and hold him prisoner in the tool shed until the mining company's signing date had come and gone.

"He asked about you at breakfast," Jess said as they passed the restrooms across from Chester's Winnebago Brave.

Despite her current anti-Mac campaign, a small bubble of happiness formed in her chest. She did her best to pop it.

"He wanted to know what your last name was."

Not exactly a question an attractive man pining for her would ask.

Manny, Chester, and Gramps sat in the shade under the awning of Gramps's Winnebago. *Damn!* She'd hoped to slip in and out without any more questions about Henry's whereabouts.

"Mac thinks you're hot."

Claire shot Jess a surprised frown. "He told you that?"

"Well, not really. But I bet if you outline your lips with my dark pink liner and use my Raspberry Sparkle glitter gloss, he'd want to do some serious snogging with you."

"Snogging?" Gramps asked, obviously eavesdropping. "What in the hell is snogging?"

Jess sighed, sounding every bit like the bored teenager

dealing with an obtuse adult. "As in, to snog."

Gramps glanced at Manny. "Is that some Spanish word?"

"Not in my dictionary." Manny ogled Claire's waist. "*Ay yi yi!* You're wearing a tool belt."

"Snogging is like Frenching," Jess clarified.

"I think she's talking about backseat bingo," Chester offered, puffing his cheeks as he blew out cigar smoke.

"Why don't you come over here and show me what's in your tool belt," Manny said and trilled his tongue at Claire.

Claire shook her head at the oversexed sixty-nine-year-old. Manny needed more than a wife. He needed a harem.

"What's backseat bingo?" Jess asked.

"Keep your hands off my granddaughter, Carrera." Gramps eyed Jess. "What's your name, kid?" He seemed to be ignoring Jess's question, or trying to distract her.

"Jessica, but you can call me Jess."

"I dated a Jessica once," Manny said, still eying Claire's hips. "She had eyes the color of the Caribbean and lovely big—"

"Manny!" Claire interrupted. "There are young ladies here."

"You're not so young, anymore," Gramps told Claire with a smirk.

"What's backseat bingo?" Jess asked again.

"I was going to say big teeth," Manny said and took a sip of what looked like cranberry juice.

"Who wants to snog with you?" Gramps asked Claire.

Chester snickered. "What's wrong, Harley? You afraid she's going to score before you do?"

"Quit flappin' your lips, you old buzzard." Gramps turned back to Claire. "Well?"

"Nobody." Sad, but true. She could use some good snogging to take her mind off her troubles. "Jess was just jabbering."

"I was not. Mac never talks about girls, and he told me that you're 'interesting.'"

Claire doubted he meant that in a positive way.

"Who's Mac?" Gramps and Manny both asked in unison.

"Never mind." Claire wished the earth would swallow her whole. She walked over and yanked open the Winnebago's door.

"He's my cousin," Claire heard Jess explain just before she slammed the door behind her.

She turned on the radio, hoping to drown out the conversation about her that was sure to follow. Hank Williams Jr. carried on about his family traditions as she grabbed a loaf of bread from the cupboard, slapped some peanut butter on a slice, and then slathered her Aunt Mary's homemade apricot jam on another.

She had a few of her own family traditions she'd like to complain about, her mother's guilt trips and blackmailing antics topping the list.

She took a huge bite of her sandwich. Her gaze landed on the picture of Henry attached to the fridge with a Yellowstone National Park magnet. Worry prickled the back of her neck. If she didn't find that dog today, she was going to catch some serious hell.

Henry and Gramps had been together for over five years now. The last thing she needed working against her with all of these Internet babes trotting around like show ponies was Gramps being lonely for another friend.

Laying her sandwich down on the counter, she opened the fridge, grabbed a chunk of squishy bleu cheese sealed in a sandwich bag, and stuffed it in the pocket of her jacket. She shoved a small bag of sour cream and onion chips in her other pocket.

The only way she was going to get Henry to come back

to her was with the proper bait—his favorite food. No need for Gramps to see what she was up to, it would just raise more doubts about her ability to do anything right.

Her notoriety for never finishing things weighed down her optimism. Gramps had never echoed what the rest of the family preached to her about following through on college, jobs, relationships, and promises, but she knew he must be thinking it right about now.

Clicking off the radio, she stepped outside, peanut butter sandwich and jacket in hand.

"—and that's how I could tell she'd had a boob job," Chester finished.

Claire almost dropped her sandwich. She glared at Chester. "Oh, that's real nice. I'm sure Jess's mom would love to know the things you're teaching her child."

"Hey, she asked me. I couldn't lie to the kid."

"It's okay, Claire," Jess said. "I already know about boob jobs. Sally James had one, and now she has to beat the boys off with a stick."

"Speaking of *chi chis*," Manny said looking at Gramps, "I hear you have a date this afternoon with DeeDee."

"They don't call her Double-D for nothing," Chester added with a laugh any dirty old man would be proud of.

Claire lifted her eyebrows. "Who's DeeDee? Is she the woman you were with last night?"

"That was Virginia," Gramps said, avoiding Claire's gaze.

"There's nothing *virgin* about that woman's hips." Manny growled like a tiger.

Jess giggled.

Claire concentrated on Gramps. "Who's DeeDee?" she repeated.

"None of your business. You focus on finding my dog. Besides, the rules state that any dates occurring outside of the Winnebago will not be discussed until twenty-four hours after the event."

Oh, yeah. She'd forgotten about that one. "Fine. Plan on talking about this love tryst tomorrow night at supper."

Gramps's brow wrinkled like one of those Pug dogs. "For your information, this is nothing so sordid."

"They're going on a picnic," Manny supplied.

"You hate picnics," Claire said.

"He's looking to get a little bit of 'Afternoon Delight,' aren't you, Harley?" Chester gave him a conspiratorial wink.

"Is 'Afternoon Delight' like backseat bingo?" Jess asked.

Claire grabbed Jess's arm and tugged her toward the store. "I'll explain later, when these three dirty birds aren't around to corrupt you any further."

"Don't be spying on me," Gramps hollered from behind her.

"I wouldn't dream of it," she yelled back.

"And don't come home without my dog!"

Chapter Seven

Where was that damned dog?

Claire tromped through a dry riverbed carpeted with sand and pebbles, following a Zebra-tailed lizard that darted back and forth between bundles of tumbleweed. Bone-cooking rays drilled down from a cloudless, cerulean sky.

If she had to spend much longer in this heat, her brain would turn crispy.

Maybe Mac was having better luck finding Henry.

She shielded her eyes and squinted up at Socrates Pit mine. The westerly sun spotlighted the steep, rugged hillside and transformed the mine into a gaping, toothless mouth. She searched for a glimpse of his white T-shirt, something she hadn't seen in over an hour.

Her idea of splitting up in their search for Henry didn't seem so brilliant now, but she'd needed some time to figure out how to talk Mac out of slapping a price tag on her grandma's valley.

So far, her plans had gravitated toward lassoing and knuckle-rubbing. However, with Mac being well over six feet tall and cold sober, common sense had vetoed those ideas. Her brain had yet to come up with a Plan B.

Keeping an eye on the mine for any sign of life, Claire plodded northward. A breeze with the scent of baking rocks dried the sweat from her skin before it had time to soak into her clothes.

Her mind bounced between wondering who owned the leg bone that had landed her in this predicament, and how far a beagle could travel in sixteen hours.

Feeling Godzilla-like, she wound through a miniature canyon, watching for scorpions, listening for any rattling sounds. A red-tailed hawk soared overhead, gliding and swooping. Its screeches echoed across the valley floor.

She tried not to think about what Gramps would say if she returned without Henry.

Something shined up ahead in the sand—glass, most likely, hitching a ride south to the Gila River. But as Claire drew closer, she slowed. It wasn't glass. It was a dog tag, surrounded by paw tracks and pointed boot prints.

Her fingers shook as she reached for it. One side read, "Henry Ford, 1309 Pilot Knob Rd., Nemo, SD 57759," the other, "Return postage guaranteed (if dog included)." The ring that looped through the tag was broken.

A renewed burst of hope tightened her chest. Squatting, she inspected the boot prints. They were small, not much bigger than hers. She chewed on her lower lip, tasting the desert's salty seasoning.

A shadow fell over her.

"What'd you find?" Mac hopped down into the dry wash.

Claire stood and dropped the dog tag into his open palm. "My guess is someone chased Henry into this wash and snagged him as he was scrambling up the other side. His tag fell off during the struggle."

Mac's hazel eyes held hers, his expression thoughtful, his glasses absent. Claire couldn't decide if he looked better with or without them. She suffered from the same indecisiveness when it came to Indiana Jones. The same fluttering pulse effect, too, dammit.

Mac lowered his gaze to the tag. "What makes you so sure that whoever made these tracks was after Henry? It could have just been a hiker."

"Two things. First, not many people go out hiking in a

pair of cowboy boots. Second, if they were just out for a stroll, why didn't they pick up the dog tag? They couldn't have missed seeing it, *unless* they were walking around in the dark. Third, Henry's prints lead only into the wash, not out."

"I thought you said *two* things."

Claire shrugged. "I changed my mind." She grabbed the tag from him and shoved it in her pocket, then noticed a red plastic wrapper entangled in the spindly arms of a nearby diamond cholla cactus. Another clue? She doubted Mac would concur. She fished the wrapper out from between the inch-long spines and stuffed it in her pocket, too.

She glanced Mac's way and found him watching her. "Did you find anything at the mine?" She fidgeted under the assessing look in his eyes.

"Lots of tennis shoe prints." He climbed out of the dry wash and held out his hand to help her up. "But no sign of Henry besides the paw prints at the mouth of the mine."

Claire took his hand, noticing his hiking boots as he pulled her up next to him. "What size shoe do you wear?"

"Twelve. Why?"

"Henry's dognapper has small feet. It must have been a woman. Or a kid. Or a man with really small feet."

"Or a tiny man with really big feet," Mac added, a cock-eyed grin on his lips.

"Exactly."

His grin slipped. "You don't even know for certain that Henry's been taken. It's a bit soon to start making presumptions."

"How much evidence do you need? A picture of Henry and his dognapper squeezed together in one of those quick-photo booths?" She should have known better than to try to convince a man of science without having the smoking gun.

The boot prints pointed westward, away from the wash. Nose to the ground, Claire trekked through groves of mesquite trees and around patches of shin-high ghost flowers covered with cream petals. Mac trailed her, silent except for the occasional sound of thorny cacti branches scratching his jeans.

A quarter mile west of the dry wash, Claire paused in the middle of what looked like a well-used wagon route. "The boot prints are gone."

Mac squatted and ran his finger through the loose, powdery dirt alongside a tire track. "A four-wheeler."

"Okay, we need to see who in the area owns one."

Shaking his head, Mac stood. "That's not going to help. Almost everyone in this county owns a four-wheeler. They practically issue them with your driver's license. Even Ruby has one."

"How come I haven't seen it?"

"You have. It's under that green tarp behind the tool shed. Jess broke a transaxle on it last fall while re-enacting an Evel Knievel stunt."

"Crap." Claire fingered the dog tag in her pocket, her hope of bringing good news back to Gramps evaporating faster than a drop of water on Death Valley asphalt. "What kind of a person steals a beagle?"

A niggling of fear poked at her belly. What if it was some freak who did twisted things to animals?

"We might as well head back." Mac rubbed the back of his neck as his gaze roamed the surrounding hills.

"Shouldn't we follow the tire tracks?"

"Kids run four-wheelers up and down this valley all the time. We're better off hanging flyers around town tomorrow morning."

"Hang flyers? That's what you do when you're selling diet pills."

"Claire."

"We're talking about someone abducting my grandfather's dog."

"Claire."

"Finding Henry may not be your top priority, but if I don't return with that dog in my arms, the only person in my family who has any faith left in me is going to be disappointed ... to say the least."

"Claire!"

"What?" she snapped back.

"Calm down."

"I'll calm down when Henry is sitting safely on Gramps's couch."

Mac put his arm around her shoulders. If he was trying to comfort her, he needed a different tactic. The scent of sun-washed desert she was beginning to associate with the long-legged, hazel-eyed hunk rubbing against her side had the same settling effect as touching the end of an electric cattle prod.

"Let's go back to Ruby's." He nudged her in the direction from which they'd come. "If you want, I'll go with you to explain the situation to your grandfather."

She peeked at him from behind her mirrored sunglasses as he led her along, his arm propelling her forward.

When he was nice to her like this, she had trouble remembering why she'd decided to stop fraternizing with him. Besides being sex-starved and nicotine-crazed, she was hungry for respect, and Mac was tossing her crumbs of it. He might not have realized that, but she did.

"Thanks for the offer, but no thanks." She'd dragged Henry out here last night, so she should take the heat for not finding him ... yet.

Pushing away from Mac, Claire picked up her pace, her thoughts more focused with each step.

They passed the dry wash again where she'd found

Henry's tags and then rounded the tailings at the base of Socrates Pit. Instead of turning left toward the car, Claire veered right.

It was time for Plan B.

"Mabel is the other way," Mac said.

"I know."

"Where are you going?"

"I want to show you something."

He followed without objection. Claire led him down a deer trail into a shallow canyon. The red sandstone walls glowed from the sun's rays. They hiked a short distance along the creek until the canyon spilled into the desert and her grandma's old cottonwood towered in front of them. She stopped under the shade of the trembling leaves.

Mac stared up at the big tree. "This must be over a century old."

"At least." Claire ran her finger over the heart and initials carved into the bark.

Plucking a stalk of desert lavender from the base of the trunk, Mac sniffed the violet flowers and glanced at the water. "It hasn't rained here in over two weeks. This stream must be spring fed."

"Ruby told me why you're here," Claire blurted.

Plan B lacked the finesse of Plan A.

Mac stared at her, his eyes narrowing.

"If she sells those mines to the mining company," she continued before her wits caught up with her, "they're gonna gut this land and dig an inverted mountain."

"This is none of your business, Claire." His voice was hard and tight, out of place in such a soft landscape.

She lifted her chin. She could feel her heart pounding in her fingertips. "I'm making it my business. There has to be some other way to save Ruby's R.V. park."

"What makes you think you can find the solution that Ruby can't?"

She smiled. It felt brittle. "I'm optimistic."

His brow furrowed. "You're naive."

"That could very well be, but I'm determined, too." She considered telling him about her grandma's ashes, but decided to keep the focus on his own family. "Ruby doesn't want to sell this land to the mining company, and I'm going to make sure she doesn't have to."

"Don't you think I've tried to come up with another solution? Ruby's backed into a corner. Selling is the only way out."

"I don't believe that."

"Believe what you want, just stay out of my way." Mac stormed off toward the car.

Claire trickled behind in his wake. She might not always make the right decisions in life, but she knew when to stop waving a red flag in front of a bull; when to hide behind a barrel.

As she strolled along admiring the abundance of fire ants and iridescent beetles scurrying along the cracked and dried valley floor, her heel came down on something hard in a pool of sandy soil.

She lifted her foot. A lighter lay in the dirt, its silver casing mostly hidden by the scattered grains of sand. She scooped it up and wiped off the dust. The letters S-A-M were etched on one side.

Sam? She flipped open the top and turned the cylinder with her thumb. It spit out sparks.

Sam was missing a lighter.

Was Sam missing a femur, too?

Monday, April 12th

"I'll be back in a couple of hours," Mac called to Ruby

as he pushed open the screen door and stepped onto the front porch.

The morning air fresh with a new day's promise lifted his spirits. He scanned the southern horizon, admiring the curves of the land. Thousands of years of weathering had smoothed the sharp angles from the valley laid out before him. For the first time since he'd driven out of Tucson's city limits, the task in front of him didn't seem so daunting.

The boards creaked under his boots as he descended the porch steps. Maybe he'd even be able to wrap up things a couple of days early and spend some time enjoying his vacation.

He paused at the base of the porch. The warm sunlight on his shoulders guaranteed another hot afternoon. The desert sun never seemed to understand that spring was a time of transition, not a matter of flipping a switch to hot.

Shading his eyes, he looked east at the northwest-trending *Tres Dedos* Mountains. A strip of cirrus clouds drifted above the large mass of Precambrian granite, nicknamed the Middle Finger, jutting out of the northern flank.

This corner of Arizona was littered with porphyry copper deposits inside masses of intrusive rock like the Middle Finger. With ninety percent of the state's copper coming from porphyry deposits, Ruby could very well be sitting on a piece of land worth ten times more than the mining company had offered.

Unfortunately, mining copper was extremely capital-intensive, and Ruby currently lived on the south side of Hard-Up-Ville.

As he walked around the corner of the porch, he dug in his pocket for the Ford's keys.

A pair of warblers perched in the crown of a nearby willow sang their hearts out. Mac whistled along with them. Not even Claire's determination to change Ruby's mind was going to pop his balloon on such a fine morning.

Then he saw Ruby's pickup.

"Fuucckk," he breathed more than spoke aloud as he skidded to a stop. He circled the truck, shaking his head. All four tires were as flat as cow pies.

He kneeled next to the front driver's side tire, scanning the tread for a screw or nail. Instead, he found a small slice in the outer wall.

Someone had gouged the tire.

Mac scooted to the back tire. It also had a gash in the outer wall.

"Son of a bitch." He pushed to his feet. This was no accident. It wasn't a prank, either. First his Dodge, now Ruby's Ford.

Somebody didn't want him going anywhere in a hurry.

Could it be Claire trying to interfere? He shook off the thought. She had her quirks, but he didn't think she'd do something that would cost Ruby money.

Maybe people at the mining company didn't want him finding something in the mines only they knew about. Then again, the bank stood to lose an easy cash crop if Ruby paid off her loan before they could take the park and mines from her.

There were too many possibilities. He needed time to think things through. More than that, he needed some wheels.

He strode back toward Ruby's front door, hesitating at the base of the porch stairs.

If he told Ruby about the flats, she'd want to pay for new tires with money she didn't have. Maybe he could take care of the problem before she took her usual morning break from schooling Jess, and she'd be none the wiser.

It was time to call in a favor.

Minutes later, Mac stood in front of Claire's Winnebago door. He could hear Johnny Horton singing the chorus to "The Battle of New Orleans" from the other side of the thin piece of aluminum.

Before he could knock, the door flew open. Claire frowned down at him, her hair tousled, her cheeks pink and pillow-lined. Oscar the Grouch stared at him from the front of her long pajama top.

"Mac?" Her voice sounded rusty with sleep.

"I need a ride," Mac blurted, his manners forgotten at the sight of Claire's bare legs and purple-painted toenails.

She rubbed her eyes, blinking. "What?"

"Ruby's tires are flat. I need you to give me a ride in your grandfather's car."

Claire leveled him with her gaze. "Of course, a ride." Pushing past him, she strode off without a backward glance across the sprouts of grass poking out of the ground.

What was that supposed to mean? He took off after her. "Did that qualify as a yes?"

She swerved around Mabel while mumbling under her breath.

Mac stopped in front of the Mercury. "Claire," he said, trying a less bumbling approach. "Would you please give me a ride to the auto parts store in Yuccaville?"

"I heard you," she shouted over her shoulder as she marched toward the concrete building housing the public restrooms.

"What's going on out there?" a deep voice said from behind Mac.

Mac whirled around. An old guy with gray, bristle-top hair poked his head out the driver's side window of an ancient, pea green Winnebago Brave.

"Nothing." He felt like he'd been caught soaping Mabel's windows. "Sorry we woke you."

"Nothing, my ass. Who in the hell are you?"

"Mac Garner." He glanced back toward Claire. She'd disappeared. He was on his own. "My aunt owns the park," he added as extra credentials.

"Are you *Señorita* Jess's cousin?" An even deeper voice thick with a Mexican accent called from the silver Airstream parked next to the bathrooms. A man looking remarkably like Jimmy Smits stepped out from under an awning draped with red pepper lights.

Mac nodded slowly. How did these guys know Jess?

"No kidding," Bristle-top said, cracking open a can of Schlitz. "Word on the street is you want to do some snogging with Claire."

"S-snogging?" Mac stuttered.

"Knock off this bullshit about snogging Claire." A third old guy, his bald head rivaling Mabel's chrome, shouted from the doorway of Claire's R.V. "It's too damned early for that kind of talk."

"Says you," Jimmy Smits Sr. said, grinning at Mac. "Some of us like our eggs over-easy with a side of sex."

Mac ran a hand through his hair. Old guys were crawling out of the woodwork. Where in the hell was Claire?

"Before you lay a hand on my granddaughter," the bald guy said as he stalked toward Mac, "you need to answer a few questions."

Mac frowned. Where had the old man gotten that idea about Claire and him? Had he caught Mac looking at her legs?

"What do you do for a living?" Claire's grandpa asked.

"Do you have any VDs?" Bristle-top shouted as he rounded the front of his Brave and waddled over on a pair of bowed legs.

"How many women have you dated in the last year?" Jimmy Smits Sr. threw out as he strolled up and leaned against Mabel's front bumper. The scent of Old Spice smacked Mac in the face, making his nose twinge.

"What are your intentions toward my granddaughter?"

"Whoa," Mac said, "I just need a ride to—"

"Do you practice safety sex?" Bristle-top cut him off.

"If you think you can get away with some kind of quick sex fling with her, you'd better think again." Claire's Grandpa's eyes narrowed. "You'll end up with my foot up your ass."

"There's nothing like a woman who wears a tool belt," Jimmy Smits Sr. said, winking, making a gargling noise in the back of his throat.

Bristle-top knuckled Mac's bicep. "When was your last physical?"

The three old men swarmed around him. A trickle of sweat ran down Mac's back.

"How did you meet my granddaughter?"

"Here's a tip, *Don Juan*. Her favorite flower is a black-eyed susan. You need to pay attention to details to win a beautiful woman like Claire."

"Have you been HOV tested in the last year?" Bristle-top asked.

HOV? Mac felt like a paper boat caught in a whirlpool. He glanced at the restroom. Damn it, where was Claire?

Grandpa crossed his arms and glared up at Mac. "More importantly, do you know how to play Bid Euchre?"

"You could have told him no," Claire said. She took her eyes off the two-lane road stretched out before her and glanced across at Mac.

"So you say, but you weren't the one surrounded by a pack of cantankerous old men threatening to remove your testicles with fingernail clippers if I harmed a hair on your head."

Claire couldn't keep her grin from surfacing. "Which is why it makes no sense why you would agree to play cards with them tonight."

"I wasn't given a choice."

She could tell by the way he sat ramrod straight in Mabel's soft leather embrace that this morning's chaos still had him strung up tennis racket-tight.

She sighed to herself. The guy didn't know how to let the world parade by without trying to corral the clowns. Loosening up a bit would do him some good. But her job wasn't to grease Mac's joints, it was to stop the mining company from turning the Dancing Winnebagos R.V. Park into another Meteor Crater, like the one up near Winslow.

Unfortunately, the *how-to* part of her plan was still hazy in her brain.

"How did your grandfather take the news about Henry?" Mac asked.

"He's worried." Claire didn't feel like talking about it. Her heart still hurt from the pain she'd seen in Gramps's eyes when she'd told him his dog had been kidnapped.

A bone, a missing dog, and now someone named Sam—her work was piling up. Which reminded her, she needed to ask Ruby if she knew anyone named Sam. "Maybe you guys could play cards at Ruby's tonight."

"Why?"

"Because I'm going to take Ruby out for a drink at The Shaft, and somebody needs to mind the store." She looked over to find him giving her a squinty-eyed stare.

"I don't like the sound of that. You're up to something, and I have a feeling whatever it is will piss me off."

"Can't two women go out for a drink with the sole purpose of sharing war stories over a cold brew?"

"If Ruby doesn't pay off the bank, she'll lose everything."

"I know," Claire replied with forced patience. While she struggled to keep her checking account from bottoming out every other month, she wasn't an idiot about finances.

"She explained the situation to me yesterday."

"Selling the mines is her ticket out of debtor's prison."

"Selling the mines is one solution. There are others."

"Such as?" Mac asked, doubt filling his tone.

"I'm still working on them."

Claire saw the *Welcome to Yuccaville* sign up ahead. *Thank God!* If she didn't pour some caffeine down her throat soon, she'd be taking the praying mantis approach to solving her difference of opinion with Mac.

Criminy, she'd shave her eyebrows for a whiff of second-hand cigarette smoke right now.

"At that first blinking yellow light," Mac directed, "take a left. The store is a block down on the right."

"Being that you're a wall builder," literally as well as figuratively, Claire thought with a slight grimace, "you must have taken a lot of geology classes in college."

"I prefer the term *geotechnician*."

"Right. Did you take any classes where they talked about how to date different rock samples?"

"Yes."

"How do you go about figuring out how old something is?"

"There are several methods." He sounded suspicious. She peeked at him. He was still giving her the squinty look. "Carbon-14, Potassium-argon, and Isotopic dating to name a few."

That got her nowhere. She needed to find out how old this bone was so she could start trying to match it to its owner. "Which did you use?" Claire asked, turning at the light.

"None. My roommate interned at a local lab for the Arizona Bureau of Geology and Mineral Resources. He did the sample testing for me."

Really? Now she was on to something. Maybe his roommate knew something about forensic anthropology, or at least someone working in that field. "Do you still keep in touch with him?"

"Why?"

"Because I need a favor, Mr. Suspicious Pants."

"No."

His immediate refusal to even listen to her needs made her want to wop him upside the head.

She pulled into an empty parking spot in front of the Roadrunner Auto Parts store. "What do you mean 'No'? Did I hesitate when you asked me to give you a ride here?"

"Your exact words the third time I asked were, 'Go fly a kite.'"

So she was a little grouchy first thing in the morning, was that a crime? "But we're here now, aren't we?"

"Because I threatened to squeal about how you scratched Mabel's bumper when you backed into that 'No Trespassing' sign."

She shut off the car and glared at him. "Quit splitting hairs. I drove you here as a favor, so maybe you could find a soft spot in your heart to do me a favor in return."

Shoving open the door, Mac climbed out of the car. He took four steps toward Roadrunner Auto Parts, wheeled around, and strode back to the car.

Claire pasted on her tooth whitener-commercial smile.

Mac leaned down, his gaze raked down her T-shirt and back up before landing on her face. "What's it worth to you, Claire?"

Sophy sipped on a glass of cold Coors, then lit another cigarette. She sat at a barrel-top table in a shadowy, smoke-filled corner of The Shaft—Jackrabbit Junction's only watering hole.

The town's resident alcoholic slouched at the bar,

slurring his tale about the wife who'd up and left him four years ago, taking his only son, their basset hound, and the kitchen sink. Sophy had been to their house several times during their marriage for lingerie parties and whatnot. She would have taken the sink, too—it was dark blue.

Happy hour was long over, but several of the mining company's first shift crew still lingered: knocking pool balls around, watching bowling on the black and white television, pumping quarters into the jukebox.

Sophy was glad Ruby Martino hadn't seen her sitting in the corner when the redhead had walked in the bar over twenty minutes ago. She didn't feel like fending off the widow's death-wish glares tonight.

"You're pretty good at this. I'll have to take you out shootin' with me." Sophy heard Ruby shout over Johnny Cash, who sang about falling into a ring of fire.

Ruby must have been talking to the brunette who'd followed her in. The two women were taking turns shooting at deer with a plastic rifle. The *Big Buck Hunter* video game was a favorite at The Shaft, so much so that Butch, the owner, had had to replace the rifle three times in the last six months.

Sophy took a long draw from her cigarette, watching the two women from behind an Amazon-sized, fake fern. No living organism could breathe day in and day out in this dark, cramped tavern, so Butch had long ago resorted to man-made products.

"Did you find your dog, yet?" Ruby asked.

Dog? Sophy froze. Her cigarette dangled from her lips.

"No. Someone kidnapped him."

"They did what, honey?" Ruby's soft Oklahoma drawl had always grated on Sophy's nerves, especially after Joe had sat in this very bar and pointed out how much more alluring it sounded than her own southeastern Arizona twang.

Nothing about her had ever been good enough for that man. But Joe sure hadn't had a problem with her working two jobs to make ends meet while he took college classes and studied all day long. By her calculations, Joe owed her that R.V. park, at least.

She wiped the sweat from the outside of her glass. Watching Ruby suffocate over the last year from the weight of Joe's medical bills had made living in Jackrabbit Junction tolerable.

"Someone took Henry."

"How do you know that?"

"I found his dog tag out by Socrates Pit, and there were boot tracks over the top of his prints." The brunette spoke in a crisp, uppity accent, like she'd lived in the city most of her life.

"Who would steal a dog?" Ruby asked.

"You tell me. It's not like he has a pedigree. Henry is just a plain old beagle who scoots on the ground to scratch his ass and spends a good half-hour every morning licking his balls."

Ruby laughed. "Reminds me of my old boyfriend back in Tulsa."

"Mac thinks Henry got lost and someone took him home to feed him. But Henry doesn't go to anyone except Gramps—unless he's bribed. I'm leaning toward the kidnapping theory."

Sophy squirmed in her seat. She stubbed out her cigarette. This chick was too close to the mark.

"How did you get my nephew to agree to help you figure how old that bone is?"

What bone? Sophy leaned closer to the plant separating her from the two women.

"I agreed to a little promise. Oh, hey, do you know anyone around here named Sam? Someone who may have lived here in the last decade or so?"

"No. But there used to be a guy living off Ocotilla Road who called his dog Sam. Why?"

Sophy knew a couple of different Sams—one ended up buried in the mine when Drift Number Four caved in thirty years back, and the other got fried by lightening while adjusting the antennae on top of his trailer. Word around town was that his fingers fell right off when they tried to pry them from around the aluminum.

"I found this lighter while we were looking for Henry yesterday. It still sparks, but the lighter fluid has evaporated."

Sophy carefully peeked through the plant.

Her heart lurched into her throat at the sight of a silver case. She knew that lighter. She'd used it several times in the past.

She knew who Sam was, too.

And now she knew one other thing—the nosey brunette needed to go away before she dug up anything else in Jackrabbit Junction.

Chapter Eight

She claims her name is Fanny Derriere," Chester said out of the side of his mouth, his lips wrapped around a cigar.

"And you believe her?" Mac asked, looking up from the two black Aces, Queen of spades, King of hearts, and nine of clubs in his hand.

A fog bank of smoke swirled under the humming florescent lights of Ruby's rec room.

Manny sat next to Mac. The older man crooned along with Waylon Jennings on the radio about going to Luckenbach, Texas and getting back to the basics of love. Hound dogs were more on key.

"If her name is Fanny Derriere, my name is Hairy Butt," Harley, Mac's partner for the night, muttered around his cigar.

While Mac, Chester, and Manny all sported T-shirts and jeans, Harley had dressed for the evening's event in a blue oxford shirt, beige suspenders, and brown and white polka-dotted tie knotted below his open collar. Add a fedora and he'd be an aged ringer for Paul Newman in *The Sting*.

"I don't care if her name is Hindquarter Helen. That's one juicy rump roast." Chester swigged a mouthful of Pabst Blue Ribbon beer.

"You should have seen her pants." Manny's eyes crinkled at the edges, his moustache smiled. "They were so tight, I could see freckles."

"On what?" Jess plopped onto the barstool between Harley and Manny. The girl didn't miss a thing, no matter how many times they sent her into the General Store on bogus errands.

"Never mind," Harley and Mac said in unison.

Chester snorted.

Harley threw a Queen of diamonds in the middle of the table. "That's trump."

"What's *trump* mean again?" Jess asked, leaning over Harley's shoulder, frowning at his cards. Determined to participate in the game, she'd badgered Claire's grandpa until he'd relented and started teaching her how to play.

"It's the suit that has the most powerful cards in the game," Manny answered for Harley. "And this," he added, his grin wide as he tossed a Jack of diamonds on top of Harley's Queen, "is the toughest *hombre* of them all."

Mac surveyed the hand Chester had dealt him—a lousy combination of cards. Of the four suits, Mac held three, and Harley had picked the odd one out. Stone-faced, he laid down the nine of clubs.

Harley grunted. "Is that the best you can do?"

"You're the one who called diamonds as trump," Manny said. He'd been acting as Mac's advocate for the last hour. Mac had yet to figure out what he'd done to earn it.

"That's because he bid two."

"What's wrong with bidding two?" Mac tossed a few salt-free mini-pretzels in his mouth, crunching.

"I thought you said you know how to play Bid Euchre."

"I do." He'd learned from a guy back in college.

Harley yanked his cigar from his lips. "Then you should know that betting two is code for telling your partner you have a red Jack and a black Jack." He shot Mac a glare. "Do you even have a Jack?"

"No table talk," Chester said and threw out a ten of

diamonds.

"Shit, boy. Everyone here has diamonds, but us."

"You shouldn't have outbid him," Manny told Harley, chuckling as he collected the four cards from the middle of the table and stacked them in front of him.

"Two is a lousy bid," Harley muttered.

"Two is a par bid," Mac said. "You didn't have to jump to four."

"Chester always bids four. I had to beat him to the punch."

Manny threw out the Jack of hearts to lead the next round. "And that's the second toughest *hombre* in the deck," he informed Jess.

"Damn you, Carerra." Harley tossed out his Ace of diamonds with a defeated sigh. A smirk hovered on his lips as he eyed Mac. "I don't know what Claire sees in you."

Mac shook his head at the mirth twinkling in Harley's eyes. "I told you guys, Claire and I are not an item."

But he wasn't blind to the way Claire kept looking at him when she thought he wasn't looking. Or to how well she filled out a T-shirt.

Okay, so maybe he was a pushover. Agreeing to take that silly femur to his buddy to analyze for nothing more than a promise from Claire to drop the possible murder notions until they received test results probably wasn't one of his smartest moves. But seeing her whole face light up when he'd consented had made him forget about Ruby's flat tires—at least until he'd handed over the cash for them.

"That's not what your cousin here told us," Chester said, throwing down the King of diamonds.

Jess had the dignity to blush at Mac's glare. "I only said it because Claire thinks you're hot."

She does?

"Jess," Mac warned, wanting to put a cork in his cousin's mouth before she said something else embarrassing.

"What else did Claire say, *Señorita?*" Manny asked.

Popping a bubble, Jess grinned. "That she really likes Mac's butt."

Wolf whistles and elbow jabs abounded from the *three amigos.*

Mac dropped his gaze to his cards, fighting the heat crawling up his neck. Damn Jess and her big mouth!

Still laughing, Chester crushed his beer can in his hand and cracked open another. "It's your turn, sweet buns."

⟶⟵ ◆ ⟶⟵

The Shaft bustled with life. Amidst the cozy cocoon of second-hand smoke, stale peanuts, and overused pick-up lines, Claire stared across the smattering of cowboy hats.

A grizzly, barrel-chested man balanced on a tea-party sized chair while he bellowed along with Tanya Tucker blasting from the jukebox. Claire struggled to listen without wincing. Judging from the amount of lighters held up in the air with flames burning, the solo performance was a hit with the rest of the bar.

"Good ol' Fernando Tortuga," Ruby said in her soft southern drawl as she slid onto the stool next to Claire. "He can't sit through *Delta Dawn* without joinin' in at the top of his lungs. Butch keeps that song on the jukebox just to hear Fernando sing along."

Claire shot her a skeptical glance.

"Entertainment in Jackrabbit Junction is sparse as glacier water."

From her barstool perch, Claire had a territorial view of the bar's cluttered landscape and the gaggle of liquor-happy patrons wandering around on wobbly legs. As she scanned the room for the jerk who'd wanted to take her out to his truck and show her his power drill, her gaze landed on a bouffant-haired brunette in painted-on red Wranglers weaving her way toward the other end of the bar. The woman's white shirt plunged hooker-low in front.

"Who's the busty bombshell with the rock-star red lips?"

"You mean the busty *old* bombshell," Ruby corrected her. "That's Sophy—spelled with a *y*, not *ie*. Sophy Wheeler. Joe told me she changed the spelling to make her name unique."

Claire frowned at Ruby. "You mean, Joe, your husband?"

"One and the same."

"Why would he know that?"

"Because she used to be Sophy Martino before Joe divorced her. But I usually refer to her as 'The Bitch.'"

Claire sat up straight. Things were finally getting exciting. "How long were they married?"

"Long enough to want to kill each other."

Claire watched as Sophy blew a goodbye kiss at the bartender, then sashayed out the door into the night with a drooling admirer in tow. The woman appeared to have a master's degree in the art of flirting. Claire would have to keep an eye on Gramps if Sophy ever stepped into his radar range.

"So, what's their story?" she asked Ruby.

Ruby sipped from her glass of beer. "They were livin' in Phoenix while Joe went to college. Accordin' to Joe, Sophy got tired of waitin' for him to finish and ran off to Las Vegas with some cowboy who promised her glitter and gold."

The hum of music and conversation around her faded as Claire's attention focused on the words spilling from Ruby's lips. "How'd Joe and Sophy meet?"

"They grew up here. Wheeler's Diner, across the street, belonged to Sophy's parents. I've never heard what went down in Vegas, but when the golden-tongued cowboy pushed her aside, he left her penniless on the street."

"She scampered home with her tail between her legs and went back to working tables for her parents. They died a few years later and left her the diner. She's been here ever since."

"Did Joe move back here after college?"

"No. I think he lived in L.A., San Diego, then Dallas for a while. But most of what he did involved travel, so he wasn't home much. I met him back in Tulsa. He was there on a business trip and came into the restaurant where I worked. When I gave him the bill, he asked me out and wouldn't take *No* for an answer."

"What did Joe do for a living?"

"I'm not sure what he was doin' back then. He never wanted to talk about it. We saw each other off and on over the next six months. Then one day, he came to my door and told me he'd bought an R.V. park for me to run in the same town in Arizona where he had an antique business. Then he handed me a bouquet of the prettiest pink roses I ever laid eyes on and asked me to marry him."

Ruby's eyes sparkled a little in the dim light.

"He owned an antique business here in Jackrabbit Junction?" Claire pointed down at the bar.

"Yep." Ruby drained the last of her glass of beer and lowered it to the bar with a clonk. "Shared the same building as the hardware store. That side of the building is still empty."

"Jackrabbit Junction isn't the most fertile place to start a business. There isn't no Wal-Marts or Taco Bells knockin' on the mayor's door."

"How long were you two married?"

"We were two weeks shy of our fifth anniversary when Joe passed. The first four years were good, the last one pure hell."

"Did he stop traveling when you got married?"

"Not right away. He balanced running the antique store and burnin' up the road for some company out of Phoenix for over a year. Selling tools to manufacturing plants all over the West."

Ruby rubbed her fingertip over the lip of her glass, a faraway smile on her lips. "He never liked to talk much about his traveling job. Said bringin' his work home made his ulcers flare up real bad-like."

She glanced at Claire. "You see, Joe was a stress case. He smoked like a diesel, drank 'til his liver floated, carried sixty pounds more than his heart could handle, and battled high blood pressure. Potato chips were his kryptonite. Never could eat just one bag."

Neither could Claire lately. She sipped her Corona fog, tasting the hint of tequila under the beer, and tried to picture Joe in her mind.

"After about a year of being married, he came home and told me he'd had a small stroke while he was in L.A. and decided it was time to retire from his travelin' sales job. He wanted just to run his store and spend his golden years with me. Talked about a little nest egg he'd tucked away that'd keep us fat and happy."

Cracking a peanut shell, Ruby frowned down at the nut resting in her palm. "Unfortunately, if there was an egg, he had it in some other nest and forgot about it."

"A couple years after his retirement, Joe was drivin' to Yuccaville for a carton of cigarettes, had a massive stroke, and rolled his Mercedes. The stroke paralyzed him on the right side, screwed up his ability to talk and write, and left his memory spotty at best."

"I watched him disintegrate over the next year, while medical expenses ate up our savings and then some. Another stroke killed him in his sleep. The next day, I woke up alone and over my eyebrows in debt. He willed me the

R.V. park, the mines, and everything that belonged to him—including his medical bills."

"So he was a little too generous," Claire said.

Ruby nodded. "First thing I did was sell everything in that antique store. Ol' Bill Taylor is a real stickler when it comes to funeral costs. He threatened to dig up Joe and drop him off on my front porch if I didn't pay him promptly for his services."

"Joe had no insurance. He was only sixty when the big stroke hit, so he didn't even have Medicare. He always said buying health insurance was like 'pissing money down a drain.' Guess he was planning on livin' forever."

A bad gamble on Joe's part, and pretty damned selfish, too, in Claire's opinion. "So, Sophy was back from Vegas and working the diner when you moved here?"

"Yep."

"And Joe had been living here, too, running his antique shop?" Something about the two of them coming back to such a tiny dot on the map stuck in Claire's craw. Her gut said there was something more between them than Ruby wanted to share. Or knew about.

"Uh, huh."

"Sophy probably wasn't beating down your door, offering any welcome-to-the-neighborhood casseroles or wanting to swap recipes."

Ruby shook her head, chuckling. "Hardly."

"And now that Joe is out of the picture, have things changed?"

"Yep. Her nails are longer and sharper."

"So, are you one of those *hombres* who likes other *hombres?*"

Mac choked on his mouthful of Saguaro Ale. "No," he

answered after catching his breath. "I like women, and *only* women."

The older man stared back, his brown eyes creased and piercing like a Mexican gunfighter of old. Mac could almost hear the cymbal sound effect used in old western movies to alert the audience that trouble was on the horizon.

Harley sure was taking his sweet time in the bathroom, and what was holding up Chester? How long did it take to grab another six pack of his favorite beer from his cooler outside the back door?

Jess snored lightly as she lay sprawled on the sofa, one leg dangling over the side, the stick of her grape sucker still clutched in her hand. She'd given up fighting the sandman right after Ruby's clock cuckooed eleven times.

"Yet, you don't like Claire," Manny said.

That wasn't necessarily true, but Manny didn't need to know that. "Claire is not the only woman on Earth."

Manny smiled. "No, but she's one of the prettier ones."

But good looks could be as deceptive as quicksand. "She's a bit unstable," Mac said.

"She's got a lot of spark."

"She's too spontaneous."

"She's the life of the party," Manny volleyed, his moustache twitching.

Mac crossed his arms over his chest. "She gives free reign to her emotions."

"She's warm-hearted and optimistic."

Harley pushed through the green curtain, his usual scowl in place, and strode toward them. "Who you talking about?" he asked as he pulled out his chair.

"Claire," Manny said as he started dealing out cards. "Mac can't get her out of his head."

Mac didn't bother refuting it. His denials had been falling on hair-filled, near-deaf ears all night.

"We were discussing what a hot babe she is." Manny added.

Harley shot a poisoned glower at Manny, then picked up his cards. "Claire is a sweet girl, and sharp, too." He moved the cards around in his hand. "She's taken more college classes than both her sisters combined, and when she's not out finding trouble, she has her face shoved in a book like a good child."

Good child? Mac had trouble buying that, although, her intelligence was evident in her speech—when she wasn't swearing. "What's her degree in?"

"She doesn't have a degree yet."

"Yet?"

Harley nodded. "The world is Claire's oyster. But," he emphasized the conjunction, "she can't decide which tool to use to pry it open."

"She's a free spirit," Manny said warmly.

"She's indecisive." Mac pinpointed.

"Her mother and aunts say she's a screw up," Harley said. "They constantly nag the poor girl, trying to bully her into taking one path in life and sticking with it. But Claire is like a dandelion seed. Her course in life is determined by the wind. In that way, she takes after her grandmother." A smile curled the edges of the old man's lips.

Chester burst in through the back door. "Hey! Guess who I just ran into outside?"

"Your ex-wife," Harley answered, grinning. "She wants your other testicle."

"A real Bob Hope, aren't you?" Chester flopped down on his chair and wiped the dripping beer can on his T-shirt. "It was Eve, all warm and pink from the shower, smelling like a bouquet of posies. She agreed to go to lunch with me tomorrow."

"Eve? Is she the retired flight attendant?" Harley asked.

Manny nodded. "A real blonde, too! Or so she says."

He closed his eyes and sucked in a deep breath. "Oh, *dios mio*. How I'd love to take a peek under her fig leaf."

"You and me both, you lousy dog." Chester lit a cigar, squinting through the puffs of smoke at Harley. "What's the latest on Henry?"

"Claire's heading back out tomorrow to the place where he was nabbed. She's pretty determined to find the old boy."

Mac stared blindly down at his cards, hearing the confidence in Harley's tone. Claire's words about not wanting to let down the only member of her family who still had faith in her replayed in his head. He could see her point now.

"She asked if she could borrow my digital camera," Manny said. "Mentioned something about wanting to take pictures in some old mine."

Mac's forehead tightened. The cut spark plug wires and flat tires had been a not-too-subtle hint. Somebody wanted him to stay out of those mines. If Claire started poking around out there, she could be in danger, too.

"Pictures of what?" Harley asked.

"I didn't ask. You think she'd let me take a few shots of her wearing that tool belt?" Manny grinned wide, tossing a wink in Mac's direction.

Mac knew better than to respond. Manny had been poking at Claire's grandpa throughout the night. Seemed to be some kind of game between the two of them. At least he hoped. The guy was old enough to be her ... he looked at Harley ... well, her grandpa.

"Carerra," Harley warned.

"What? I was just thinking of Mac. He's still young enough to pitch his tent without the help of Viagra."

Harley glared at both of them in turn.

Mac shook his head, beyond embarrassment after three hours of jabs and jokes on his account. At least they'd saved the worst for after Jess fell asleep.

"Harley, are you going to bid sometime before I turn eighty?" Chester asked, tapping his fingers on the table.

Harley turned his gaze back down at his cards. "I thought Mac and Claire were not an item."

"We're not," Mac confirmed. But the memory of her smooth thighs and purple toenails made him wonder what she'd been hiding under her Oscar the Grouch pajama top. Did she smell like watermelon all over?

"Right," Harley said, sounding unconvinced. "Well, while you're busy not being an item, you'd better be sure to treat her with respect. I may be old, but I can still pull the trigger on my shotgun."

⸻✦⸻

"If I hear this damned song one more time," Ruby groaned, "I'm gonna dump this glass of beer over Jerry Joseph's head!"

Claire rubbed her eyes, trying to clear the alcohol from her eyesight. Right now she had about 20-80 vision— twenty percent alcohol, eighty-proof tequila. She had switched to water a half hour ago. Much more of that Mexican fire in her belly, and she'd be *adios*-ing the Pleasantly-Numbed-Lips city limits and stumbling across the Can't-Find-My-Pants county line.

While trying her damnedest not to act tipsy, she must have missed whatever had Ruby all riled up.

On the jukebox, Ronnie McDowell sang about older women being beautiful lovers. Claire blinked several times as she glanced around the bar for the man about to receive a beer shower. "Who's Jerry Joseph?"

"That tall, gangly redhead leaning against the pool table, staring at me with that Jethro-like grin on his face."

"That guy?" Claire frowned. The cowboy couldn't be

much older than her thirty-three years.

"Yep. He's young enough to be my son, and just can't get it through his dense skull that I'm not fixin' to sleep with him."

"You don't go for the younger guys, huh?"

Claire couldn't blame Ruby. She'd once dated a guy several years younger, and all he wanted to do was lie around in bed and lick peanut butter from between her toes. He might have smelled like sun-dried sheets and been red hot in the sack, but a girl can only stand so much sex before the need to eat interferes.

"No way. I've always liked my men older, more experienced. Joe was eight years older than me."

Joe's name brought to mind a question that had rattled around in her brain since Ruby had told her the story of his death. "What do you know about the history of your mines?"

"Only that Joe bought them from some old prospector when he first moved back to Jackrabbit Junction, and now they're my headache."

"Do you think the local library would have any information on them?" If she was going to try to deter the mining company, she needed to know the story behind those holes in the ground and if the femur played some part in that history.

"They might have some copies of the blueprints for the mines, but you'd probably have better luck diggin' through Joe's office in the basement. Don't mind the dust, though. I haven't had the time or inclination to clean in there since I hunted for Joe's nest egg."

Claire had planned on dragging her sorry ass back up to Socrates Pit tomorrow afternoon to take some pictures of Henry's tracks and any other prints around them, but maybe she could do that after supper. It shouldn't take her more than an hour. She could be in and out before the sun drooped behind the horizon.

The thought of hanging out in Socrates Pit after dark made her feel a bit skittish.

"Perfect," Claire said, her voice back to speaking volume as Ruby's song came to an end. "I plan on finishing up that woodpile fence in the morning. I'll find you as soon as I—"

"That damned fool!" Ruby jumped up off the barstool. *Older Women* had started up again, drowning out the bells ringing in Claire's ears. "He just doesn't get that 'No' means 'I'd rather eat raw toads and drink snake piss!'"

Ruby yanked her drink off the bar, spilling a third of the beer on the scarred oak.

"Wait!" Claire reached out to grab Ruby's arm, but missed.

She overbalanced, tipped sideways off her stool, and torpedoed head-first toward the peanut shell and sawdust-covered floor.

Relief washed over Mac at the sight of Ruby striding in through the back door. The smoke and bullshit-filled air had his eyes and ears burning. The next time someone asked him if he knew how to play Bid Euchre, he would run the other way.

"Where's Claire?" Mac asked Ruby, dropping his cards on the table. He needed to talk her out of going near the mines.

"Walking back to Harley's Winnebago."

Mac didn't wait to say good-bye. He raced out the back door, catching sight of Claire at the edge of the General Store's drive. "Claire, wait."

She stopped and turned as he jogged up to her. The porch light colored her cheek with a yellow glow.

Frogs croaked their nightly tune down by the creek, joined by a chorus of crickets.

"I need to talk to you about something." As he drew closer, he smelled The Shaft's *eau de toilette*—a strong blend of cigarettes and alcohol, mixed with a hint of sawdust.

She looked at her wrist, where no watch existed and probably never had. "Okay, you've got five minutes before I turn back into a hairy godmother."

Mac opened his mouth to correct her, but noticed an underlying smell drifting from her—a scent that reminded him of Mabel. He grinned. "Why do you smell like banana air freshener?"

"I didn't want Gramps to know I was drinking."

The air freshener wasn't going to cut it. "But you told him you were taking Ruby to the tavern."

"What's your point?" Her words slurred a little.

He glanced at the store's second-story windows and saw Jess peeking out through a split in the curtains. Ruby must have roused her from the couch and sent her to bed.

Great, an audience. He didn't need Jess hearing what he was about to tell Claire. Jess shared secrets in tabloid style.

"Never mind." He drew Claire by the arm into the shadows under the willow tree. "Listen, I want to talk to you about tomorrow."

"Let me guess, you need another ride?"

"Not quite. I need you to stay away from the mines."

"No. Why?"

"Because ..." He hesitated, not sure how much he should tell her about his suspicions.

While the shadows blurred many of her features, her eyes glittered up at him. He didn't need to see the determination in her gaze—he could feel it in the rigid muscles of her upper arm, which he still held.

He might as well spill the truth. "Because I think

someone is trying to stop me from working in the mines. If they see you going in them, they may think you and I are working together."

"I can handle myself."

"That's the alcohol talking."

She tilted her head to the side. "Why should I believe you're looking out for my welfare? This could be your way of keeping me from interfering with Ruby selling those mines."

"If I thought you even had a chance of saving Ruby's ass, I'd—"

"Wrap me up in a blanket like a burrito and drop me off on the other side of the border?"

He frowned down at her. "No, I'd help you. You think I want to see Ruby lose her land?"

"You'd really help me?" Her voice had lowered, turned silky.

Mac didn't like the way his pulse picked up speed at just the sound of it. He lifted his hand from her arm. "Of course, but there's no way out of this for her."

She smiled, her teeth white in the dappled shadows. "Says you."

"Stay away from those mines."

"No, Ruby gave me permission to trespass."

"Damn it, Claire. Stop being so—"

She grabbed him behind the neck and pulled him down to her level. "Shut up, Mac," she whispered, all breathy.

Then she smothered his lips with hers.

Chapter Nine

Tuesday, April 13th

S ophy dried a rack of coffee mugs, one at a time, as she stared blindly out at the tables she'd waited since her tenth birthday.

Wheeler's Diner had been established two months after her father crawled off the train that carried him home from the war. He'd pinched, he'd saved, he'd planned. First, the marriage to her mother; second, the diner; third, a child. He'd succeeded—his blue-collar American dream.

Now it was Sophy's inherited, blue-collar American nightmare.

With its grease-hazed air, sun-faded curtains, brass hanging lamps, and the longhorn skull over the door, the diner weighed heavy on her shoulders. She knew every crack in the water-spotted ceiling, the yellowed linoleum, and the orange vinyl booth seats.

The early afternoon sun spotlighted the old radio she'd bought her father the year before his heart gave up the fight to keep pushing blood through his hamburger-clogged arteries. Glen Campbell sang about being a rhinestone cowboy.

Vegas ... With a hungry sigh, she placed a white mug on the shelf and picked up another wet one. Glen wasn't the only one who wanted to be where the lights were shining on him.

Joe ... She rarely thought of the neon lights without

feeling the pinch of losing him. Thirty-five calendars had hung on the diner's wall since that first summer. At twenty-three, Joe had been thick with rip-cord muscles he'd built from swinging a pickax every night at the mine. With his slicked-back, black hair and movie-star eyelashes, he could make girls swoon with a wink.

Growing up together in the choke-hold of Jackrabbit Junction, Sophy had spent most of her early teens engraving Joe's name on crispy paper napkins, tracing it in the warm sandy banks lining Jackrabbit Creek, scribbling it across the narrow lines of her diary.

Every day, she'd stare out the fingerprint-smudged diner windows, watching for his midnight blue El Camino to race up and down U.S. Route 191. Every night, she'd pray he'd push through the glass door, sweep her up, and make her his.

Joe ... His neck laden with purplish maroon love bites, a pack of cigarettes wrapped mummy-tight in his shirtsleeve.

During the summer of her seventeenth birthday, while the sun fried the blacktop until it rippled, sticky and gooey, like flypaper under foot, her body budded, blossomed, and dangled fruit. Tank tops became outer layers of skin, nipples hard as juniper berries. His brown eyes seared her skin through the flimsy cotton.

Sophy picked up another cup, her towel now damp throughout.

Joe ... His palms scratching over her inner thighs while *The Great Escape* crackled through the drive-in speakers. A hint of Brylcream sweetened the sweltering air.

Those sultry dog days of August with Sophy lying on a buttery soft cotton blanket under the stars in the back of Joe's El Camino, still breathless from his skilled hands. He whispered Vegas sweet-nothings in her ears. High-rise condos, bright lights, and fancy five-star hotels—her imagination painted the rest. She cut out color pictures of Vegas from her parents' *Life* magazines and tacked them to her bedroom walls.

His words became her bible. He'd lobbied that high school was for girls with nothing to offer the world. With her experience at the diner, she could land a job anywhere in the big city.

She threw her American Lit textbook out the El Camino's window at passing greasewood trees on their way to Phoenix. The memory of her pop's fury and mama's tears a passing cloud.

Three months later, struggling under the weight of two greasy-spoon jobs while Joe juggled full-time classes at a community college, she shared her secret with him—the one growing inside of her, a reason to stay at Joe's side forever.

"Order up!"

Sophy jerked back to the present, a mug nearly slipping out of her fingers. She carefully placed the cup on the shelf with the rest of the mugs and threw down the towel.

But she'd lost the baby, and *forever* had only lasted a handful of years. Baskets of burgers, plastic ketchup bottles, and pastel pink and blue sugar packets had filled her days for the last thirty years.

Carrying two plates loaded with the usual Tuesday special—meatloaf, Sophy weaved through the tables. Chester Thomas lounged in a booth, his arm drooped over the back, across from a skinny blonde.

He winked at Sophy as she placed his plate in front of him. Two years back, she'd given in to his pestering and made the mistake of sitting next to him in a dark theatre. Before the second movie trailer had finished, Chester had a sprained wrist and a black eye. It had cost her a broken nail.

She hoped the blonde carried mace.

At the corner booth, she paused, her order pad in

hand. "What can I get for you boys?"

Manuel Carrera's puppy love gaze worshipped her 36 double-D's. "Do you know how to tango?"

"Only between the sheets, sugar, but don't pop any Viagra on my account."

She'd had her share of men over the years. Age and color made no difference to her, but the Latin lovers she'd had tended to chatter away from the first drink to the kiss goodbye, and she preferred not to mix words with sex. It ruined her fantasy.

"I'll have the special." Harley Ford was a "usual" kind of man. He liked his coffee black, his eggs scrambled, and his pie without the *a la mode*. She'd already told the cook to prepare a plate of meatloaf for him.

"I'll take a fry bread taco with pork and a side of you, minus the apron." Manny winked at her as she took the menu.

"Sweetie, you're too much man for me," she lied, but added more umph to her sway as she walked away from his leer. Nothing wrong with wetting a man's whistle.

"*Ay, mi corazon.* I've changed my mind," he called after her, "bring the apron, too. I'll wear it."

Sophy pushed through the kitchen door. "Add a pig in a Navajo rug to that meatloaf order," she shouted to her line cook over the constant whir of the stove hood fan. She raced for the safety of her office, her soft-soled shoes crunching across ever-present crumbs.

The hollow wooden office door dulled the clattering sounds of the kitchen. Sophy painted on another coat of lipstick, smacking her lips together, then spritzed the back of her knees, the inside of her elbows, and the shadow of her cleavage with Tabu.

Joe hadn't been able keep his hands off her when she doused herself with Tabu, even after he'd moved back to Jackrabbit Junction with that no-good, rat of a cousin. At least not until he'd dragged that redheaded whore from Oklahoma to town.

First Ruby, then her nephew.

Sophy yanked open her desk drawer, needing something for her frazzled nerves. She'd almost driven into the ditch when she saw Ruby's old blue Ford bouncing along the old trail leading to Two Jakes mine this morning. Tossing three ibuprofens in her mouth, she chased them with a hit of vodka.

The nephew, the dog, and now the brunette.

The lights of Vegas twinkled behind her eyelids, beckoning with every blink. She slammed the bottle down on her desk. Vodka splashed out onto her Tucson Electric Power bill.

Glaring down at her latest broken fingernail, she growled under her breath.

Where did Joe hide that goddamned loot?

---◆---

Mac stomped on the brakes at the sight of Mabel parked in front of Wheeler's Diner. Ruby's new tires screeched in protest, burning a thin layer of rubber onto U.S. Route 191's asphalt.

He and Claire had some unfinished business to argue about. He cranked the wheel and slid into the gravel parking lot. The old Ford shuddered to a stop. After having forced it part way up the rutted, wagon trail to Two Jakes mine, Mac expected steam to hiss from the radiator.

The plug wires for his pickup were supposed to be in today. Tomorrow, he'd scale the path to Rattlesnake Ridge in four-wheel drive style with all his tools in tow. There'd be no more half-ass prospecting.

Two Jakes had been a bust. Dead end tunnels painted pictures of repeated false starts. Four different shafts had been sunk off the main adit leading from the mine's mouth, which was one more than was drawn on the blueprint he'd copied. Two of the holes brimmed with water, their sodden wooden ladders descending into the cold, inky depths.

To search those sections of the mine, he'd need scuba gear and balls of steel, neither of which he'd brought with him on this trip.

The other two shafts were filled with shadows and stale air, but Mac didn't trust the toothpick thin ladders heading down into their pitch blackness. He needed some nylon rope, anchors, and the rest of his rappelling equipment to slide into those oversized snake holes.

A wake of dust drifted past him as he hopped out of the Ford. Inside the diner, the smell of hamburger, onions, and fries beckoned. His stomach gurgled.

"Mac!" two voices called out in harmony.

Shit.

Claire was nowhere in sight as he strolled over to the booth where Harley and Manny lounged, their plates scraped clean. Coffee steamed in front of them.

"Howdy." Mac dug in his front pocket and tossed a twenty-dollar bill on the table in front of Harley's coffee cup.

"What's that for?"

"Gas money. Claire's been chauffeuring me around the last couple of days at your expense."

"What can I get ya?" The red-taloned waitress with the Kathleen Turner voice had slipped up behind him, a stiff wallop of perfume her calling card today.

"Nothing. I was just—"

"Have you eaten?" Harley asked.

"Well, no, but—"

"He'll have the special," Manny said as he scooted across the booth seat to make room for Mac.

"Listen, guys, I need to—"

"And a coffee," Harley added.

"Make it a Coke," Mac told the waitress. Sometimes it was easier to drown than fight the undercurrent. He dropped onto the cracked vinyl bench. It creaked under his Levi's. "And add their total to my bill, please."

The hard, icy glare in the brunette's eyes didn't match the warm, flirty smile on her lips. "Will do," she said tightly, quickly bussing the table before sashaying back into the kitchen.

From the radio next to the cash register, Johnny Cash cranked out complaints about the hardships for a boy named Sue.

"She must not like the way you part your hair," Manny told Mac.

She probably hadn't appreciated the way he'd rammed into the parking lot. Some women didn't take kindly to testosterone displays, unintentional or deliberate.

Mac shrugged off her coolness.

"If you're buying me lunch, take your twenty back." Harley pushed the money toward Mac.

"Speaking of Claire," Manny said, grinning.

"We weren't," Mac interjected. He had learned his lesson—sex and Claire were two subjects to shun in the company of these men.

"I hear you two got caught locking lips last night."

Heat shot up Mac's neck, frying his cheeks.

Not a single doubt clouded his mind about who had played the town crier. Jackrabbit Junction's nosiest nark had made it her business to see exactly what was going on under that willow tree, her mouth a geyser of fable, fiction, and fantasy whenever she had an attentive audience. Unfortunately for him, this time she'd been spouting facts.

The truth was that Mac still wasn't sure what had happened under those drooping branches. One minute he was warning Claire to stay away from the mines. The next, her mouth was exploring his.

Between the banana air freshener and tequila, she'd smelled like a tropical margarita, and Mac had wanted to lick so much more than just her sweet, soft lips. But before he'd had a chance to taste-test further, she'd pulled free, stumbled over to Ruby's patch of daisies, and thrown up all over them.

"So much for you two not being an item," Harley muttered.

"We're not." Induced vomiting was not a reaction he'd label as "progress" in any kind of mouth-to-mouth experiment.

"Come on, cough it up." Manny elbowed Mac's ribs. "Did she let you get to second base?"

Harley's lips tightened. "What's your definition of second base?"

Second base? With Claire, even practice swings while standing on deck tempted bad mojo. That woman was the cover model for *Trouble* magazine, but dammit, he couldn't stop thinking about what she'd look like in a wet T-shirt and Daisy Dukes.

"Second base means tuning her radio," Manny explained.

Harley shot Mac a frosty glare. "There will be no radio tuning until you ask for her hand in marriage."

"Not a problem," Mac said, happy to see the waitress carrying meatloaf toward him. A plate of food would give him something to bury his burning face in.

"Come on, Ford. How are the kids supposed to have any under-cover *fiestas* if you keep laying down these nineteenth century laws?"

The waitress dropped Mac's plate in front of him. The cheap China clinked. A fork clunked onto the table next to it. After shooting him a withering glare, she strutted away, wordless.

What in the hell had he done to her? He brushed aside her animosity and turned to Harley. "Ketchup, please."

"Hey, sweet buns," Chester said, standing over the table.

Mac groaned, glancing up at the third musketeer.

"Word on the street is that you scored a little tongue action last night." Chester shoved in beside Harley.

"Where'd Blondie go?" Harley's scowl showed his unhappiness with being pushed toward the window.

"The little girls' room." Chester eagerly leaned across the table toward Manny. "Did you see Sophy's garters today? They're pink."

"*Ay yi yi,*" Manny chewed on his knuckle. "Such a classy chassis. What I wouldn't do to lube her engine."

"Who's Sophy?"

"The long-legged brunette who brought you your dinner," Chester said. "She owns the joint."

"You're kidding me."

"Nope," Harley said. "She's been here for decades."

"I usually eat at Ruby's place."

"Maybe you should lay off my granddaughter and spring for Sophy. I've seen her leave The Shaft with men too young to grow sideburns."

Cringing, Mac shoved a forkful of meatloaf in his mouth.

"Now that you've had a chance to cop a feel with Claire," Chester waggled his eyebrows at Mac, "Carerra and I have a little wager we need your help with. Harley, plug your ears."

Mac stopped chewing. This couldn't be good.

"You weren't exaggerating when you talked about the dust in here," Claire told Ruby while glancing around Joe's office.

The dust fairies had thrown one hell of a wake for the man, liberally coating the mahogany Queen Anne-style partners desk and everything else in the basement room. Doily-like cobwebs draped across a tall bookcase, screening faded cloth book spines and various antique knick-knacks.

"Yeah. I'd rather do anything than dust," Ruby said, setting a plate of brownies on the corner of Joe's desk.

Claire grabbed a warm brownie. "I used to date a guy who was into antiques." She stuffed half of the brownie in her mouth and leaned back in the leather swivel chair. It squeaked in protest at being forced out of retirement, or from the weight of her ever-growing ass. Damn Ruby and her need to bake when stressed.

"What kind of antiques?" Ruby asked, blowing the dust off a 1900s black Kodak box camera and placing it on a bookshelf.

Claire's nose itched from the dust.

"The Marilyn Monroe kind. Autographed photos and one-sheets, a mauve and teal pair of her spiky-heeled pumps, three big round hair curlers with strands of her hair still stuck in them, a pair of diamond teardrop earrings she'd worn to the debut of *The Seven Year Itch* in 1955, and a tiny gold pillbox full of what he swore up and down were her toenail clippings."

Ruby's eyebrows wrinkled. "Toenails?"

"Yep, cranberry red nail polish and all." Claire swallowed the last of the brownie, wiping her fingers on her blue jeans. "He gave off kind of a creepy-weird vibe, you know." Almost as creepy-weird as knowing the last person to sit in this office was now six feet underground. "But he had these Paul Newman blue eyes that made your heart skip a beat."

"Kind of like your grandfather's?"

Claire shot Ruby a surprised glance. Ruby was too busy

drawing stars in the dust blanketing Joe's desktop to notice. "Yeah, sort of."

"Sexy peepers or not," Ruby said, "I'd have been racin' out the door as soon as I laid eyes on those toenails."

"I should have. But after years of being accused of suffering from commitment phobia, I was determined to stick it out, even after he tried to clip my toenails while I was sleeping."

"But when he arrived for the showing of *Some Like It Hot* at the old Pluto Theatre wearing a blonde wig, a painted cheek mole, and a knock-out replica of Marilyn's famous white, exhaust vent dress, I ran for the door."

"You're kidding!" Ruby grinned wide.

"Nope. And you know what? That rotten, cross-dressing bastard looked better in a dress than I did."

Even Ruby's laugh sounded southern. "Speakin' of boyfriends, Jess said she saw you and Mac kissin' under the willow last night."

If Claire had the ability to create a black hole in the floor of Joe's office, she'd have dived into it head first. Her face burned, no doubt turning the shade of chili powder. "Uhhh, about last night—"

Ruby waved her off. "No need to explain yourself. Mac's a big boy. He could use someone to shake up his life, make things happen."

Claire sat forward in Joe's chair. "Listen, we're not—"

"And I've seen his legs—he'll never look better in a dress than you, honey" Ruby added, winking.

That was a relief. Claire tried again. "Last night was—"

"I best mosey on back to the store. I left Jess in charge, and a flea has a longer attention span than that child lately." Ruby closed the door behind her.

Claire groaned and thumped her forehead on the desktop. When was she going to learn not to mix alcohol and men? The hangovers were humiliating.

Pulling open the left-hand desk drawer, she decided to get down to business. She'd deal with the *Mac Situation* when she had time for self-abuse.

Thumbing through bank statements, stock dividend results, and credit card bills, she found nothing extraordinary. Joe may have been reckless about his health, but he kept his finances semi-organized, at least until his stroke, judging by the dates on everything.

She moved to the middle drawer and shut it after seeing nothing more than the usual jumble of paper clips, rubber bands, pens, and thumbtacks. In the right-hand drawer, she rifled through a stack of doctor and lab bills, most with outstanding balances and dates less than two years old.

Under the bills was a yellow envelope with "Mercedes" scrawled on the front. Inside was the original sale's receipt, a 30,000 mile check-up receipt, and a warranty for the alarm.

She paused, frowning, then looked at the sales receipt, again. $95,655.92 was typed next to *Total*. She scanned the receipt. From what she could tell, not only had he paid a large chunk of change for the car, but he'd paid for it with a wad of green.

No financing for Mr. Joe Martino when it came to buying luxury cars. No, sirree.

She had assumed the Benz Joe had wrecked was older, used, with faded carpet in the back window and stone-chips on the bumper. Not a brand-spanking new, silver metallic SL500 Roadster filled with luxury conveniences like charcoal gray leather seats, multi-function keyless remote, automatic climate control, and concierge services.

Where did a traveling salesman come up with these liquid assets? She'd have to talk to Ruby, see if she knew anything more about the car.

Too bad he'd totaled the Mercedes. Selling it might

have helped Ruby limp along a little longer. The man apparently had been allergic to the word *insurance*.

After stuffing everything back into the drawer, Claire moved to the bookcase and ran her finger along several worn book spines. The blue gilt-stamped cloth was frayed at the edges, the gold print on *Moby Dick* and *Treasure Island* rubbed and faded.

She pulled out *Treasure Island* and flipped open the cover. The binding creaked, like an old ship rocking. Her eyes skimmed the words, *London Cassell 1883, First Edition*, her grip tightening on the book. A first edition! How much was a classic literature first edition worth these days?

Her mom might know. The woman watched *Antiques Roadshow* religiously every Monday night.

Deftly drawing out *Moby Dick*, Claire opened the slightly tattered, blue cloth cover, and under her breath read, "Harper & Brothers, 1851. First American Edition." Blowing out a low whistle, she gently tucked the books back onto the shelf.

Did Ruby have any idea of the value of some of the antiques sitting in her basement? Claire doubted it. If Ruby liquidated, she'd probably add a hundred to a hundred and fifty thousand to her savings account. That wasn't enough to pay off the bank, but it was a hell of a running start.

Stepping over to the modern, black filing cabinet, she tugged on the top drawer, expecting it to be locked. It rolled open, the tracks smooth.

She flicked through folders, months and years scrawled across the manila tabs. Nothing unusual, just folders with old electric, water, and other month-to-month bills. She shut the drawer.

The bottom drawer opened as easily as the top. Many years' worth of *Antique Collector Monthly* magazines were stacked in the front of the drawer. Toward the back, unlabeled folders leaned against the magazines. She grabbed a handful.

Most of them were empty, but one contained two articles. The first one read:

Gold Boxes Stolen from Waddesdon!

At approximately two a.m. on Tuesday, June 10, Waddesdon Manor in Buckinghamshire England experienced a break-in and theft. Over 100 gold boxes and other precious items, mainly 18th century French and some English, were stolen. All of the items are unique and immediately identifiable. The National Trust is offering a reward up to £50,000 for the safe recovery of these objects and for information that will lead to the arrest of the people responsible for the theft.

The bottom of the article listed the contact information. Claire flipped through eight stapled pages containing pictures and information about each of the boxes.

The second article was written in German, which meant it could have been in Martian for all she knew of the language. The black and white picture on the front looked like some medieval castle, all gray stone and turret-topped.

Why had Joe collected these tidbits and stored them in his filing cabinet? Curiosity?

She shrugged, stuffed the articles back in the folder, and shoved it with the others. Shutting the drawer, she glanced around at the antiques cluttering the room.

A profile picture of Johnny Cash painted on black velvet hung on one of the two interior walls. An image of a safe tucked away in the drywall popped into her head.

She crossed the room. Johnny's frame lifted easily in her hands, the wall behind him seamless. Well, it had been worth a try. Her grip on the picture slipped as she tried to hang it back up. She caught it halfway to the floor, the paper backing tearing under her tight grip.

She placed Johnny face-down on Joe's desk. The paper backing had torn loose from the upper left corner. She lifted the thick paper. Maybe Elmer's glue would fix it.

Something blue under the brown paper caught her eye. She tore the paper backing a little more and found three passports, duct-taped to the back of the portrait.

"What have we here, Mr. Martino?" she said.

She carefully lifted the passports free and flipped one open. A round-faced, black-haired man stared up at her, his eyes narrow, his lips thin. His face looked squished, like he'd had his head stuck in a vice clamp for too long.

Funny, she'd figured with the weight issue Ruby had told her about, Joe would've had jowls, or at least a double chin. The man in the picture had slight hollows under his cheekbones. She scanned the name below the photo: Anthony Peteza. *Who?* The rest of the book was empty—no stamps from foreign countries.

She grabbed the second passport. The same face stared up at her, this time with a goatee. She looked down at the name—Alonzo Basilio. This one had a stamp from France.

The third passport had the same guy wearing a sad excuse for a moustache and a green shirt instead of blue. He'd changed his name again—to Arturo Enzo. Two stamps from Japan were the only other contents.

"What the hell?" She tossed the passport on top of the other two.

Leaving the three passports lying on Joe's desk, she leaned Johnny Cash against the wall, next to a wooden box with a keyhole in the front. She squatted next to the box and ran her pinky over the hole—it wasn't made for a typical key. It looked more like a skeleton key hole.

She swept her palm down the smooth, dark wood. Walnut, she guessed by the grain and color. She picked it up. It was as heavy as a ripe watermelon. Setting it back down on the olive shag carpet, she tried to pull it open, but the lock held tight.

She'd seen a box similar in shape and size once in the

Sioux City Museum on a field trip for her "History of Midwestern Pioneers" class. That one had been unfolded and spread out—a small writing desk for travelers, if she remembered right—the 1800s equivalent of a laptop.

Ruby's clock cuckooed five times from the other room, snapping Claire back to the present.

Dang it! She needed to go to Socrates Pit to take some photos. Grabbing the plate of brownies, she closed Joe's office door behind her. She would nose around some more tomorrow.

She slipped out the back door and stopped short at the sound of someone crying. Walking around the back of the store, she found Jess sitting cross-legged on the grass, her hands covering her face.

"Hey, kiddo." Claire squatted next to her. "What's wrong?"

"Nothing." Jess sniffed, brushing the tears from her lashes.

"Nothing, my butt. Come on, out with it."

Jess handed her a piece of paper.

"What's this?"

"A letter from my dad. He's so busy with his new wife's kids that he doesn't want me around."

"Oh, sweetheart." Claire squeezed Jess's shoulder. "I'm sorry."

"My mom doesn't want me, and neither does my dad."

Claire knew better than that. Ruby didn't spend all day home schooling Jess for the hell of it.

Glancing up at the hills, Claire blew out a breath. She needed to get a move on if she wanted to make it to the mine and back before sunset, but the thought of leaving Jess wrenched on her heart.

"Hey, if it's okay with your mom, how about you and I go to Yuccaville for pizza."

Jess nodded, standing up. "That'd be cool."

Claire draped her arm around the girl's shoulders as they strolled toward Gramps's Winnebago. "Afterwards, maybe we'll grab some ice cream." The seams in Claire's jeans bulged just at the mention.

"Sure."

They walked several steps in silence, Claire feeling Henry's trail growing colder and colder.

"Claire, what's it like to kiss a boy?"

Claire wasn't sure it was her place to be explaining anything even remotely birds-and-bees-ish to Jess, but she decided to give it a whirl. "Sometimes it's slimy and uncomfortable, full of jabbing tongues and gobs of slobber."

"Eww!"

"Sometimes it makes you feel all warm and cozy inside, like a cup of hot cocoa with marshmallows."

"Oh."

"And sometimes ..." a certain hazel-eyed, long-legged man came to mind, "sometimes it makes your heart race and your skin tingle."

"Really?" Jess grinned. Sunlight sparkled in the tears drying on her auburn lashes. "Is that what it felt like when you kissed Mac?"

Chapter Ten

Wednesday, April 14th

Mac strode down Ruby's porch steps and marched toward Claire's R.V. He'd been in Jackrabbit Junction for four days now, and he was still spinning his wheels, no thanks to Claire's shenanigans. This morning was no different, only hotter.

The park's road was already cooked and crispy, smelling of Arizona's finest sun-baked powder. A pair of woodpeckers chatted with each other high above him in the cottonwoods. Their quick, stuttering trills and squeaky peeps scraped his nerves.

He now realized that Claire's biggest threat to him as an adversary was her ability to frustrate the hell out of him by just being in the same state.

He rapped on her door. The woodpeckers quieted, as if waiting with him for the door to open.

Silence issued from inside the Winnebago.

A high-pitched, yappy dog rattled off a warning on the other side of the campground.

Mac knocked again, harder.

Seconds later, Claire wrenched the door open. "Criminy!" She stood there in a skimpy, hot pink pajama tank top with Tweety-bird's head and the words, "Got Milk?" plastered across the front of it.

Mouth suddenly dry, eyes ogling, breath temporarily nixed, Mac's blood pressure red-lined. All thoughts evaporated from his mind.

"Let me guess," she said, her vocal chords still husky with sleep. "You need a ride."

Sleep-wrinkled, soft-lipped, and bare-skinned, she was one hundred percent TNT—the old, unstable kind, sure to go off in his hands when he lit the fuse. Definitely hazardous to his mental health.

"Mac."

"What?"

"You're staring."

Mac dragged his gaze away from the two perky points pushing out the soft cotton beneath Tweety's smiling face. *Sweet Jesus!* He'd add his money to Manny's wager—those had to be real.

He wiped his damp palms on his jeans. "I was just ... uh ... wondering if canaries really drink milk."

Lame excuse. Hall of fame lame.

"Right." Her smirk had a "bullshit" tilt at the corners.

"Jess said you're skipping work this morning and hiking to Socrates Pit."

Her silky shorts left a lot of bare leg available for examination.

She crossed her arms over Tweety and leaned against the doorframe. "Maybe."

He pretended not to notice as the hemline of her pajama top crept up her stomach, showing an inch of bare flesh. "Did you hear a word I said the other night?"

Her face reddened several shades. "Yes, I did."

"Then what are you thinking?"

"None of your damned business."

"If it involves you and that mine, it is my damned business. If anything happens to you while nosing around alone up there, I'm responsible."

"Nothing's going to happen to me. I'm going to hike up there, take a few pictures, and be back before anyone realizes I'm gone."

"I doubt that," he said, unable to hold back a grin. "Not with the way you climb."

"Oh, bite me."

He'd love to, starting with her creamy thigh. He held out his hand. "Give me the camera. I'll take the pictures for you."

She lifted her chin. "Absolutely not. I'm going to find Henry on my own, thank you very much."

"Claire," he warned.

"No, Mac. You're not stopping me. Get that through the thick wall in your skull."

He held her stare. The wind chimes on Manny's awning clinked out a ding-ping melody. The slam of a car door echoed across the park.

"Fine." The stubborn woman left him no choice. "Get dressed. We're leaving." Having her along would force him to adjust his plans for the day, not to mention test his tolerance for all things Claire. But at least he could make sure she made it there and back.

"Now you listen here," she started.

He climbed the first step and stood nose-to-nose with her. "Claire, you have five minutes to put some clothes on before I do the job for you."

She grinned, a devilish glint in her brown eyes. "Tempting."

Siren! "In front of your grandfather," he added.

"Eeek!" She slammed the door in his face.

⇢ ✦ ⇠

The hike up to Rattlesnake Ridge reminded Claire why she needed to stop eating fried pork rinds before bedtime.

By the time they'd reached the mouth of the mine, her trachea had become a steam pipe leading away from the boiler furnace in her lungs.

In addition to struggling under a sun that was doing its damnedest to turn her brain to ashes, memories of her idiotic behavior the night before last kept her in a constant state of silent humiliation.

Keeping two eyes out for the ridge's notorious namesake—rattlers, she stepped over prickly barrel cacti and tufts of yellow primroses. The air smelled of super-heated rocks, and she fantasized about taking a quick dip in one of the water-filled mine shafts Mac had warned her about.

While the inside of Rattlesnake Ridge offered respite from the blistering ball in the sky, the entrance was still warm enough to melt a slab of butter given time. Sunlight flowed in through the toothless mouth.

Mac had promised they'd hop over to Socrates Pit as soon as he grabbed a couple of samples he'd left Saturday night. He'd told Claire she could save her breath and wait for him in the pickup, but curiosity to see one of Ruby's mines propelled her out under the blue sky—that and the need to wipe the smirk off Mac's lips.

She mopped her face with her T-shirt and glanced over at Mac, who kneeled next to a red plastic crate full of rock chunks. His unzipped pack lay at his feet with funky gadgets and gizmos spilling out of it.

"You sure have a lot of toys." Claire picked up a fancy-looking compass and turned in circles, trying to figure out what the numbers encircling the pointer represented.

Mac plucked the compass from her fingers and slipped it into his shirt pocket. "They're very expensive tools, not toys."

"It's just a compass."

"It's a Brunton 5010 GeoTransit Compass with a hinge clinometer."

"A Geowhatzit?"

"This little baby gives me the ability to calculate horizontal and vertical angles from a single point."

"Makes you sound like Superman. You know, 'able to leap tall buildings in a single bound.'" Claire chuckled at her own cleverness.

Mac didn't even crack a grin.

"Maybe not," she said, sobering. "How does it work?"

"I measure a couple of angles, and with the use of a little trigonometry, I have the answers I need. It's pretty simple."

Simple, her ass. Claire couldn't believe she'd found someone who used trigonometry in everyday life. She hadn't used it for so long she couldn't remember how long ago she'd forgotten it.

She watched him organize rock samples and make notes in his waterproof field book for a while before giving in to the question dancing on the tip of her tongue. "How well did you know Joe?"

"Ruby's husband?"

"Uh-huh."

"Not very. I only saw him twice." Mac continued writing, not sparing her a glance. His pencil scratched across the waxy paper.

"Did you know he drove a Mercedes?"

"I know he crashed one."

"Let me rephrase that. Did you know he drove a $90,000 Mercedes?"

His fingers scribbled away. "How do you know it cost that much?"

"I found the sales receipt in Joe's office."

Mac shrugged. "He drove a pricey car. That's not a crime."

"He told Ruby he inherited it from a favorite uncle."

"So, he's a liar. He probably had a logical reason for not telling her the truth."

"He paid cash for the car."

Mac's pencil stopped. "Maybe he inherited money from his uncle and bought the car with it."

Good point. She hadn't thought of that. "Have you ever been in his office?"

He looked at her, his gaze guarded. "Nope. Not my business."

She brushed off the innuendo. "What about that antique store he had in town? Did you ever go in there?"

"Never had a need to."

Mac wasn't making this easy for her. "Do you have any idea of the kind of antiques he sold there?"

"Old ones." A grin surfaced on his face for the first time since they'd left the R.V. park.

"A real one-man Laurel and Hardy show, aren't you?"

"You bring out the best in me, Claire." Laugh lines spread from the corners of his eyes.

"Do you think it's odd that he didn't share anything about his sales job and antique business with his wife?"

"No. He was old school, didn't think a man's job was his wife's business. She served another purpose."

"Thank God for bra burners everywhere."

His gaze dipped to her chest for a split second. "Besides, Ruby had enough to keep her busy fixing up this place. The campground was in pretty bad shape when Joe bought it. She didn't have the time to get involved with his other business ventures." Mac scribbled in his field book again.

"He has some pretty valuable stuff in his office. First edition books, a traveling writing desk, and an old camera, to name a few." Claire didn't mention how valuable, because she wanted to hop on the Internet in Yuccaville's library before tossing out figures. It didn't take a psychologist to see that while Mac would swallow facts whole, she'd have to cram guesses down his throat. "Ruby could really cash in on some of that stuff."

"Unless you find a satchel of cash, none of those antiques can help Ruby. It'd take too much time to liquidate it all."

No shit, Claire thought, fighting the urge to reach out and knock him upside the head. Was it too much to ask for a little participation in her game of delusional suspicions?

"I found a couple of articles on some valuable antique thefts in Joe's filing cabinet." When Mac didn't say a word, she added, "I wonder why he kept them in there."

Mac snapped shut his book. "Claire, you're making something out of nothing, just like with Henry. Face the facts: the dog ran off and Joe liked to dabble in antiques. End of story. Nothing dubious. Just plain, white-bread life in Jackrabbit Junction."

Frustrated with how black and white he saw the world, she decided not to tell Mac about the passports—not until she could identify the squished-face man in the picture.

Maybe Joe's antique store could offer some answers. Ruby had said she'd cleaned it out, but there might be clues to Joe's past still hiding in the corners.

Claire cleared the dust from her throat. "Have you heard anything back from your lab friend regarding that leg bone?"

"Not a word." He picked up a fist-sized rock, turned it over, and studied it.

Rather than grab Mac by the earlobe, drag him outside, and throw him down the steep hillside, she decided to do some exploring. She flicked on the spotlight in the hard hat Mac had given her to wear and stepped further into the mine.

"Where are you going?" he called after her.

"To see what's around the bend."

"That's not a good idea."

She sighed. "I've been in mines before." The Black

Hills were honeycombed with old silver and gold mines, leftover from bygone days of hope, sweat, and despair. "I'll just be a couple of minutes."

"Yeah, right. Be careful. And don't pick at the walls."

Claire drilled his profile with a dirty glare, and then hiked into the blackness. A set of rusted steel rails led the way.

Ore carts, rather than pack mules, must have carried rock debris from the mine. She'd seen similar sets of tracks in several of the silver mines back home in Galena, some leading to a bored-out cavern, others to dead-end tunnels. And sometimes, they disappeared into dark, chilly water.

Over the years, she'd collected trinkets—like a pick-ax with a splintered handle, a miner's lamp with a candle still in it, a handmade leather glove—pieces of history solid in her hands.

To the right of the tracks, a small cavern had been carved out of the wall.

A shaft, fenced off by four one-by-eight inch boards, sank into the earth not ten feet from the rails. Claire edged over and shined her hard hat light into the hole. Water, still as a sheet of black ice, rimmed the lip. A wooden ladder rose out of the watery depths. The square-headed bolts pinning it to the rock were barnacled with rust. She dropped a pebble into the water, watching it sink out of sight, and shuddered.

Deciding to explore a little further, she followed the tracks around another bend, and another, and another.

She slowed when she came upon a straight stretch dotted with shallow cavities—called *stopes*, if she remembered right—in the ceiling and walls.

Standing on her tiptoes, she peeked into a pair of wall craters. The first was two feet deep and sprinkled with pebbles and dust. The second was three times deeper, and littered with dried twigs, sagebrush scraps, and cactus spines—a nest, probably home to a rat, squirrel, or skunk.

Her light bounced off something shiny in the bedding. She blew into the nest, coughing when dust whirled up her nose and down her throat. Waving away the dust, she withdrew a brass knob from the debris. Under her light, she admired the bevels and shape.

How it had ended up inside Rattlesnake Ridge mine was beyond her.

She stepped backwards, her gaze glued to the knob, and tripped over the rails. Arms flailing, hard hat flying, she slammed back-first into   the opposite wall where a rock gouged her left hip. Her hat crashed to the ground, a clink of breaking glass followed by darkness confirming its demise.

Way to go, Grace. She rubbed the knot already forming on her upper butt cheek. At least she'd managed to hold onto the knob. She stuffed it into her pants pocket.

A scraping sound came from deeper within the mine. She held still, blood thundering in her ears, suddenly aware of a rancid, foul odor under the smell of stale dirt.

Something clacked—a stone smacking into another maybe; then clinked—like rock on steel rails. Gulping past her suddenly-dry tongue, she stared into the depths of the mine, but saw only blackness.

The clacking sound continued, interspersed with the tapping sound like hooves crossing the rock floor. Huffs of breath merged with the racket. Darkness squeezed tight around her, sweat coated her upper lip.

Holy fuckballs! Something was coming her way, and she doubted it was selling Avon.

Without light, she felt like a mouse cowering in the corner of a snake tank. Stinky armpits were her only weapons.

Then she remembered Manny's camera.

Scrambling, she dug in the leg pocket of her khakis.

The compact body of the digital camera was cool to the touch, ready to aim and shoot. She slid open the lens protector, wincing as the whir of the camera grinding to life resonated off the walls.

The clicking and clacking stopped, the huffing and puffing muted. Whatever was coming had heard the camera.

Claire stared blindly at where the LCD window should be, her fingers feeling for the shutter release button as she pointed the camera in what she hoped was the right direction.

She pushed down on the button, waiting as the dim meter light spilled from above the eyepiece and bounced off the rails in front of her. Then a fake shutter sounded and a bright light flashed.

An image displayed on the LCD screen, glowing in the blackness, showing two rails leading around the bend up ahead. Besides the brown rock walls and ceiling bracketed by shadows, the picture was empty.

The clicking started again, mixed with clattering, coming closer, faster than before.

Huffs of breath, steam-vent loud, pulsed.

Claire pushed down on the button again, the metering light measuring ... measuring. "Damn it, take the shot!"

Suddenly, the racket ceased, and she was no longer alone.

The hairs on the back of her neck and forearms screamed, 'Retreat! Retreat!' Stench hit her like a serving tray, making her eyes water, her stomach recoil.

Then the camera finally cooperated and a flash whitened the mine for a split second.

Before she could do so much as take a breath, a high-pitched, deafening squeal blasted her eardrums.

In the LCD screen, red eyes stared at her. A pair of two-inch long canine teeth, bright white amidst the mine's brown innards, speared out of the jaws along the sides of the beast's snout.

As if spurred by some unseen demon, its hooves smacked onto the rock floor as it raced toward her in the pitch black.

Claire stood Popsicle stiff, the camera clutched in her hands, and screamed along with its squeals.

A dull thud of muscle and bone connecting with solid rock cut through the pandemonium, followed by a deep grunt.

Claire swallowed her next scream, her ears straining to hear what her eyes could not see.

A short burst of snorts came from her right—too close.

The flash must have temporarily blinded it, confused it. She needed to get the hell out of there!

Turning her back to the beast, she snapped off a shot, cursing through the metering hesitation. As soon as she could see her exit path on the screen, she ran, stumbling into walls and over loose rocks and steel rails as she snapped pictures.

Snorts raged from behind her, driving her forward, gaining on her.

She blindly rounded yet another bend, her shoulder knocking into a support timber. She pinballed off it, careening over the rails, and slammed into a solid body with a grunt of surprise.

Mac's familiar scent registered in her panic-soaked brain as they tumbled to the floor, where a board did a lousy job of softening their fall.

The sudden silence that followed was broken by two things: a plop as something fell into the water-filled shaft beside her, and a steady whoosh of breath through a four-inch snout.

Claire clambered to her feet. Mac's penlight lay on the

floor next to him. Scooping it up, she shined it in the direction of her attacker. "Mac, get up!"

Mac cautiously rose. "Jesus." He grabbed the light and pushed her behind him. "That thing reeks like rancid meat."

"What the hell is it?"

"A *javelina*."

"It looks like a pissed-off pig with fangs to me."

"Stay back." He tucked her further behind him. "It's a sow—a pregnant one. They leave the herd to have their piglets. You probably stumbled onto her as she was burrowing in, preparing to squeeze a couple out, and scared her."

"She scared me back, so we're even. Now tell her to leave."

"Maybe we should do the leaving. She was here first."

As if it understood what they were saying, the *javelina* slowly backed up, keeping its gaze locked on them as it slipped back around the bend, deeper into the mine.

"What's she doing?" Claire whispered against his shoulder.

"If she came here to have babies, she's probably already in labor. Now that you're out of her territory, she's going to go back and finish what she started."

The *javelina* gave them one last snort, then left.

"Whew!" Claire pocketed the camera, then pinched her nose shut. "It's too bad she didn't take her smell with her." She moved up beside Mac and glanced down at the shaft next to them. "We came close to taking a swim." Then she remembered the plopping sound she'd heard after they'd fallen. "Shine the light down there. I heard something drop into the water."

"That shaft is hundreds of feet deep. You're not going to see any further than ten feet, fifteen most, with this light."

Why must he fight her on everything? "Just shine the light down there. Please."

He stood close to the edge and pointed the penlight toward the water. Several feet down, something silver glinted.

Claire leaned further over the shaft. "Is that—"

"My compass," Mac finished, his tone clipped.

"Uhh ..." Claire licked her lips. Guilt warmed her cheeks. "Just how expensive was that particular toy?"

"Five hundred dollars. On sale."

"Oops."

Later that afternoon, Claire parked Mabel next to a beat-up, green VW—the old slug-bug kind—in front of Creekside Supply Company, Jackrabbit Junction's hardware, gun, and liquor store. Everything a cowpoke or miner needed for a hunting expedition or a romantic date could be found under one roof, including perfume and several varieties of mule deer piss.

She left the car windows down to keep the interior from reaching meltdown and crossed the gravel toward the glass entry doors. Despite Mac's attempts throughout the morning to convince her otherwise, she still had trouble swallowing the idea that Joe was just a traveling salesman.

Pretending to admire the landscape, she checked to make sure nobody had noticed her, then slipped around the side of the white cinderblock building. Charlie's Angels had nothing on her.

Two-foot high shrubs of flat-top buckwheat waved pink flowers while tiny blue and orange butterflies danced from bloom to bloom. Patches of knee-high thistles tipped with pinkish purple blossoms scratched across Claire's khakis as she tromped through them to the back of what used to be Joe's antique store.

Standing on her toes, she peeked through a dust-ridden screen into the empty store. Sunshine poured in through the two large storefront windows and spilled across the wood slab floor and white stucco walls.

The place was empty all right. Not a single Louis XVI armchair or French oval side table in sight.

Claire slunk around to the far side of the building. A tall grouping of paloverde trees with long branches hid her from U.S. Route 191. The ground inclined several feet as she moved toward the front; the window at eyelevel.

She peered in at a small rectangular room, probably

eight feet wide by ten feet long. A monster-sized, 1970s style metal desk and an aluminum chair with green padding furnished the room. A cardboard box had been shoved into one of the corners.

Above the desk hung another painting of Johnny Cash on black velvet, straight on instead of his right profile, like the one in Joe's office back at Ruby's. Joe must have had a thing for the man in black.

What was inside that desk? Without ripping the screen and breaking the window, Claire wasn't going to find out.

She skirted the trees and stepped onto the boardwalk that spanned the front of Joe's store and the Creekside Supply Company.

Maybe she could meet with the realtor, see about touring the place, fake interest in starting some kind of business. Southwest pottery and dreamcatchers would be believable, or a cheap cigarette shop.

She walked past the front door, pausing in front of the steel plate where a deadbolt used to reside. Or maybe, just maybe ...

She raced to Mabel and swiped Gramps's laminated picture of Tammy Wynette from the visor.

Back at the front door, Tammy's picture slid smoothly into the doorjamb. With a little jiggle, the knob turned freely and the door popped open. "Thank you, Ms. Wynette," Claire whispered and stuck Tammy in her back pocket.

After glancing both ways, she sneaked in and locked the door behind her. The air inside, slightly cooler than outside, smelled of beeswax with a hint of varnish. The floor creaked under her feet as she crossed to the backroom.

Fingers tingling with excitement, she hauled open the middle desk drawer. The drawer was empty except for a notepad advertising Motel 6 on every sheet and a yellow pencil with a chewed eraser. The two drawers on each side held only paper crumbs in the corners.

Crap.

She moved to the box in the corner. An old pair of canvas tennis shoes filled with spider webs leaned against a wire coat hanger.

That left Johnny. Claire lifted him from the nail and flipped him over onto the desk, tearing into the backing. No duct tape secured anything to the back of this one. Maybe Joe had jammed something between the painting and the frame.

She dropped the frame to the floor, stepped on one corner, and yanked on the opposite. The wood splintered and cracked. The velvet peeled away from the boards like skin from a ripe peach. Nothing, again.

"Sorry, Johnny." She leaned the broken frame against the box.

Scanning the floor, the walls, and the ceiling, she searched for any crack or bulging seam or loose board, but came up empty. Out in the main room, she found an earring back and a handful of dead flies.

Deflated, she trudged back to the front door.

Maybe Mac was right. Maybe she was trying to stir up some exciting mystery in Jackrabbit Junction to keep from twirling her hair all day.

An old boyfriend had once said she had the uncanny ability to create fiction out of fact. Even if the bastard had been lying about sleeping with his boss's wife at the time, he had a point. Her imagination shouldn't always run the show.

After making sure the coast was clear, Claire stepped out, shut the door behind her, and crossed the parking lot. The hot sunshine on her shoulders beat her into the ground.

Ten feet from Mabel, she stopped so fast her toes crunched against the front of her shoes. *Holy frickin' moly!*

Henry sat in the driver's seat, looking out at her.

She blinked, then coughed out a laugh. "Henry! Where in the hell have you been?"

He wiggled and whined in excitement, tail wagging back and forth, swishing against Mabel's white leather. He looked like he'd been dipped in a vat of mud and hung out to dry, but his eyes were as bright as ever.

Claire grinned and grabbed his face, raining kisses over his bony head, then caught a whiff of him and paused. She leaned into the car and sniffed again.

"Ran off my ass," she told Henry, remembering Mac's words as she scratched the dog behind the ears. "If you ran away, why do you reek of perfume?"

Chapter Eleven

Sophy sat in her Suburban, binoculars up, staring across the valley at the dark hole in the side of Apache Mountain. A sinking crescent-moon bathed the valley in dim blue light.

From her birds-eye view on the opposite hillside, she watched as a flashlight beam bounced around inside the black mouth of Socrates Pit, like a firefly fluttering inside a soup can.

Ruby's nephew was very busy in there, nosing around where he didn't belong. On her way to the mine, Sophy had spotted his white pickup, mostly hidden behind a grove of mesquite. If he was trying to be sneaky, he needed lessons.

According to her watch, ten o'clock had just come and gone. That left her three hours to get some work done, if Mac Garner would just remove his ass from the mine.

She popped a couple of NoDoz and took a swig of cold coffee. Spending her nights in Socrates Pit for the last month had her feet swollen and her joints screaming every morning, but finding that loot would be worth the pain.

A cool breeze wafted through the open window.

Ever since Mac had come to town, Sophy had been hiding her tools near the mine's mouth. The chance of him finding anything valuable in its walls was slim, but it didn't pay to be careless this late in the game. She'd already underestimated that damned beagle's digging abilities.

She'd about dropped a tray of burgers and fries when she saw that mud-covered mutt bee-line across U.S. Route

191 toward Harley Ford's Mercury, parked in front of Creekside Supply Company. Through the diner window, she'd watched Ruby's brunette friend rumble off toward the R.V. park, the dog on the seat next to her.

Lowering the binoculars, she took a deep drag from her cigarette. If that mutt came nosing around again, she'd see if it could find its way home from the other side of the Mexican border.

An owl hooted nearby, breaking up the monotony of cricket chirps. She lifted her binoculars for a quick look. Light flickered briefly inside the hole. There was no sign of Mac leaving anytime soon.

She tapped her cigarette ashes out the window. There was no way she was going to sit here every night while Mac tried to figure out what those holes in the ground were worth.

Sophy already knew that answer. It was just a matter of digging up the proof.

---+ + +---

"What do you mean I have to leave?" Towel-drying her hair, Claire stepped out of the Winnebago's cramped bathroom. "It's a quarter-after-ten, for crissake."

Gramps, dressed in an orange Hawaiian-style shirt and green Dockers, lounged on the couch. Next to his bare feet, Henry lay sprawled out, cleaning his doggy jewels—the one area on the little shit that Claire had refused to scrub earlier.

"Are you in preschool? Ten isn't late," Gramps said. "Hell, most stag parties don't even get hopping 'til midnight."

"I don't care about stag parties. I have to work tomorrow."

"You can sleep at my place," Manny offered. He rested his feet on the opposite booth seat, a Cheshire cat grin on his lips. "I have a big bed."

"Not big enough," Claire said.

"I'm not asking you to stay away all night, only a couple hours."

This "couple hours" to romance a woman business was bullshit. What happened to the good old days of ten-minute, backseat romps? Getting kicked out of her bed every other night so Gramps could do things that Claire would rather gouge out her eyes than think about was making her fingers itch to strangle someone—any old man would do.

She hung her towel on an empty peg next to the door. A petite-sized, yellow knit sweater hung next to Gramps's bomber jacket. "Is this hers?" she asked, holding the sweater up by her index finger.

"Whose?"

"The woman coming over tonight."

"That's none of your business. Rule number five states that questions regarding clothing left behind are not allowed."

On a whim, Claire buried her nose in the sweater.

"What in the hell are you doing, girl?" Gramps asked.

The fabric, downy-soft against her skin, smelled of lavender and hyacinth. "Seeing if she smells like Henry did."

"¿Por que?" Manny asked.

"Don't ask," Gramps muttered.

"I'm looking for his dognapper." Claire returned the sweater to the peg. "He smelled like a French whore when I found him."

"I told you to drop it, Claire. I like French whores."

Manny chuckled. "I can vouch for that."

"Besides, Henry's back, so there's no need to go pointing fingers. It'll only ruffle feathers."

"Ooh la la. I wouldn't mind seeing Hot Cheeks with her feathers ruffled." Manny winked at Gramps.

Gramps grinned, blushing slightly.

"Who's Hot Cheeks?" Claire asked.

"Rosy Linstad—the owner of that sweater you're holding," Manny said. "Chester gave her the nickname. He's got a thing for her ass."

Claire shook her head. Chester needed a hobby—collecting toy trains or building model airplanes, something besides chasing skirts. "Am I being ousted because Hot Cheeks is coming?" she asked Gramps.

"I told you, it's not your business."

"No," Manny answered for him. "Nasty Nurse Nancy is making a house-call tonight. Harley needs a physical."

"Damn your bucket mouth, Carrera."

Claire grabbed her jean jacket from the wall. "I can't believe you're kicking me out of my bed so you can perform some kinky procedures with a nurse."

"Oh, Nancy's not a real nurse." The smirk on Manny's face said a thousand dirty words. "She's just good at playing one."

"Oh, come on." Claire yanked open the door. "That's just icky."

"Don't come back until after midnight," Gramps hollered at her as she stepped outside.

"Hey, what about Henry?" Manny asked.

She glanced back to see Manny holding up the dog's leash. "Henry stays here. You two can get your rocks off by watching Nasty Nurse Nancy take his temperature." Claire slammed the door behind her.

"Thanks again for taking me in," Claire said to Ruby fifteen minutes later. "Gramps, uh ..." She didn't want to tell Ruby that while they were drinking Coke floats in Ruby's rec room, Gramps was playing doctor with some

Internet floozy.

Earlier that afternoon, Ruby had off-handedly prodded Claire regarding Gramps's dating life. Claire had a sneaking suspicion there was more smoldering under the Arizona sun than the top of her head.

"Gramps and the boys smoked me out," she finished.

"Please, Claire. I appreciate you tryin' to spare me the truth." Ruby placed three different bottles of perfume on the bar in front of Claire. "But I'd have to have my head buried in a pile of sheep shit not to see what your grandfather and his friends are fixin' to do, what with all of these brassy broads swarming around here."

Claire picked up a tall, skinny bottle and spritzed the inside of her wrist.

"I know he's lonely," she told Ruby, "and I don't have any problems with him dating, but I wish he'd take things a bit slower, get to know these women first. Find out what they did in the past, what they hope to do in the future."

She sniffed her wrist—jasmine. Too sweet. It must be Jess's.

"Honey, what makes you think he's not asking those questions?"

"He's a man. I don't think questions are a top priority when he's alone with a woman."

Ruby sat down on the stool next to Claire. "I've known your grandpa for several years now. Unlike Chester, Harley likes to take his time and test the water first."

"I hope you're right." Claire's mom would have her scalp if Gramps crossed back over the South Dakota state line wearing a wedding band.

"So, what's the story with you and these perfumes?" Ruby pointed at the bottles. "If you're fixin' to find yourself a man around these parts, you'd be better off dabbing some beer behind your ears and wearing a locket filled with chewing tobacco."

Claire grinned. "Henry's kidnapper flea-dipped him in perfume. Determining the brand of perfume is the first step to figuring out who abducted him."

"Then what?"

"Then I'm going to pay a friendly visit to each of your visitors and see which one of them wears the same perfume."

Ruby poked at the scoops of ice cream floating in her glass. "You really think one of these crazy ladies kidnapped Henry?"

"Possibly. But it could also be someone who lives around here."

"Why would someone take a dog?"

"Ransom money, animal cruelty, black market sales—Henry kind of looks like a purebred, you know."

Claire sprayed her wrist with another bottle. She sniffed and sneezed. It smelled like she'd buried her head in a bouquet of gardenias. Eyes watering, she pushed the bottle away.

"And you're determined to find out who the dognapper is in order to stop them from committin' the same crime again?"

"No. I'm just pissed. These last few days have been hell. Vengefulness has always been my worst trait."

Claire tried the last bottle. No luck. Tomorrow, she'd drive up to the hardware store and test their supply. If she couldn't find the brand there, she'd head over to Yuccaville.

An American history book sat on the end of the bar. "Where's Jess?" she asked Ruby.

"Upstairs. She's supposed to be studying for tomorrow's health test, but she's too busy being mad at me for giving birth to her."

Jess had chilled last night after gorging on ice cream, but Claire knew it was only a temporary fix. Sugar might dull the pain Jess's dad had inflicted, but only time would heal the wound. "Did you see the letter her dad sent?"

Ruby nodded. "I peeked at it last night while you two were out."

"How did you ever hook up with Jess's dad?"

Sighing, Ruby frowned. "I was lonely, drunk, and about to turn forty, and he looked great in a pair of Wranglers. We had one night together, and a month later, I found out I was pregnant."

Claire frowned. "Did he want anything to do with the baby?"

"Nope. When I looked him up and told him, he laughed in my face and said the kid was my problem."

"Nice," Claire stirred her float. "Real nice."

"Over the years, he's tried *not* to help out with Jess, but the law has forced him to pay his part."

"What a jerk."

"Damn straight. But try to say anything even slightly bad about the man in front of Jess and she'll tear you a new one." Ruby sipped her float. "What's funny is that she's never even met him."

"Really?" Jess had acted like she'd seen him off and on over the years.

"He's sent her a couple of letters, mostly responses to the hundreds that she's written to him, but he's never called or tried to actually visit her."

Claire's heart ached for the kid.

"If I ever see him again, he's gonna suffer for the emotional rollercoaster he's dragged my little girl on."

Claire pushed her empty glass away, licking the last of the sweet foam from her lips. "Did Jess get along with Joe?"

"She didn't hate him." Ruby shrugged. "But with him traveling and her at school, they hardly saw each other."

"Jess mentioned she got kicked out of school. She said something about giving another girl a black eye."

"Yeah, she has my momma's temper. Lucky for me, the girl's parents didn't want anything more than an apology. But the school gave me the names and numbers of several therapists and told me to send Jess to one of them for help."

"Do you think she needs help?"

Ruby shook her head. "I think she needs a father, but there's not much I can do about that right now. I've got my hands full with stopping the bank from rippin' this place out from under me."

"I know you don't want me to sell the mines, but with the profit I'll make, I can keep the park going and provide more opportunities for Jess's future—like a private school."

The air conditioner kicked on, rattling loudly until Ruby walked over and punched it.

"Sounds like you need a new air conditioner," Claire said.

"Nah. It just likes attention. It takes after Joe."

That reminded Claire of another question. "Did Joe keep paperwork anywhere else around here? You know, stuff from when he was a salesman?"

"Not that I know of. What he didn't keep in his office, he carried with him in his car."

"The one he totaled?"

"Yep. He had this fancy metal briefcase with a motion detector and alarm. If some guy stole it from him, he could pull out a remote, click a button, and zap him through the handle with one hell of an electrical shock. He told me he bought it on a whim at a sportsman's show. Was real proud of it, too."

Something told Claire that Joe had stored more than just sales contracts in that briefcase. "Do you still have it?"

"It disappeared the last year he was alive. I figure he forgot where he put it. His memory was so sketchy at the end."

"What happened to the car after Joe totaled it?"

"I cleaned out the glove box and trunk, and then we sold it to ol' Monty Kunkle. He owns a junkyard east of Yuccaville."

"Did you find anything interesting in the glove box?"

"Nah. Just the usual stuff—registration, nail clippers, pens."

Damn. "What about under the seats? In the trunk?"

"The trunk had a spare tire and a jack. I only glanced in the back seat. Why?"

"No reason," Claire lied. "Just curious." And suspicious as hell, but Ruby didn't need to know that yet.

"You're welcome to take a look for yourself."

Claire frowned. "What do you mean?"

"The car is still sittin' out back in Monty's junkyard. He couldn't find it in his heart to crush such a classy car, so he's been partin' it out piece by piece over the Internet for the last two years."

Thursday, April 15th

"You look like you ate one too many chili peppers," Manny told Claire as he dealt cards facedown around the table.

After spending most of the afternoon mowing, weed whacking, and stacking firewood, Claire's skin glowed as red as a branding iron. With her head throbbing, the last thing she wanted to do this evening was sit stuffed between Chester and the Winnebago's wall in a room choked with cigar smoke.

"I'll bid two," Gramps said, lowering his cards to the table. "I noticed a small scratch on Mabel's back bumper."

From under her eyelashes, Claire could see him staring

across the table at her. She'd sooner offer to hand wash Chester's boxer shorts than cough up any information on the origin of that scratch.

"I ran into Skinny Minnie at the General Store this afternoon," Chester said while staring at his cards. "She was loading up on chocolate-covered cherries and Coors light. Three."

"Maybe someone backed into Mabel when you were eating lunch at Wheeler's Diner." Claire moved a couple of cards around in her hand and avoided Gramps's gaze. "I'll pass." She threw down her cards.

Gramps frowned. "That's the fourth time in a row you've passed."

And the fourth time in a row that he'd bitched at her about it. "I can't help it that I have shit for cards tonight."

"Skinny Minnie, huh?" Manny interrupted their bickering. He knocked twice on the table, passing as well. "Did you offer to help her with her cherries?"

Chester grinned. "She asked me to stop over later tonight for a nightcap." He threw down a Jack of spades. "That's trump."

"Are you going to introduce Chester Jr. to the *Señorita*?"

"Hell, no," Chester said. "She's all skin and bones. Sex with Skinny Minnie would be like screwing a bag of antlers."

While Manny and Gramps roared, Claire shook her head and threw out a nine of diamonds.

She gulped half her can of Budweiser. The taste of beer made her tongue happy tonight, but the rest of her wanted to crawl under some cool cotton sheets and not come out until morning.

Manny dropped a Queen of spades on the pile. Gramps tossed a Jack of clubs on Manny's card. The frown he'd been wearing all evening was firmly back in place.

As Chester raked in the cards, someone knocked on the door.

"It's open," Gramps called.

Jess stepped into the Winnebago, waving her hand in front of her face as she walked through the wall of smoke. "Hi guys." In her pink, pansy-covered pajamas, she barely looked twelve, let alone fifteen going on sixteen.

Claire smiled at the kid. "Hey, girl." What was Jess doing out this late on a school night? Claire opened her mouth to ask, but then thought better of it. She didn't want to embarrass Jess in front of the "old dudes."

"What's up, *chica?*" Manny asked.

Jess shrugged, sidled up to Gramps, and stared at his cards over his shoulder. "Mom's on the phone with Dad, yelling at him something fierce, so I decided to come see what's happening with you guys."

Claire grimaced at Jess's situation.

Except for Elvis Presley singing "Suspicious Minds" on the kitchen radio, and Henry—stomach up, legs splayed — snoring as he lay sleeping on the couch, they played the next two rounds in silence.

Chester won both with high, non-trump cards, and the wrinkles in Gramps's brow sank deeper with each card Claire threw down.

"What's your cousin up to?" Claire asked Jess, trying to sound cool and casual and not desperate for any word on the guy who'd occupied her thoughts all afternoon. She ignored the big smile that creased Manny's lips.

"He's still in the mines. He didn't even come home for supper."

Chester started the next round with the ten of spades. Claire dropped her King of spades on top of the ten, and then lifted her beer to her mouth.

"Damn it, Claire!" Gramps shouted.

Claire jerked in surprise and spilled beer down her T-shirt.

"What are you thinking, girl? Why did you throw off trump on that first round if you had that King setting in your hand?"

She wiped her shirt. "I guess I wasn't paying attention."

"Well, you'd better start."

She slammed her cards down on the table. "I don't know what crawled up your ass and died tonight," she told Gramps, "but I'm tired of you taking your frustrations out on me. Move it, Chester."

"You can't leave in the middle of a game," Chester said, rising.

"Watch me." She slid across the booth seat.

"Claire, where are you going?" Gramps asked. The anger sapped from his voice. He sounded tired, worn smooth.

She grabbed her jean jacket from the peg and opened the door. "For a walk. Don't wait up."

With a goodbye nod to Jess, she stepped outside.

The breath of fresh air in her lungs unlocked the tension pinching her neck. Her shoulders dropped an inch at the sight of Ursa Major hanging out in the sky. A near half-moon painted the trees, tumbleweeds, and picnic tables in shades of gray.

The dirt poofed from under her tennis shoes as she passed in front of the General Store. The lights were on inside. Ruby paced behind the counter, the phone pressed to her ear.

Claire kept to the shadows and marched across the bridge and out of the park. She barreled along, thigh muscles humming, her sunburn keeping the need to slip on her coat at bay.

The chirping of crickets faded with every step away from the creek, replaced by the rustling of sage bramble as the desert breathed around her.

Since she'd arrived at the Dancing Winnebagos R.V. Park, her days had been filled with dead-ends and frustration. First the bone, then Henry, then Mac, then Joe; now Jess, and Gramps, and Ruby.

She rooted through the pockets of her jacket. Where was that emergency cigarette she'd tucked away? She searched each pocket twice, marching past the junction for the road heading to Socrates Pit and Rattlesnake Ridge mines.

Seconds later, she heard a vehicle approaching from behind. She glanced over her shoulder at a familiar white pickup. Her heartbeat picked up the pace.

Mac rolled down his window. "What are you doing out here?"

"Taking a walk." *Alone!* She'd met her quota for frustration today, both sexual and platonic.

He stared at her, his eyes seeming to search her face for something. "Hop in the truck. We need to talk."

Chapter Twelve

Mac watched Claire settle onto the bench seat next to him. The dashboard lights cast a glow across her cheekbones and nose, softening the shiny sunburn he'd noticed under the dome light. Her white T-shirt hugged her chest, outlining her soft curves in the semi-darkness.

He groaned in his head, frustrated with wanting something he shouldn't.

Claire turned and caught him staring.

At her raised eyebrows, he whipped his gaze back to the road, where it belonged.

Sage bushes, ghostly under the headlights, flashed past as he accelerated.

Silence reigned inside the cab, broken only by the thwump-thwump of the tires rolling over the tar-patched lines that criss-crossed the road.

Now that Claire sat within touching distance, smelling like watermelon and cigar smoke, Mac couldn't find his tongue. He tapped the brakes as a coyote darted across the road. The pedal felt a little soft under his boot.

"So," Claire said, "what do you want to talk to me about?"

"Henry's dognapping."

"Bzzzt. Wrong answer. After roasting my head under the freakin' sun all day, wise-cracks and criticism could result in a sledgehammer to the knees—yours, not mine."

Grinning, Mac glanced at her. She was busy massaging the side of her neck. His fingers itched to help her.

"How about we stick to the weather," she said. "Or how many girlfriends you've had in the last decade. Your choice."

Mac chuckled. Talking about his ex-girlfriends was the last thing he wanted to do while sitting in the dark with Claire.

He drummed on the brakes again, dodging a Texas-sized pothole that the county hadn't bothered to fix since Nixon was in office. The brake pedal felt very squishy this time.

He pushed on it twice more, his stomach tightening when the pickup barely stuttered.

"But I know about the weather, so ..." Claire trailed off.

The sage bushes whizzed by faster as the pickup rolled down the four percent grade toward Jackrabbit Junction, less than three-quarters of a mile away.

Mac stomped on the brake. The pedal slammed against the floor—no resistance at all.

"Put your seatbelt on," he told her.

"Why are you going so fast?"

"Just put your seatbelt on. Now!"

"Fine, but I think you should slow down."

He waited until he heard a click. "I can't."

Out of the corner of his eye, he saw her open-mouthed stare. "What do you mean you can't?"

Up ahead, he could almost make out the STOP sign where the road dead-ended into U.S. Route 191. "The brakes are out."

"Out? Brakes don't just go out."

"Well, these did."

"Why don't you down-shift into second?"

"We're going too fast. I'd rather not leave my tranny in our wake."

"Shit."

"Don't worry," he assured her. "I have a plan."

The seat shifted as Claire shoved back into the cushions. "If it involves opening my door and jumping out, I want to hear Plan B."

"I'm going to use the emergency brake." Mac just hoped it was still working. The STOP sign was visible now, a glimmer of red in the distance.

"Will it stop us?"

"Not immediately, but it should slow us down enough."

"Enough for what?"

He pushed lightly on the emergency brake, feeling the minor effects of friction as the brake shoes rubbed the drums. "Enough for us to swerve without rolling the truck rather than crash through the front windows of Wheeler's Diner."

He pushed the emergency brake further. The pickup lurched, slowing down to the posted speed limit—about thirty miles per hour faster than he'd prefer this close to U.S. Route 191.

"Then how are we going to stop?"

"I haven't worked that out yet." He could just make out the letters on the STOP sign. They weren't slowing fast enough.

"Uh, Mac." Claire's voice sounded a bit higher than normal. "We need to stop."

"I know that, Claire." He white-knuckled the wheel.

She grabbed his forearm and squeezed, hard, her fingers digging into his muscle. "We need to stop now!"

"What do you think I'm trying to do here?"

Her fingers burrowed deeper into his flesh. "Mac?" A humming noise started in her throat. She pointed out her window.

Mac glanced over for a split-second and nearly swallowed his tongue at the sight of an eighteen-wheeler, barreling down U.S. Route 191. At the rate they were slowing, they'd be in the middle of the intersection just in time for the rig to smash into Claire's door.

The humming noise in Claire's throat grew louder, higher.

Mac stomped on the emergency brake. It hit the floor.

The STOP sign was less than ten feet away, the rig seconds from crossing their path. Its headlights blazed into the cab.

Claire shielded her face and screamed.

The blast of an air horn drowned her out, and five sets of wheels thundered past in front of the windshield.

Mac jerked the wheel to the right.

The front left fender of the pickup skimmed the tail of the semi-trailer. They screeched sideways across U.S. Route 191 and spun into the gravel-filled parking lot in front of Wheeler's Diner.

Mac turned into the skid, fishtailing. Gravel flew. He straightened out the truck just in time to swerve left to keep from crashing through Wheeler's front door, but smashed into the *Tucson Daily* and *Phoenix Sun* newspaper dispensers. The boxes of metal and glass crunched, scraping through the gravel, stopping them before the truck reached Jackrabbit Creek.

Mac's heart walloped in his chest as clouds of dust swirled around them. The smell of burnt rubber filled the cab.

Claire had stopped screaming. He looked at her. "You okay?"

A strangled squeak leaked from her mouth.

"Claire?" He pried her fingers from his forearm. Her breath came in short bursts. What were the signs of shock? Enlarged pupils? Mac leaned toward her, and then he heard the click of her seatbelt latch.

A split second later, she was out the door.

He pushed open his door. Claire was already halfway across the parking lot. "Where are you going?" he called.

"To get a drink," she yelled over her shoulder, "and change my goddamned underwear." She jogged across U.S. Route 191 and slipped inside The Shaft's wooden door.

Running both hands through his hair, Mac slowly exhaled, happy to still be breathing; happier yet that Claire was still yelling and cussing, like usual.

He turned back to his Dodge, frowned, and grabbed a flashlight from behind the seat before scooting under the pickup. The gravel bit into his shoulder blades.

Everything looked fine where the brake lines came down out of the engine compartment.

He followed one of the lines to the caliper. "Son of a bitch," he whispered and ran his index finger over two small punctures, not much bigger than the tip of a sharp punch, then rubbed the pads of his finger and thumb together. They slid smoothly over each other.

He sniffed his finger. Brake fluid. Holes that small would allow the fluid to drip slowly while his truck was parked, but spray out each time he pushed on the brakes.

Checking the other brake line connections, he found similar holes at each one. He crawled out from under the pickup and wiped his hands on his pants. Somebody had punctured his brake lines while he was parked out at the mine—probably the same person who'd flattened Ruby's tires.

But why?

The thought of what could have happened to Claire tonight made him nauseated.

He threw the flashlight back into the cab.

First the spark plug wires, then the flat tires, now his brakes.

Somebody wanted him to go back to Tucson, and not necessarily in one piece.

Claire had downed half a glass of Budweiser by the time Mac pushed through The Shaft's front door. Her pulse revved as he strode toward her, his gaze stormy, holding her prisoner.

She kicked out the chair across from her. "Have a seat."

Mac spun it around and straddled it, resting his forearms across the back. With a lock of honey brown hair falling over his forehead, he could wipe the floor with Han Solo, although Brad Pitt—shirtless—still ruled.

Drawing invisible circles on the scarred tabletop, she tried not to ogle him.

"Are you okay?" he asked.

"I will be after another beer. How's the truck?"

His lips thinned. "Somebody punctured the brake lines."

"Jesus." She took another swig. "I'm beginning to think folks around here don't take kindly to out-of-towners."

"Someone doesn't want me in those mines."

"Maybe you should consider hiring a bodyguard."

He raised an eyebrow. "You applying?"

Her stomach flipped and flopped. She'd watch his body all right, but there wouldn't be much guarding involved.

"I don't think so." She shoved her glass of beer toward him. "Have a drink. It'll shave the hard edges off this evening's events."

He took several swallows, frowning as she rose to her feet. "Where are you going?"

"To get us two more beers."

"I'll get them."

"You can get the next two. What's on your fingers?"

"Brake fluid." He stood and glanced toward the *Bucks* room. "I'll be right back. I need to wash my hands." His gaze bore into her, his eyes piercing, assessing. "You sure you're okay?"

She saluted him with her empty glass. "I'm working my way back up to cloud nine. The way I see it, after nearly becoming bug-splatter on the grill of an eighteen-wheeler, my day can't get much worse."

"You're one of a kind, Claire." He dropped a kiss on her cheek and then threaded his way toward the men's room.

Claire stared after him, feeling like her head was floating about three feet above her shoulders, until reality slapped her back to Earth. Those were hardly words of undying pining and heartfelt need. And the kiss was just a peck, really. She'd seen him give Ruby similar quick kisses on the cheek.

She weaved her way over to the bar and flagged down the owner, who was busy drying glasses. "Hey, Butch, I'll have two—"

"Hey, sugar," Joe's ex-wife interrupted, leaning over the bar. Her over-inflated boobs nearly spilled out of her slinky tank top. "Will you grab Billy and me another couple of Coor's Lights?"

"Hey!" Claire glared, bristling like a pissed off porcupine.

Sophy flashed Butch a mega-watt smile. "Make sure you get a lot of head on those—Billy likes to lick the foam off my lip."

Claire slammed her glass down. "I don't know who you think you are, but I was here first." Claire shot Butch a warning look. If he valued his life, he'd make Sophy wait her turn.

"And you'll be here last," Sophy said, looking down her nose at Claire. She turned to Butch. "Just go ahead and fill those quick. I'm holding up a pool game."

"Listen, you cradle-robbing, huss—" Claire started.

"Don't get your panties in a wad, bitch."

A burst of rage rocketed through Claire's skull. She cold-cocked Joe's ex with a hard right. Her fist smashed into Sophy's cheekbone with a solid *thwap*, knocking the woman flat on her ass on the wood-planked floor.

A hush spread through the bar, broken only by Barbara Mandrell on the jukebox whining about sleeping single in a double bed.

Claire sniffed, wiping her hand on her pants. "Now, about those beers, Butch."

She kept her eyes on the older woman, who used a bar stool to pull herself to her feet.

Glowering, Sophy touched her cheek where an angry-looking red welt was already surfacing. "You're going to pay for that, you stupid cow." She rushed, red talons extended.

Claire lifted her arm to shield her face. Sophy's body collided with hers, sending them both flailing and crashing to the floor with Sophy on top. Rolling around under the elk horn chandeliers, Claire grunted and growled, peanut shells cracking under her. The smell of cigarette ashes and the bitch's perfume nearly suffocated her.

Sophy grabbed a handful of Claire's hair and yanked, then dragged her nails down Claire's cheek.

Eyes watering from the pain, Claire rolled on top of the woman, aimed for her nose, missed, and belted her in the chin instead.

Suddenly, a strong pair of arms hauled her off Sophy and dropped her onto her feet. Claire shoved her hair out of her face, ignoring the cheers shouted by the crowd surrounding her, and glared across at Sophy.

Butch held Joe's ex—barely—with the help of a skinny blond cowboy.

Claire tried to twist free of her keeper, wanting to

finish the job she'd started.

"Damn it, Claire! Quit struggling," Mac said in her ear.

Strong-arming her out of the stuffy, smoky bar into the cool clear desert night, he directed her through the parking lot over to a halo of light cast by a streetlight. Once there, he lifted her onto the hood of an old Chevy Nova, and then stepped back, arms crossed. "What in the hell happened back there?"

Claire tried to comb her hair out of her eyes and came away with a palm full of it. "Sophy pissed me off."

"So you tackled her?"

"No, I decked her. She's the one who tackled me."

Mac shook his head. "Christ, woman."

She felt something dripping down her cheek and touched her finger to it. Blood, dark and wet, smudged her fingertip.

"Don't move a muscle," Mac ordered. "I'll be right back."

While he jogged across the road to his truck and back, Claire pulled another handful of hair from her crown.

Mac dropped a first aid kit on the hood next to her and popped it open. "Remind me never to piss you off," he said as he dabbed her cheek with cotton. Then he sprayed something on the scratch that made it sting like a horsefly bite.

Claire sat quietly, coming down from her adrenaline rush, while Mac patched her up. Anger seeped out of her bones as his fingers brushed over her skin. She kept her gaze lowered, not wanting him to see the hunger gnawing at her for something more than just casual contact from him.

He moved closer, tipping her head to one side and then the other; inspecting, touching. His breath, warm and beer-tainted, fanned across her lips and nose.

She peeked up at him. He stared back, his eyes mirroring the frustration grinding inside of her. "You look like you want to kiss me," she whispered.

"You know I do." His voice was smooth, like butter-soft suede.

Shifting closer, she tilted her head to make room for his lips. "So, do it."

"You're nothing but trouble, Claire."

"Yeah, but you seem to like trouble."

He chuckled under his breath, his eyes zeroing in on her lips. "Not as much as I like you."

His lips brushed hers, tentative, testing. Then a low growl rumbled in his throat and his mouth grew bolder, his lips seeking.

Claire moaned, tasting him, breathing him in. The touch of his tongue to hers just about blew the sneakers right off her feet. She leaned into him and ran her palms down his ribcage. Her fingertips pressed into his abs, fingers clinging to his shirt as she hung on for dear life and tried to keep her head from spinning right off her neck.

"Claire," he said hoarsely against her mouth, tipping her head higher, his fingers cupping the back of her head.

"Umm." She slid her hands under his T-shirt, her thumbs skimming along the trail of soft hair leading up the center of his chest. His skin was firm, warm under the pads of her fingers. She scooted closer, squeezing her inner thighs around the outer seams of his jeans.

His mouth slid along her jawbone, leaving a trail of heat in its wake. He nibbled the skin below her ear. "You smell like watermelon," he whispered.

"It's my shampoo."

"I want to sink my teeth into you."

Claire tipped her head back, staring dazedly up at the blinking light of a passing satellite. Much more of this and she was going to slip down off the side of the car and lie panting at his feet. Her toes curled as he traced the outer shell of her ear with the tip of his tongue.

"I hate to break up the show, lovebirds," a deep, nasally voice said from behind Mac, slicing through the haze in Claire's brain. "But you're sitting on my car, and if I don't get home in the next ten minutes, my wife is going to lock me out."

Mac pulled away from Claire, his breath uneven. "Sorry about that," he told the guy and helped Claire to the ground. He grabbed his first aid kit. "Come on, Slugger," he said to Claire, taking her by the hand and tugging her along behind him across U.S. Route 191.

As they neared his pickup, he let go of her hand. "I'm going over to the gas station to give Ruby a call to come pick us up. Wait for me at the truck."

Claire nodded, her voice box scorched from the inferno still raging inside of her.

"And try to stay out of trouble," he said with a lazy grin, and then strode over to Biddy's Gas and Carryout.

Claire floated to his Dodge.

Between the beer, the after-burn of adrenaline, and Mac's blistering kisses, her head hovered somewhere between the Big Dipper and Cassiopeia. But by the time Mac strode back across the gravel, reality had seeped back in, along with the need for a cigarette.

She rested against the closed tailgate of the pickup and watched him approach, a question waiting on her lips.

"Howdy," Mac said as he leaned against the truck next to her. "What's on your mind?"

"How did you ..."

"Your eyes. You're not very good at hiding what's going on behind them."

That sounded like a bunch of hooey.

"It's the truth," he said, apparently reading her eyes again.

She looked away quickly. That could be dangerous when it came to him.

"So spit it out," he prodded.

"When you picked me up outside of the R.V. park, you wanted to talk to me about something. What was it?"

He grabbed her hand, flipping it palm-side up, tracing the outline of her fingers.

Screw the cigarette, she needed sex. Claire quickly batted that notion out of her mind. Sex with Mac would be a problem of Chernobyl proportions.

"I found some small boot prints up in Socrates Pit," he said. "Like the ones we saw out where Henry's dog tag was lying."

She watched as he laced his fingers with hers and lifted her bruised knuckles to his lips.

Little stars danced behind her eyes. She blinked, several times, rapidly. Hadn't she read somewhere that sexual frustration could cause blindness?

"I also found something else."

He reached into his back pocket and pulled out something that crinkled, sounding like flimsy plastic. He unlaced his fingers from hers and dropped a wrapper in her palm. Under the pale orange streetlight, she could see a familiar label.

"Remember the wrapper you found stuck in that diamond cholla cactus?"

She nodded, surprised he'd remembered she'd grabbed it.

"This is the same kind of beef jerky."

She licked her lips. Suspicions raced through her mind. "You know what this means, don't you?" she asked, stuffing the wrapper in her back pocket.

"That Henry likes beef jerky?" Mac answered with a cocky grin.

"Henry likes food period—beef jerky included. You know what else it means?"

Mac grabbed her by the arm and drew her toward him,

his hands dropping to her hips as he settled her between his long legs. "That Henry is a litterbug?"

She chuckled as he brushed his lips over her chin, her breath suddenly heavy in her chest. "Not quite. Guess again."

"Hmmm," he said as he nuzzled the hollow at the base of her neck. "What will I get if I say it?"

"You should be more worried about what you'll get if you don't," she said, fighting for oxygen as his mouth slid along her collarbone. "I've been known to throw a mean right hook."

"Mmmmm, yes, you have." He nibbled his way up to her earlobe, tugging on it with his teeth.

"I believe," he spoke against the sensitive skin of her inner ear, sending chills spiraling down her arms, "what you're looking for are the words, 'You were right about Henry.'"

Her legs nearly buckled as blood rushed to muscles that hadn't been exercised for much too long. "Something like that."

As she dissolved against him, a voice of wisdom nagged at the back of Claire's brain. They needed to stop for some reason.

Mac gripped her hips tighter, pulling her even closer.

"Ruby!" Claire suddenly remembered and yelped. She jumped out of Mac's hold a split-second before a pair of headlights spotlighted them.

Gravel crunched under the old Ford's new tires as it slowed to a stop.

Ruby, wearing a white bathrobe and fluffy slippers, tore out of the pickup. "What do you mean someone sabotaged your truck?"

Friday, April 16th

Claire rolled into the R.V. park, Mabel's V-8 rumbling as she crept along. The afternoon sunlight reflected off the chrome window edging, ricocheting UV rays straight into her skull. She switched the vent to full blast, gritting her teeth in the whoosh of hell-hot air, and cursed Gramps for being too stubborn to install air conditioning.

Up ahead, Mac stepped from Ruby's front porch and flagged her down.

Claire's libido gurgled to life at just the sight of his long legs. What was it about kissing a gorgeous guy that made the birds start singing Disney tunes and the clouds morph into fluffy tufts of cotton candy floating in a powder blue sky?

She shifted into Park.

Mac rested his forearms on the passenger's side windowsill. "I need your help."

"It'll cost you."

He flashed her an X-rated grin. "Name your price."

Claire fanned the front of her shirt. "We're playing with fire, you know."

"I like the heat." He winked.

"If anyone finds out about what we were doing last night outside The Shaft, we'll never hear the end of it."

"I know."

"Not to mention that we have different opinions about Ruby selling the mines."

"That's true."

"So why do you keep smiling at me that way?"

He shrugged. "I'm an avid fan of the Pink Panther."

Claire glanced down at the Pink Panther iron-on covering the front of her T-shirt. Something tingled in her gut, and it wasn't the Pop Rocks she'd eaten for breakfast. "You said you need my help," she reminded him, changing the subject before she slid down the seat and melted into a pool of sexually charged protons.

He dragged his gaze up to her eyes. The heat was still there, but slightly banked. "My truck is ready to pick up, and Ruby is at a doctor's appointment with Jess in Tucson."

Claire glanced behind Mac and saw the *Be Back Soon* sign hanging in the General Store's window.

"I need a ride to Yuccaville."

Perfect. She needed someone to act as a lookout. "Sure."

He crawled in, sniffing as she reversed and drove out of the R.V. park. "What's that smell?" he asked, sniffing again.

"It's me." She'd spent the last half-hour over at Creekside Supply Company, spraying and spritzing every spot of bare skin with cheap perfume, and she'd only made it through half the rack.

Thank God Henry hadn't smelled like mule piss when she'd found him.

"You trying out new perfume?"

"No. I'm trying to figure out what Sophy was wearing last night."

"Why?"

"She smelled like Henry did when I found him sitting in Mabel the other day." She cringed, waiting for Mac to start berating her about her half-assed suspicions.

He draped his arm across the back of the seat, his fingertips brushing the bare skin of her upper arm with every little bounce and bump. "Did you figure out the brand?"

What? No comments on her hare-brained scheme? "Not yet."

In spite of the sweat trickling down her spine, goose bumps speckled her arms.

She glanced at Mac from under her eyelashes. Did he

have any idea how dangerous it was to flirt with a woman who'd started sniffing pepper on a daily basis after *Cosmopolitan* rated sneezes second to orgasms on their "Pleasure Scale."

At the U.S. Route 191 junction, she turned right.

"Yuccaville is the other way," he said, frowning at her.

"We're taking a detour." Claire pulled the folded phone book page from her pocket and tossed it into Mac's lap.

"What detour?"

"The one that runs by Sophy's house."

Chapter Thirteen

I don't think this is a good idea," Mac told Claire as they pulled up in front of Sophy's gray, single-story, cinderblock home. There was something about the lack of another house within sight that made him feel like he'd stumbled onto one of Hitler's secret hideouts.

Claire shut off the car. "I didn't figure you would." She pushed open her door and stepped out into the early afternoon sunshine.

Mac followed, hesitating at Mabel's front bumper. The urge to drag Claire back to the car and haul ass out of there vibrated through his body. Glancing around at the orange-brown hills speckled with daisy patches that barricaded Sophy's place from the road below, he wondered if Claire's wild imagination was rubbing off on him.

As warm sunshine blanketed his shoulders, the tinkling of wind chimes merged with the sound of Claire's footsteps on the pebble drive. Soft puffs of hot air filled with the smell of seared clay and baked dirt rose through the small canyon from the valley below, whipping her hair about as she crossed toward a shed.

The small building was a sure-fire magnet for a woman bent on proving her suspicions. With its corrugated steel roof spotted with surface rust, and the cedar boards flanking it faded gray with weathering, it was a haven of possibilities.

Mac growled and took off after her. While creeping around Sophy's property made him feel as warm and fuzzy as bending over to touch his toes in a proctologist's office, the idea of Claire casing the place on her own made his gut burn.

Claire was frowning down at the yellow padlock fastened to the door latch when he reached her. "It'll take a .44 slug to open this door," Mac said.

"Damn it."

He glanced at Mabel, her chromed-toothed grin sparkling in the sunshine. "What time do you think Sophy leaves the diner?" he asked.

"Feeling flighty?" She jiggled the lock. It didn't budge.

"I'm new at this trespassing business."

"Who says we're trespassing?"

"That sign hanging on the gate at the end of the drive." He wouldn't be surprised if Sophy carried a six-shooter. Most everyone did around these parts.

"What sign?" Claire cast him a mischievous smile. "I didn't see any sign." She disappeared around the side of the shed.

Mac followed, cursing the weak half of his brain that kept him scurrying along after her like a lovesick Gila monster.

"Ah, ha!" She stared at the base of the wall where dirt had been disturbed recently. "Look at that."

"What? Loose dirt?"

"No, proof. This must be where Henry dug his way out."

Mac squatted down, pushing a potato-sized chunk of igneous rock to the side. "You said he was muddy?"

"Yep."

Mac scooped up a handful of the loose soil and let the dirt trickle through his fingers—reddish-brown, powdery, no clumps—clay with a mix of alluvial sand. "If the ground had been wet, we should be seeing some paw prints." But there were none.

"Maybe it's muddy on the inside?"

"Or maybe Henry splashed through Jackrabbit Creek and rolled around on the muddy bank before hopping in Mabel," he rationalized.

"Then why is the door padlocked?"

Mac rose and wiped his hands on his pants. He glanced around, noticing a chicken crib on the other side of the house. "Maybe she throws her chickens in here at night to keep them safe."

"It's mid-afternoon," her tone was blatantly skeptical.

"My point is there could be a logical explanation for the lock."

Claire rested against the shed and squinted at him. "If you're going to tag along with me, you need to at least try to play along with my suspicions."

He placed his hand next to her head, leaning into her, breathing in the smell of her sun-warmed hair. "If you'll remember, I'm not here by choice."

She smiled, lifting her chin, her eyes wicked and inviting.

Mac gulped. "Now is not the time, Claire." He pushed away from the shed. "Sophy could be home at any moment, and what I want to do to you will take several hours to do right."

He heard her suck in her breath and nearly slammed her up against the wall, anyway—Sophy be damned, but he had no desire to be caught with his pants down. He grabbed her hand and pulled her away from the wall. "Come on. Let's go get my truck. Rattlesnake Ridge is waiting for me."

She tugged on his hand, stopping him. "I don't think that's a good idea. Not after what happened to your brakes."

"I reported the incident to Sheriff Harrison in Yuccaville this morning. He can't arrest anyone until whoever is doing it is caught in the act. What more can I do?"

"Not go out to the mines."

"Claire, I'm not going to sit on my hands while you convince Ruby not to sell those mines."

Her eyes narrowed, flashing in anger. "That's not what I meant, you big bozo."

"Then what did you mean?"

"Working in those mines is dangerous."

The warmth tingling under his skin had nothing to do with the spring sunshine. He draped his arm over her shoulders and led her toward Mabel. "So is spending time with you, but I can't seem to stop."

She elbowed him lightly, chuckling when he grunted. Halfway to the car, Claire ducked out from under his arm and jogged toward Sophy's house.

"What are you doing?" he called after her.

"Running a security check." She slipped around to the back, out of view.

"Damn your curiosity, Claire." Mac chased after her, wondering why he couldn't be attracted to meek women who were afraid of their own shadows.

He rounded the corner just as the screen door slammed shut behind Claire. Mac paused on Sophy's back stoop, rubbing his jaw. Why would Sophy padlock her shed but leave her back door unlocked?

Opening the screen door, he stepped inside a plain old laundry room—no bubbling cauldrons, crystal balls, or pentagrams chalked out on the cement floor. The smell of stale cigarette smoke filled the still air, no doubt from years of it drifting throughout the house, clogging every porous surface.

"Claire?" When she didn't reply, Mac squeezed through the half-opened door leading into the kitchen.

The window above the sink looked out at the cedar shed, yellow padlock and all. Wayne Newton salt-and-pepper shakers sat centered on the sill. Magazine cutouts and postcards of Las Vegas plastered the refrigerator and surrounding cupboard doors.

Dragging his gaze from the images of gaudy fountains and flashy casino fronts, Mac tiptoed across the vinyl flooring, wincing with every creak.

The dining room was ticking.

With the blinds shut snugly, soft shadows lurked in the room, especially the corners. Mac skirted the round oak table to get a closer look at the clock. Red dice took the place of the numbers and two elongated Greta Garbo cigarette holders made up the hands. *Viva Las Vegas* was painted on the face. A classic piece, he mused, undoubtedly available only at Tiffany's.

A chest-high stack of newspapers sat on the table. Mac picked up the top one—the *Las Vegas Sun*, dated three months ago. What was with Sophy's obsession with Vegas?

A dull thud came from the next room, followed by a "yowch!"

He dropped the paper back on the pile. "Claire?" he whispered and stepped through the archway leading into the living room.

Beige shades diffused the sunlight blasting through two big windows and cast a tan-colored glow. The smell of smoke mixed with perfume filled this room. A glass coffee table sitting askew—that must have been what Claire bumped into—separated a brown couch, worn on the armrests, from the huge 1970s console television. Above the T.V., one of those light-up pictures hung on the wall.

Mac peered closer, shaking his head as he recognized the Las Vegas Strip. Maybe Sophy was an ex-showgirl.

A gasp of surprise resounded from a hallway lined with four doors, all closed except for the one second from the end.

"Claire?" Mac headed down the hall, stopping abruptly

in the open doorway. Stacks of furniture packed the room in sardine-style. Green drapes shuttered out most of the sunlight.

"Look at all of this," Claire said, rising on to her toes to squeeze between a tall armoire and a large dresser chest—both unquestionably antiques.

The room smelled of old varnish and stale upholstery. The gloom and heat felt almost tangible, claustrophobic.

Several more antique dressers were squeezed into the center of the narrow room, along with a fancy, tasseled couch. Three pansy-covered chairs, a glass door bookcase, a large desk, a dark-colored sideboard, and two identical nightstands stacked on top of a round, claw foot table edged the room.

"Why does she have it all packed in here?" Mac asked.

Letting out a low whistle, Claire leaned over the large desk. She pulled open one of the drawers and closed it, the wood gliding smoothly in its track. "These aren't just any old antiques, you know." She glanced from piece to piece, rubbing her hands together. "These are worth a pretty penny."

"Let me guess, Antiques 101, right?"

"No, smartass. My mom records every episode of the *Antiques Roadshow*. She plays that show 24/7."

"So how old are we talking?"

Claire pointed at the tall armoire. "That's a Louis XV Walnut Armoire, probably dated around the late 1700s. I bet it'd run close to $17,000 at Sotheby's. This dresser is a George III 'Secretary' Chest-On-Chest, made sometime around 1800. I'd price it around $15,000."

Mac didn't doubt Claire's estimates, but why were these expensive antiques in the spare bedroom of the owner of a small-town diner? Had Sophy been in business with Joe, and Ruby didn't realize it?

He watched Claire's gaze bounce around the room.

"Would you look at that ..." she said, her eyes locked on the nightstands stacked on top of the claw foot table. With a frown etched on her brow, she scrambled over the writing desk toward them.

"What?" Besides the top drawer missing a knob, he didn't see anything striking about them. "Hey, what are you doing?" he asked as Claire unscrewed the knob on the lower drawer.

"Nothing." She pocketed the knob and crawled toward him.

The sound of tires crunching on the gravel outside made them both freeze.

Claire's eyes were as wide as quarters as she stared back at him. "Uh, oh," she whispered.

"Don't move." Mac crept back to the living room and peeked outside. A white Chevy S-10 with a Tucson Electric Power decal on its door sat parked behind Mabel.

He stepped back from the window at the sound of footsteps crossing the wood porch.

Someone knocked on the front door. Mac stood still, holding his breath.

The screen door creaked open, then more knocking followed by a deep "Hello?"

If he and Claire made it out of this without getting caught, Mac was going to bury her up to her neck in sand and not dig her out until he was finished with the mines.

The screen door slammed shut. Footsteps thudded across the porch. Seconds later, the pickup growled to life and the truck disappeared back down the drive.

His heart still rattling in his chest, Mac returned to the room. "Claire, we are leaving." His tone allowed no arguments.

"I can't."

"Why not?"

"I'm stuck, and I think I ripped my pants."

"What are you stuck on?" Mac squeezed between the fancy armoire and the expensive chest of drawers, careful not to scratch them with the rivets on his jeans.

"A beaded, Italian, three-arm chandelier."

"Can't you just pull yourself free?"

"And break it? This thing was made in the late 1800s."

Mac inched closer. "Is the chandelier caught on your pocket?"

"No, my hair."

"Then why are your pants ripped?"

"Because I ate a pint of fudge nut brownie ice cream last night after I got back to the Winnebago."

Mac chuckled.

"It's not funny, Mac."

"Sorry," he said, still laughing. He crawled over the desk.

Claire held onto his ribs as he untangled her hair, its corn-silk softness feathering through his fingers. He nudged her back across the desk in front of him. As she slipped down over the desktop, something fell to the floor with a dull whop.

"Crap," she muttered.

"I'll get it." Mac crawled over the desk.

He picked up what looked like a book with a snapped flap holding it closed. He unsnapped it and flipped open the book—only it wasn't a book. Instead of bound pages, there were holes for coins. Labels marked the date and type.

"What is it?" Claire asked.

"A coin collection."

Mac stared at the coin holes. There was one empty slot in the set. The label below it read, *Double Eagle, $20 Liberty (gold) d.1879.*

He frowned. "I'll be damned."

Sophy peered out through the kitchen order-window as Dory Hamilton squeezed into his usual booth, the one that overlooked Jackrabbit Creek.

Tucson Electric Power had been good to the man, obvious by Dory's big belly, fat gold wristwatch, and multiple log-chain style necklaces.

She grabbed her order pad and walked over to where the Mr. T wanna-be stared out at the cottonwood trees. "What can I get ya, Dory?" She clicked her pen.

Dory turned, a surprised smile creased his thick cheeks. "What are you doing here?"

Sophy raised her eyebrows. She'd spent almost every day in this godforsaken diner for over three decades. What did he think she was doing there? Holding dance classes?

"Why wouldn't I be here?"

"I figured you were home with your company. I just stopped by your place to read the meter and saw a sweet-looking hotrod in your drive, with lots of chrome and a flaming paint job."

Fear and rage cramped her stomach.

Dory's chubby forehead crinkled into deep wrinkles. "What happened to your cheek? That's a nasty bruise."

Sophy ignored his question. "What color was the hotrod?"

"Blue with yellow and red flames up the side. Reminded me of a car my old man had back—"

"What kind of car?" She played dumb. There was only one car in this corner of the state that fit that description, and Sophy was ninety-nine percent certain that Harley Ford wasn't behind the wheel today.

The bruise on her cheek began to throb.

Dory shrugged, his jowls bouncing along with his shoulders. "A late '40s or early '50s Mercury. You know the owner?"

She swallowed the lump of fury in her throat and forced a smile to her lips. "Sure do. Now what can I get you?"

Sophy jotted down his order and pegged it in the order-window. Grabbing a knife, she quartered a lemon and took several deep breaths. The sharp smell of citrus cut through the grease-filled air. She was going to have to teach that nosy bitch what curiosity did to the cat.

"Hey, Sophy," Dory called across the diner. "What's up with your newspaper boxes? Was some stupid kid spinning doughnuts in your parking lot again?"

No. "Probably."

She'd seen Ruby's nephew's pickup parked in her lot when she'd left The Shaft last night. She had little doubt as to who'd crushed the boxes. And why.

"Order up," the cook called.

Next time she would deliver more than just a warning.

Sophy stabbed the knife into the butcher block.

⸻ ✦ ⸻

"You look like hell," Gramps said, frowning up at Claire through a haze of cigar smoke.

"It's good to see you, too, you old fart." Claire dropped into the lawn chair next to Manny.

The sky was filled with dark pinks and soft purples as the sun vanished below the horizon. Patsy Cline's sweet voice rang out from inside Gramps's Winnebago, singing about walking after midnight.

"What happened to your cheek, *bonita?*" Manny asked.

The screen door slammed. "Mom said she walked into a barbed wire fence last night," Jess said, stepping down from the Winnebago with a bag of fried pork rinds and two Budweisers. "But I think she looks like Tammy Marshal after Jane Miller scratched her with her nails."

Gramps gave Claire a squinty-eyed stare, Dirty Harry fashion. "Did you get in a fight?"

"No, of course not." Claire was grateful that the remnants of her sunburn hid her blush.

If Gramps found out the truth, he'd probably tell her mom. Then all hell would break loose. She turned to Jess. "Your mom's looking for you."

Jess handed Gramps and Manny the beers, then dropped onto the ground at their feet and started crunching on the pork rinds.

Gut rumbling, Claire swallowed the hunger-spurred saliva pooling in her mouth. The fried-food madness had to stop. Her clothes were bursting at the seams. She'd sooner run around in her polka-dotted skivvies than don a muumuu for the remainder of their trip.

"Mom's trying to send me off to Tucson to some boarding school." Jess lifted her chin. "I'm not going."

Manny shook his head, his usual grin absent.

Gramps took another hit from his cigar and looked off toward the setting sun as though he had one last chance of seeing it tonight.

Claire leaned forward, dangling her hands between her knees. "How about I walk you home?" Somebody needed to help the girl sort fact from fiction.

Jess sighed. "'Kay, but can we wait just a little longer?"

"Sure." Claire pushed to her feet. "I'll take a shower first."

"Are you planning on sticking around here tonight?" Gramps asked as she passed in front of him.

Claire nodded. If he told her she had to leave, she was going to wallop him upside the head. Respect for elders aside, the old man didn't need that much freakin' sex. If she wasn't getting any, he shouldn't, either.

"Good. I'd hate for you to run into any more barbed wire fences." The grin on his face fell in the wisenheimer class.

"You mean you don't have a date coming over?" She dug back.

Gramps didn't answer.

Manny chuckled. "Oh, he has a date all right. He's going out with Rosy Linstad again."

"Shut it, Carrerra."

"Again? How many times is this?" Claire asked.

"None of your business."

"Three," Manny supplied without hesitating.

Three? Claire's heart panged for a certain redhead she'd grown very fond of.

"Way to go, dude," Jess said, crunching away.

Claire crossed her arms over her chest. "According to the rules, one more date and I get to meet her in person."

"Don't count your chickens before they've hatched," Gramps said.

Manny wolf-whistled, loud and clear.

Claire turned and stared as a long-legged, black-haired beauty strutted past in a seersucker shirt, a short skirt, and black boots that rimmed her thighs. With a toss of her waist-long hair, the Cher look-alike shot Manny a flirty smile and winked.

"*Ay yi yi,*" Manny said under his breath.

Claire watched the woman strut away, the wag in her hips practically rattling the windows of Chester's Brave. "Who is that?"

"Kat Jones," Gramps supplied. "Ex-dancer and Pilates instructor extraordinaire."

"With that hair," Claire said, "she looks like she has some Latino in her."

Manny chuckled. "If I have my way, she'll have some more Latino in her by the end of tonight."

Claire shook her head. She should have seen that one coming.

With a grunt, Manny clambered out of his chair, his joints snapping like an automatic cap gun, and raced after Ms. Jones—well, as fast as a sixty-nine-year-old man can race.

Claire glanced back at Jess. "I'll be back in a jiffy." She shot Gramps a warning look. "Be good."

"What? I'm always good."

"Your nose is growing." Claire stepped inside the Winnebago.

Fifteen minutes later, she walked out of the bathroom in the midst of towel-drying her hair and paused when she saw Gramps grabbing Henry's leash off the wall.

He glanced over at her. "I'm taking the kid home."

"Why?"

"It's on my way."

"To Rosy's?"

"Like I said before, mind your own business." Without another word, he left.

Claire rolled her eyes and squeezed more water out of her hair. If she'd stuck to minding her own business during this trip, she wouldn't have found the room full of antiques in Sophy's house.

Speaking of antiques ... Fishing the brass knob from her pants, which now sported a three-inch tear along the inseam, Claire laid it on the counter. Then she dug in her backpack for the other knob.

She held them both under the florescent light above the kitchen sink.

"Well, well. Looks like we have a match."

Chapter Fourteen

Saturday, April 17th

W hat do you mean Mac is gone?" Claire asked Ruby.
She shut Ruby's cash register drawer and opened the soda pop she'd just bought. Not smoking would be the death of her. She was working her way up to a six pack of Coke a day—the legal version of injecting sugar and caffeine straight into her veins.

Mac's absence left her with an empty ache inside. Like Gramps's favorite country star, Ronnie Milsap, she was having daydreams about night things in the middle of the afternoon ... and the evening, and around midnight, and close to dawn.

On top of that, the torture device she slept on nearly propelled her Mac-induced fantasies into the sadomasochistic realm; eyebolts and barbed wire were the only things missing.

"He left about an hour ago, after breakfast," Ruby said as she emptied her purse on the counter. "Damn it, where are my keys?"

She sifted through the pile of purse paraphernalia—hand lotion, a Swiss Army knife, nail clippers, and several flavors of ChapStick.

"Jess!" she yelled up at the ceiling. "Come on, it's time to go."

"Did he go to the mines?" Claire asked.

"No." Ruby stuffed a nail file back into her bag. "He

went to Tucson."

Tucson! Claire's jaw hit the countertop. No "good-bye," "see you around," or even a "catch you later" from the guy. What a waste of a sexy-underwear day.

"Like I said at breakfast," Jess's voice rang down through the overhead, wrought iron vent. "I'm not going, *Ruby!*" The vent cover practically rattled with emphasis.

Ruby paused, a bottle of Visine in her hand, and took a deep breath. "That child isn't gonna make it to her next birthday if she doesn't knock off the attitude. And to think, I'm doing this for her future. I must be into self-torture."

"You and I both know those are the hormones yelling." Claire waved off Jess's behavior. "So, did Mac leave any message for me or ..."

She purposely trailed off, trying to sound breezy, carefree; as if word from Mac ranked below the weather report in everyday life.

Ruby swept the rest of the stuff into her purse and dropped the bag onto the counter. "Not that I remember."

Well! Claire huffed mentally, drumming her fingers on the wooden counter. See if she shaved her legs again anytime soon for Mr. Love-'em and Leave-'em.

"Jessica Lynn Wayne!" Ruby hollered. "Get down here now!"

Silence reigned overhead for several seconds. Then heavy footsteps pounded across the second floor. Indiscernible muttering echoed down through the vent.

Claire brushed invisible crumbs off the counter. "Did he say why he went to Tucson?"

"Something about work." Ruby dug in her coat pockets, a frown etched on her forehead. "Darn it. I swear I put my keys right next to my purse just a half-hour ago."

The sound of Jess stomping down the stairs reverberated throughout the house. A parade of hippos in tap shoes would have been quieter.

"Did he mention when he'd be back?" Claire pressed. *Or if he is coming back at all?*

"Nope."

"Damn it, Mom," Jess said as she pushed through the curtain. "You never listen to a word I say. Harley was right about you."

Claire blinked in surprise at Gramps's name.

"You watch that cussin', girl." Her hands on her hips, Ruby asked, "What do you mean Harley was right? About what?"

Claire's shoulders squeezed tight. Just what had Gramps told Jess last night on their walk home?

"He said you like to screw up my life."

"Really?" Ruby shot Claire a tight-lipped, see-what-I-have-to-deal-with look. "How exactly am I screwing it up today?"

Jess lifted her chin. "By trying to ship me off to some lousy boarding school. Honestly, Ruby, I don't understand why you had me. You've done nothing but shove me off on other people since birth. It's no wonder Dad didn't want to marry you."

A flush crept up Ruby's neck and over her cheeks. She glared at her daughter.

Jess's bottom lip quivered slightly—the only visible sign of fear in the kid's stance.

Claire could hear herself swallow in the thick silence.

"Go get in the truck right now." Ruby's voice was low, her soft southern drawl razor sharp around the edges.

Jess's face contorted in rage for a split-second. "Fine!" She tromped toward the door, pausing on the threshold to shoot a hate-filled scowl back at her mom. "I'll go with you to this stupid school today, but I'm driving!" She held up a set of keys, jingling them, and then slammed out onto the porch.

"That little shit took my keys," Ruby said, shaking her

head. "What do you think I'd get for her on the black market?"

Claire grimaced. "I'm sorry for what Gramps told Jess."

"Don't be. Those weren't his exact words."

"How do you know?"

"He told me," Ruby answered.

"You mean he stayed to talk when he dropped off Jess last night?"

Ruby's brow wrinkled. She gave Claire a puzzled look. "Well, yeah. That was the idea."

The idea for what? "What are you talking about?"

"Harley coming over."

"When he dropped off Jess?" Claire purposely didn't add, *on his way to Hot Cheek's love shack.*

"Yep."

"So, he stayed for a few minutes to talk to you?"

"No, he stayed for a few hours."

Claire did a double take. "He what?"

The Ford's engine rumbled to life out front.

"Damn that little hellcat!" Ruby snatched up her purse and raced for the door. "Thanks again for watching the store. We'll be back around two."

Speechless, Claire stared after Ruby. The screen door bounced in the older woman's wake.

So, Gramps had been with Ruby last night, huh? That meant he'd either lied to his cronies about his date or stood up Rosy Linstad.

Claire chuckled. Oh, how she'd make him squirm with the truth the next time they were neck deep in cigar smoke and cards.

She chugged the rest of her soda pop and bank-shot the can into the recycling bin.

As for the hazel-eyed hunk who haunted her dreams, he'd better have a damned good reason for leaving, or he was going to be doing some squirming, too!

The late afternoon sunshine spilled through Creekside Supply Company's front windows, drenching Aisle One's row of pick axes, shovels, garden hoses, and post-hole diggers in diluted radiation.

Claire split off from Gramps and cruised down the middle aisle that divided the store in half, taking a hard right into Aisle Ten: Housewares, Hosiery, and Hygiene—aka the Ladies' Department.

Short of breaking into Sophy's shed, which Claire hadn't scrounged up the courage to do yet (breaking and entering was a bit more ballsy than trespassing), she could think of only one way to prove that Sophy had kidnapped Henry: perfume.

She stopped in front of the shelves of perfume. Scanning the familiar boxes of Charlie, Emeraud, and Stetson for Women, her gaze zeroed in on the smoking gun—Tabu.

Inside the white and black box, a skinny bottle with a black cap looked exactly like the one she'd found in Sophy's bedroom yesterday. Not that Mac had given her a chance to fully inspect Sophy's room before dragging her out of the house.

Claire sprayed the inside of her wrist and sniffed the aromatic mix of roses, orange blossoms, and jasmine on her skin. She grinned. Add a dash of dried mud and a sprinkle of dog fur, and she had a batch of dog-stealer brew.

She stuffed the bottle back in the box.

"You're not woman enough to wear that," a familiar, low-pitched, voice said from behind her.

The hair on the back of Claire's neck bristled.

The last time she'd heard that voice, she'd ended up

rolling around on a peanut shell-covered floor.

Claire looked over her shoulder at her red-taloned nemesis dressed in her usual bar ensemble: a low-cut tank top and sausage-skin-tight jeans. She flashed Sophy a fake smile. "Why, if it isn't Sophy Wheeler, Jackrabbit Junction's oldest calendar girl."

Sophy's expertly outlined eyes narrowed. "Real funny. Just like those fingernail scratches on your cheek."

In no mood to get into an insult match, especially with Gramps wandering around the store, Claire went straight for the brush off. "Unless you're here for Round Two, I have better things to do than waste time listening to you."

The Tabu box in hand, Claire walked away from the woman Ruby warmly referred to as *The Bitch from Hell.*

"Watch yourself, sugar," Sophy called after her. "Folks from around these parts don't take very kindly to trespassers."

Claire stopped in her tracks, gulping. She turned back to the red-lipped redneck.

The glare in Sophy's gaze made it crystal clear that she knew where Claire had been yesterday. There was no use formulating a denial.

"You tell the folks from around these parts that I don't take kindly to dognappers."

Sophy lifted an over-tweezed eyebrow. Her reaction didn't shout *guilty*, as Claire had hoped, but it didn't declare her innocence, either.

"What's that supposed to mean?"

"I think you know." Claire held up the box of perfume and shook it. "Funny thing about Tabu, it sticks to dog fur the same as skin."

Sophy smirked. "That explains your trouble attracting men. You're not supposed to spray it on your dog."

No amount of playing dumb on Sophy's part was going to veer Claire off course. She'd bet her grandma's wedding ring that the floor of Sophy's shed was sprinkled with Henry's hair.

"I'm on to your little game, Sophy." Claire felt like a puffed up kitten hissing at a St. Bernard. "I'm not going to quit until I figure out your motive."

Sophy's eyes glittered menacingly. "If you have an ounce of sense in that foolish little brain of yours, you'll scuttle back to whatever hole you crawled out of. You seem to forget that you're a stranger in town—*my* town."

"Threats don't scare me." Claire's heart beat in triple time.

"Maybe a 12-gauge shotgun would."

"Maybe a 12-gauge shotgun would what?" Gramps asked, breaking the tension between Claire and Sophy.

Sophy turned to Gramps, her sneer and glare replaced by a sultry smile and bedroom eyes. She ran her red nails down Gramps's arm. "Hello, Harley. You're looking awfully handsome this afternoon."

Claire made a gagging gesture at Gramps. His lips twitched.

"Sophy," he replied with a brief nod. "I didn't realize you knew my granddaughter, Claire."

Sophy's smile faded slightly. "We don't really 'know' each other. We just had a little chat the other night at The Shaft."

"What happened to your cheek?" Gramps asked Sophy, his sharp gaze bouncing back and forth between Claire and Sophy's faces.

Claire braced herself for a future lecture, sure he'd already added one and one together.

"Just a little accident at the diner."

"Odd things, those accidents," Gramps said. "Claire had one recently, too."

"I noticed." Sophy grabbed a box of Tabu and dropped it into her basket. "It's always nice to see you,

Harley." She paused next to Claire and glanced back at Gramps. "You'd better keep an eye on this girl. She's gonna get herself into trouble if she's not careful."

With a flip of her hair, which moved as a solid mass—no doubt due to the various cans of hairspray Claire had found cluttering Sophy's bathroom vanity—Sophy sashayed away.

Gramps shot Claire a frown. "What did you do now?"

"What? I didn't do anything." Claire made a last-ditch attempt at playing the 'I'm-innocent-I-swear' routine.

"Child, I wasn't born yesterday. When I walked up here, you two were circling each other like a pair of hungry hyenas hovering over a hunk of raw meat."

Claire sighed. "Couldn't you compare me to a prettier animal? A cat would be nice. Maybe even a swan. Do swans fight?"

"Claire," he warned.

There'd be no sidetracking him on this one. "What can I say?" She raised her hands in the air. "I don't like the color of her lipstick. Besides, she started it. I just wanted to refill my beer."

"Sophy Wheeler is one creature you shouldn't poke with a stick. Rattlers have less venom."

She crossed her arms. "How do you know so much about Sophy?" Most men couldn't see past a pair of big boobs, especially a pair on the verge of falling out of a tank top.

"I pay attention to details."

Claire pursed her lips. "Or has a little red-headed bird with an Oklahoma drawl been whispering secrets in your ear late at night when you're supposed to be over in Hot Cheeks' love nest?"

Gramps's face reddened. "Get your ass in the car."

Claire snickered all of the way to the cash register.

Sunday, April 18th

The woodpeckers were at it again.

Mac stood outside the door of Harley's Winnebago, listening to the rat-a-tat-tat as they drilled their way into one of the willow trees lining Jackrabbit Creek.

A sprinkling of dew covered the grass in a sparkling veneer. The desert seemed to be holding its breath ever since the sun had crested the *Tres Dedos* Mountains and doused the cool night breeze. The rosy, pre-dawn glow he'd raced through from Tucson in order to reach the R.V. park—and Claire—had melted into an early morning, powder-blue sky.

The faint smell of bacon tinged the air, reminding Mac that he'd skipped breakfast in his haste to return.

Claire had been in his thoughts since he'd left yesterday morning, the vision of her in that Pink Panther T-shirt unshakable. Common sense said to nip this attraction in the bud.

But, damn, she looked hot in a pair of jeans.

Tired of this growing debate in his head—the same one he'd covered several times since leaving the city over two hours ago—Mac rapped on the door and listened for movement on the other side of the aluminum.

The door opened.

Claire stood there, barelegged in her Oscar the Grouch pajama top. All anti-Claire sentiments flew from his head.

Her eyes narrowed at the sight of him. She crossed her arms over her chest. "You left without even saying good-bye."

Mac tugged on the hem of her top. "Did you miss me?"

"Absolutely not."

"Liar."

"Quit reading my mind."

"How about I show you how much I missed you?"

Her lips curled slightly. "I'm trying to be mad at you."

Mac climbed the step and stood nose-to-nose with her. She smelled like fabric softener, flowery soap, and everything Claire. He tucked a tendril of hair behind her ear, trailing his finger down her neck.

Her breath caught when he feathered his fingertip along her collarbone. She caught his hand. "Gramps is awake," she whispered.

"What are you talking about? I can hear him snoring."

"That's Henry. Gramps is in the bathroom."

"I didn't know dogs could snore that loud."

"You should try sleeping in the same room with the damned mutt."

She still held his hand, rubbing his fingers with her thumb, and had no idea how close she was to being taken advantage of up against the side of a Winnebago. A man could withstand only so much sexual frustration in one week's time.

"I brought you a present." He leaned closer, his lips almost touching hers. Tiny flecks of gold speckled her brown irises.

"Think you can buy my affection?" Her eyes sparkled. She tried to peek behind his back to see what he was hiding.

"They say the way to a woman's heart is through a man's wallet." At least that's what his last girlfriend had read to him out of some *Rules of Dating* book.

"Really? I've always felt it had to do with the size of his ..." Claire trailed off, blinking in exaggerated seduction, "truck."

Mac chuckled, lacing his fingers with hers. "Oh, I've got a big truck, Slugger."

The softness of her laughter filled him with heat that

had nothing to do with the morning rays drilling into his back.

"So what's my present?"

"Close your eyes."

She lowered her eyelids, a smile hovering at the creases of her mouth.

Mac withdrew his fingers from hers and brought forward the leg bone he'd picked up from Steve at the lab in Phoenix.

"Is that a bone in your hand?" Chester shouted in his raspy voice from the driver's side window of his Brave. "Or are you just happy to see Claire?"

Eyes wide and cheeks reddening with guilt, Claire took a step back from Mac, straightening her pajama top.

God damn it. Was it too much to ask to have a discussion with Claire on her doorstep without the peanut gallery watching?

Mac held the bone in front of him. "I brought your bone back. Well, most of it, anyway. Steve kept a sample for further analysis. He sent it to an old girlfriend who works in the state medical examiner's office."

Claire lifted the bone from his hand. "What did he say about it?"

"Hey, Henry's bone is back," Gramps said from behind Claire. "Come here, boy."

The sound of toenails on linoleum announced Henry's arrival just before he appeared next to Claire's bare legs. When the dog saw the bone, he whimpered, then growled when Claire held it out of reach.

"How old is it?" Claire asked, nudging Henry away with her foot.

"He said—" Mac started.

"*Ay yi yi, bonita,*" Manny's suave voice came from directly behind Mac. "What sexy legs you have."

Mac looked at Claire's legs. Manny was right.

She grabbed the bottom hem of her pajama top and tugged it down, still trying to hold the bone out of Henry's reach. The beagle had a good four-foot-high jump.

"Stop looking at my granddaughter's legs, Carrera."

"Did he find any old fractures?" Claire asked Mac between Henry's leaps.

"Would you rather I focus on the fact that Claire isn't wearing a bra?" Manny shot back at Harley.

Mac focused on the new objects of discussion.

"It is a human leg bone, right?" Claire crossed her arm over her chest, doing a very inefficient job of covering that lovely part of her anatomy.

"You should've seen the hooters I got up close and personal with last night." Chester said, sidling up next to Manny. "I could've floated across the English Channel on those fun-bags."

Mac felt laughter bubbling inside of his chest. Now that all the clowns were present, the circus could begin.

"Mac?" Claire pressed, curiosity burning in her brown eyes.

"You can't float on bags of saline," Manny said.

"Wanna bet?" Chester goaded.

"How big of bags?" Harley asked Chester.

Mac had a feeling that life with Claire would always be this chaotic. "He said you need to find the rest of the body."

He felt all eyes turn in his direction.

"And how am I supposed to do that?" Claire asked.

He'd been trying to come up with an answer to that question all morning, an answer that didn't interfere with his plans in the mines. But so far, only one came to mind: "With my help"

Chapter Fifteen

Sighing in relief, Mac parked his truck in front of Ruby's store. Behind the drooping crown of the old willow, the horizon glowed with the day's last light.

Lately, he cringed every time he stuck the key in the ignition. No amount of what he'd come to think of as his pre-flight inspections eased the tension that tightened his shoulders after flying across U.S. Route 191 the other night.

Whoever wanted him to stay away from the mines must have noticed he was still poking around. How long until he received another not-so-subtle "No Trespassing" hint?

He grabbed his pack and headed around the side of the store. Bullfrogs croaked their nightly serenades down by the creek, sounding like a symphony of squeaky bed springs.

As he stepped through the back door, a wall of cigar smoke smacked him in the face. Coughing, he waved a path through the haze.

"So I told Fanny it's only a heat rash," Chester's voice rose above Garth Brooks's, who was crooning about having friends in low places. "But she still wouldn't touch it."

Mac grimaced. He didn't blame Fanny.

"Howdy, Mac," Ruby called from her seat at the card table. "There's beer in the fridge and chips on the bar."

Harley, garbed in his usual cigar and suspenders, card-playing attire, lounged directly across from her. Manny and Chester bracketed her on either side. Each of them had three cards left in their hands.

Food sounded good. Beer, even better. Mine dust still coated his throat.

"Where's Jess?" Mac asked, grabbing a cold Corona from the fridge. It was too early for her to be in bed already.

"Upstairs," Ruby said. "Probably plotting against me."

Where was Claire? The question weighed on his tongue, but any answer from these jesters would be dealt with plenty of ribbing, and his ribs still hurt from this morning's jabbing.

"Let's see you try to take this, you lousy bastard," Chester said to Harley, and flung an Ace of hearts on the table.

"Any trouble tonight?" Ruby asked Mac, her gaze piercing.

She'd made it clear at lunch that she wanted Mac to stop fooling around with the mines. The multiple attempts to deter him hadn't gone unnoticed, but, like his aunt, obstinacy ran in Mac's blood.

"Nope."

"Trouble with what?" Harley asked around his cigar.

"With—" Ruby started.

"Coyotes." Mac cut in, not wanting to cause alarm.

Harley eyed him for several seconds, then turned back to his cards and threw out a ten of hearts. "Thanks for dealing me such a shitty hand," he told Chester.

Chester smirked back at him.

"Mac's a lousy liar, worse than Claire." Manny tossed a Queen of hearts on the pile.

"Did you finish with Two Jakes?" Ruby asked.

"Almost." Mac wetted his whistle with a swig of Corona.

Last week, while gathering samples, the ones he'd exchanged for the bone yesterday when he visited Steve in Phoenix, he'd noticed the mine maps he had copied from the library were outdated. Several drifts and chambers near the main adit in Two Jakes weren't shown, and he'd bet more sections of the mines weren't mapped, either.

While he waited for feedback on the samples, he planned to fill his time with spelunking and mapping—in addition to figuring out why somebody was so anxious to keep him out of those mines.

Ruby tossed a King of clubs on top of the pile.

"You trumped my ace!" Chester shouted and banged his fist on the table. The cards bounced. "Damn, woman. I thought you said you weren't any good at Bid Euchre."

Ruby smiled. "Oops."

Chuckling, Harley watched Ruby rake the pile toward her.

"Ah, *mi amor*." Manny ran his finger down Ruby's arm. "Have I told you how much I adore feisty redheads?"

Mac caught the glare Harley shot Manny a split-second before Harley masked it behind a tight smile. Blinking, Mac wondered if he'd imagined it.

"Harley, this one's yours," Ruby said, leading the next round with a ten of diamonds. She glanced up at Mac. "Claire was looking for you earlier."

Mac swigged a mouthful of beer. Just the mention of Claire's name made his gut flop. This had to stop.

Chester trumped Harley's King of diamonds and pulled in the pile, grinning at Harley as he threw down his last card.

"She has more questions for you about that bone of hers," Ruby added as she slammed her last card down on top of Chester's with a victory cry.

"Damn it!" Chester scowled at her.

"Ha! She set you, you blustering jackass," Harley said, smiling at Ruby. His blue eyes glittered with something more than triumph.

Mac turned back to his aunt. "Where is Claire?" If she was out hiking around those mines on her own in the dark, he was going to shackle her to his side.

"The Shaft." Ruby shuffled the cards like a Vegas dealer. "She said something about needing to breathe some second-hand smoke. Apparently, this stuff," Ruby gestured at the cloud of smoke hovering overhead, "isn't strong enough for her lungs."

"And you let her go alone?" The last time Mac had left Claire alone in the bar, she'd wound up in a wrestling match with Sophy.

"Of course not," Harley answered. "Henry's with her."

"Word around town is that you want to talk to me about a bone," Mac murmured, his voice low, velvety in Claire's ear. His breath singed her neck as his lips brushed over her skin.

The Shaft's steady roar of voices, laughter, and jukebox jingles dulled as blood flooded Claire's extremities.

Mac's warm, desert scent filled her, sending goose bumps rippling up her arms and making her tingle all over. The Poker Party arcade game she was in the midst of playing blurred as he wrapped his arm around her stomach and pulled her back against him.

Sweet Mary Lou! She reached for her bottle of Bud, needing something to douse the flames suddenly raging under her skin.

"Yes, well, I ..." her words stuck in her throat when he nipped her earlobe. Claire closed her eyes, fighting to keep from jumping the guy right there in the bar's backroom.

"We have an audience," Mac whispered, pulling away, taking his fire and her beer with him.

Claire opened her eyes to find Sophy glaring at her from across the room.

Two pool tables and several cowboy hats bridged the

distance between them, but the hatred radiating from the other woman had the air crackling. The heat coursing through Claire, thanks to Mac's touch, tempered.

Mac leaned against the Poker Party game, sipping her Bud, looking delicious in his faded Levi's and dark green button-up shirt. "You like to play strip poker with the ladies, huh?" He nodded toward the game's video screen.

"It was this or shoot at Bambi's mom and dad," Claire answered, referring to the Big Buck Hunter game next to her. "Removing women's clothing seemed more environmentally friendly."

"Nice shirt." Mac glanced down at her T-shirt. "I've always been fond of Daisy Duck, even more so now." The hungry look in his hazel eyes made her mouth dry. "Where's Henry?"

"Sleeping in Mabel's backseat."

"You want to talk here or outside?"

"Outside—out of earshot." Claire grabbed her jean jacket from a nearby stool and slid her arms into the sleeves. "But no touching until I'm finished asking questions."

He grinned, wicked, sexy. "Where's the fun in that?"

Claire led the way, returning Sophy's menacing glare as they passed by the tramp in her skin-tight Wranglers, white tank top, and pink cowboy boots.

In spite of her small show of bravado, Claire was happy to have Mac on her heels as she left the place.

Outside, the clean air burned her lungs. The Milky Way filled the sky with a pale band of speckled light, the half-moon dipping toward the horizon. Claire and Mac weaved through pickups and cars toward the shadows where Mabel sat, out of range of the orange nightlight. Mac had parked next to her.

While she checked on Henry, who was busy sawing logs like a veteran lumberjack, Mac lowered his tailgate.

"Fire away." He motioned for Claire to sit beside him.

She complied, keeping a couple of inches between them. "So, was your old roommate able to determine the age of the bone?"

"Not as precisely as you'd have liked, I'm sure. That's why he's sending a sample to his ex-girlfriend. She'll do a chemical analysis of the bone and give a more precise age."

"What did he say about it?"

"He said it looked 'fresh'."

"How fresh?"

"Less than a century."

Claire frowned. "That's not fresh."

"It is if you're used to dating samples that are at least several thousands of years old."

"Oh, right. So how do we find the rest of the body?"

Mac shrugged, rubbing his chin, the rasping of whiskers cozy in the cool darkness. "Joe had a metal detector. I think it's still in the tool shed. There's a chance that whoever we're looking for was carrying a piece of metal on him—a button or snap, a filling, or even some coins—when he died."

"Henry could help, too; use that hound dog nose of his for something besides food for once," Claire said. "We could take him to where he found the bone and have him help search the area."

"Good idea." Mac gently tugged on a tendril of her hair that had escaped her ponytail. "I've always had a soft spot for smart women."

Smiling in the shadows, Claire asked, "How many smart women are we talking about here?"

He chuckled. "How about we start the hunt on Tuesday?"

"Why not tomorrow?"

"I'm busy."

Doing what? She wanted to ask, but decided not to push

it. "Tuesday, then," she agreed.

But would finding the rest of the body save her grandma's valley? At what cost? Ruby's financial ruin? Claire wasn't sure she could handle the weight of that on her shoulders.

She glanced at Mac and found him watching her, the black of night no shield for his magnetism. "Um," she fought to net the butterflies flapping around in her chest and shucked her jacket to keep from sweating. "Did your buddy have anything else to say about the bone?"

"That you're right—it's a human femur, and based on its size, most likely from a male." He laced his fingers with hers, scooting closer until their legs touched.

Claire gulped, the reins on her body's reactions slipping. Too long without a man had turned her into a wobbly blob of Jell-O when faced with Mac's sexual onslaught.

"Then he asked if you were single and available."

"Really?" She peeked at him from under her eyelashes. "And what did you tell him?"

"That you were too smart for his worthless ass."

"Oh," Claire whispered, staring at his lips, leaning toward him. "Good answer."

A squeal of female laughter cut through the night, severing the winch tugging her toward him. Claire turned, spotting Sophy climbing into a black Chevy pickup.

"Why does she lock her shed and not her house?" Claire asked the question that had bugged her since her visit to Sophy's. And what was in that damned shed? Her curiosity escalated every time she ran into Sophy.

"She's probably just storing more antiques in there," Mac answered as the truck growled to life, spun out of the lot, and chirped its way onto the blacktop. "Maybe she forgot to lock up that day, and it was just a coincidence that we happened to be out and about, trespassing."

Bullshit. "Why would she keep all of those expensive antiques closed up in that room? There has to be something illegal about the whole thing. Especially considering her attitude yesterday in the store."

"What are you talking about?"

"I ran into her at Creekside Supply Company. She warned me off, threatening me with a 12-gauge shotgun."

"You're kidding."

Claire shook her head, aware with every red and white blood cell in her body that he still held her hand in his. "Nope. When I said I was onto her about kidnapping Henry, she went a little crazy, getting all squinty-eyed and Medusa-like. Scared the crap out of me."

"All because of a dog?" Mac's question held disbelief.

"Exactly, which seemed a bit much. But back to the shed—what could be in there that would cause such a strong reaction from her?"

"What makes you certain it's the shed? Maybe it has to do with the kidnapping. If you think back to the night Henry disappeared, he was up by the mine when you lost track of him. Then, later, I found boot prints by the mine, looking exactly like those where you found Henry's tag. If those prints were Sophy's, what was she doing in the mine that night?"

Mac pulled something from his back pocket.

"Probably something she didn't want anyone else to know about," Claire surmised. It didn't take a smoking gun to make her suspicious of Sophy's motives. "Maybe that's why she took Henry. He'd tracked her once and she knew he could do it again, only with someone in tow."

Mac squeezed her hand. "That would explain the beef jerky wrappers in both places. She lured him with food and used it to keep him busy while we looked for him in Socrates Pit. You're pretty good at this detective stuff."

"Thanks." His compliment made her heart swell.

Flattery would get him everywhere, including into her pants if she wasn't careful.

"Okay," Mac said, "so explain this." He dropped a coin in her palm, the metal still warm from his touch.

She held it toward the light. The shadows hid the details on it. "It feels like a fifty-cent piece, but heavier." She ran her thumb over the raised surface on both sides. "What is it?"

"A twenty-dollar, Double Eagle, Liberty gold coin. Part of the collection you knocked on the floor in Sophy's spare room."

"You took it from her?" That wasn't Mac's style.

"No. I found it in Socrates Pit while searching for Henry."

"And you're just now telling me about it?"

"When I found it, I barely knew you. Hell, I figured some old prospector lost it in there. I had no idea it was part of a set."

"So, how did it get up there?" Claire had asked herself the same question several times already about the drawer knob she'd found in the Rattlesnake Ridge mine.

Mac shrugged. "I don't know. Maybe she had the whole collection up there at one point. As to why, I have no idea."

"She could have stolen them from Joe and hidden them up there. According to Ruby, there was no love lost between them." Claire chewed on her lips. "I need to search inside those mines, see what else I can find."

"I don't think so, Slugger. Not alone, anyway. Somebody is doing their damnedest to keep me away from Ruby's mines right now. I don't need you out there with a target on your back."

"Maybe Sophy is the one sabotaging your pickup." Claire had no qualms about pinning everything on the red-taloned bitch.

"Are you kidding? Have you taken a look at the woman? She has 'High Maintenance' stamped all over her. I doubt she's ever seen a tool, let alone picked one up." Mac slid off the tailgate and cozied up between Claire's knees, running his hands over her thighs, leaving a smoldering trail in his wake. "Whoever messed with my pickup knows his way around a vehicle."

"Who, then?" Claire rasped, her throat suddenly parched.

"I have a feeling folks from the mining company found something in those mines that I've missed. Before the signing deadline, I'm going to find whatever it is and make sure they pay Ruby the right amount for the claims."

Which meant Claire had a week to figure out a way for Ruby to keep the mines and to save her grandma's gravesite.

She needed to do more digging into Joe's past. With all of the expensive antiques floating around this dust-bunny of a town, Joe had to have some kind of a nest egg tucked away somewhere.

Mac lifted her hands to his mouth, kissing each of her knuckles in turn before moving to the inside of her wrist.

"Hey, I'm not done asking questions." Claire squirmed on the tailgate, her knees squeezing his hips.

"Yes, you are," he said, his lips soft, hot.

Claire squeezed her eyes shut, trying not to let him derail her train of thought.

If she was right about Sophy stealing from Joe and hiding the goods in those mines, Joe couldn't have been just a traveling salesman. That furniture would have been out of his price range. The stuff stacked away in Sophy's house was Sotheby's material, not from some rinky-dink antique store out here in the middle of nowhere.

Tomorrow, the junkyard would be open, and Claire could go take a look at Joe's Mercedes, see if she could find that briefcase hidden somewhere. Briefcases didn't get up and walk away.

Mac's mouth traveled up the inside of her arm and all of her coherent thoughts headed for Splitsville.

Something growled from the shadows under the pickup.

Claire looked over her shoulder in time to see Henry leap from the open car window and tear after a white cat through the tangle of parking lot traffic.

"Shit!" She hopped to the ground and chased after him, weaving through darkened pickups. "Henry, come back!"

The blare of a horn made her freeze. Wincing, she watched in horror as Henry raced after the cat across the road, a minivan slowing just in time to miss his tail.

Claire rushed after the dog, only to be yanked backward as she reached the highway shoulder.

A Corvette trying to match the speed of sound whizzed in front of her, the whoosh of air trailing it pelted her face with dust.

"That was close," she breathed, her heart jackhammering in agreement.

"Too close," Mac said from behind her, letting her go.

Looking twice this time to make sure the road was clear, she zipped across the asphalt and skidded to a stop in front of Sophy's diner. She squinted in the thick shadows, looking for a glimpse of Henry's little white butt, listening for his panting.

Mac jogged up next to her.

"Did you see which way he ran?" she asked between gasps.

"Yep." Taking hold of her hand, he dragged her around the back of the building.

Mac halted around the corner, shining a flashlight into the trees bordering Jackrabbit Creek.

Henry stood on his hind feet at the base of a cottonwood, his front paws on the trunk as he growled at the rustling leaves.

Claire wheezed and bent over while trying to catch her breath. Mac wasn't even the slightest bit winded, damn him. "Do you carry ... a flashlight on you ... all of the time?"

"No, I grabbed it from inside my truck when you ran after Henry."

Henry tried to climb the trunk and slid back down.

The cat hissed. A low branch wavered from more than the breeze.

"Crap, I forgot his leash."

"I noticed." Mac held out the strip of nylon.

"How did you grab both a flashlight and the leash and still catch me before I crossed the road?"

"You're no Olympic sprinter, Claire." Mac chuckled at the cosmopolitan gesture for "get bent" she directed at him. "You want me to grab him?"

"No." She needed to cling to what little dignity she had left. Henry was becoming an expert at making her look like a total ass in front of Mac.

Holding the stitch in her side, she hitched her out-of-shape hiney over to where Henry sat whining up at his tormentor, the beam of light from Mac's flashlight spotlighting the scene. She strapped on the leash and tugged.

The dog refused to move.

"Fine, we'll do this the hard way." She picked him up and carried him away.

Every muscle in the dog's body was wiry and tense as he struggled, but not quite hard enough to get free.

"Ready?" she asked as she returned to Mac's side.

"Hold on a minute." He flashed the light at their feet, centering on a cigarette butt. He bent down and picked it up by the tobacco end.

"You found a cigarette. Congratulations."

He held it out to her. "Red lipstick."

"Sophy probably comes back here to smoke. What's the big deal?"

"I saw one with red lipstick in another place last week."

"Where?"

Mac dropped the butt. "Socrates Pit."

━━━◆━━━

Monday, April 19th

"Explain to me again why we're digging around in this nasty car," Jess said from the backseat of Joe's Mercedes.

"We're looking for clues." Claire wiped a drop of sweat rolling down her temple, ignoring the tone in the kid's voice.

The midday sunshine reflected off the other old, dead cars watching Claire and Jess. Millions of pieces of broken glass littered the oil-stained ground around them and raised the temperature to bone melting level. Joe's car stunk of musty foam padding and baked leather. A hint of something dead and rotting wafted through the smashed windows.

"Ewww!" Jess shrieked. "I just touched a mouse turd! Wait, it's a raisin—no, a chocolate chip. How long are chocolate chips good for?"

Claire frowned back at Jess. "Chocolate would have melted long ago."

"Then it's a raisin." Jess stuck her hand under the passenger's side seat, or what was left of it.

Something seemed to have spent a season burrowing into the stuffing previously covered by very expensive leather—the same leather that was now nothing more than strips piled on the faded carpet at Claire's feet.

"We're looking for clues for what?" Jess asked.

"Joe's past."

"Wouldn't it be cool if we found a bloody finger or a dried up eyeball somewhere in here?"

"Yeah, real cool." The last thing Claire wanted to find was a body part—human or any other mammal. Unfortunately, she wasn't having much luck finding anything at all.

Someone had gutted the trunk already, and the engine had been sold long ago. All that was left was what remained of the interior.

Ruby had been wrong. Old Monty Kunkle wasn't selling parts from this crinkled trashcan. He was offering it as a sacrifice to all gods and creatures of the Arizona desert, sun and beast and insect alike.

Claire had about swallowed her tongue when she'd opened the glove box and a scorpion had scrambled out at her. After that, she and Jess donned the leather gloves Ruby had wisely recommended and took great care when reaching into shadowy places.

Jess sat up, using the back of her arm to push back wisps of red curls that kept catching in her lashes. "Nothing under here, except more potato chips." She dropped the chips in the palm of her glove and held them out for Claire. "Look, sour cream and onion flavored. That was Joe's favorite, you know."

Henry's, too.

"Great detective work, kid." Claire grinned despite her disappointment.

She started to climb out of the driver's seat and paused when a flash of white between the seat and the center console caught her attention. She pulled out a crumpled pack of cigarettes in a red and white wrapper. Marlboro, the leaded kind.

"Did you find something?" Jess asked from behind

Claire, the girl's shadow blocking out the sun for a reprieving second.

"Just a cigarette pack wrapper." Claire smoothed out the pack. She tapped it against her palm and two cigarettes—wrinkled slightly from wear and tear—fell into her hand. She sniffed one. The tobacco smelled old, stale, but still smoke-worthy.

"You're not actually thinking about lighting up, are you?"

Claire looked at Jess. The girl had a disgusted sneer on her lips.

Maybe. "Of course not. I was just trying to see if I could figure out how old they were by smell."

"What's that?" Jess pointed toward Claire's lap.

"What's what?" Claire glanced down, ready to scramble out of the car if the object in question had legs and/or antennae.

"That." Jess lifted a small piece of paper from Claire's thigh. "It must have fallen out when you tapped the cigarettes on your hand."

"Really?" Claire stuffed the pack in the side pocket of her cargo pants while Jess frowned at the paper. "What is it?"

Shrugging, Jess handed it over. "Some dude's name and number."

Letters and numbers were scrawled on the inside of the gum wrapper. "Is this Joe's writing?" she asked Jess.

"How should I know? I hardly ever saw the old guy."

Claire folded the paper and shoved it in her pocket. Finally, another clue.

"So, like, what are you gonna do with it?" Jess asked, eyes sparkling with anticipation.

Claire climbed out of the car. "Call the number and see who picks up." She tried to keep her tone level, bored sounding. No need to drag Jess into more trouble than the girl managed to stir up on her own.

"Cool! Maybe we'll find out that Joe had another wife and kids. You know, more family—brothers and sisters."

"Yeah, right." For Ruby's sake, Claire hoped not.

"Or maybe it's the name and number of a rich uncle."

Or maybe, Claire thought, forcing a smile to her lips for Jess's sake, the guy on the other end would be able to answer a few questions about Joe and the real business she suspected he'd been running out of Jackrabbit Junction's only antique store.

Chapter Sixteen

D amn it!" Sophy threw her pickax across the shadow-filled chamber. Her words, along with the clatter of steel hitting rock, echoed off the walls of Socrates Pit.

Where had the bastard hidden it?

She tore off her gloves. Between the dust clouding the air and twenty minutes of swinging a pickax, her lungs burned. With just a few hours left until she had to open the diner, another setback didn't fit into her schedule.

She glared down at the ore cart partially buried in the rubble. She'd followed his slurred instructions, finding the cart right where he'd sworn it would be. But it'd meant hacking her way through several feet of ceiling that had collapsed over the last few years thanks to that damned copper company and their nighttime blasting.

The "loot" he'd bragged about that night at The Shaft was supposedly stashed under the cart. Her hands shook as she wiped the sweat from her brow. Her dreams, her future—so close.

But the loot wasn't there.

Sucking in a gulp of musty air, she remembered his last words, his last gasps and pleas. He couldn't have lied. The fear filling his bulging eyes had been too real.

Uncertainty festered in her stomach, the dark silence of the mine squeezing her in its grip.

But what if he had?

Joe had been an expert at masking the truth. He'd whispered sweet nothings of Vegas, its neon lights;

promised a desert oasis—a high-rise condo dream. And she'd been a first-rate fool. A smile plastered on her lips day in and day out as the hot and dusty reality of low-income housing and food stamps enveloped her.

The hope that had flourished in her heart, along with her belief in his tinsel-town vows, had carried her through the poverty. But after years of double shifts and swollen feet, she'd seen through his lies.

Yet, she'd stayed.

It had taken a tall slick-talker in a white Stetson hat and snakeskin boots to pry her from Joe's side. Whispering promises of poolside martinis, high-roller rampages, and red satin sheets while he held her in his arms, Mr. Stetson had convinced her to pack her meager belongings and chase after her dream again.

But he was no different than Joe. The whipped-cream world he'd guaranteed melted into a pool of sticky lies. Within a week, he'd left her, bruised, penniless, flat on her ass in a dark Vegas alley.

They never showed those alleys on the glossy pages of magazines.

Sophy dug out a cigarette. The flame of her lighter danced in the semi-darkness. She inhaled, the nicotine taking some of the bite out of her gnawing frustration.

Too many years of dreaming. Way too many.

After scurrying home from Vegas with her tail between her legs, she'd picked up her greasy-spoon life where she'd left it.

Two decades of cleaning tables and filling napkin dispensers lined her face by the time Joe had returned through that diner door. Her parents were long dead, their bones left to rattle in their coffins with each dynamite blast over at the copper pit.

Visions of reconciliation had danced in her head, flamed by Joe's need for her during those first few months after his return to town. But she'd confused lust for love yet again.

He'd laughed when she'd mentioned renewing their wedding vows. Then he'd stopped coming by her house late at night.

The pain of watching him set up shop kitty-corner from her diner, seeing him come and go, day and night, drove her to the liquor cabinet more often than not. But those nighttime outings convinced her that selling antiques wasn't his only racket, and months later all of her spying paid off.

Her tears long-dried by then, she'd aimed for Joe's throat, and this time, he'd bled. But not for long, and Sophy had been ready—she'd expected retaliation.

What she hadn't expected was Joe dragging that redheaded bitch to town.

Watching Joe moon over Ruby, freely giving the woman the love Sophy had begged him for burned deep.

She dropped her cigarette and crushed it with her boot heel, grinding it into the floor, her thoughts festering on Ruby's smiling face. She looked at the empty ore cart and swallowed the acrid memories coating the back of her tongue.

The loot had to be close. She'd followed his directions to the letter.

Squatting, she shined her light under the cart again. The dust had settled. Her beam seemed brighter this time.

Her breath caught at the sight of another wheel further back in the rubble. *Another cart!*

She sat back on her heels. He hadn't mentioned more than one cart. Then again, he hadn't been in much shape to chit-chat at the time.

Her pulse slowed as she looked at the pile of rocks she'd need to hack through to reach the second cart. With less than a week until Ruby sold the mines, time to find the loot was disappearing fast.

And Ruby's nephew kept getting in her way. The last two nights, she'd seen his pickup below Two Jakes mine. How long before he was back snooping around in Socrates Pit?

She picked up her cigarette butt and tucked it in her pocket.

Mac Garner didn't seem to understand that playing in mines was hazardous to his health.

Maybe it was time to put an end to his snooping for good.

Tuesday, April 20th

Claire hung up the phone and glared at the receiver. "I'm going about this Joe thing all wrong," she told the wall and anyone else listening. "I should have called in a psychic. I hear that past life readings are the rage in Southern California now."

A sun-warmed, mid-morning breeze puffed through the General Store's screen door, carrying the scent of fresh cut grass and desert lavender. The soft ting-pings of Ruby's front porch wind chimes chased the breeze.

It was a regular desert paradise.

Claire contemplated tearing out her hair.

"What did he say?" Ruby asked from behind her.

Claire turned around, but held her tongue, not sure where to start and what to omit.

Yesterday afternoon, as soon as Claire and Jess had crossed the threshold, Jess had broadcast to Ruby the fact that they'd found a name and number on a slip of paper in Joe's car. Not that Claire had planned to hide this tidbit of information from Ruby; she just hadn't intended to say anything until after she'd made the phone call.

Jess was oblivious to how Joe's dirty laundry could affect Ruby's life.

Ruby paused in the midst of stocking a shelf with Moon Pies and frowned at Claire. "Spill it, girl."

Claire pasted a chipper smile on her face. "He didn't say anything. He wasn't there."

"Then who were you yelling at over the phone?"

"His mom." The last person Claire had expected to answer the phone was the guy's mother. Judging by the crackle in the lady's voice and her inability to hear anything below a shout, the woman had to be pushing ninety.

"When's he going to be back?"

Now came the tough part. "Not for another seven years, unless he makes parole."

Ruby's mouth fell open. "What?"

"Funny story—he got nailed for grand larceny. Seven to ten years in the state penitentiary."

"You're kidding."

"But according to his mom, he's completely innocent."

"Let me guess, they got the wrong guy?"

"Isn't that always the case?"

Ruby cocked her head to the side. "But ten years? That's a little harsh, isn't it?"

"Oh. Did I forget to mention the grand theft auto, illegal possession of a firearm, assaulting a police officer, and contempt of court charges? Apparently, the Miami judicial system doesn't take too kindly to obnoxious criminals."

Ruby tossed Claire a Moon Pie. "Sounds like a nice guy."

"A real angel, to hear his mom talk." Claire bit into the chocolate-covered cookie and marshmallow pie. "Thanks for breakfast. I skipped my usual half a grapefruit this morning," she joked, hoping to divert the questions sure to follow.

"Why did Joe have this guy's name and number in his car?"

Claire needed to work on her diversion techniques. "Your guess is as good as mine."

But she was pretty sure her own guess was based on a much darker, more criminal origin than Ruby's.

Ruby shoved the last Moon Pie on the shelf and tossed the empty carton into the trashcan on her way to the counter. "Manny's right, you're a rotten liar." Her green-eyed gaze locked onto Claire's. "What was my husband really doing in that antique shop?"

Claire froze, her Moon Pie halfway to her lips. "Honestly, I'm not sure." *Yet.* Her suspicions were still in the larvae stage, and she didn't feel comfortable sharing them with Joe's widow. "But I'm working on an answer for you."

"An answer for what?" Mac asked as he pushed through the velvet curtain while buttoning up his shirt.

He strolled up to Claire and dropped a quick kiss on her mouth, stealing her breath and leaving the minty taste of toothpaste on her lips. Then he grabbed her hand with the Moon Pie in it and took a bite of her breakfast.

She frowned, glancing toward Ruby. "Ixnay on the isseskay."

He waved her off, leaning against the counter. "Ruby probably knows already."

"Humpf. Well, she does now."

"Mac's right," Ruby called over her shoulder as she headed toward the bathroom in the back of the store. "I'd have to be blind as a mole not to notice the way Mac ogles your backside every time you leave the room."

The bathroom door slammed behind her, leaving Claire alone with the hazel-eyed devil.

"Not to mention that love bite on your neck." Mac

pinned her against the wall.

"I have a hickey?" Great. She was walking around, looking like some billboard for Sex-on-the-Sly, Inc. Claire's cheeks burned hotter.

"Not yet, but you will in just a second." He pushed aside her lapel and nipped her collarbone.

"Mac." Her gaze darted to the closed bathroom door.

He slipped his hands under her shirt, his calloused fingers skimming across her stomach and ribs.

Claire's knees wobbled and trembled, joining the mutiny the rest of her body waged against the voice of reason shouting orders from the helm of the ship—as it sank.

"I can't stop thinking about doing all kinds of wicked things with you," he murmured against her flesh. His tongue seared her skin as his lips trailed across her shoulder.

"So quit trying."

He pulled back and stared down at her, his eyelids lowered to half-mast. "You are such a Siren."

Sandwiched between him and the drywall, she wrapped her arms around his neck and nibbled on his smooth-shaven chin. "Say I were to take off my shirt." The spicy aroma of his aftershave made her toes tingle. "What would you do next?"

With her lips pressed against his throat, she felt the rumble of his groan as much as heard it.

"Okay, you two. I'm coming out," Ruby yelled from the other side of the bathroom door.

"Ah, hell." Mac planted a kiss on Claire's lips before stepping back. "You and I are going to continue this when I return from the mine tonight."

"Tonight?" She frowned up at him while straightening her shirt, trying to look like she hadn't been rubbing all over Ruby's nephew. "I thought we were going to search for more bones this afternoon."

"Here I come," Ruby yelled, opening the bathroom door.

"I want to finish with Two Jakes first."

Fine. She'd just go out on her own.

"Don't even think about going without me," Mac warned.

"Going where?" Ruby asked as she neared the counter.

"Stop reading my mind," Claire told him. He was welcome in her pants, but not her brain.

"I mean it, Claire. If I hear you went out searching alone, I'll rescind my offer to help."

She huffed a sigh. He didn't play fair. The male protective gene was overrated. "Okay, I'll wait until tomorrow, but after that, I'm going with or without you."

"Good," Ruby said to her. "Because I need your help here, today. Jess has to have a physical before she can go to this new school."

Claire winced to herself at the scene that was sure to preclude the trip to the doctor.

"And while I was in the bathroom just now, I remembered something I forgot to tell you about Joe and his store." She smiled at Claire, her eyes sparkling.

Claire wasn't so sure if Ruby's sudden interest in helping her solve the mystery surrounding Joe was a good thing or not, but she leaned forward despite her reservations. "What?"

"There's a box of stuff from Joe's store that he kept in a locked filing cabinet. I sold the cabinet right after his stroke, but I think the box is still in the attic."

For such a small town out in the Arizona boonies, people here in Jackrabbit Junction sure liked to use locks.

Claire glanced at Mac and found him staring back at her with a thoughtful frown on his face.

"I'll go up in a bit and see if I can find it," Ruby told her. "You can look through it this afternoon while holdin' down the fort."

Later that afternoon, Claire sat next to the cash register, papers spread over the counter and on the floor behind her where the afternoon blasts of hell-furnace air had blown them. A drop of sweat ran down her back. Her deodorant had melted an hour ago.

What in the hell happened to spring? Had she slept through it?

For the life of her, she couldn't get Ruby's damned air conditioner to kick on. The duct-taped piece of shit was just lucky her toolbox wasn't close by, or she'd have gutted it and offered its innards to the sun god in exchange for a few clouds.

If Ruby didn't come home soon and rescue her, the candy bars would be nothing more than pools of chocolate on the floor.

After covering her face with a cold, wet washcloth again for a few breaths, she returned to the general ledger propped open in front of her. Judging from the figures scrawled on the pages, Joe's store had barely broken even. The pile of receipts and bills of sale on the counter seemed small for him having been in business for almost a decade.

Her first thought had been that Ruby had another box of Joe's stuff shoved somewhere, but the papers' dates spanned from the store's opening until Ruby sold the remaining inventory for a paltry amount after Joe's big stroke. Claire had seen garage sales that fared better.

The bells over the screen door jingled. Claire glanced up at a familiar pair of pale blue eyes and wrinkled brow.

"What are you doing here?" Gramps asked.

Claire sat up straight, stretching her lower back. "It's good to see you, too, Grumpy Smurf."

His brow crinkled even more. "You know what I meant. I just expected ..." He blinked, and then shook his head. "Never mind."

"You just expected Ruby to be sitting here," Claire finished, grinning at the way his face turned lobster pink.

"I said never mind." He walked to the beer cooler and yanked open the door.

Claire dropped the general ledger on the pile of the other accounting paperwork in the box and dug under half a ream's worth of sales slips, merchandise receipt confirmations, and quarterly tax statements.

Her fingers brushed against the corner of something hard. Carefully, she pulled out an eight-by-ten inch frame and stared down at a yellowed newspaper photo of Joe, looking younger than he did in the wedding picture on Ruby's dresser. He stood in his antique store sporting a goofy smile.

Claire read the print below the picture.

Local Man Profits from the Past

Jackrabbit Junction's first antique store is having its Grand Opening on Saturday, June 1st. Located next to Creekside Supply Company, Joe Martino offers great prices on late 19th and early 20th century American antiques. Be sure to come and check it out.

American antiques? Claire stared at the picture again, holding the frame so close that her breath steamed the glass. Her heart thudded in her ears. "Ah, ha."

"Ah, ha, what?" Gramps dropped a six-pack of beer on the counter.

Claire lowered the frame and frowned at the cans. "I thought you didn't like Miller Light."

"It's not for me."

"Then who's it for?"

"None of your business."

Claire shook her head and rang up the beer. "You're growing harder to live with by the day. What's going on?" She had a feeling it had something to do with a certain redhead.

Gramps grunted. "Nothing."

Bullshit. Claire decided to try another route. "Ruby must like Miller Light."

"No, she likes Corona."

"Really?" Claire smiled, taking the money he shoved at her. She wiggled her eyebrows at him. "What else does she like?"

"Claire," he warned.

"Okay, okay, I'll back off for now." She picked up the picture again. "But don't think I didn't notice the way you were watching her the other night."

Gramps nodded at the picture. "What's that?"

She held up the newspaper piece. "It's Ruby's husband, Joe."

"I know what her husband looked like," he said, nearly snarling, and then sighed. "Sorry."

Claire grinned at the obvious jealousy. She pointed at the picture. "Take a look at the cupboard he's standing next to."

Gramps pulled his wire-rim glasses out of his shirt pocket and slipped them on, staring at the photo for several seconds. "What about it?" He looked over the top of the lenses at her.

"It's a 19th century American jelly cupboard."

"You've been watching too much of that damned antiques show your mother plays every waking moment." He turned back to the photo. "Like I said before, what about it?"

"Its value is notably less than the 18th century French

..." she trailed off, suddenly remembering whose company she was in; or rather, whose company she wasn't in. "Never mind."

His eyes narrowed. "I know that look, Claire Alice Morgan. You're getting into some kind of trouble again."

She pulled the picture away from him. "I'm not." At least not yet.

Gramps snorted.

"I'm just noticing some stuff in this old picture."

He grabbed his beer. "Some detective you are."

"What's that supposed to mean?"

"You're so busy naming the furniture that you didn't even notice the guy behind the counter in the back of the store."

"Guy behind the counter," Claire repeated, frowning.

"The one standing next to the picture of Johnny Cash."

"I wonder who ... Hey, he kind of looks like ..." She squinted at the picture. The man looked a lot like that guy in the passport photos. An awful lot.

She glanced up. Gramps was giving her one of his suspicious, gunslinger stares.

"I wonder if Ruby knows who he is," she said, trying to deter him.

"I doubt it."

"What makes you so positive?"

"First of all, this picture is almost ten years old. Ruby has lived here for five. Second, she told me that Joe worked alone. He never had a partner."

"When did she tell you that?"

He glanced at the screen door. "Lately."

"When?"

"None of your business."

Claire sighed. Spooning her way out of Alcatraz would be less maddening than interrogating Gramps. She'd have to corner Ruby.

"So how am I going to find out who this guy is?" she asked as Gramps pushed open the screen door.

"Well, if I were you, Kojak." His smart-ass grin was back. "I'd visit Joe's neighbor—the owner of Creekside Supply Company."

⇥ ⊹ ◆ ⊹ ⇤

Mac peered down at the map of Two Jakes mine. The light on his hard hat spotlighted the notes he'd made over the last two days about several missing tunnels and subchambers.

Pebbles rattled a few feet in front of him in the shadows. A rat the size of a brick watched him, eyes glittering. Mac grimaced at its hairless tail as it scurried away.

Damn, he hated rats.

With midnight quickly approaching, he needed more time. He had three more tunnels to map and who knew how many side tunnels shot off from those. But he'd promised Claire he'd help her tomorrow.

Besides, after her teasing this morning, he had plans involving a hotel room, a bottle of watermelon wine he'd found in Tucson a few days ago, and Claire—preferably unclothed.

He didn't want anything to screw up his plans for getting her alone. Certainly not a musty old mine, and especially not three crusty old men.

He rolled up the map and started toward the main adit, following the orange spray paint marks he used as breadcrumbs.

A loud boom echoed through the mine.

He froze as the earth rumbled around him. Tiny pebbles rained from the ceiling, clattering on his hard hat.

Then the rumbling stopped, and a stale breeze

whooshed past him, cooling the sweat that had sprung out on his flesh in the last few seconds.

Shit! Fear weighed cannonball heavy in his stomach. Clutching his pack, he sprinted through the side tunnel, his boots thudding on the hard-packed dirt. He rounded the bend where the tunnel attached to the main adit and raced up the slope toward the exit.

The dust, now fog-bank thick, coated his throat. Coughing, he turned another corner and slid to a stop.

His heart pounded, raged, then fluttered.

"Mother fuck!" he whispered.

A pile of rocks and timbers separated him from the rest of the world, entombing him under the desert floor.

Chapter Seventeen

Wednesday, April 21st

Claire marched into the General Store, chased by a midmorning breeze heavy with the scent of warm greasewood and filled with sizzling promises.

"Where's your mom?" she asked Jess, who was sitting behind the counter with her school books scattered around her.

"In back." Jess nudged her head toward the curtain without looking up from the colored pages of her U.S. History book. "She's busy ruining my life."

Spoken like a true teenager. Claire bit back a smile. Ever since Ruby and Jess had returned from Tucson, the decibel level in the house hadn't dropped much below fire-whistle intensity.

Playfully messing up Jess's hair as she passed, Claire pushed through the curtain, noticing the faint smell of cigar smoke clinging to the velvet—the same smell that permeated the sofa cushions in Gramps's Winnebago. That might explain Gramps's red cheeks last night when he'd scampered in with pink lipstick on his collar.

Ruby sat on a stool at the bar, pouring over a stack of papers, a pencil in her hand and a furrow on her brow.

"What are you doing?" Claire plopped onto an adjacent stool.

Ruby tapped the eraser on the bar. "This damned new school of Jess's has more paperwork than an IRS 1040 with twenty attachments."

Claire shoved the framed newspaper photo of Joe's grand opening toward Ruby. "Do you know who this guy is?" She pointed at the man standing next to the Johnny Cash painting.

As she stared at the picture, Ruby's frown deepened even more. She took the frame from Claire and lifted it closer to her face. Several seconds passed. "No. Who is he?"

"According to Willis Rupp," Claire threw out the name of the owner of Creekside Supply Company, "he's Joe's cousin."

Ruby's gaze whipped to Claire. "Joe's *what?*"

"Cousin. Did Joe ever mention having a cousin?"

Shaking her head slowly, Ruby handed the frame to Claire.

Claire sighed and tossed the picture on the bar.

She'd figured as much. Ever since she'd started digging into Joe's past, there was something about Ruby and Joe's relationship that had bothered her.

She took a moment to form her next question, choosing her words carefully. "I know you didn't really get into Joe's business dealings, but were you ever curious about where he was and what he was doing while he was off on his sales trips?"

"Of course I was curious." Ruby rested her jaw on her palm as she leaned on the bar and stared at Claire. "But in a marriage, there's a thing called trust, and I had a lot of it."

Claire nodded. That made sense. Ruby had trusted her from the moment Claire had walked in carrying the Help Wanted sign. But still ...

"Plus," Ruby continued, "I had this park to keep me busy. When I took over, the store on the verge of collapse, the river flooded the campsites every spring, and the ground was riddled with rattlesnake holes. It took two years just to get the store and campsites back in shape."

"Then we had the rare White-Eared Hummingbird flutterin' around that summer, and the bird lovers flocked here in masses to see it." Ruby paused, staring down at the pencil in her hand. "My momma got sick the third year I was married to Joe, so I spent most of that winter driving back and forth to Oklahoma. She passed away in the spring, my pop followed nine months later."

Her eyes a little watery, she looked back up at Claire. "By the time I found a spare moment and was fixin' to get curious, Joe had retired from the traveling sales job and cut back on hours at the antique store."

Claire pushed off her stool and nabbed a soda pop from the small fridge behind the bar. "What about after he'd had that last stroke?" She cracked open the pop and took a sip.

"What about it?"

"When you had to sell off his inventory and delve into his finances to pay off creditors, didn't you wonder where he got the stuff in the office downstairs?" Stuff like all of the expensive antique furniture and books, or the $90,000-plus Mercedes Benz. Ruby was a smart cookie, she couldn't have just overlooked all of these signs of hidden wealth.

"Wonder?" Ruby asked, her tone held a mixture of acid and soft, southern twang. "Had I had the time, I'm sure I would have enjoyed a moment to wonder about a lot of things. But my husband was wheelchair-bound and completely incapable of doing anything on his own, even emptyin' his bladder, and we could only afford a nurse on a part-time basis."

"Then there was Jess—acting up at school, fighting with other kids, stressing the hell out of me with her monkey business. Six months into Joe's illness, I couldn't afford to pay for help around this paradise of mine. Just keeping my head above water spiked my blood pressure to levels that made my doctor sweat."

Hearing about Ruby's rough-and-tumble history with the park lit a fire in Claire. Ruby was kind and generous, warm-hearted, quick to grin. She deserved better than a handful of memories of Joe and the huge mess he'd left behind. Mac's willingness to come to Ruby's aid, even if it meant helping her sell her land, made more sense every day.

Claire squeezed Ruby's arm. "But you did keep your head above water when a lot of people would've drowned. That takes a hell of a lot of strength."

Ruby shrugged. "My pop didn't raise a quitter."

"Back to this picture." Claire grabbed the frame. "You've never seen any other pictures of this guy?" The passport photos couldn't be the only other evidence of Joe's cousin.

"Nope. What did Willis say his name was?"

"He couldn't remember."

Ruby snapped her fingers. "Maybe that's whose name and number—"

Claire shook her head. "I thought the same thing, but Willis said the cousin used to come and go a lot, heading home to L.A. in between visits. The guy I tried calling is from Florida, his mother is the treasurer of the Key Largo Estates Association."

Ruby whistled. "Sounds fancy."

"It's a trailer park."

"So, we know the cousin is from L.A. Anything else?"

Claire wasn't ready to tell Ruby about the three passports. If the truth turned out to be ugly, it could make Ruby's life even more complicated.

"That's it," she lied, hoping she didn't sound like she was up to her ears in bullshit.

Ruby seemed to believe her. "What are you gonna do next?"

"I don't know. I figured I'd talk to Mac about it and

see if he had any ideas." That, at least, was the truth. "I saw his pickup out front. Is he around here somewhere?"

Ruby pointed overhead. "Still sleeping. He must have got home late last night. I didn't even hear him pull up."

"Well, he'd better be up and moving when I finish mowing." Soda in hand, Claire walked backwards toward the curtain. The image of Mac, all skin and no clothes, lying on white cotton sheets, made her throat dry. "Because we have a date this afternoon, and if he's running late, I'm going bone hunting on my own."

⸻ ◆ ⸻

Down in the dark, hand-burrowed caverns under the desert hardpan, Mac stared at the mine map. With his lamplight no brighter than a jar of fireflies, the scribed measurements and numbers melted together, the ruled lines crisscrossed.

He closed his eyes and rubbed his palm over his face. Dirt, sweat, and salt coated his skin, making it slick and gritty at the same time.

His bad luck was multiplying; his batteries were dying. The light on his hard hat had faded a few hours ago, and as soon as his lamplight battery died, he'd be left with two green glow lights, his lighter, a book of matches, and the candle he carried in place of a canary to test for poisonous gases.

He smiled in spite of the gloom, remembering Claire's reaction when he explained candles didn't react to gases the way canaries did, but they burned slower with less squawking.

Blinking, he shook his head, trying to focus on finding a way out of this tomb. Life was too interesting these days for him to rot away underneath this mountain.

The main exit was a bust. With the tons of rock and

timbers blocking the path, there'd be no digging through the rubble. He'd tried that already, and wasted several hours and precious sips of canteen water only to have more of the ceiling crash around him.

That left two of the unmapped tunnels as his only chance of escape. The third, which was closest to the front, he'd ruled out after spending two hours exploring the labyrinth of side tunnels and false starts. The two shafts he'd found within it were filled with thick shadows his light scarcely pierced. His hundred-foot stretch of nylon rope probably would leave him dangling in them like a worm on a hook in a deep pool of blackness.

The other two unmapped tunnels forked off the main adit further back in the mine—where he stood at the moment.

After a game of eenie-meenie-mynie-mo, he stared down the tunnel on the left. "Looks like you win." His voice sounded crusty, the back of his mouth coated with a layer of mine dust. The dull thud of his boots on the rock floor comforted him in a way only someone who'd spent the last eighteen hours alone in the stomach of a mountain would understand.

Every few steps, the floor dipped in elevation, how much he wasn't sure. The mine's musty scents had become commonplace, expected. The sight of a rat would have been welcome, another beating heart in the shadows. But not even rats strayed this far from sun and food.

He tramped deeper into the network of channels branching off from the main tunnel, pausing with every twist and turn to spray a directional mark in case he needed to backtrack. As he walked, the walls drew close around him until his shoulder brushed the rocks on either side and he had to bend over to keep his hat from knocking against the ceiling. Much too soon, his back started to groan in protest at being hunched.

Five minutes after that, the floor turned to water.

At the water's edge, Mac lifted his lamp, searching for the opposite coastline. He found none. The only way across was to slosh through. But without any idea of the depth or distance of the pool, he hesitated. For all he knew, a hundred-foot-deep shaft could be the drain in this tub of water.

He stuck his fingertip in the glass-smooth liquid and sighed. Freezing—that figured. Not that he'd been expecting hot tub temperatures, but something an ice cube would melt in quickly would have been nice. The mine was root-cellar cold already. Add wet clothes to the mix, and hypothermia would surely follow.

Mac didn't want to think about how many hours he had yet to play around in these passageways. Maybe he should go back and check out the last tunnel.

Toenails clicked on the stone floor in the darkness ahead.

What was that? Mac leaned out as far as he could without falling face-first into the water, his lamp dangling at arm's length, and squinted into the shadows. Something glittered in the narrow band of darkness between the water and the ceiling.

Pebbles clattered up ahead, the sound echoing off the walls and water. Holding his breath for several seconds, he waited for a splashing sound to follow. It didn't come. There was an end to the pool, but how far to the other side he didn't know.

Mac sniffed. Over the smell of stale earth, he picked up a tinge of foulness and stepped back. The urge to get the hell out of there made his muscles burn, but logic held him still. It was a long way back in the mine for anything to be making a nest—except for bats, but that hadn't sounded like a bat.

The clack of stone hitting stone echoed past him again.

Mac stared at the black water. The fact that there was something moving up ahead meant there might be another way out. If he ever wanted to see the sun again, he was going to have to get wet.

He grabbed a green glow stick in case his lamp died mid-pool, then shucked his clothes, except for his boots, and stuffed them in his pack. Now was as good a time as any to test if the bag was waterproof like the salesman had claimed.

Crouched, with his pack held above the water's reach, Mac stepped into the dark pool. His breath caught as the cold liquid sloshed against his kneecaps. As he moved deeper, the water lapped at his thighs and the ceiling dropped, crunching him even lower.

He turned up the wattage on his lamp and searched for the opposite shore. The sight before him made him groan.

He should have brought his scuba gear.

──◂ ◆ ▸──

"Where's Mac?" Claire asked Ruby. She walked toward the cooler in the back of the General Store. "We have a date with a dog and a bone."

She stood in front of the open cooler door while cold air chilled her arms, shoulders, and face. After spending the last several hours mowing, her sinuses felt stuffed full of wheat-grass and dirt.

Claire grabbed a can of Diet Coke and shut the cooler door, then snatched a bag of Bugles and a pack of Twinkies from a shelf on her way to the counter. The concern etched in Ruby's brow made Claire pause. "What?"

"I thought he was with you," Ruby said.

"With me?" Claire threw a five-dollar bill down for her goodies. "His truck is still sitting outside."

"I know. I thought you two headed out looking for

more bones in Harley's car." Ruby rubbed the back of her neck. "I haven't heard a single floor board creak all morning. Then again, Jess has been here more than I have."

Fear tickled Claire's chest. She headed for the backroom. "Maybe he's still in bed," she said over her shoulder.

Jess pushed through the curtain before Claire reached it. "If you're looking for Mac, he's not here." Either the kid had been eavesdropping from the other side of the curtain, or she had the hearing of a fox.

"Where is he?" Ruby asked.

Jess shrugged. She grabbed a Snicker's bar from the shelf and tore it open. "How should I know? I'm just a kid, remember?"

Ruby and Claire stared at each other across the room. Ruby's gaze mirrored the worry clenching Claire's gut. The clock in the rec room cuckooed.

"His pickup didn't just drive here on its own," Ruby said.

"Maybe somebody drove it home for him," Jess piped in, seemingly oblivious to the undercurrent of fear rippling through the room.

Her skin suddenly clammy, Claire chewed on her lower lip. That would mean Mac was still at the mine.

Best case scenario, he was sitting in the shade, waiting for someone to come pick him up.

Worst case scenario ... she gulped, wincing. "Give me the keys to the old Ford," she told Ruby.

"No." Ruby burst into action, racing from behind the counter. "Come on, I'm driving. Cover the store, Jess," she yelled and rushed out the screen door.

Claire followed, tight on Ruby's heels.

⟶ ◆ ⟵

Lips quivering from the cold sinking into his bones, Mac forced his breath out slowly, evenly.

Water lapped at his neck as he squeezed through the narrow walls. The ceiling scraped the top of his hat. He felt like Alice in Wonderland, chasing that damned white rabbit through a doorway that kept shrinking.

Five crouched steps later, the ceiling dropped another two inches. Water rimmed his lower lip.

Six more inches and he'd be swimming underwater through a narrow pipeline of rock, a thought as relishing as a solid kick in the balls.

He lifted the green glow stick. The water level was too high to use the lamp, which was probably toast now that water had likely seeped into every crack in its casing.

His heart stuttered as the sound of more pebbles clattering rippled over the water, much louder this time. He was close. Not close enough to see anything in the dim, pale green glow, but close enough to know the stench blanketing him was from something that had once lived and breathed and was now slowly decomposing.

Swallowing the bile that kept creeping up his throat, Mac took another step.

But his foot didn't connect with rock.

Surprise robbed him of breath as he slid completely under the water.

The glow stick slipped from his grip as he struggled to swim back to the surface of the shaft. The weight of his bag dragged him down deeper. He kicked hard, his hiking boots heavy as anchors, the inky blackness swallowing him whole.

His hand slammed against one of the shaft walls, the pain dull in his near-panicked state. Grabbing onto a ledge and pushing off from it, Mac propelled upwards with every ounce of strength in his bones. He broke the surface fast—too fast—and crashed into the ceiling.

"Oww!" He cursed in the pitch black, rubbing the new

lump on his head. His hat must have floated off during his struggles.

Coughing out inhaled water, heavy with the taste of minerals, he paused long enough to hear the sound of whatever waited ahead for him and to get his bearings, then swam forward until his knee scraped against the mine floor. His heart hammering, he pulled himself out of the pit.

After his pulse returned to normal, he moved forward blindly, still crouched, not wanting to open his pack to grab the other glow stick until he could keep the water from seeping into the bag. His matches were waterproof, but his clothes and equipment weren't.

Ten steps later, the water level dropped as the ceiling lifted.

Eight more steps and standing up straight was an option again. His bare knees shivered in the cool air. He breathed through his mouth to keep from gagging on the smell of rotting flesh.

The sound of wet chewing was noisy—too noisy. Whatever he was sharing the tunnel with didn't seem to mind company.

As his soaked boots connected with dry floor, Mac unzipped his bag and pulled out his last glow stick, leaving the matches and candle stub as his backups. If this tunnel didn't lead out of this hellhole, he was in some deep shit.

He cracked the stick and shook it. A rat the size of a Chihuahua, sitting not six feet in front of him, paused with its snout half-buried in the entrails of a maggot-covered porcupine.

Two beady eyes stared up at Mac for several seconds, then the rat hissed and returned to its lunch. It kept a close eye on him as it chewed.

Stomach lurching, Mac reached for the wall. His palm landed on a hard, sharp point. "Shit!" He yanked his hand away, rubbing it on his leg, and held the pale green light up to the wall.

"I'll be damned," he whispered, smiling at the sight before him.

Ruby and Claire bumped along the dirt road toward Two Jakes mine. The shocks on the old Ford squeaked in protest while dust filled the cab of the pickup, coating Claire in a gritty veneer.

Ruby slid to a stop on the shoulder and cut the engine. She turned to Claire, her face pale. "You ready?"

Claire didn't waste time on an answer. She shoved out the door and was halfway up the hill before she remembered her blood was full of Ho-Ho deposits, and that there was an easier trail around the side that led up to the mine.

Lungs burning, she continued onward and upward, pushed by her need to see Mac again, alive and smiling.

Ruby was waiting for her at the top. Claire shielded her eyes from the sun. "You took ... the lazy ... way up," she said between gasps.

A quick smile flitted across Ruby's mouth as she caught Claire's arm and pulled her up the last few feet. "Nice climbing, Rocky Balboa. You fixin' to train for another fight?"

Gramps must have spilled the beans to Ruby about Claire sparring with Sophy on the bar floor. It was too hard to talk between ragged breaths, so she gave Ruby the finger instead.

Ruby patted Claire on the back and then stepped into the mine. Claire stumbled in behind her, but both of them stopped just inside the shadows. Claire's limbs grew ice-cold at the sight of the rock and rubble piled high before them, plugging the mine.

"Oh, my God," Ruby said, her voice weak, her usual spark missing.

Claire leaned against the wall, still working on catching her breath. "Now what?"

"I have to get him out." Ruby grabbed a football-sized rock from the pile and threw it behind her. "It's my fault. He's in there because of me."

"It's not your fault. Mac's a big boy. He can take care of himself, even in dark places." At least Claire hoped so.

She watched Ruby pull another rock from the pile. "Ruby, stop. We don't even know if he's in there." She glanced around, searching for some clue that would prove Mac wasn't on the other side of God knew how many tons of rock.

"What do you want me to do?" Ruby rolled another rock from the pile. Her panic showed in her wide eyes and quick breaths.

"I'd suggest trying Morse code," Mac said from behind them.

Chapter Eighteen

Thursday, April 22nd

The windshield of Harley's Winnebago gleamed like a sheet of chrome in the midmorning sunshine. Mac pushed his sunglasses higher on the bridge of his nose. After spending the last fourteen hours passed out on Ruby's spare bed, he was suffering from a post-hibernation hangover.

As he rounded the R.V.'s bug-splattered front bumper, a warm breeze smelling of cigar smoke wallpapered his T-shirt to his chest. A full-fledged sweat welled just below the surface of his skin, making him wish he'd thrown on shorts instead of jeans.

"Well, if it isn't Sleeping Beauty," Harley said as Mac paused in the shade of the R.V.'s awning. The aluminum lawn chair creaked as Harley leaned back and squinted up at Mac.

"It looks like good ol' Sweet Buns has risen from the dead." Chester spoke around his cigar as he dealt cards across the plastic patio table.

Jess sat across the table from Harley with her back to Mac with Manny and Chester bordering her on either side.

Claire was nowhere to be seen. A pang of disappointment flitted through him.

"Howdy, Mac," Jess said, turning around in her chair to smile at him, her cheeks dimpled.

Mac smiled in return. "Is Claire inside?"

Manny fanned his cards and shot Mac a conspiratorial wink. "Romeo is searching for his Juliet, I see."

"Why are you looking for Claire? What kind of trouble has she stuck her nose in now?" Harley's tone held suspicion.

"They're going bone hunting," Jess supplied in a sing-song voice while rearranging the cards in her hand.

Mac winced at her choice of words in front of this crowd of hecklers.

Gramps glared at Mac, while Manny snickered and Chester wheezed. Seemingly oblivious to the elbow jabs and choked laughter, Jess hummed under her breath as she adjusted the straps of her pink *Hello Kitty* tank top. Her ponytail swished over her freckle-spattered shoulders as she bee-bopped to whatever bubble-gum tune played in her head.

"A little early to be hitting the cards, isn't it boys?" Mac hoped to change the subject before the old sparkplugs added several raunchy phrases to Jess's vocabulary.

Jess laid her cards face-down on the table. "They're teaching me how to play." Her eyes twinkled like Ruby's used to before Joe's death.

"Aren't you supposed to have your nose buried in an Algebra book right now?" Mac asked, and then regretted his question when a cloud shadowed her face.

"Ruby kicked me out until eleven. Some guy from the bank is coming over." Jess pushed back her chair. "Watch these," she told Mac, pointing at her cards. "I have to use the Ladies room."

She skipped across the dirt drive, puffs of dust trailing in her wake. Apparently, his comment about schoolwork hadn't had a lasting effect.

"I heard you had an accident Tuesday night," Chester said.

Mac turned back to find three pairs of keen eyes staring

him down. How much did they know about the last forty-eight hours? Hell, Mac wasn't even sure yet how much he knew. And without evidence to prove someone threw a lit stick of dynamite in the mine with the intention of sealing him in there, he had nothing to hand over to Sheriff Harrison besides theories and suspicions.

Lucky for him, his would-be murderer had no idea about the man-hole-sized air vent past the rotting porcupine that some miner had hacked into the hillside. The blinding sun had been a welcome sight, the fresh, dry air coaxing the musty moisture from his lungs. When he'd heard the rattle of Ruby's old Ford on the road below, his knees had nearly buckled.

"*Señorita* Jess said someone stole your pickup and left you stranded at the mine overnight."

Mac nodded, but kept his lips sealed. While poking holes in his brake lines, his wanna-be assassin must have found the spare key hidden in the wheel well. Stealing his pickup was a minor crime compared to using it as a decoy; the former ruled by greed, the latter by a much more malicious intention.

"You've really run into a patch of bad luck lately, boy," Harley said, his gaze locked onto Mac's.

"Sure seems like it."

Harley cocked his eyebrow. "What's your take on the value of those mines?"

His "take" was that he'd have a better chance at guessing the value of the moon. With just four days until Ruby's deadline, uncertainty hung around his shoulders like a lead cape. "Until I get results back on those samples I took to Phoenix last week," he said, rubbing his forehead, "I'm not drawing any conclusions."

"What happened to your hand?" Chester pointed at Mac's hand, the one he'd gashed on a sharp edge of amethyst in the mine's wall after wading out of the pool.

"Just a little accident." Mac stuffed his hand in his pocket.

"Hmpff. He's as bad as Claire," Harley told his buddies.

The amethyst find was nothing to blab about. It could play a bigger role in Ruby's future than the sample results. If it had been just a thin vein, he wouldn't think twice about its effect on the mine's value, but a ten-foot wide section of grade-A purple quartz was nothing to shrug off. If that vein extended into the last unmapped tunnel, Two Jakes might be worth more than the other three mines put together— maybe not to the copper company, but surely to a gem seller.

Chester let out a wolf whistle.

Footsteps crunched on the drive behind Mac. He turned to see what had all three boys grinning like village idiots and was blinded by sunlight ricocheting off a rhinestone-peppered bikini top.

"Ms. Derriere is strutting her stuff again." Harley said, his voice hushed.

Mac shielded his eyes from the walking disco ball. The woman would have made Liberace scream with envy. He dragged his gaze back to the boys.

Manny stared after the woman, his grin tiger-like. "How did your date go last night with Fanny, Chester?"

Chester grunted. "We played strip poker. She stripped, and I poked her."

Laughter filled the afternoon air.

"What's so funny?" Jess asked from behind Mac.

"Chester's love life," Mac said.

Jess wrinkled her nose, and Mac couldn't have agreed more.

"So where's Claire?" Mac asked after they'd quieted down.

"Probably running into barbed-wire fences again,"

Harley said.

Manny chuckled and sipped his Corona.

"Claire is playing with fire," Harley continued, shooting Mac a glance. "Sophy is dangerous."

Mac got the impression he was being warned. "Are you referring to those three-inch claws?"

Manny made a purring noise in his throat. "Mmmmm. Red nails. She's dangerous all right—dangerously sexy."

"I bid three," Jess said, then peered over the top of her cards at Manny.

"Pass." Chester threw his cards face-down on the table. "Sexy, yes. But she's also dangerously deceptive."

"Exactly." Harley knocked twice on the table to show he passed, too.

"Deceptive how?" Mac asked. Besides hiding behind too much makeup and what had to be one of those inflatable bras, Mac couldn't imagine Sophy doing anything that would get dirt under her red fingernails.

"I'll pass, too, *gatita*," Manny said, patting Jess twice on the head. "You get to call trump."

"There's more to Sophy than short skirts and red lipstick." Harley lit a cigar with a silver-plated lighter.

"Hearts is trump." Jess threw down the Jack of hearts. "Are you guys talking about that old lady who works at the diner? The one who always has hickeys on her neck?"

Chester tossed out the Queen of hearts. "She once broke a guy's arm for trying to steal second base without her approval."

Jess's mouth fell open. "She broke his arm for trying to French kiss her?"

"What are you saying?" Mac asked. "The woman is no light-weight in the ring?" Judging from the way Claire was throwing punches while rolling around on the bar floor, she wasn't either.

"Yes, and something else—something that may interest

you in particular." Harley threw a nine of hearts on top of Chester's Queen. "A couple of years ago, Mabel was sputtering every time I started her up. One day, when I was leaving the diner, Sophy was outside smoking and heard Mabel do her coughing routine. The next morning, when Sophy brought me my usual, she told me I needed to get Mabel's idle jets cleaned. The woman could tell just by listening."

Mac's gut twisted as the meaning behind Harley's words sunk into his sleep-hung-over brain.

Manny took another swig of his Corona, then cleared his throat. "She told me her father was in the 89th Infantry Division as a mechanic for the regimental motor pool. He taught her how to put together an engine piece by piece. When I asked her why she didn't run a garage instead of the diner, she told me kitchen grease is easier to wash off." Manny dropped a ten of hearts on top of the pile and grinned at Jess. "Good job, *señorita*. You won that round."

"Yay!" Jess clapped her hands.

As he watched Jess rake in the cards, Mac's thoughts raced. Looking at Sophy, he'd never guess she could be the one sabotaging his truck. But if what the boys were telling him was true, he now knew his number one suspect. What to do with this knowledge had him spinning in circles.

Harley smiled across the table at Jess. "Nice work, kid. Now do it again." He looked up at Mac and the wattage of his smile dimmed. "You get my point then, boy?"

Mac nodded. "Where's Claire?" He didn't hide the urgency in his voice. Claire had better be more tender-footed around Sophy. If Sophy was capable of trying to bury him alive in Two Jakes, she'd stop at nothing to get rid of Claire.

"She's cleaning out the tool shed," Jess supplied while throwing out the Ace of hearts.

"Thanks." Mac tipped his head to the boys before

turning to leave.

"Oh, Mac," Jess's voice stopped him. "I heard Claire tell Ruby she's going out looking for more bones with or without you this afternoon. She's tired of waiting around."

No way in hell was she going out there without him.

"It's not nice to keep a lady waiting," Chester told Mac. "Gets them all hot and bothered."

"You'd know," Harley said. "That's part of your technique."

"Isn't that what Mac wants from Claire?" Manny asked.

Mac escaped before they could hold him over the coals any longer.

Five minutes later, he stood outside the open shed door listening to Claire bumping around inside.

He stepped into the shed. The stagnant heat trapped under the steel roof made him pause to acclimate to the oven-like air. As his eyes adjusted to the shadowed interior, the smell of grease, gas, and dust filled his sinuses.

Claire stood at the far wall of the shed, her back to him as she struggled with something that had her spewing curses auctioneer-style. Her orange T-shirt, darkened with sweat along her spine, clung to her like a faded sunburn, a slice of her porcelain-pale skin visible just below the bottom hem. Her jeans hung low on her hips, a tool belt slung around her waist.

Mesmerized by the belt wrapping around her hips, Mac strolled toward her. His palms itched to trace the curves under her jeans. As he reached for that crescent of bare skin, a loose floor board creaked under his weight.

Claire whirled around, her eyes wide, a wrench in her hand.

Mac grinned. "Morning, slugger."

"Damn it, Mac," she tossed the wrench behind her on the bench. "You scared the shit out of me."

His focus returned to her hips. "Nice tool belt you've

got there." Manny was right—the sight of a woman in a tool belt could drop a man to his knees.

Mac's gaze crawled up her T-shirt to where Porky Pig smiled back at him, the words *Men are Pigs* scrawled in blue underneath the mug shot. The orange cotton hugged the soft swells beneath. He gulped.

Claire's eyes narrowed. "Mac." She stepped back, her butt bumping into the workbench. "Stop looking at me like that."

"Claire," he managed to say around the thick lump of flesh that was his tongue. He reached for her.

"Freeze, buster." She whipped a drill out from behind her and held it between them.

He paused, the tip of a bit poking into his chest. "Drop the drill."

She shook her head. "I don't trust you. I've seen that wicked gleam in your eyes before, and it's always followed by your lips kissing me senseless."

"And you object?"

"Right now I do. I have a few questions for you, and it'll be impossible to ask them if your tongue is in my mouth."

He knew a brick wall when he hit one. He stepped back and rested on his heels. "Okay, shoot." The quicker they got this over with, the sooner he could sink his teeth into that sweet spot on her shoulder.

"Well, to start with, are those mines worth more than the mining company is offering?"

Mac shrugged. "Right now, I don't know." Which was the truth.

He wasn't going to clue Claire in on the amethyst cache until he did some research on the value of gem mines. He didn't need her running to Ruby and convincing her not to sell if the vein in Two Jakes turned out to be nothing more than a small pocket of amethyst.

"When will you know?"

"After Saturday, I hope."

"What's Saturday?"

"I'm heading back to Phoenix for the samples and results."

She seemed to chew on that for several seconds. "Are you going to go back in those mines?"

"Yes." As much as he'd rather not, he had to.

There was that last tunnel in Two Jakes to explore, as soon as he found the nerve. The only way into that mine was back through the air vent and past the rotting porcupine. The thought of swimming across that inky pool again made his ball sack shrink.

Rattlesnake Ridge had about a mile of drifts to check out, and he had yet to step foot in the Lucky Monk. Plus, Socrates Pit held something Sophy was willing to kill to protect.

"You're insane."

"I have a job to do."

"You're willing to risk your life to do it?"

He nodded once. "Whatever it takes."

She wiped at a drop of sweat trickling down her forehead. "Who drove your truck home the other night?"

"I don't know," he said, but he had a strong suspicion.

Claire shot him one of her "bullshit" glares.

Until he found out why Sophy was trying to remove him from the picture, he wasn't going to waste time speculating with Claire—she was too quick to act for his comfort.

"Who trapped you in Two Jakes?"

"The mouth caved in—no big deal. These kinds of accidents happen periodically. Years of heat and cold waging war on the fractures in the rock tend to weaken them." Neither Claire nor Ruby needed to think it was anything more than an accident. "The copper mining company's nighttime blasting probably triggered the whole thing."

"Spare me the geology lesson, Mac." She dropped the drill on the counter behind her. "I saw the debris. Cave-ins don't imbed pebbles two inches deep into ten-by-ten inch slabs of timber." She crossed her arms over Porky's face. "I also saw boot prints outside Two Jakes that were too small to be yours."

The woman was sharp—too sharp. She wasn't going to let him off with a few head scratches and shoulder shrugs. What he needed was a distraction.

Mac grinned. "You look sexy as hell in that tool belt."

"Mac," she warned, reaching behind her.

He closed the distance between them and pinned her against the workbench, clamping his hand down on top of hers over the drill. "And there's nothing hotter than a beautiful woman with big ...," he cupped the back of her head, "... brains," he finished, his lips almost touching hers.

"Don't patronize me." Her breath fanned his chin. "And distracting me is not going to work."

He palmed her hips and tugged her tight against him. "I'm not patronizing." He reinforced his words with an unwavering gaze. "You're a very intelligent woman, which you've proven repeatedly in the two short weeks I've known you. And as you can tell," he glanced downward, "I find that fact a huge turn-on."

"Oh." Her voice sounded strangled. She cleared her throat. "Thanks."

Mac heard her suck in a breath as he trailed his lips down the tendon bridging her ear and collarbone.

"But ..." she moaned when he nipped her shoulder, "I still want to know who trapped you in that mine."

He slipped his hands inside her shirt. Her stomach trembled under his fingers as he inched them up her ribcage. The softness of her warm, silky skin made his knees weak.

He wanted to touch her—all of her—and he was tired of fighting what he wanted.

"And I'm not going ..." her eyes widened when he unhooked her bra. "I'm not going to stop ..." her breath hitched as he licked the sensitive hollow between her neck and shoulder. "Stop asking you ..." her voice quivered as his thumbs caressed the damp skin where her underwire had rested. "Oh, screw it."

She hopped up on the workbench and wrapped her legs around his hips. "Mac," she whispered, trailing her fingertip down over his Adam's apple. "Take your shirt off."

"Yes, Ma'am." He lifted it over his head and dropped it on the bench next to her.

Her finger took a circular course down to his navel. He caught it at the waist of his jeans and lifted it to his mouth, then ran his lips along her wrist up to her inner elbow. "Claire," he said against her soft flesh.

"Yes?" she licked her lips as he stared at her mouth.

"Kiss me."

"I thought you'd never ask," she said and slid her fingers in his hair, pulling his mouth to hers. Her tongue coaxed his, her hands sliding over his bare shoulders.

Mac pulled away from her mouth and rained kisses down her chin and neck, making his way south. She smelled of grease, tool shed, and sunshine, and he wanted to taste every sweet and salty inch of her.

He palmed Porky the Pig's rounded cheeks, the soft weight of her filling his palms. The ache inside him cinched tighter.

Her nails scraped down his bare back.

"Christ," Mac said slipping his hands under her shirt. "When you wiggle your hips against me ..." he paused as his thumbs hit paydirt. *What would she taste like?* "I can't think straight."

"Really?" Her tone teased. "What happens when I do this?" She reached down and ran her palm over his zipper.

He groaned and pushed back against her.

"I want you, Mac," she whispered, pressing harder, her teeth grazing his earlobe. "I want you to—"

"OH, MY GOD!" Ruby's cry stopped Mac cold, like a bucket of ice dumped down the front of his pants.

He yanked his hands out from under Claire's T-shirt, keeping his back to his aunt.

"I'm so sorry," Ruby said.

Mac peeked at her over his shoulder. Her hand was clamped over her eyes.

"I didn't see anything, I swear."

Liar! Her fiery blush told the truth.

Mac turned back to Claire, who was trying to fasten her bra. He reached out to help and she batted his hands away, shaking her head vigorously.

Was it too much to ask to ravish Claire without an audience? "What do you need, Ruby?" he asked through gritted teeth.

"Claire."

So did he, something fierce. His aunt could wait in line.

"I have to go to Yuccaville for a couple of hours, and I need her to watch the store."

"I'll be there in just a second." Claire hopped down from the workbench, still adjusting her bra.

Ruby sprinted out of the shed like her hair was on fire.

Picking up his shirt from the workbench, Mac took a deep breath. "Claire, if I don't see you naked soon, I'm going to lose my mind."

He watched her straighten the tool belt on her hips. "On second thought, lose the clothes and keep the tool belt." He grabbed her hand and tugged her toward him.

Chuckling, she pulled free of his grip and backed

toward the door. "Tell me who trapped you in that mine, Mac Garner, and I'll make every one of your tool belt fantasies come true."

Friday, April 23rd

Claire's luck had gone the way of the Dodo bird.

She slouched on a stool behind the counter in the General Store, frowning out the door at a pair of Spotted Towhees playing tag in the early morning sunshine.

The heat had yet to catch up with the morning, but warm drafts of sagebrush-scented air pushing through the screen held the promise of sweaty backs and stinky armpits.

The sound of Jess screaming at her mother drowned out the soft jingles from the wind chimes. Claire closed her eyes and tried to block out the anger raging down through the overhead vent.

Yesterday had been a bust. Mac, Henry, and she had spent the afternoon nosing around the valley adjacent to her grandma's valley, combing over the area where Henry had found the bone and she'd found the lighter. Not only had she been wound up cross-bow-tight with sexual frustration and not a cigarette in sight, but they hadn't found a single atom of evidence to support her theory that the bone belonged to a murder victim.

Mac had continued to play dumb about his saboteur, hiding behind another one of his mental walls.

She didn't believe the mine had caved in without human interference. There were too many facts that supported her theory, facts on which Mac refused to comment.

The stubborn, irritating, hard-headed, too-sexy-for-his-own-good man. Men like him made women cast aside their six-figure Wall Street careers and daydream about crocheting baby booties and canning tomatoes.

Okay, that was exaggerating a bit, but the thought of returning to her old life in South Dakota held as much appeal as eating a handful of tree grubs.

Mac had dropped her off back at the store late yesterday afternoon with nothing more than a peck on the lips. Then he'd dashed off to Yuccaville to "take care of some business." One way or another, before this day was through, Claire was going to find out what "business" he was up to.

"Jessica Lynn Wayne," Ruby yelled as she shoved through the curtain into the store. "Get your smartmouth down here right now, or I'm going to come up there and make you wish you'd never taken a breath of oxygen after you popped out of my womb!"

A crash rang from overhead, followed by a run of muffled curses.

Ruby dropped her purse on the counter and sighed. "I swear to God, I'm fixin' to throw that child to the wolves and shoot the stork that left her on my doorstep." Her left eyelid ticked as she stared at Claire. "We'll be back around three."

Claire nodded. "Don't worry about me. I've got Chester's newest *National Enquirer* to read, and Manny gave me one of his vampire-romance books. I'll just be sitting back and enjoying the cool breeze from the air conditioner all day."

As if on queue, a loud rattling issued from the rec room.

Claire shook her head. That worthless piece of duct-taped scrap metal was flirting with execution via sledgehammer if it didn't perform up to par this afternoon.

"Manny reads romances?" Ruby asked.

"He says they enrich his love life. I think he studies the

sex scenes, working on more ways to coerce women into bed."

Ruby grinned. "Whatever works." She dug her keys out of her purse. "Too bad they don't make romances that get men all hot and bothered."

Claire wondered if Ruby was referring to a certain crotchety, old man who'd told Claire she could use Mabel tonight if she agreed not to come home before midnight, because he was going to be *busy*. "They do. You can find them in the Forum section of *Penthouse*."

"Ruby!" Jess yelled through the vent, making her mother wince. "Where are my yellow PRINCESS shorts? I'm not going to that stupid school with you unless I have those shorts!"

"They're in your closet on the floor where you threw them last week." Ruby hoisted her purse on her shoulder. "I'm tellin' you, that girl was touched by the devil at the age of three."

Claire followed Ruby to the door and onto the porch. "Maybe she'll get to this school and see it's not such a bad place," Claire said, not believing that for a moment, but it never hurt to pretend the glass was half-full.

Jess wanted to stay with her mom, something Ruby seemed to be blind to. But on such a sunny, blue-skied day, it would take a hot poker to motivate Claire to step in and attempt to reconcile the two wildcats.

"Nice try," Ruby smirked. "But we both know how today will go. I hope she doesn't set the school on fire while I'm signing papers."

The familiar sound of Mabel's engine rumbling up the drive snagged Claire's attention.

She watched as the blue beauty rolled by, while her chin hit the boards below her feet at the sight of someone with a beehive of silver hair and a familiar yellow sweater sitting in the passenger seat.

What in the hell was Gramps doing with Rosy Linstad? Is that why he didn't want Claire home until after midnight?

Claire glanced at Ruby's face. Her stomach tightened at the sight of the pained expression in Ruby's green eyes.

That two-timing, cantankerous, son of a bitch! Unless Gramps had one hell of a good explanation as to why Rosy's cheeks were planted in Mabel's front seat, Claire was going to light the old man's shorts on fire with him in them.

The Shaft pulsed around Sophy with cigarette smoke and patrons—cowboys and miners alike, along with the leather-decked bikers, who often filled the tables on warm spring and fall evenings. Shelly West belted out "José Cuervo" on the jukebox while frothy beer poured from the tap.

Sophy sipped at the bittersweet foam rimming the lip of her glass and glanced at her watch—nine-twenty.

Old Dick Webber should be finished checking on his cattle by now. She'd run into him once, about a month ago, on her way up to Socrates Pit with a pickax and a flashlight in her hand. Lucky for her, he didn't ask too many questions, just talked about his collection of petrified animal shit. But she didn't need him seeing her heading up to that mine twice.

"So," Billy Ray's slurred voice cut through her thoughts. "How's 'bout you and me head back to my place for some rough ridin', if ya know what I mean."

Sophy looked into the red-rimmed eyes of the blond thirty-six year-old. She'd ridden Billy before. She had nothing but praise for the size and girth of his saddle horn, but the boy always stumbled out of the gate and had trouble reaching an even stride. And more often than not, he tended to keep chasing the rabbit long after the race was over, leaving her saddle sore by the time he returned to a canter.

Patting Billy on his stubble-roughened cheek, she winked. "Not tonight, sugar. I have—" The rest of her sentence stalled on her tongue at the sight of Ruby's nephew walking in the door followed by Harley's granddaughter. Her teeth snapped closed.

"You all right, Sophy?" Billy Ray squeezed her hand. He grabbed her chin, forcing her to face him. "You look like you seen a ghost."

Gulping down the panic crawling up her throat, she whispered, "I wish I had."

⟶ ◆ ⟵

"All I'm saying is if Sophy's dirty glares could kill, you'd be pushing up daisies," Claire told Mac, tapping Mabel's brakes. "Why are you being so adamant about Sophy, anyway?"

From the moment they'd left The Shaft, Mac had been lecturing Claire about why she should treat the she-devil like a rabid coyote.

"Because I don't trust her." Mac said as Claire pulled

off the dirt road leading to Socrates Pit and stopped on the wide shoulder. "Just promise me that you'll stay away from her in the future."

"Okay, okay." Claire shifted into Park. "I promise I'll try." But she didn't promise to stay away from Sophy's shed.

She shut off the engine.

"What are you doing?" he asked.

"Parking." Claire turned the key counter-clockwise until the glow of the dash lights flickered back to life.

The full moon peeked in through the front windshield.

She took a deep breath, trying to slow her pulse. Sitting alone in the dark next to Mac did funny things to her heartbeat. The smell of Mabel's leather and his spicy cologne produced an olfactory nirvana that had Claire's synapses sparking like firecrackers.

Leaning over his long legs, she popped open the glove box and dug through papers and napkins until her fingers brushed Gramps's CD case.

"Do you mean *parking*, as in Chester's version of backseat bingo?" Mac's breath fanned her cheek.

She closed the glove box, and then flipped through Gramps's CD collection. "Here we are." She slipped the Conway Twitty CD into the player and skipped forward to *Slow Hand*.

"Claire?"

She could feel Mac's stare. "Who trapped you in that mine?"

"I already told you back at the bar—"

"And I said you were full of shit, and that I wasn't buying your explanation."

She turned up the volume. Conway's husky voice filled the car.

Wrangling out from under the steering wheel, she scooted across the bench seat.

Mac's eyes widened as she straddled his lap somewhat inelegantly, bumping the back of her head on Mabel's roof. Her boot heels knocked against the dashboard and her elbow whapped on the window.

"Claire, what—"

She covered Mac's mouth with her palm and sank down onto his thighs. "Since you refuse to tell the truth of your own free will, I'm going to resort to torture."

Scrambling around in such a tight place while hopped up on pheromones had her overheating—and not the sexy kind of sweating. She rolled down the driver's side window a couple of inches, and then did the same with the passenger side.

He grabbed her hips and adjusted himself under her weight. "So you're going to sit on me until I tell you what you want to hear?"

"Something like that." She shot him her most wicked grin—the one she saved for beefy firefighters and bronzed construction men—and reached for the button on his jeans.

"Whoa there, Speed Racer." He caught her hand in the act and pulled it away, his lips curled in a sexy smirk. "Like the song says, no heated rushes. Only slow hands."

The blaze radiating from his eyes melted the elastic in Claire's underwear. Her earlobes started to perspire.

"If you insist." Her voice came out sounding raspy. "But it will just drag out your torture."

She moved to the buttons on his shirt. As she bared his skin, her feet began to tingle—whether from the anticipation of skin-on-skin wrestling with Mac or the lack of blood supply below her bent knees, she couldn't tell.

His flesh felt hot beneath her fingertips. She rubbed her palms down his chest and brushed across the sprinkling of hair that arrowed down his abdomen and disappeared under his waistband.

Mac shifted under her again.

"Mac," she whispered in his ear, licking a trail along his collarbone, tasting his salty skin.

"What?" He clamped onto her hips and pulled her even closer.

"Tell me what you know." She dragged her fingernails up his ribcage, one by one.

"I know that I want you," he said, his voice ragged as she squirmed strategically against him.

His palms skimmed up over the front of her T-shirt and covered Pink Panther's chubby cheeks.

"So I gathered." She tipped her head back, eyes closed, as he spread kisses down her throat, leaving a burning trail in the wake of his mouth.

"More than I've ever wanted a woman in my life."

Claire's eyes popped open, the pin-sized holes in Mabel's leather ceiling blurring at such a close range. Her seductress role forgotten for a moment, she frowned down at the crown of his head. "Really?"

"Definitely," he said, his focus on her chest. "You're an amazing," his hands slipped under her T-shirt, "intelligent," he paused to pop the clasps on her bra, "beautiful woman."

Claire leaned into his hands. Oh, man. If he never stopped, it'd be way too soon.

"And if you don't finish what you've started here tonight," his tone dropped to a sexy growl that made her skin ripple with goose bumps. "I'm going to have to join the Polar Bear club."

The feel of Mac's hands, caressing, rubbing, and stroking, zapped every notion of rational thought from Claire's overheated brain. Even if her toes fell off from a lack of blood flow, she wasn't budging from Mac's lap until the hunger she'd been beating back for the last week had been satiated.

Grabbing him by the ears, she plastered her lips on his,

exploring his mouth until they were both gasping for oxygen. She wiggled on his lap again.

"Damn it, Claire," he whispered, unbuttoning her khakis and reaching for the zipper, "you're killing me here."

"Hurry." She dug her fingers into his shoulders, clinging as each click of zipper teeth brought her closer to what she wanted more than anything right now.

"CLAIRE ALICE MORGAN!"

Claire jerked upright at the sound of Gramps's voice blaring in her ears and whacked her head on the roof.

Heart hammering for reasons having nothing to do with Mac's hands inside her waistband, she gawked at the driver's window.

Gramps and Manny, faces pressed against the partially-open glass, peered back at them.

"What in the hell are you two doing in *my* car?" Gramps's nostrils flared wide enough to fit a wine cork in each.

Manny chuckled. "Looks to me like he's checking out her chassis."

Chapter Nineteen

Saturday, April 24th

Mac rapped on the door of Harley's Winnebago. From the grove of cottonwoods down by Jackrabbit Creek, a woodpecker let out a high pitched laugh and then rattled out a steady drum roll against the bark, mimicking Mac's knock.

Even the birds in this section of the R.V. park were a pain in the ass.

The door squeaked open and Harley stood there, grizzled with gray stubble, frowning. "Claire's not here."

"Any idea where she is?"

Harley shook his head and crossed his arms. His eyes narrowed, making Mac squirm in his boots. Claire's grandfather was obviously still pissed about last night.

"What are your intentions toward my granddaughter?"

Oh, shit. Mac was already running late this morning. He should have been on the road to Phoenix a half-hour ago. This was a bad time to look into the future.

"His intentions are to get her into the sack," Chester called from the window of his Brave.

"No," Manny said from where he was shaking out a floor mat outside the shade of his Airstream's awning. "Mac's not a dog like you. He's after her heart."

Harley grunted and held the door open wide. "Come in. I need to talk to you for a moment." He glared at his buddies. "Alone!"

Mac hesitated. He'd rather have marched into a grizzly's den in the spring, playing a trumpet. He gulped and stepped into the R.V.

The smell of bacon greeted him as the door slammed shut behind him. Henry lay sprawled out on a green couch, his eyes drooping shut, his back legs twitching.

Mac scanned the place, searching for signs of Claire amidst the trophy fish hanging on the wall, the newspapers piled on the table, and the empty beer bottles in the sink.

"Have a seat." Harley nodded toward the couch. Stiff-legged, he limped over to the radio and turned down Willie Nelson singing the original version of "On the Road Again."

Mac dropped onto the soft, fur covered cushions next to Henry. The dog didn't even flinch.

"Okay, let's try this again." Harley leaned against the kitchen counter, his arms crossed. "I'd have to be blind and stupid not to see that you are warm for my granddaughter."

Warm? More like red hot. Mac nodded, waiting to see where this was heading.

"What I want to know is if you're in it for the long run."

"You mean marriage?" Mac weighed the feel of that in his thoughts.

"Not necessarily," Harley answered, waving off the idea. "I mean ..." He wrinkled his brow, then sighed. "Let me put it this way. Claire has a small problem when it comes to men. She won't let any of them get too close." Harley stared at his feet, looking uncomfortable with the subject at hand.

"You mean she'll dump me before things get too serious?"

"More like she'll hike up her skirt and run for the hills like the devil is at her heels."

"Oh." Mac leaned back into the cushions, considering

Harley's words. To date, he had yet to receive a single brush-off from Claire. If anything, she'd played the pursuer as often as he. At what point was she going to start running? "Why are you telling me this?"

Harley shrugged. "You seem like a nice kid, and you're Ruby's nephew. I wanted to give you a sporting chance."

"Does that mean I have your approval?"

"Maybe."

Mac grinned. This must be killing the old guy.

Harley snorted. "But don't go getting all cocky. Just because you have a better understanding of your enemy doesn't mean you'll be the victor. If you want to keep Claire from running, you're going to have to come up with a strategy."

"A strategy?" Mac sat forward.

"Of course. You can't win a battle with just wishes and dumb luck. I don't know if you've noticed, but Claire is one smart girl."

"Oh, I've noticed."

Harley smiled for the first time. "It's good to know you've looked beyond the surface. After last night, I wasn't sure."

Mac's neck warmed. He kept his lips clamped shut. He had a feeling the ribbing about last night had only just begun.

"There's only one way to get through her defenses."

"What's that?" Mac asked. Wine? Roses? Poetry? Moon Pies?

"You need to storm the beach."

"Storm the beach?"

Harley nodded. "Barge in with your horns blaring and your guns cocked and take no prisoners."

"Guns cocked?" Mac was beginning to feel like a parrot.

"Yep. Then you need to dig in, hole up, and wait."

"Wait for what?"

"The rumble of her tanks."

"She'll have tanks?"

"Of course! She's not going to give up easily. When the tanks come, that's when the real battle begins. She'll stop at nothing to blow you away. But don't give an inch. You hold firm, call for an air raid, and level her defenses. The rest is rice, lace, and wedding bells." Harley paused, his eyes taking on a piercing glare. "You do eventually plan to make her an honest woman, right?"

Uhhhh ... "Sure," Mac said.

"Good." Harley walked over to the door and pulled it open. "So, now that you know what to do, go out there and get started."

Mac pushed to his feet, not sure at all what to do about Claire. One thing was certain, he needed to get the hell out of Dodge and ponder the inside information Harley had just shared—after he deciphered it.

He hesitated at Harley's side. "While we're discussing intentions this morning, maybe you'd like to explain what yours are in regard to my aunt."

Harley's eyes widened for a second, then narrowed. "That's none of your business, boy."

"As Ruby's nephew, I think it is. Despite the fact that you went out with another woman last night, I'd have to be blind not to notice that you're warm for my aunt." Mac crossed his arms over his chest. "What I want to know is, are *you* in it for the long run?"

⊷◆⊷

Claire escaped the magnifying glare of the late morning sunshine and slipped into the shadow-filled tool shed. She was beginning to feel like the greasy-smelling sweat hut was her home away from home, what with the Winnebago being

Gramps's territory and all.

As usual, the floor board creaked as she walked to the workbench.

Something had crashed through the fence in the north end of the canyon, and Ruby wanted Claire to fix the broken rails before some local rancher's stock explored the campground and left cow pies as calling cards.

Claire grunted as she lifted the metal toolbox from the bench top. She took three steps toward the door and the heavy chunk of steel dive-bombed to the floor, corner first, the handle still clutched in her grip.

The resounding crash of metal tools clanging together made her ears ring as the guts of the toolbox spilled across the floor.

"Well, shit," she muttered, then noticed that in the impact, the box had broken the creaky floor board in half. The opposite end had been forced up, pulling the nails free of the subfloor.

Great, now she needed to fix the floor, too.

Squatting, she righted the toolbox and shoved the wrenches and chisels and screwdrivers back into it. With the claw end of a hammer, she yanked the splintered floor board completely free and stopped, board in hand.

Under the subfloor, tucked away in a lidless cardboard box, was a briefcase.

"Holy Peter, Paul, and Mary," she whispered, gaping down at the silver piece of metal while bees buzzed excitedly in her stomach. Joe's briefcase! She'd found Joe's briefcase.

Claire brushed off the spider webs and blew off the layer of dust, coughing as it coated her lips and tongue and filled her throat and nose. Okay, so that wasn't her smartest move of the day. She searched twice for scorpions and black widows before hoisting out the briefcase.

Both latches were locked, the combination dials on

each side showing different numbers. She flicked them to all zeros, but the latches still didn't budge.

On to Plan B—a chisel and a hammer. The first latch gave way in five blows, the second in just four. There was more than one way to open a briefcase.

The hinges squeaked in protest as she lifted the lid, her heart thumping in her ears. The black, velvet-lined interior was stuffed with Baby Ruth candy bar wrappers and empty potato chip bags. She should've had Henry sniff around in the shed.

Claire picked up a sour cream and onions bag, grimaced at the crumbs lining it, and tossed it onto the floor.

"Crap." She glared at the crinkled wrappers and bags. Another brick wall. This was getting old.

She kicked the briefcase, sending it spinning across the floor. Wrappers flew and bags fluttered, and when the case stopped, a dark tan book lay in the bottom.

Claire grabbed the leather book, holding her breath as she unzipped it. She opened the front cover, and a matchbook dropped into her lap. The front cover had a pink flamingo on it with *Key Largo Estates* written in fancy cursive writing underneath. She recognized the name immediately—it was the same community where the Florida convict's mom lived, the woman she had talked to several days ago.

Inside the matchbook cover, written in pen were the words:

Jackrabbit Junction
The Shaft
9/28 8 p.m.
Joe Martino

The handwriting wasn't Joe's. She'd seen his penmanship on several of the documents in his office, and this was more round and loopy than his. She guessed it belonged to the guy currently sitting in a Florida prison cell, which meant he'd been right here in Jackrabbit Junction at one time. But why? What would Joe need with a convict? Claire had a feeling the answer to that question would in no way benefit Ruby.

She tucked the matches in her shirt pocket and lifted the book. It was a day planner, and a fancy one at that. Gold-edged, thick paper, and a soft, cow-hide exterior. Joe had expensive taste, as she already knew from the Mercedes.

Fanning the pages, she scanned the dates, her brow tightening as her eyes searched for ink.

"Hi, Claire," Jess said.

Claire jerked. A defibrillator would have caused less of a jolt to her heart. She needed to hang a bell around the kid's neck

"What're you looking at?" Jess skipped over and stared down at the day planner.

Claire snapped it closed. She didn't want Ruby to know what she'd found until she had a chance to look through it and judge the possible effects any contents could have on Ruby's life. "Uhhh, it's just a diary—my diary."

"You keep a diary, too?"

"Sure," Claire lied, tossing the book into the toolbox and gathering the remaining tools scattered about the floor.

"What do you write in yours? Do you talk about Mac?"

Claire paused, a screwdriver in hand, and frowned.

Apparently, there was no such thing as a secret in Jackrabbit Junction. "Of course not. Why would I want to write about him?" she said, as if her mind hadn't been busy lately conjuring all kinds of wicked ideas involving the hazel-eyed man.

Grabbing the tools she needed and throwing the rest in the handle-less toolbox, Claire walked out into the sunlight.

Jess followed and waited next to Ruby's old Ford as Claire placed the tools in the bed. "Because I saw him kissing you."

"You did?" Claire wiped her dirty palms on her shirt, trying to act like sharing sugar with Mac was last year's news.

"Uh-huh. Just like I saw your grandpa kissing my mom."

"He was?" There was hope for the ornery old coot yet.

"Yep. On the lips. I think he stuck his tongue in her mouth, too."

Claire winced. Grandparent sex—ugh. She'd been able to block out the idea of Gramps with a woman since they'd arrived. No need to break through that barrier now. "Don't tell me any more. I don't think my stomach can handle it."

She ruffled Jess's hair and dropped her arm over the girl's shoulder, leading her toward the cab of the Ford.

The itch to scan through the day planner tugged on Claire, but she could tell by Jess's attitude that the girl was going to stick to her side like peanut butter for the day, or at least until lunch. Claire would have to save the book until later. Maybe lock herself in Gramps's bathroom and then delve into it.

Jess climbed into the cab, then flashed Claire a devilish grin. "Manny said they caught you snogging with Mac last night."

Claire blushed clear down to her purple toenails. "Manny has a big mouth," she muttered and climbed behind the wheel.

Jess giggled and peeked at Claire from under her eyelashes. "So have you gone to second base with Mac yet?"

"What'll ya have, Willis?" Sophy asked as she set an

iced tea on the counter in front of the hardware store owner. He'd bathed in English Leather again. The sharp tang of his cologne overshadowed the ever-present grease hanging in the air.

"Just the usual today." He took off his cowboy hat and dropped it on the barstool next to him.

Sophy yelled through the order window. "Two German pigs, make 'em cry and smother 'em with Wisconsin wax." She turned to find Willis frowning at her over the top of a copy of the *Yuccaville Yodeler*.

"Why don't you just say sausage and onions, covered with cheese?" he asked.

Sophy smiled. "Wanna chase that with a bucket of cold mud?"

He lowered the paper. "Now you're doing it on purpose."

Winking, she tossed a packet of Nutrasweet in front of him.

He tore open the packet and dumped it in his tea. "Oh, hey, do you remember that guy who used to work with your ex-husband at the antique store?"

Sophy froze, ketchup bottle clutched in her grip. "Why?"

"Some girl came in the store the other day asking about him. She had that picture they ran in the paper years ago. You know, the Grand Opening one?"

Sophy knew exactly which picture, and she knew exactly who was asking. Claire was at it again. The girl didn't know when to stop.

"She wanted to know his name, and for the life of me, I can't remember. This damned steel plate," he knocked on his forehead, "makes my brain short out."

Pretending to think, Sophy placed the ketchup bottle down in front of Willis.

"Anyway, I thought you might remember who he was,

being that he was so chummy with your ex."

Sophy remembered all right, but there was no way in hell she was sharing that information with Willis, or that interfering woman. "Can't say that I do. It's been a long time since I thought about Joe, not since the funeral." *May he rot in hell, the lying bastard.*

"Order up!"

She grabbed Willis' meal from the order window and dropped the plate in front of him with more of a clang than she'd intended.

Willis didn't seem to notice. "Well, let me know if it comes to you." He lifted his newspaper with one hand and picked up his fork with the other, digging into one of the sausages.

"Sure." *Never.*

Beads of sweat formed on the back of Sophy's neck. She busied her hands drying cups to hide her shaking.

Time was short, her luck in the mine was running dry, and Mac had somehow managed to dig his way out. Sophy didn't need Claire poking around in her past, but stopping the nosy bitch without drawing a crowd was going to take some finesse.

Sunday, April 25th

Mac parked his pickup in front of Ruby's store. He glanced at the sky as he crossed the drive. The sun hadn't taken on its hard-pan glare yet, but the cobalt sky held the promise of another road burner.

His boot heels thudded on the porch. The smell of bacon hung in the air, making his mouth water. He hadn't stopped for breakfast on the way through Tucson.

"Don't you walk away from me, Jessica Lynn!" Mac

heard Ruby yell as he reached for the door handle.

Jess shoved out through the screen door, nearly slamming Mac in the nose with the screen. Her face was red and blotchy, tears threatening. "I hate you, Ruby!" she screamed, leapt down the steps, and grabbed her ten-speed leaning against the porch. Without a backwards glance, she sped across the bridge and peddled toward town.

Mac shook his head. Poor kid. Growing up without a father was tearing her apart. He stepped inside the General Store, letting the screen door bounce shut behind him.

Ruby burst through the curtain, a yellow dishrag thrown over her shoulder. Her mouth was tight, her face looked tired. "Listen, Je—" She paused when her gaze hit Mac. "Oh. Hi." Her mouth twisted into a grin. "Welcome back to Serenity Haven."

"What was that about?" Mac nodded toward the door.

"Just the usual breakfast chatter. You know—I'm an evil, heartless bitch bent on destroying everything good in Jess's life."

"She doesn't want to go to school in Tucson, I take it."

"She'd sooner have me pull her teeth out with pliers."

"Why are you pushing her to go then?"

Ruby sighed and pulled the dishtowel from her shoulder. "The high school in Yuccaville doesn't have the extra programs offered by city schools. I want her to have opportunities I never had."

"But what about what Jess wants?"

She folded the towel and dropped it on the counter. "This parenting business feels like eating nails some days. Worrying about her future keeps me awake at night. All of these 'what-ifs' instead of fluffy white sheep leaping around in my head." She frowned, her green eyes looked troubled. "How do you do what's best for your child and not hurt her at the same time?"

Crossing the floor, Mac grabbed the damp dishtowel.

"I don't know anything about raising kids," he said, gently nudging Ruby back through the curtain and following behind her. "But I do know a thing or two about being an only child. Jess wants to be with her family—namely you. You're all she really has. Now you're threatening to take that away again. If I were her, I'd be doing some kicking and screaming, too."

Ruby leaned against the bar. "But what if she winds up pregnant, poor, and stuck here in Jackrabbit Junction?"

"Better here than pregnant, poor, and stuck in some strange city all alone. Besides, Jess is too smart to get herself into that situation. She's like her mom."

"Yeah, I'm real smart. I'm nose-deep in debt with the bank calling me every other day. I wouldn't wish that on her even when she's tellin' me what a rotten mom I am." She looked over at him. "What did you find out about those samples?"

Mac schooled his features. While the news hadn't been overwhelmingly positive when it came to extracting the copper at a minimum cost, there was an unusually large amount of high-quality turquoise in those chunks he'd taken from Rattlesnake Ridge and Socrates Pit. He still needed to get out to Two Jakes and see how deep that vein of amethyst ran before giving Ruby the red or green light.

"I need to go over the figures, do some math, read up on the market forecast for raw material." Slipping behind the bar, Mac grabbed a soda pop from the mini-fridge and opened it.

He also wanted to figure out why Sophy didn't want him in the mines. Suspicions buzzed in his head, tainted with myths he'd heard over the years of lost and hidden treasures. Had Sophy found gold? Buried treasure? Odder things had happened in the Arizona mountains. He sipped the sweet soda.

Ruby's eyes widened. "Mac, you know I have to have

an answer for the mining company tomorrow at five. How long is this going to take?"

"As much time as I can find." He squeezed her forearm. "Trust me. I'm not going to let you lose this campground." Even if it meant him taking out a second mortgage on his house and cashing out his retirement funds—all of which were now in reach. After spending most of yesterday at the bank and on the phone with his stockbroker, it was just a matter of a few signatures.

"I just want to make it through this next week without collapsin' into a ball of weepy putty." Ruby squeezed her temples. "Claire was right—damn Joe and his lack of foresight. He hadn't thought about anyone but himself."

The mention of Claire's name made Mac's chest tight. She was the other topic horning in on his thoughts over the last twenty-four hours. If he told Ruby to sell, he'd be helping the mining company, and Claire would be pissed. Add Harley's warning to the growing list of Mac's Claire-based anxieties, and the tension knotting his shoulders and back cinched up another notch.

"Where is Claire?" he asked, hungry to see the Siren in spite of his apprehension.

"I don't know. She asked for the day off. Said something about needin' to run some errands."

Mac frowned. What kind of errands? Most stores in Yuccaville were closed on Sunday. It sounded like a typical Claire distraction.

"You want some bacon and eggs?"

"Sure." His stomach growled at just the mention. "Did Claire take Harley's car?" He hadn't seen Mabel in town.

Ruby flashed Mac a knowing grin. "No, she took my old Ford. After catching you two exchanging good vibrations Friday night, Harley grounded her from driving his car."

Chapter Twenty

Claire stared into the dark mouth of Rattlesnake Ridge mine, sucking in musty air while clutching the pain in her side. Eating that jelly doughnut for breakfast this morning probably hadn't been the best idea.

At least this time she wasn't seeing shooting stars, unlike a couple of hours ago when she'd climbed to Socrates Pit.

Any fear she'd had of being watched by an unseen nemesis had evaporated under the rays of sunshine burning holes in her skull. She'd thrown stones at the vultures that had circled mockingly overhead, taunting her with screeches.

As luck would have it, no Al Capones or Cruella DeVilles had been waiting for her inside Socrates Pit. Unfortunately, no clues about Joe's past had been waiting, either; nor had any sign of Sophy's presence. At the rate Claire was going, her odds were better at finding the Holy Grail.

She used her T-shirt to dry the sweat on her face and scanned the valley below, looking for any followers. Though Sophy should still be waiting tables at the diner, Mac might be back from Phoenix. If he caught her in the mines, she expected he'd chain her to the tool shed and feed her gruel and moldy bread for the next week.

The coast was clear as far as she could tell.

Claire grabbed her pack and the rope she'd dragged along and crept into the mine. She moved deeper down the throat of the main tunnel, shadows lurking just beyond her flashlight's beam.

She sniffed, then sniffed again, pausing every few feet to listen in the quiet dark. The last time she'd trekked back in this mine, she'd gone head to head with a vile smelling she-pig from hell. Another encounter like that would cost her a clean pair of underwear.

Grimacing with guilt as she passed the shaft where Mac's compass had fallen to its watery grave, she continued around several more bends before reaching the craters dotting the walls and ceiling.

Her thorough inspection of each cavity produced nothing but rat turds, nests of dried sage, and a furry ball of coarse gray hair—which she promptly threw down.

Next, she examined the floor, hiking even deeper into the mine, but discovered only aged pieces of timber and a rusty pickax. Her feet heavy with defeat, she trudged back toward the mine's entrance.

After pouring over the pages of the day planner she'd found yesterday in Joe's briefcase and finding no names or information whatsoever, Claire's hope for saving Ruby's land was sinking faster than a cement duck in a swimming pool. Maybe it was time to give up and tell Ruby to sell to the mining company. She recoiled at the thought of them destroying her grandmother's burial ground, but Jess and Ruby's welfares were at stake.

As she lumbered along the rusty rails, Claire's thoughts turned to last night's phone call with her mom, and her right eye started its twitching.

First she'd been chewed out for "forgetting" to call home last week. Then her stutter-filled yarn about there being no women prowling the campground, just the boys with their cards and cigars, earned her a lecture about lying to her mother—a skill she had yet to perfect, unlike her younger sister, Kate.

Claire figured next week's phone call would be about as fun as sticking a bobby pin in a light socket.

As she drew closer to the shaft, she slowed. Guilt returned to gnaw on her stomach some more. Who paid five hundred dollars for a freaking compass? Hell, she could have gotten one for the cost of just two UPC symbols from a Fruity Pebbles box.

She tiptoed to the edge of the shaft and shined her flashlight into it. The crystal clear water allowed a translucent view down to where the compass lay on a rock ledge about eight feet down. But watery depths could be deceiving.

She glanced at her rope. Maybe there was a way she could rig some kind of scooping device. Mac's jaw would surely hit the floor when she handed him back his expensive little toy ... uh, tool.

Rolling up her sleeve, she kneeled at the shaft's edge and stuck her arm into the water. The cold stole her breath. Her flashlight clenched between her teeth, she stared into the shaft while balancing her weight on one of the boards lining it. She'd been wrong. It wasn't eight feet down. Closer to twelve from the looks—

"Claire!" A high-pitched voice squealed from behind her.

Claire jerked so hard, her teeth cut into the rubber grip on the flashlight. A loud crack resounded from the rotted board she clutched before it snapped off in her hand. She tottered over the rim of the shaft for a second before plunging head-first into the freezing water.

Jess's scream followed Claire into the dark depths.

The cold water squeezed a gasp from her, and her flashlight slipped from her jaws and sank beyond reach. With water burning her sinuses, Claire struggled to the surface and burst through, panting, coughing.

"God! It's freezing!" She grasped the rusty ladder at the

edge of the shaft, which squeaked in protest at being used as a life-ring. There was no way it would hold her weight if she tried to climb out.

Jess hovered over Claire, blinding her with a bright beam of light. "Sorry 'bout that. Are you okay?"

Claire's lower lip quivered from the cold. She shielded her eyes. "If you ever sneak up behind me and scream my name again, I'm going to tell your mom about you and your buddy trying a cigarette last year."

Jess grimaced. "I'm really sorry, Claire."

The humble tone in Jess's voice along with the freezing water soaking into Claire's pores tempered her anger. "How'd you find me?"

"I was riding by on my bike and saw Ruby's truck. Why did you park down in that ravine?"

So nobody—namely Mac—would see what she was up to.

Claire chose not to answer that question. "Where did you get the flashlight? And quit shining it in my eyes."

Jess lowered her beam to the water's surface and dropped to her knees in front of Claire. "When I saw you climbing up to the mine, I grabbed it out of the glove box of the pickup."

So much for her commando-like attempt to sneak up the hillside without anyone seeing her. Claire hoped nobody else had been paying attention, especially now that Jess was with her.

"How are you going to get out of there?" Jess asked.

Claire glanced at her pack. Thank God she hadn't pulled it down with her. "You can pull me out with that rope secured to my pack."

"I don't know." Doubt clouded Jess's tone. "I'm not *that* strong."

Claire grunted, trembling in the cold water, fighting back the urge to splash the kid. "Okay, then tie it to one of those beams—"

"Hey!" Jess leaned over the shaft and shined the light into it. "There's some kind of treasure down there."

"—and I'll p-pull myself out," Claire finished, her voice starting to waver from the icy cold seeping into her bones.

"What do you think it is?" Jess continued, seeming to ignore the fact that Claire's toes were turning into frozen tater tots.

"Mac's compass."

"How do you know?"

"I was here when it f-fell into the shaft." That was a nice skewing of the truth. She'd have patted herself on the back if she wasn't busy turning into a human Popsicle.

"What's that other black thing on the shelf?"

"What black thing?" Claire stared past her waterlogged tennis shoes.

"That square black thing sitting next to the compass, close to the wall." Jess angled the beam slightly. "See it?"

Claire did, despite the fact that the water was growing slightly murky from her splashing around in it. She stopped kicking for a few seconds. The ladder groaned in protest at the added weight.

That "black thing" looked like a box. Claire's heart picked up speed. "Jess, you think you can hold that light still for twenty seconds?"

"Probably, why?"

"I'm going to d-dive down and see what it is." And grab Mac's compass while she was at it.

"What if something grabs you while you're down there?"

Good question. Panic rose up from her frigid toes, but Claire slammed the door on her imagination before things got too freaky. "Nothing is going to grab me. Just keep the light on the box, okay?"

"Ten-four."

After a deep breath, Claire performed a little dolphin dive and kicked toward the shelf, her hands in front of her. Her eyes burned in the mineral-laden water. She avoided looking into the blackness further down.

The light grew matchstick dim as she neared the shelf, and pressure had her ears aching.

She grabbed the compass, then the black box, only it wasn't hard like a box. It was soft, like leather. With her lungs nearing a campfire-hot intensity, she kicked for the surface.

"Now," Claire said between wheezes as she handed Jess the wallet and the compass, "help me out of this damned hole."

Jess tied the rope to a beam and dropped the other end into the water. Claire's whole body shook uncontrollably from the cold as she braced her feet on the inside edge of the shaft.

With a lot of heavy breathing, she hauled her waterlogged ass out with help from Jess, who almost yanked Claire's arm out of its socket in the process.

As Claire sat at the shaft's edge, shivering, she held out her hand. "Let me see the wallet."

Jess obliged and spotlighted the black leather. "You think somebody dropped it in the shaft by accident?" Jess asked. "What if there are thousands of dollars in it? I could buy my own ticket to go see my dad."

Claire held her tongue, not wanting to thunderstorm on Jess's parade. She sat up and unfolded leather. A California driver's license, still in perfect shape thanks to lamination, sat behind a clear piece of plastic.

"Well?" Jess's voice brimmed with excitement.

Claire stared at the face in the picture, her forehead tightening. "You've got to be kidding me."

Warm fingers of afternoon sunshine reached inside the mouth of Socrates Pit where Mac kneeled, studying an old map of the mine.

A lot had changed since the map had been created, and none of those changes appeared on the paper in front of him. Piercing screeches from a pair of hawks in the valley below added to the frustration making his head throb.

Despite the mine's cool dampness, his shirt was soaked, and he stunk like the inside of a boxing glove.

Over the last hour, he'd hiked through one side tunnel after another and found no sign of Sophy—no boot prints, jerky wrappers, or cigarette butts. Either she'd stopped visiting Socrates Pit, or one of the dozen unmapped tunnels held all of the answers.

Mac sat back on his heels. With Ruby's deadline just a day away, he should be researching the gem stone market and checking out that third tunnel in Two Jakes, not hunting Sophy's trail.

Maybe Claire was right. Maybe selling to the mining company wasn't Ruby's best bet. With the stash of amethyst in Two Jakes, and whatever booty Socrates Pit held for which Sophy was willing to kill, these mines could be worth more than the mining company was offering. Hell, the mining company execs could even be trying to put one over on a desperate widow, morality taking a back seat to greed.

Speaking of Claire, where the hell was she? When he left the store after lunch, she still hadn't shown up. His gut instinct said she was out stirring up some kind of trouble, but Ruby's Ford was nowhere to be seen.

Mac checked his watch—ten after four. If Sophy stuck to her usual routine, she'd wait until nightfall to show up at the mine, which meant Mac had another few hours until he had to get the hell out of there. After the stunt she'd pulled at Two Jakes, he didn't relish the idea of her finding him sniffing around in her lair.

He focused on the map again and decided to start with the network of tunnels near where he'd found her cigarette butt weeks ago. Rolling up the map, he grabbed his pack and flicked on his flashlight. If only he had more time.

With the newfound wallet stuffed in the waistband of her jeans, Claire holed up in the only place she could think of to escape from Jess's curious gaze, Ruby's worried glances, and Gramps's watchful stares—the Winnebago's bathroom. Nobody dared to follow her into the stifling, cramped quarters.

From where she sat on the closed toilet lid, she could hear the drone of the boys' voices as they swapped anecdotes outside under the awning. Periodically, Jess's high-pitched peals of laughter interrupted the hum.

Sweat rolled down Claire's spine as she pulled the wallet from her jeans. While the sun had almost slipped under the western horizon, the heat inside the motor home was still building after baking under the hot rays all day.

She flipped open the wallet and fished out the California driver's license. The man in the picture was the same man she'd seen in the three passports and the newspaper photo from Joe's grand opening. *Sidney Arnold Martino*.

How many other Martino family jewels could there be? Joe's mom and dad were dead, and he'd been an only child, so this had to be the cousin she'd heard about.

If this wallet did belong to Joe's cousin, where was the guy now? Ruby hadn't heard of him, so he must not have shown up at Joe's funeral. Was he back in California? If so, why had his wallet been left to soak in a shaft? Had Sidney been up in the Rattlesnake Ridge mine with Joe at one time?

A chill rippled down her arms. Or had Joe done something to Sidney to make him disappear, then ditched his wallet in the shaft to get rid of the evidence?

That would mean Ruby had been married to a killer, and Claire wasn't sure how to break the news to the woman. She couldn't very well just say, "Oh, by the way, I found out your dead husband murdered his cousin," over a beer at The Shaft.

Claire dug through the rest of the wallet. Besides a wad of waterlogged twenties, she found a laminated membership card to *Sugar Shack Adult Movie Rentals* in Tucson; a red business card for *Madeline's Escort Service* in Las Vegas; a Bank One Visa card for someone named Anthony Peteza (which Claire thought might be a name she saw on one of the passports); several illegible business cards all stuck together in a gooey paper glob; a red, white, and blue NRA membership card; a Nevada driver's license with a picture of Sophy on it; and a ...

Wait a second.

She returned to the Nevada driver's license. Sophy looked very pretty and much younger.

Why in the hell was Joe's cousin carrying Sophy's driver's license from Nevada?

"Hmpff." Claire sat back. Who said small towns were boring? Jackrabbit Junction seemed to be filled with closeted skeletons.

From her shirt pocket, Claire pulled one of the crinkled cigarettes she'd found in Joe's Mercedes—her emergency supply—and stuck it in her mouth, savoring the taste of tobacco. She needed a light.

Reaching into the back corner of the under-sink cabinet, behind the rolls of toilet paper and bottle of Pepto Bismol, she pulled out her box of tampons. In the bottom laid Sophy's two antique drawer knobs and the lighter Claire had found weeks ago lying in the sand.

The metal casing felt cool in her hand. Then Claire remembered its lack of lighter fluid and groaned, frowning at the initials engraved on it. *S—A—M.*

SAM? She blinked. "Well, shit," she mumbled around the butt in her mouth. SAM—Sidney. Arnold. Martino.

The slam of the screen door made her jump.

She banged her elbow into the back of the plastic stool and pain shot down her arm. *Yowch!* She needed to get a handle on her nerves. She was getting as skittish as a three-legged cat in a dog pound.

"Claire!" Gramps shouted from the other side of the bathroom door. "I need to use the latrine."

Claire shoved the cigarette back in her shirt pocket. "Why don't you use the campground bathroom?" It wasn't even forty feet from where he'd been sitting a moment ago.

"Because I want to use MY bathroom."

"I'm busy in here." She stuffed everything back in Sidney's wallet as fast as she could.

"Either shit or get off the pot, girl, because I have about a forty second window before my plumbing lets loose."

"Classy." She shook her head at his brashness. She had no idea what Ruby saw in Gramps.

Claire stuffed the lighter in her pocket, tossed the tampon box under the sink, and shoved the wallet back into the waistband of her jeans. She flushed the toilet for sound effect and slid open the door.

"Jessica said you found a wallet in the mine this afternoon," Gramps said as she pushed past him.

"Jessica talks too much." Claire grabbed a bottle of water from the fridge. She looked back to find him watching her from the bathroom doorway, his blue eyes drilling into her.

"What were you doing up in the mine?"

"Looking for something."

"Looking for trouble?" Gramps pressed.

She grinned. "I never go searching for it."

"But it always finds you."

She chomped her teeth together to keep from giving a sarcastic reply. Gramps being right all of the time was getting old. "Don't you need to use the bathroom?"

His lips thinned. "That's it. You're grounded, young lady. No more going to The Shaft unless I'm with you."

"What?" Her mouth fell open. "You can't ground me from a public place. I'm thirty-three years old, you know."

"If that public place is frequented on a regular basis by Sophy Wheeler, I can do whatever I damned well please."

"You've spent too much time in the sun. It's melted your brain."

"If it wasn't for me, you wouldn't even be on this Earth!" he bellowed. "It's my job to do whatever it takes to make sure you arrive back home in one piece."

With a parting glare, he stepped into the bathroom and slid the door closed with a loud *thwack*.

Sophy paused outside the mouth of Socrates Pit when the beam of her flashlight locked onto fresh tennis shoe prints in the sand on a trail she thought only the deer knew about. Those prints hadn't been there last night.

Creosote branches on the hillside rattled in the cool, night breeze, drawing a shiver from her. Upon closer inspection, she recognized the shoe print. She'd seen it several times before: behind her diner, outside her home, and up close and personal while wrestling on The Shaft's floor.

Claire had been to the mine.

Sophy's face and neck steamed.

Slinging her small duffle over her shoulder, Sophy

trailed the shoe tracks to the mine's entrance, where they disappeared on the rock outcropping.

She hesitated, the desert fresh air blowing wisps of her hair around. Most likely, Claire was long gone, but it wouldn't hurt to be cautious.

A few minutes later, as she crept along the main adit, she heard the faint clatter of stones ahead of her. Her heart drumming in her ears, she lowered her bag to the floor and fished out her 9mm.

A slug to the head should do the trick, then she'd dump Claire's body in a shaft and get to work.

She was out of time. Tomorrow, Ruby would sign over the land to the mining company and Sophy would be shit out of luck. No more Vegas hopes and neon dreams, unless she could find Joe's stash tonight.

With her 9mm leading the way, she inched deeper into the adit.

That bitch should have known better than to play in a mine after dark.

Chapter Twenty-One

Y ou've been a busy girl, Sophy," Mac said, holding his flashlight beam on the stash of tools partially tucked away in an ore cart that probably hadn't seen sunlight for over a century.

He lifted the short-handled pickax, noticing a Creekside Supply Company price tag stuck on the handle, the black ink still crisp on the UPC number. The ore cart was old, but not the tools.

He returned the pickax to where he'd found it next to a pry bar and shovel, then squatted to study the pile of igneous rocks on the other side of the ore cart. The ceiling of the chamber must have caved in, burying everything in the back of the cut out, but it was impossible to tell how long ago.

Flashing his light around the room, Mac focused on the big pile of rocks on the other side. Most of the stones bore white scratches and scars where a pickax had connected with them.

What was Sophy looking for?

His flashlight dimmed and flickered. He knocked it against his leg a couple of times until it brightened. When he focused the beam on the ore cart again, he noticed a second ore cart, half-buried, further back in the debris. Its rusty sides were camouflaged by the surrounding rocks.

Was that what she was trying to unearth?

Mac raised the beam to the cavernous ceiling. Fissure cracks branched across the surface. He'd seen fewer lines on a road map of Los Angeles. Turquoise—Mother Nature's neon sign for copper—coated the rocks, much like several other sections of Socrates Pit.

Loaded with copper ore, this mine was a bonanza. But extracting the copper would take a pool of capital, one Ruby wasn't exactly floating in at the moment. The mining company execs must be salivating at the thought of getting their hands on this hillside.

His thoughts and flashlight returned to the second ore cart. Sophy had cleared a small section underneath it. Rocks covered the top of it and cascaded over the side.

His light dimmed again until he banged it against the palm of his hand.

Under the cart, he found a critter's nest stuffed up where an axle connected to an iron wheel. He brushed away the dried greasewood twigs, coughing from the dust he'd stirred up, but found nothing more than the sticky remnants of stale-smelling axle grease. Rust coated the bottom and the wheels.

Frustration burned in his throat along with the dust. There was something in this mine—in this very room—that Sophy was willing to kill to protect, but what?

A glance at his watch drove him to his feet, his heart hammering. He'd been in the mine for too long. He needed to get the hell out of there before Sophy showed up to start digging.

Without a backward glance, he rushed from the chamber. He'd learned his lesson the last time Sophy had shared a mine with him. Cave-ins were not his idea of a good time. He preferred to face the deranged broad under the open sky.

The tunnel stretched before him.

Several bends in the mine later, his flashlight dimmed again, glowing no brighter than a cigarette lighter. He knocked the light against his leg.

The beam faded even more.

Dropping to one knee, he unzipped his pack and dug out a spare pack of copper tops. He flicked off the light, total darkness blinding him. He dumped out the old batteries and slipped the first battery into the body of the flashlight.

Light glimmered off to his right.

The second battery still clasped in his palm, he didn't move a muscle, barely breathing.

A beam of light bounced off the wall ahead.

Sophy! Shit, he was too late.

Hands sweaty, he pushed the last battery into the light, scooped up his pack, and slinked back toward Sophy's lair, trying not to scuff his boots as he stepped.

He kept the light off until rounding the next corner.

Two bends before the chamber, he slipped into a shallow passage, fifteen or so feet deep. Earlier, he'd checked out this short tunnel with a flash of the light. Now, he raced to the back of it and leaned against the wall behind a rock that jutted out of the wall.

Killing his light, he waited in the pitch black.

Several silent seconds passed, then the outline of his nose became visible. The light was growing.

He couldn't hear her footsteps, her breath, nothing. If he'd dicked around a few more minutes back in that chamber, Sophy could have snuck up on him and removed him from this whole equation.

If luck wasn't on his side tonight, she still might.

Mac peeked past the outcrop. As he watched, a flashlight came into view, then the hand holding it. Then another hand—this one holding a 9mm.

Holy. Fucking. Shit.

Mac's grip on his pack tightened so much one of his knuckles popped, sounding ten times louder in the shallow passage.

The flashlight whipped in his direction. He retreated a fraction of a second before the beam crossed over the outcrop, the shadow of it blackening the wall over his shoulder. He plastered himself against the cold rock, jagged edges digging into his lower back.

The beam bounced around the cave for several gut-wrenching seconds before sweeping away.

Mac counted to twenty, breath held, and peeked out.

Sophy, wrapped in shadow, slipped out of sight.

His breath whooshed from his lungs in a silent blast. Blood roaring in his ears, he stood there, trying to become one with the wall for a bit longer.

That was close. Too close. He needed to get the hell out of Socrates Pit before that crazy broad and her 9mm blocked the exit.

With his flashlight still off, he edged out to the lip of the short tunnel and peered around the corner in Sophy's direction. The dim glow from her flashlight and the faint smell of her perfume seeped around the bend toward him.

Dousing his flashlight with his palm, he tiptoed in the opposite direction. Several corners later, he pulled his hand away from the lens and picked up his pace, careful not to let his boot heels clop down on the stone floor.

Sweat ran in rivulets down his back. Every so often, he glanced behind him to make sure there wasn't a 9mm pointed at his head.

The touch of the cool night air on his face and arms eased the tension in his shoulders, the wide-open sky made breathing easier. Then he remembered Claire's mysterious absence all afternoon, thought about Sophy's 9mm, and tightened up all over again.

He clambered down the hillside, uprooting prickly pear cacti bunches and daisy clusters, scared shitless he wouldn't find Claire safe and sound at the R.V. park.

Way too many heart-racing minutes later, he killed his

pickup in front of the dark windows of Ruby's General Store.

His white-knuckled grip on the steering wheel relaxed at the sight of Ruby's old Ford parked under the cottonwood tree. Claire had made it home. She wasn't lying face down in some chamber with a bullet hole in her forehead.

He climbed out of the pickup and eased the door shut to keep from waking Ruby and Jess. The porch's wood steps creaked under his boots. The forty-watt porch light flickered, moths peppering it.

As he reached for the screen door, it opened. Mac moved back to let Harley step out.

The older man closed the door. He nailed Mac with a squint. "Your aunt is worried about you." He sniffed and wrinkled his nose. "You smell ripe. Where the hell have you been?"

Mac didn't want to talk about it. "Did Claire make it home okay?"

An owl cooed in the cottonwood tree.

Harley nodded. "You haven't answered my question." He crossed his arms and leaned back against the door, blocking it. "Where have you been?

In other words, Mac wasn't getting inside until he gave a sufficient answer.

"Out," Mac said, rubbing the back of his neck.

He needed to figure out what to do about Sophy, and until then, he didn't need Harley and his posse of old buzzards shoving their beaks into this sticky situation.

"Out where?"

"Just out." He didn't like the way Harley was staring him down, like he'd been busted with joints in his sock drawer. Two could play this game. "What are you doing here so late?"

Harley bristled. "I told you, your aunt was worried

about you. She wasn't fit to be left alone."

Ruby was no daylily. Underneath that soft southern drawl, she was as tough as the hardpan soil on the valley floor.

"Right. And judging by the lipstick smeared on your jaw, neither were you."

⬩⬥⬩

Monday, April 26th

Sophy's body hummed with anticipation.

As she lifted the last rock from the bottom of the ore cart, she nearly dropped it on her toe at the sight of a small, metal box. With a victory cry, she threw the rock toward the pile and lifted the box, its casing cold and dented.

"*Viva Las Vegas*," she sang, Elvis's voice echoing in her head as she used the tail of her shirt to wipe dirt from the lid. She ran her fingers over the small keyhole on the front, then shook the box. Something rattled inside, sounding like a handful of small stones—rubies, emeralds, diamonds?

While fishing a pocketknife from her jeans, she glanced at the chamber opening for the umpteenth time since she'd given up searching for Claire.

Dark and empty, the doorway looked the same as it had five minutes ago. But that didn't ease the tension in Sophy's neck. The nosy bitch could still be poking around in the mine somewhere, even at three-thirty in the morning.

She snapped open her knife and dropped to her knees. Her hands shook as she twisted the skinny blade in the keyhole.

Sweat trickled down the length of her spine, the muscles in her back and arms warm from hefting rocks about for the last couple of hours.

She'd searched high and low throughout Socrates Pit

for this box. The old map of the mine had been about as useful as a limp dick, since the passageway leading to this chamber didn't exist on it.

She'd scoured tunnel after tunnel, chamber after chamber, searching for the ore cart he'd told her about. Over the years, she'd dug out three different rooms, thinking the ore cart might be under all of the rubble, only to end up empty-handed.

Finally, hours shy of the mining company taking over the land, she held the loot in her hands.

The bright lights of Vegas glittered behind her eyelids, the sound of coins clinking in the slot trays filled her ears. No more suffocating under the stench of kitchen grease, day after day. No more faded orange curtains and torn vinyl booths, button-fumbling hicks with chew stuck in their teeth, dingy watering holes and one-horse towns.

She'd served hard-time for Joe. He'd stolen her youth. Now she'd take what she'd earned.

With a rusty-sounding clink, the lock broke under her blade. She dropped the knife on the floor and sat back on her heels, rubbing her palms on her jean-clad thighs.

She'd have red silk sheets, rhinestone-studded dresses, and a solid granite bathtub full of champagne.

Her hand trembling, Sophy touched the lid. It creaked as it flipped back onto the floor.

She'd dreamed about this moment for so ...

A gasp exploded from her lips.

Her heart flash-froze into a chunk of ice in her chest.

Reaching down, she scooped up a handful of marbles, squeezing them in her grip. Her breath grew ragged, a scream building in her lungs.

She backhanded the box, knocking it onto its side, and whipped the marbles across the chamber. The box's remaining marbles spilled across the floor, rolling every which way.

A glint of gold on the floor next to the now-empty box caught her eye.

A ring.

She picked it up and held it under the battery-powered lamp.

It had writing engraved on the inside. She squinted without her reading glasses, and pulled back a little until the words came into focus.

Forever your girl—Sophy

"No, no, no," she cried, staring in horror at the wedding band she'd bought for Joe with the money her parents had sent for her eighteenth birthday.

She covered her face and screamed into her palms.

The rotten, thieving, son of a bitch!

He'd fucked her over again.

⸺⸻✦⸻⸺

Mac stepped inside the General Store and found Jess behind the counter, scribbling down algebra problems on a notebook page.

The cool shadows inside the store were a welcome relief from the blazing sun holding court high in the afternoon sky. He could hear the rattle of the air conditioner coming from the other side of the curtain. The smell of cigar smoke—Harley's calling card—lingered in the air.

"Where's your mom?" he asked.

"In back." Jess nudged her head toward the curtain. She didn't look too happy to be stuck on cash-register duty. "With the others."

"What others?"

"The old dudes." Jess shoved a red curl behind her ear

and focused back on the algebra book. "Harley, too."

"What are they doing?"

Jess shrugged, which he figured in teenager-speak meant she cared more than she wanted him to see.

Mac tugged playfully on her ponytail as he passed her. He pushed through the curtain and hesitated at the threshold, blowing away the finger of cigar smoke drifting toward him. In the midst of a card game, the four of them seemed oblivious to his presence.

He cleared his throat. Heads turned and four pairs of eyes drilled into him.

The mining company's deadline was two hours away, and the lines streaking across Ruby's forehead made it clear she hadn't forgotten.

"Where have you been, boy?" Chester asked.

"Selling your secrets to your ex-wife," Mac replied and slipped behind the bar to grab a Corona from the fridge.

"Which ex?" Manny asked as Mac strolled up to the table. "The long-legged blonde who filled his pickup bed with cement, or the top-heavy brunette who chopped his favorite fishing pole into matchsticks and drilled holes in the bottom of his boat?"

"Don't forget about Bernadette and the time she tried to run him over with her '71 Monte Carlo," Harley added.

Chester smiled, his gaze taking on a faraway look as he lowered his cards. "That feisty redhead shot me in the ass with a BB gun, too. More than once." He slapped an Ace of spades on the table. "Damn, I miss her, especially in the sack."

Harley frowned and threw down a Queen of spades. "That woman was a couple of chickens short of a coop."

Ruby grabbed Mac's arm. "Well? Am I signing?"

The others quieted, their cards still in front of them, their attention riveted on Mac.

"Do you want to talk about this here?" Mac wasn't

certain this was something she wanted the boys to hear.

She shrugged. "I have nothin' to hide. They know what today is. Shoot, this place has been their home away from home longer than mine."

True, but they weren't the ones who'd been hanging onto it by their fingertips for the last year.

Mac swigged the cold Corona, savoring the flavor as he went over the words he'd contemplated on the way home from the Yuccaville library. He took a deep breath, uncertainty rumbling in his gut. "Don't sign the papers."

Ruby's brow pinched. "Are you saying ..." She trailed off, her mouth opening and closing like a malfunctioning garage door.

"I'm saying don't sell the mines to the mining company."

"But an hour ago," Ruby said, "Claire came in here and told me I should sell. She said you were right all along."

Surprise made him step back. Claire had said that? What had changed her mind?

"No disrespect to Claire, but she doesn't know that the land and those mines are worth more than the company is offering. I do. Don't sell."

That sounded a lot more confident than he felt inside at the moment.

"I have to do something about the bank. I need to have that money to them by Friday at closing time."

"Leave the bank to me."

Her green eyes sparked. That had gone over like a truck with square wheels. "I don't like the sound of that."

He hadn't figured she would, but since she was paddling up Shit Creek, she didn't have much choice. "Trust me."

"Where are you gonna get that kind of money by Friday?"

"It's already taken care of."

Her nostrils flared, and her lips compressed into a tight white line. "MacDonald Abraham Garner."

Mac winced at the sound of his full name.

"I will not take your charity."

Dropping a kiss on her pink cheek, he said, "Just trust me, Aunt Ruby. I won't let you down."

Ruby sighed. "Okay, but if this comes out of your pocket, your name goes on the papers as the land owner."

"No way. If I'm right about what those mines are really worth, the amount you owe to the bank doesn't equal half of it."

"Fine. You'll be part land owner, then." When he opened his mouth to refute her, she held her palm up. "On this, I get final say."

Mac glanced at the boys. Harley stared at Ruby so intently that he didn't notice Chester cheating, peeking at his cards. Manny smiled like a proud father.

"Let's talk about this more later," Mac said, turning back to Ruby, "after the mining company knows you're not falling for their line of bullshit."

"Okay," she said.

"Now," Mac tossed his empty bottle in the garbage. "Where's Claire?"

They had some unfinished business to attend to.

⊷⊷◆⊶⊶

Down in Ruby's basement, Claire sat slouched at Joe's desk, staring at the turn-of-the-century Rayo lamp that had been "electrified" to fit modern light bulbs. A faint buzz of electricity hummed from the lamp.

For the last hour, she'd hunched over five pictures of Sidney Arnold Martino—his driver's license, three passport photos, and the newspaper photo.

And for the last hour, she hadn't come up with a single

idea on how Sidney fit in with Joe and Sophy.

When it came to sharp detectives, she fell in the butter knife group.

Then there was the bone. She squeezed the bridge of her nose, not wanting to think about the damned bone that had lured her into this whirlpool of bullshit.

She slumped in Joe's office chair, the springs squeaking as her weight shifted, the scent of aged leather enveloping her.

She'd failed. Failed her grandmother, failed Ruby.

Telling Ruby she should sell to the mining company had left her with an ache in her chest. She'd sell her soul for a cigarette about now.

She had been so determined to follow through on something in her life, to finish what she'd started and come up with the right answers. Answers that would make the eight years she'd wasted in college classrooms add up to something, anything of value.

Instead, she'd ended up mired in a slough of clues with no idea on how to link them together.

Blowing her hair out of her face, Claire picked up the day planner she'd found in Joe's briefcase and fanned through the pages. There had to be something she'd missed that explained why some of the dates were circled in red.

Who kept a day planner with practically nothing in it?

Claire's older sister, Ronnie, carried a planner with her wherever she went. She wrote down everything in that damned book.

Then there was Claire's Aunt Mary, her mom's sister, who carried a day planner for the sole purpose of wanting people to take her more seriously. Aunt Mary liked to wear silver glitter eye shadow and hats with life-sized, foam pieces of fruit gracing the brims. A planner wasn't going to cut it.

She snapped the book closed. She'd run head-long into

another dead end.

With a grunt of frustration, she hurled the book at the door. It hit with a satisfactory *wump* just as the doorknob turned and the door opened a crack—no further.

"What?" Claire didn't even try to tone down her annoyance. She'd told Ruby and the boys she needed some time alone—a rare commodity over the last few weeks.

"Is the coast clear?" Mac asked through the crack.

Claire crossed her arms. She'd missed the smell of him over the last couple of days, even resorting to sneaking into his room and sniffing his pillow a couple of times. But just because she was hungry for the sight of him didn't mean she'd forgotten that he was deliberately withholding information from her. "That depends."

"On what?"

"Whether you came here to give me some answers, get hot and heavy, or just frustrate me more."

The door opened a bit further and his hand slipped through, her tool belt dangled from his fingers. "Does this answer your question?"

Her pulse stuttered. A flame flickered to life clear down in her toes. There was only one reason he'd be carrying around her tool belt, and it had nothing to do with repairing fences.

"I believe that particular deal involved you telling me who trapped you in Two Jakes mine. Are you going to spill?"

"If you let me in without throwing anything at me."

Claire narrowed her eyes. She didn't quite trust him, but the fire had already spread to her knees and was rushing northward. After the rotten day she'd had, she really, REALLY wanted him to spill. "Okay."

Mac stepped in and shut the door behind him, leaning against it with the tool belt still dangling from one finger. His eyes raked over her, his grin extra wolfish as he locked the door.

She gulped, her lower belly now a glowing furnace.

"You're locking the door," she said. It was a statement, not a question. She hoped that meant what she thought it meant.

He nodded slowly, his eyelids fluttering low and sexy-like as he eyed her mouth. "I'm storming your beach."

"You're what?" That sounded like something she'd hear Gramps and the boys say.

Mac dropped the tool belt on the desktop and rounded the side. "I said, I'm storming your beach."

He pulled her from the chair and tugged her against him, the desert-fresh scent of his cologne enveloped her, mixed with a hint of beer and cigar smoke. He must have said hello to the boys before coming downstairs.

"Okay." Whatever he meant, she liked the sound of it. Her body felt so wired she could jump-start a blender. Her skin burned, her fingertips tingled. She wanted every inch of him ...

His lips lowered toward hers. "Daisy Duck looks very sexy spread across your chest like that."

But *not* before he answered a couple of questions. She covered his mouth with her hand. "Hold it right there, Romeo."

Mac grunted, his hazel eyes smoldering with promises of wicked deeds.

"We need to clear a few things before the clothes start flying."

Mac raised an eyebrow.

"Who trapped you in that mine?" She lifted her hand, but didn't step back. Breathing him in felt too damned good.

The heat in his gaze cooled a couple of degrees. "Sophy."

"I knew it!"

"But you have to promise me you'll stay away from her."

Her eyes lowered to his Adam's apple. "Of course," she said, which she mostly meant.

But she didn't promise to stay away from Sophy's shed. Knowing for certain that Sophy was behind the attacks on Mac shot Claire's curiosity into the stratosphere. Something important was in the shed, and tomorrow she was going to find out what it was.

"Claire." Mac cupped her chin and forced her to look in his eyes. "I mean it. Sophy is dangerous—way more than you know."

"Why do you think she did it?" She veered from the subject before she started to fidget under his warning glare.

He rubbed his thumb over her chin. "She's looking for something in one of the mines, and I was poking around, getting in her way."

"I knew she was sadistic, but I had no idea she'd take things that far. Sealing someone in a mine is up there with cement blocks and gravel pits. That woman needs to be serving pie in a sanitarium."

"She's running out of time," he frowned, "well, as far as she knows. Had Ruby signed those papers today, the mining company would have been in those mines by the end of the week, and whatever Sophy wants would be out of reach forever."

Claire barely caught the end of his sentence.

She stepped back, needing distance to focus properly on the conversation. "What do you mean *had* Ruby signed those papers? I thought she was going to sign and hand them over today."

Mac leaned against Joe's desk. "I told her not to."

"You what?" A mouse's sneeze would have knocked Claire on her ass. "What about ... You said ... I mean ...Why not?"

"The mines are worth more than the mining company offered."

"How much more?"

"Enough that selling for the amount they're offering to pay would make Ruby look like a fool."

Claire plopped into the chair, her weight rolling it back several inches. "I'll be damned." Her grandmother's ashes were safe from the steam shovel after all. "But how is Ruby going to pay the bank?"

"I've got it taken care of."

"That's a lot of money."

"That's my business."

"I'm sure Ruby would disagree with that."

Shrugging, Mac said, "She and I will work things out."

"So what comes next?"

"You. Me. No clothes."

"I mean with Ruby and her mines."

Mac captured Claire's hands and hoisted her out of the chair. "I know what you meant." He dropped his hands to her hips and settled her in front of him, between his thighs.

"So what's your answer?"

"My answer, hmmm ..." he ran his fingers up her arms and buried them in the hair at the nape of her neck, drawing her in. His lips brushed over hers, then returned, hard and demanding, stealing her breath. He leaned back. "My answer is that Daisy needs to go."

In one quick sweep, he hauled her T-shirt over her head.

"Wow," Claire chuckled as he tossed her shirt behind him. "You're good at that."

"These need to go, too," he said, unbuttoning her shorts and pushing them to the floor.

His mouth claimed hers before she had a chance to react. She stepped out of her shorts as his tongue teased her. Her knees wobbled in anticipation, her head soaring.

The feel of hard, stiff leather against her stomach pulled her back down to Earth. She glanced down as he cinched the tool belt under her belly button.

"Now," he said and nudged her back a step. "Let me look."

Claire crossed her arms, not sure what to do with her hands while she stood in front of him in nothing but her satin bra, butterfly-covered panties, tool belt, and tennis shoes. Wishing she'd skipped the king-sized Snickers bar she'd eaten to ease her anxiety about her inability to help Ruby with her woes, she straightened her spine and sucked in her stomach.

Mac ogled, and then ogled some more. He twirled his finger. "Spin around."

Claire shuddered. *Dear Lord, the butt view.*

Now was the moment of truth.

She turned. "I'm not exactly Victoria's Secret catalog quality," she said over her shoulder, "but I'm handy with a torch, and can weld better than most—"

Mac grabbed her, spun her back around, and lifted her onto Joe's desk. The pictures she'd been looking at went flying. The lighter engraved with SAM dug into her ass. "Hey," she protested, pulling the lighter out from under her.

Then Mac was all over her, touching and rubbing and licking and kissing, whispering promises of the things he'd do to her, blasting rational thoughts from her head.

She tore off his shirt, popping buttons, and smiled at the sound of fabric ripping.

"God, Claire." He shed the remains of his shirt. "I've been thinking about this—about you, naked—for so damned long."

"Then hurry up and take off my bra."

He obliged in one swift move, then groaned as he stared down at her, tracing her skin with his eyes. His hands followed. Then his tongue.

She leaned back onto her elbows, allowing him more access.

"Your skin is so soft," he said against her stomach. "So sexy."

Claire wiggled against him, eager for what came next. "Mac," she whispered.

"Mmmmm?" he answered against her skin.

"Take your pants off."

His teeth nipped her hip bone. "I'm a little busy here."

Claire grabbed the sides of his head and forced him to look up at her. The dark hunger in his hazel eyes nearly turned her to Jell-O from the waist down. "Take them off now."

He shucked his boots and pants with Superman speed. She managed to kick off one tennis shoe before he found the inside of her knee with his lips and made her eyes roll back in her head.

"Mac." She moaned.

His mouth moved up her inner thigh.

She twisted and clenched. "Mac."

His finger slid up under her tool belt and lined the inside hem of her underwear. She was surprised the flimsy fabric didn't combust.

The delicious heat from his tongue circling her belly button made her shoeless foot shoot out straight, toes rigid in her sock.

The tremors started deep within her core. She knew where this was leading, and as tempting as it was to lift her hips to his mouth, she wanted him inside of her this first time. Foreplay would get its due next time around. "Mac!"

"What?" He pushed the tool belt higher on her waist and then cupped her hips.

She latched onto his bare shoulders, holding tight. "It's time." She gasped as the tips of his fingers brushed over her.

"Okay." He caught a butterfly on her panties in his teeth and started to pull down the thin piece of fabric.

She laced her fingers through the hair on his crown and yanked his head up so she could look at him eye to eye. His pupils were big, black pools. "If you'd like to participate in today's event, then you need to take action now. Otherwise, I'm going alone."

He nodded. "Take them off."

Claire needed no second bidding. She wiggled out of her underwear in world record speed. Joe's desk was cool under her bare skin.

A smile curled the edges of his mouth. "I meant mine."

"Oh."

She obliged. Then she stared. Then she melted.

"You better hurry up with that," she pointed at the condom in his hand, glad he'd thought ahead, because she sure hadn't and wasn't sure she could have stopped at this point without it.

He did and followed with a kiss that made her head spin.

"Wrap your legs around me," he whispered in her ear.

She locked her ankles behind his back. "Mac, there's something I've been wanting to tell you since you patched me up after the bar fight."

"What?" he paused right before entry, ready, his eyes searching.

"I really like you."

The corners of his lips twitched. "You don't say."

"And I really want to feel you deep inside of me."

He obliged in one swift shove. "Like this?"

"Yes." Her ankles tightened.

He moved in and out again. "And this?"

"God, yes." She leaned back on her elbows.

His mouth explored her cleavage, his tongue tracing

circles as his thrusts drove her higher and higher. She tightened around him and wiggled, increasing the friction.

A groan rose up from his chest. "Claire."

"You like that?" She did it again.

"Too damned much." Then he touched her with the pad of his thumb and the stars spun behind her closed lids.

She started to cry out and then remembered she was in Ruby's basement and moaned behind sealed lips as the waves of pleasure rippled through her.

Mac wasn't far behind, his lips on hers as he groaned into her mouth and shuddered under her hands.

"Holy shit," she said, smiling at the ceiling tiles. A warm glow lit her from the inside out. "That was freaking incredible."

Mac rested his forehead on her sternum. His hands still cupped her hips under the belt. "Slugger?"

"Hmmm?" She combed his hair with her fingers.

"We're going to do that again."

"Yes."

"Only slower."

"Yes."

He pushed upright. "And on something soft."

"Definitely." Her tailbone had practically dented Joe's desk.

"But you still have to wear the tool belt."

She laughed and turned her head, her gaze traveling from the Johnny Cash painting beside the door to the floor where the day planner had slid half out of its leather binder. Her fingers stilled.

"What're those?" she said under her breath, frowning at the two pieces of paper spilling out from between the planner and its leather sheath.

She scrambled free of Mac's hold, despite his protests, and rushed to the book. Her hands trembled as she scooped up the papers.

Chapter Twenty-Two

Tuesday, April 27th

Claire couldn't find her underwear.

"Where are you running off to so early this morning?" Mac's voice, gravelly with sleep, stopped Claire at the bedroom door.

Clad in her wrinkled T-shirt and shorts, sans the tennis shoes she clutched and her missing panties, Claire fished for a believable lie. Unfortunately, without caffeine, she had trouble just baiting the hook.

"Uh ... I was just ... Yuccaville," she answered. Pathetic, but after a night of sheet-burning sex, it was a wonder her synapses were even firing.

"The sun isn't even up yet."

"Yes, it is. Your eyes are closed."

Mac patted the mattress next to him.

She caught sight of her butterfly undies sticking out from under his pillow.

"Come back here," he said. "I haven't thanked you properly yet for getting my compass back."

Tempting, Claire thought, what with him sprawled on the yellow sheets, looking all tan and finger-licking yummy in his birthday suit. But she had a date with a padlock and a pair of bolt cutters.

"Where's your tool ..." Mac's breathing slowed, lengthened, "belt?"

Claire remained cemented to the floor until she saw his

chest expanding and collapsing rhythmically. Then she tiptoed over, pulled out her undies, and stuffed them in her shoes. The door hinges creaked as she slipped out of the bedroom.

She tiptoed down the hall toward the stairs, sniffing for a whiff of brewed coffee. If Ruby was already up, Claire was busted. At this point, the fewer who knew she'd spent the night rubbing skin with Mac the better.

As she hit the bottom stair, the door to Ruby's bedroom opened. Claire paused, her bare foot hanging in midair.

Gramps stepped out of the room and quietly pulled the door shut behind him. He jolted in surprise when he saw her standing so close to him.

"Jesus Christ, girl," he whispered and backed against the closed door, holding his chest. "You shouldn't sneak up on an old man like that."

Claire noticed the stubble covering his cheeks and jaw and grinned. "You were in Ruby's bedroom."

"So?"

"What were you doing in her bedroom?"

Gramps narrowed his eyes. "None of your business."

Her grin widened. The man needed a new line.

His gaze lowered to the shoes she was still hanging on to. "Why are your skivvies stuffed in your shoe?"

Without looking down, Claire shoved her butterfly panties deeper into her tennis shoe. "They aren't mine," she lied for the second time in less than five minutes. She was on a roll this morning. At the rate she was going, she'd be roasting in Hell by mid-afternoon.

"Your shirt is buttoned crooked," she said to distract him and pushed past him as he frowned at the buttons that were done up correctly.

She was down the hall and halfway through the rec room by the time he caught up with her.

"My shirt is just fine," he said to her back.

"What was it doing off in the first place?" She wondered what Rosy would say if she found out he'd been rolling around in Ruby's sheets all night.

Gramps followed her out the back door into the morning air, already stale with heat. The sun warmed her like a towel straight from the dryer.

"You have enough trouble of your own brewing, no need to nose into mine," Gramps said.

"What are you talking about?" She hobbled over the sharp gravel toward Ruby's old Ford. With Gramps tight on her tail, she'd sooner walk across a bed of nails than take the time to dig out her underwear and slip on her shoes.

"You spent the night with Mac."

"Yeah, so what?" Unlike Gramps, she had no problem owning up.

"What happens whenever you jump into bed with a man?"

Claire didn't really see how this was appropriate subject matter before breakfast, especially since the other participant was her grandfather, but she answered anyway. "I don't know. I have sex with him?"

Ah, sarcasm—her favorite.

"Quit being smart with me and answer the question."

The door handle on Ruby's pickup gleamed in the sunlight. Claire yanked open the door with more force than necessary, wincing at its rusty scream. "What? I turn into the Wicked Witch of the West?"

"No, you lose interest."

She slid behind the wheel. "I do not."

"What about that Higgins boy?" Gramps blocked the door so she couldn't slam it shut. "You broke up with him less than a week after your mother caught you two in the pool shed."

"He was immature." The guy had cartoon rockets

wallpapering his bedroom. Claire was willing to overlook peculiar tastes in exchange for a chest of rock-solid muscles, but when he'd called her "mommy" in the midst of sex, she'd zoomed out of there faster than the Road Runner without even a courtesy "beep beep."

"And what about that boy with the old Chevy you were so fond of?"

So she had a weakness for classic trucks, especially 1959 Chevy pickups painted Plum-Crazy Purple. "He liked his guns more than his girls," she explained. With over eighty pistols, rifles, and shotguns hanging on the guy's basement walls, she hadn't wanted to stick around to see how he ended arguments.

"Then there was that foreign kid ..."

She dragged her fingers through her hair, tugging on it, growling deep in her throat. If they were going to analyze each and every relationship she'd bungled over the past two decades, they'd be there until sunset.

"Gramps, he was from Hawaii. Part Samoan. That's not foreign. And I broke up with him when I found out he was just using me to get closer to Natalie."

"Leave your cousin out of this. She has plenty of her own problems when it comes to men. "

Claire'd had just about enough of Gramps's version of *This is Your Life*. "What's your point with all of this shit?"

"That you're going to ride out of here with me in a couple of weeks and leave Mac in the dust with a broken heart."

Claire inhaled a big breath of desert-fresh air. Why had she ever quit smoking? "Since when did you get all soft-hearted about my boyfriends?"

"Since you chose Ruby's nephew as your latest mark."

Okay, truth or not, that stung. "Oh, I see. It's all about Ruby and you. Who gives a damn about good ol' Claire's feelings. Her heart's made of rubber. She'll bounce back like usual."

His blue eyes clouded over. "That's not what I meant."

"While we're being so honest," she gripped the steering wheel like it was bendable, "let's talk about what you're doing sleeping with one woman while screwing around with another on the side."

Gramps stepped back, his face flashing an angry red. "Watch your tongue, young lady. That's no way to talk to your elder."

He was right. Her grandma would've dragged her through the house by the ear if she'd heard Claire talk to Gramps that way.

"Fine." If he was done rubbing her nose in her past failures, she had a job to finish.

She slammed the door shut and cranked the window halfway down to keep the air flowing. Her internal radiator needed all of the help it could get to keep a meltdown at bay.

Claire would be the first to admit that her history with men rivaled Mt. Rushmore in rockiness, but this thing with Mac felt different, more comfortable—like well-worn cotton. But only fortune tellers and palm readers had a clue what the future held for her and Mac, and she'd be damned if she'd spend any more time bickering about it with her grandfather.

She started the engine.

"Where are you going?" Gramps asked.

"Yuccaville." The lie came easily this time.

She shifted into gear and spun out of there, glancing back once to catch a glimpse of her grandfather's puckered brow as he watched her drive away.

Half a mile down the road, she pulled onto the shoulder and let the engine idle while she dug out the two pieces of paper that had been hidden in the day planner.

With Mac watching her last night when she'd first

picked up the papers, she'd barely had time to do more than give them a glance before he was wondering what was more interesting than taking turns getting carpet burns. She'd managed to distract him with her mouth long enough to cram the papers in the pocket of her shorts lying on the floor next to them.

With the rest of the evening and wee-hours of the morning spent tasting every inch of scrumptious male flesh and writhing around under Mac's electric touches, there'd been no time for reading.

No time for cigarette cravings, either.

No time for anything but sex and sleep and more sex and less sleep. She needed a few hours to regroup both mentally and physically before seeing Mac again. A few hours to work through some of the crazy thoughts and emotions he'd ignited in her last night.

Claire glanced in the rearview mirror as she unfolded the papers. Sun shimmers and lizards garnished the cracked asphalt. The old Ford rumbled low and deep, grumbling at being forced to sit still. She locked the doors.

The first sheet turned out to be a hotel bill for one Señor S. Martino from somewhere called *El Gato Verde*.

She flipped the bill over and found the same handwriting as the signatures on the passports. After the hours she'd spent pouring over those pictures and names, she'd recognize those squished little "o's" with the curly loop-strings anywhere. Sidney Martino must have liked to write in cursive.

The words on the back of the bill made about as much sense as those on the front.

Chichis Cantina
Los Conejos
Fri, 9
box 10 carrots

Didn't anybody write full sentences in the Martino family? Claire tossed the sheet of paper across the bench seat, which left her with the other piece of paper. It looked like a letter or note, the handwriting feminine, or done by a man with serious closet issues.

> *I've been watching you. I know what you're up to and have pictures for proof. Unless you want me to tell the sheriff, meet me tonight at midnight up on Juniper Ridge at the Cowlick Creek bridge. Don't tell Joe!*

Don't tell Joe?

Claire chewed on her lower lip. The day planner must not have belonged to Joe, but rather to Sidney. But why had Joe hidden it in the briefcase? And if Joe had been the one who had hidden it, did he know about this letter?

Claire flipped the paper over, finding nothing but fold marks. Then she noticed the faint smell of something sweet, exotic in the cab. She lifted the paper to her face, practically wiping her nose with it, and sniffed.

"Holy frijoles," she whispered under the sound of the rumbling motor. She knew that perfume—Tabu, still clinging to the paper after all of these years. The leather day planner must have preserved it.

So, the letter was from Sophy. But why would she want to meet with Sidney? Now Claire had two links between Sophy and Sidney—the driver's license in Sidney's wallet and this letter. But what did that prove besides that they'd known each other?

Claire scanned the words of the letter again, searching for something between the lines, but found nothing more than white space.

With a grunt of disgust at her inability to figure out what the hell had been going on ten years ago between Joe, his cousin, and Sophy, she shoved both the bill and the letter back into her pocket. There was one other place to check, and the bolt cutters she'd hidden under the seat yesterday were her entry ticket.

A loud bark beside the truck made her jump and hit her elbow on the horn.

A blaring honk spliced through the clear desert air. So much for sneaking about; she might as well have tied cans to her bumper.

Two more barks followed, then the sound of toenails scratching on metal.

Claire leaned her head out the window and gave the mutt sitting outside the door a fur-scorching glare. "Henry," she used her boss-the-dog-around voice, "go home."

Henry cocked his head to the side and stared at her.

"Go! Shoo! Get outta here!"

The dog glanced toward the R.V. park and whined. He turned back to her and barked again.

What did he want? Most days, he didn't even spare her a glance. "Dammit, Henry. Go home!"

Henry crouched on his haunches then leaped into the bed of the pickup in a single bound.

Claire gawked at the ground where he'd been sitting. Gramps needed to lay off watching those professional dog shows—Henry was getting too big for his britches.

Whirling in the seat, she stared at the mutt through the dirt-fogged back window.

Henry circled twice before dropping onto his belly. He lowered his head onto his paws and peeked up at her briefly before closing his eyes and pretending to go to sleep.

What did he think? She'd graduated from the Stupid Academy?

She grabbed the door handle. The sight of a car heading toward her from town made her pause. She didn't want anyone stopping to see if she needed any help. "Screw

it," she said and let go of the handle. The dog would have
to join the search party. She just hoped he didn't freak out
when he realized where she was heading.

Grinding into first gear, she dumped the clutch,
stomped on the accelerator, and spit gravel into the ragged
bunch of sage lining the ditch.

It was time to find out what Sophy had locked in that
shed.

Ten minutes later, she killed the engine in front of
Sophy's place.

Nothing had changed since Claire had last trespassed—
same cinderblock house, same patch of daisies in the front
yard, same shed with a yellow padlock. So how come chills
were crawling up her spine?

Judging from the growl coming from the pickup bed,
she wasn't the only one feeling a little apprehensive.

Claire checked the watch Ruby carried in the ashtray—
six forty-five. She had hours until Sophy finished at the

diner, she needed only twenty minutes.

Stuffing her undies in the glove box, she slipped her shoes on. With a grunt of courage, she climbed out of the pickup and grabbed the bolt cutters from behind the seat.

Mac reached across the bed for Claire and found nothing but cool sheets and an empty pillow.

His lids shot open. As he stared at the popcorn ceiling, a hazy memory of Claire standing at the door replayed in his head. Where had she said she was headed?

His stomach tightened and twisted, and it had nothing to do with the smell of Ruby frying bacon down in the kitchen.

He shoved back the sheet and reached for his jeans. Minutes later, he buttoned his shirt as he trod across the rec room, the shag carpet tickling the skin between his toes. He could hear Ruby singing in the kitchen.

He paused in the doorway and watched his aunt flip bacon in the cast iron frying pan. She was smiling, her cheeks glowing. He hadn't seen her looking so happy in years. Not since she'd first married Joe.

"Morning," he said, smiling back at her. He crossed the green and white checkered linoleum, crumbs sticking to the bottom of his bare feet, and kissed her cheek. "What are you so happy about?"

"Oh, nothin' much. Just the typical stuff this morning. You know: the sun is shining, the jays are singing, and the old willow's branches are swinging in the breeze."

Sounded like the setting for a Disney movie. Mac had an idea her mood had more to do with the crotchety old guy he'd run into on the way to the bathroom in the middle of the night than the weather.

"What time did Harley leave last night?"

Ruby's face flushed. She kept her eyes on the pan in front of her. "I'm not sure. You want some eggs?"

"Thanks, but bacon and toast are plenty. Have you seen Claire this morning?"

"Nope, but she took the pickup."

"Without asking you?"

"She asked last night. Said she had some errands to run this morning."

Mac frowned. He didn't like the sound of that.

Claire was hiding something—something she'd seen on those two pieces of paper that had mysteriously disappeared while she'd turned him inside out with her mouth. Knowing Claire, it was probably something that would make his blood pressure shoot sky high. He needed to speak to the one person who would know all the details on where Claire had headed off to this morning. "Is Jess up?"

Ruby shook her head. "I heard her alarm go off, but she probably won't drag her butt down here for another half hour."

Until Jess got up, he might as well sit and enjoy his breakfast. He poured himself some orange juice and dropped into one of the kitchen chairs, the padded vinyl hissing under his weight.

"How'd you sleep last night?" she asked.

Mac grabbed the *Arizona Daily Star* newspaper from the opposite side of the table. Sleep had taken a back seat to exploring Claire's body.

"Fine," he lied, swallowing the juice, flipping to the For Sale section.

Ruby carried the pan over to the table and dropped a piece of crispy bacon on his plate. "Really? Just 'fine'?"

Mac looked up to find her grinning at him. "Yeah, why?"

"Because your neck looks like you spent the night fighting off my vacuum cleaner."

Claire stood in the bright morning sunshine, heat pounding down on her like a sledgehammer. Sparrows chirped and chattered around her while goose bumps raced up and down her limbs.

Now that she stood in front of the cedar-planked shed, her nerve wavered. Her feet wanted to turn around and climb back in the pickup, with or without the rest of her.

There was something in the shed that Sophy didn't want anyone else to see.

Was it dead? Worse, was it still alive?

Claire rubbed the back of her neck, not sure she really wanted to find out.

Henry whined at her feet.

Maybe rushing over here wasn't the wisest action to take. Maybe she should have stayed and tried to convince Mac to come with her.

Nah. He'd never have gone for it. This was something she was going to have to do on her own.

She squashed the flutters of fear flapping around in her gut and strode to the shed door. With one strong squeeze, she cut through the yellow padlock and dropped the broken lock and the bolt cutters on the ground.

Henry whined again.

She looked back at the mutt. The old boy crouched in the shade next to the front tire, his snout resting on his front paws, his eyes glued to the shed like it might shudder to life and attack him at any moment.

"You big wimp," she said, while a shrill voice in her head brought up the fact that the dog had already been inside the shed and might be the wiser of the two of them.

Taking a deep breath, she pulled open the door. The screech from the rusty hinges echoed across the valley. She winced, feeling about as sneaky as a rhino on roller skates this morning.

Shadows waited for her on the other side of the jamb.

Something brushed against her leg. She glanced down to find Henry standing next to her, his back quarter leaning against her calf as he stared into the shed's gloomy interior.

"Shall we?" she asked the dog, as if someone who liked to clean himself in front of mixed company could talk any sense into her.

He growled deep in his throat.

A tremor shot through her before she could hold it back. "Oh, knock it off."

Without further hesitation, she stepped into the cool, dark building. Its metal roof hadn't had a chance to soak up the heat yet, but in another couple of hours, the place would rival the Sahara.

As her eyes adjusted to the semi-darkness, she sniffed—stale air and old grease, but no dead bodies. Well, at least no rotting ones. That didn't rule out skeletons, though.

Something scurried along the packed dirt floor in the far corner—a sound effect she could have done without. Henry barked twice and raced over to investigate.

Where was the light? There had to be a light.

She felt along the wall for a switch, her fingers brushing over sticky cobwebs. Something with too many legs to be friendly scuttled over the back of her hand. She grimaced and yanked her hand back, wiping it on her pants as she wondered how many scorpions could live in a shed this size. What about brown recluses or black widows?

She didn't even want to think about the snakes down in these parts.

With an involuntary shiver, she pulled out the small penlight she'd found in Ruby's glove box and wished Jess had put the other flashlight back.

Not five feet in front of her was a tarp-covered El Camino. The shape of the bed gave the secret away. The wire-wheels peeking out from underneath sparkled like chromed Ferris wheels.

Claire rounded the front of the car, bypassing a long workbench covered with cans and bottles containing everything needed to wash a car and then some.

She shined the light on the far wall. No pentacles or pentagrams, no symbols for the four elements or four seasons, no upside-down crosses or Latin words scrawled in pig's blood, or any blood for that matter. Just tools—a shovel, post-hole digger, hand saw, pair of loppers—nailed to the wall.

So much for her notion that Sophy was making animal sacrifices in here. Claire was beginning to feel like a first-rate fool for making such a big deal of this shed.

She walked around the back of the car and shined her light on three, fifty-gallon oil drums sitting in the corner. A pair of thick leather gloves lay on top of one of them. She slipped them on, they were a size too large.

Holding the penlight between her teeth, she grabbed the metal lid on the barrel closest to her, squinted, and braced herself mentally for what she was about to find.

The lid lifted off like it had been blown off from the inside. It slipped out of her loose gloves and clattered onto the packed dirt floor, sounding like she'd dropped a tambourine in a porcelain tub.

Henry trotted over and let out a quick bark, staring up at her as if telling her to knock it off.

She pulled the pen light from her mouth and spotlighted his white and brown face. "Like you're one to talk." She glared at him, daring him to reprimand her again. "Your snores could wake the dead."

He walked away from her and started sniffing one of the car's back tires.

Turning back to the oil drum, she shined the light down into it. It was filled with rocks the size of her fist. She blew out a breath of relief, happy as hell not to find pieces of anyone floating in some kind of formaldehyde.

She picked up one of the rocks and held it under her light. Purple-tinged crystals glittered in the veins coursing through the granite. Another rock was littered with speckles of turquoise, flecks of greenish-blue copper peppered it.

The other two oil drums contained rocks as well, all similar in size, all with veins of turquoise or quartz of some kind. Sophy had been digging around in those mines for a while it looked like.

What had she been searching for?

Claire circled the rest of the car, her light bouncing off a roll of chicken coup wire, a weed eater, and several empty gas cans.

Her disappointment welled with every step. She'd been so sure there was something in here Sophy hadn't wanted anyone to see. Answers to all of Claire's questions.

She came to a section of floor along the wall where a hole had been filled in. The dirt was disturbed, not packed down like the rest of the shed's floor. A two foot chain was still attached to an eyebolt screwed into one of the two-by-four supports.

She squatted and lifted the chain. White hairs were stuck to the rust-flaked links. Her blood boiled. The odor of urine was strong enough to notice above the musty dirt, stale grease, and hint of Tabu. Claire dropped the chain. It rattled against the cedar wall, swinging by the eyebolt.

Poor Henry. While he wasn't her favorite dog, he didn't deserve to be chained and forced to sit in his own piss.

Something rustled in the canvas behind her.

She whirled around. Henry's little white ass and tail stuck out from under the canvas covering the back bumper.

"Henry," she whispered loudly. "Get out of there."

Henry ignored her, as usual. He crawled up over the tailgate and into the bed of the El Camino. The lump of his body under the canvas showed his progress, like Bugs Bunny tunneling for the South Pole, as he walked across the bed and stood on his hind legs at the back window.

Then the lump disappeared, and Claire could hear him sniffing and scratching at something inside the cab of the car.

"Shit!" She didn't need Sophy finding any evidence of her being here, especially not dirty paw prints on the seat.

She raced around to the back of the car and pulled at the strings that held the tarp on. Her fingers fumbled with the knot. She stopped, took a deep breath, and then untied the damned thing.

After loosening the rigging, she unrolled the canvas a few feet over the bed. Blue paint, so dark that it looked black without the penlight, shined back at her. She let out a low whistle and ran her hand along the porcelain smooth surface of the tailgate. No wonder Sophy kept this puppy inside and under wraps. Claire knew a hand-rubbed paint job when she saw one.

The muffled sounds of scratching and growling came from somewhere under the tarp, reminding her that she hadn't come here for the car show.

She rolled the covering back to the middle of the bed. Careful not to scuff the paint, she climbed into the bed and ducked under the tarp. The smell of dry-rotting canvas coated the back of her throat with a musty veneer, making her cough.

She crawled along the grooved bed to the back window, which was open just enough for a beagle to squeeze through. She pulled it open wider and stuck her head inside, shining her light through the window.

"Oh, you rotten little shit," she whispered when she

saw the clawed and shredded mess Henry had made of the cherry-red vinyl seats. Clouds of stuffing littered the cab. "Henry!"

The dog paused, looked up at her, and licked his nose. Then he buried his snout back in the hole he was making and tore at the seat some more.

Opening the window wider, Claire made a grab for him. But he dodged her hand and backed up against the passenger side door.

"Come here."

He stared at her with small pieces of stuffing stuck in his whiskers and eyebrows. Add a few more tufts to his chin and he'd be Santa's canine twin. She could have sworn he was grinning.

Shoving the windows open as far as they would go, Claire squeezed her shoulders inside, but her hips didn't make the cut, leaving her butt hanging out the window. She stuck the penlight between her teeth and reached for Henry again.

He hopped to the floor.

"Damn you! That's it. When we get home, I'm going to take you to the vet and tell them you want to be a girl-dog."

He whimpered, but didn't budge.

She lowered one hand to the shredded seat cushion and tried to pull her hips further through the window. Her hand slipped down into the hole full of stuffing, her index finger catching in a spring and bending backwards.

"Ouch! Shit! Son-of-a ..." Her ring and pinky finger collided with something solid and cool.

Bracing herself on the seatback, Claire carefully removed her index finger from between the coils, then pulled out several more tuffs of stuffing. "What have we here?" she mumbled around the penlight at the sight of a small black box.

She pulled it out, gently maneuvering it around the

coils. The box was heavy for its size, which was about the width of her palm and two inches high. A small pop-latch held it closed.

The window sill was trying to slice her intestines in two. She un-wedged herself from the window, adding a few bruises to the growing list on her way out, and sat down in the bed.

Penlight in one hand, she tried the box's latch. It popped open. Her fingers shaking slightly, Claire opened the lid. "You've got to be fucking kidding me," she whispered. A potato chip bag? She lifted the folded snack-sized bag from the box. Sour-cream and onion—Henry's favorite. No wonder he was shredding the seat to get to them.

But the bag was heavy and bulky. If it held chips, they must have turned to stone judging by the weight of it.

She unfolded the bag and tipped it slightly toward her palm. Out tumbled several stones, pebble-sized. Her breath caught as they sparkled under the penlight.

Henry whined beside her. She glanced up to find him panting, his head sticking out the window, staring all googly-eyed at the potato chip bag. Some people—or dogs, in this case—just had no will power.

Claire picked up one of the stones and inspected it. It looked real enough.

Holy Chinese chickens! Could they really be diamonds? A whole snack-bag full of them? Why else would someone have hidden them inside the seat cushion?

Her heart rattled loud enough for everyone down in Jackrabbit Junction to hear.

She dropped the three gems back in the bag and shoved it in the box. "Come on, boy. We need to get out of here." Scrambling out from under the tarp, she held it up long enough for Henry to follow her.

He paused at the edge of the tarp and growled.

"Come on. I'll buy you a bag of potato chips on the way back to Ruby's."

He still didn't move.

"Jumbo-sized," she added.

Something clicked behind her and the light overhead flickered on.

Claire's heart stopped beating.

Henry whined.

"I warned you about trespassing." Sophy's voice, hard as the diamonds Claire clutched in her hand, chased the blood out of Claire's face. "I guess you need me to show you what I meant."

Chapter Twenty-Three

Mac was sitting at the kitchen table, eating the last of his bacon while waiting for Jess to come down for breakfast, when all hell broke loose.

"Jessica Lynn Wayne!" Ruby yelled from the rec room. Mac nearly knocked over his cup of coffee in surprise. "Get your ass down here this instant!"

The I'm-gonna-kick-some-ass tone in his aunt's voice left little room for doubt that she was about to go off on her daughter like a stick of dynamite.

Jess hit the bottom stair step at the same time Mac crossed over the threshold into the rec room.

The girl's eyes were wide, startled, as she stared at Ruby, who stood in the middle of the room, looking as if she was about ten seconds away from critical meltdown. When Jess's gaze landed on the paper clutched in Ruby's hand, her face paled.

A pepper-red blotch dimpled both of Ruby's cheeks.

"Care to explain why I found this in your backpack?" Broken glass couldn't compete with the sharpness in Ruby's voice. The paper shook in her fist.

"I ... I ... uh," Jess wrung her hands together.

Mac risked a step closer to Ruby, trying to see what was written on the piece of paper. One of Ruby's Betty-Boop checks was stapled to the bottom of it.

"You what?" Ruby asked through clenched teeth.

"What were you doing touching my backpack?" Jess crossed her arms over her chest and lifted her chin. "You have no right to be digging through my stuff. That's an invasion of my privacy."

Mac rolled his eyes. When confronted with a pissed off grizzly, only a teenager would be stupid enough to reach out and give it a hard pinch.

"I was taking care of your dirty jeans and T-shirts—the ones I asked you to throw in the wash *three* weeks ago!"

"I told you to stay out of my backpack," Jess continued recklessly. "You know it's off limits."

"As long as you live in my house under my care, nothing of yours is off limits. Now quit trying to change the subject and tell me why in the hell you thought it was okay for you to steal this application out of the mailbox?"

Jess's eyes filled with tears. "Because I'm not going to that damned school of yours!"

"Yes you are!"

"No, I'm not!" Jess's voice hit steam whistle decibels, making Mac wince. "And you can't make me!"

Jess ran over, snatched the application out of Ruby's hand, and tore it in half and then in half again. "I hate you, Mother!" she screamed, tears streaming as bits of paper fluttered to the carpet like oversized pieces of confetti. "I hate you for ever having me!"

Ruby's mouth fell open as Jess raced out through the velvet curtain. The front door jingled and slammed, then footsteps pounded across the porch and down the front steps.

The silence of Jess's wake was pierced only by the bells still clanging in Mac's ears.

He rubbed the back of his neck as he walked over to his aunt, who stared at the shreds of paper on the carpet. "Something tells me she's not very keen on attending that school," he said, trying to lighten the heavy air.

He scooped up the pieces of paper and dropped them in Ruby's palm.

Ruby's shoulders slumped.

In the blink of an eye, she looked every single one of her fifty-five years, and then some. "Do you think she really hates me?" The fire was gone from her voice. It sounded brittle, like someone had hollowed out her vocal chords and made the walls too thin in spots.

"No." Mac put his arm around her shoulders and pulled her against him in a gentle squeeze. "She's just using the only method she knows to make you listen to her."

"What am I going to do? It's too late now to get her into that school. We've missed the deadline."

"Enroll her in school in Yuccaville. Let her live here with you."

"I can't give her what that private school could have."

"That private school can't give her what she wants— you."

Ruby slogged over to a bar stool. "And what if she ends up living in Jackrabbit Junction for the rest of her life?"

"She'll still have you."

An engine rumbled to life outside the back door. Mac's ears perked, recognizing that gravelly purr.

"Is that your truck?" Ruby asked.

Jess must have grabbed his keys off the counter.

"Shit!" He sprinted for the back door.

⊷ ⊷ ◆ ⊶ ⊶

Sophy stood just inside the open shed door, a double-barrel shotgun in her hands. Claire wasn't sure how Henry felt, but she didn't plan on sticking around long enough to find out what gauge of shells were in the chamber.

"Nice car you have here," Claire said, patting the dusty canvas tarp covering the bed, as if they were just two people shooting the breeze and she hadn't been caught breaking and entering. "A real classic."

Some way or other, she had to distract Sophy long enough to run for her life with her tail between her legs. "Did you buy—"

Sophy cocked the shotgun.

Claire gulped. Her mother was going to be mortified when the paramedics called and explained that her daughter's body had been found wearing no underwear at all.

Henry whimpered, leapt to the ground, and scuttled behind Claire's legs.

Great. Splendid. What a brave guard dog Gramps had. Lassie and Rin-Tin-Tin just rolled over in their graves.

"It's Joe's." Sophy stepped further into the shed, bracing her hip against the front quarter panel of the El Camino.

The length of the car separated them.

A breeze drifted through the door, carrying a whiff of Tabu Claire's way—she was really starting to hate that perfume. "Joe's what?"

"Joe's car."

"You mean Joe Martino?"

"Yes, Joe Martino, you two-bit idiot."

"As in your ex-husband?"

Sophy sighed. "As in the bastard who promised me glitter and gold, but didn't deliver horseshit."

"How'd you get his car?" Had she stolen it from Ruby? That would explain why she was hiding it behind a padlock.

"I bought it after the asshole was worm food."

"Ruby sold it to you?" Claire had trouble believing Ruby would sell anything to Sophy.

Sophy sneered. "Of course not. She sold it to a fella over in Yuccaville, or so she thought. But it was my money, not his. And now it's my car."

Sophy must have bought the car not knowing about

the diamonds hidden in the seat, which meant they'd belonged to Joe. Why else would Sophy still be slaving away in that faded diner every day?

Claire squeezed the box tighter in her hands. If she could just get the stones back to Ruby ...

Sophy raised the shotgun.

Claire almost peed her pants.

Henry zipped out from the other side of the car and beelined out the open door.

"Sounds like your knight in shining armor just hightailed it on outta here," Sophy said, her eyes never leaving Claire.

"You should have shot him first."

"Why waste a shell? I'd rather save it for you."

Claire raised her free hand in front of her, as if her fingers could block the spray of lead when Sophy pulled the trigger. The sight of those two dime-sized barrels locked onto her chest gooped up the gears in her brain. She had to stall Sophy somehow.

"Why'd you buy Joe's car?" Claire waged her bet on spite.

"Because he loved it."

Pay the winner, Claire thought. "More than his Mercedes?"

"Joe didn't love that Mercedes. It was just his way of flashing his dirty money in front of us poor rednecks. He thought expensive cars and Armani suits could make everyone forget his father slaved in the copper mines while his mother fucked any man with a five-dollar bill in his hand."

"Dirty money? You mean he stole money from someone?" Maybe, finally, she'd find out the truth about Joe.

Who'd have guessed she'd be hearing it from Joe's ex-wife?

Sophy lowered the shotgun. "He fenced high-priced, stolen antiques."

Blood traveled north of Claire's collarbone again. "For whom?" Claire pressed. The magazine article about those stolen gold boxes she'd found in Joe's filing cabinet came to mind.

"Some fancy suits out of L.A. They'd steal expensive antiques from ritzy houses throughout Europe and the United States. Joe would haul the goods here to hide in the mines until the insurance companies gave up the hunt. When the time was right, he'd move them to wherever the buyer wanted."

"Like Florida?" Claire was thinking of one man in particular who was currently serving time in a Florida prison while his mother took his phone calls.

Sophy shrugged. "Florida, New York, South America, Mexico. You name it and he probably knew a buyer there."

Mexico? That hotel bill from the day planner had been from Mexico. It had mentioned something about ten "carrots" too, which made complete sense now that Claire was holding a box of diamonds in her hand, some of which were undoubtedly ten *karats* in size.

But how did Sophy know so much about her ex-husband's business when Ruby hadn't even recognized Joe's cousin in that newspaper article?

Cousin ... a subject that might buy Claire even more time while she waited for some brilliant escape plan to pop into her head. Lord knew Henry, the chicken shit, wasn't going to come back and save the day. "Did you know Joe's cousin, Sidney?"

"Maybe." Sophy's eyes narrowed. "Why?"

Maybe, my ass, Claire thought. Sidney had had Sophy's Nevada driver's license in his wallet—that kind of connection didn't just happen by chance.

"Was he as dirty as Joe?" Those three passports sure

made it look like it.

"Dirtier. But dumber than an inbred chicken."

"He worked with Joe on this antique fencing business?"

If that silver lighter with the S.A.M. initials was anything to go by, Sidney's fingers had definitely been in somebody's pocket. And if he'd been helping Joe move antiques in and out of those mines, that might explain the lighter lying in the valley below Rattlesnake Ridge. But there was still the matter of the man's wallet. Dropping a lighter in the sand is one thing. Dropping a wallet down a water-filled shaft didn't seem nearly as random.

"Whenever Joe would let him."

"Then he disappeared," she guessed, hoping Sophy would fill in the huge blank that had stumped Claire for weeks.

Sophy nodded, a sharp-toothed grin on her lips.

Claire back-stepped until she was even with the rear bumper. There was something in that grin that made her knees wobble.

"You know what happened to him, don't you?" It didn't take a Sherlock Holmes wanna-be to figure that one out.

Sophy nodded again.

"What?" That came out more breathless than Claire would have liked. She didn't want to sound frightened. Squeaking would only excite the snake.

The shotgun swung up.

"He knew too much, so I killed him."

"Oh." That was an answer Claire hadn't considered. Silly her.

"And now, so do you."

Claire had trouble hearing Sophy's voice clearly over the whooshing sound of fear flooding her skull. Her legs, seemingly of their own volition, took another step backwards.

"Say goodnight, Claire."

So much for following through on something and finishing it for once. Sophy was going to blow a hole through her. What kind of a frickin' reward was that?

Sophy squeezed the trigger.

———◆———

"Give me the keys," Mac said over the guttural rattle of his truck's engine.

He leaned against the warm driver's side door, the smell of exhaust thick in the air. Sunshine reflected off the chrome mirror next to him, spotlighting Jess's face. "Give me the keys and I'll forget you even thought about taking off in my truck."

Jess's lower lip trembled. Her hands were locked onto the steering wheel with a white-knuckled grip. So far, she hadn't had enough guts—or stupidity—to put it in gear.

"I don't want to go to Tucson."

"You don't have to."

"*She* keeps trying to make me."

"Your mom didn't understand how important it was to you to stay with her. Now she does."

She turned to him, her eyes filled with tears. The last time he'd seen such a sad expression was at the dog pound. "I don't want to go away, anymore."

"I know." He squeezed her chin, shaking her head slightly. "Now go inside and tell your mom that."

"She won't listen."

"She will this time, I bet."

Jess sniffed, then turned off the engine and dropped the keys in Mac's palm. "I wasn't really going to steal your truck," she said as she stepped to the ground.

"Good." He watched her as she walked toward the

house, her feet seeming to drag through the dirt more and more as she neared the back door. He couldn't blame her. Even if Ruby and Jess did reach some kind of understanding about school, Jess had still stolen her mom's mail. Ruby wouldn't let that go unpunished.

As she reached the door, he remembered what he'd been waiting to ask her all morning. "Hey, Jess?"

She turned toward him. "Yeah?"

"Do you know where Claire went this morning?"

"No."

"Damn," he muttered under his breath.

"But yesterday I saw her put those big scissors behind the seat of Mom's truck."

"Big scissors?"

"You know. Those scissors you used to cut through that rusted slider bolt on the back gate last year."

A warning trumpet blared in Mac's head. "You mean the bolt cutters?"

"Yeah, those."

"God damn it!" As soon as he found Claire, he was going to lock her in Ruby's basement for the rest of her life.

"What?"

"Never mind. I'll be back in a bit."

Mac climbed into his pickup. What part of "stay away from Sophy, she's dangerous" did Claire not understand?

⇥⇥◆⇥⇥

"Come out, come out wherever you are," Sophy taunted in a singsong voice. She slowly edged along the driver's side door, the shotgun cocked and ready.

Two more twelve gauge shells sat in the chamber, both reserved for Claire's hide.

A scuttling noise came from behind the tailgate. Sophy paused in her tracks. Sunlight trickled in through the splintered, grapefruit-sized hole in the plank wall. The girl's reflexes had been quick, she'd give her that. But the next shot would not miss.

"Sophy?" Claire's voice sounded froggy, like she'd swallowed a handful of dirt.

"What?"

"What did Sidney know that made you need to kill him?"

"Curiosity killed the cat, Claire."

"Well, since I'm going to die anyway for knowing too much, I'd like to hear the full story. Consider it a last request."

Sophy smiled. Sure, whatever it took to distract Claire. Sophy didn't have the time or patience to play hide and seek around Joe's car. "Arnie got greedy."

"Who's Arnie?"

"Joe's cousin—Sidney *Arnold* Martino." Sophy inched toward the back bumper, moving slow so she didn't spook Claire. "He went by Arnie all his life. It wasn't until that last year he started wanting to be called 'Sidney.' He tried to get sophisticated on us, wearing knock-off Armani suits, driving a used Lexus, carrying a leather notebook everywhere."

"He carried a day planner?"

"Yep. Although, I never did see him write a single word in it. He wasn't the organized type, had trouble matching his socks on a daily basis. He thought carrying that stupid thing made him look smarter. But what Arnie never figured out was that dressing and acting like Joe didn't make him as good as Joe."

"Ya see, fencing required people skills and patience— two things Arnie'd been born without. Until Joe came along, Arnie'd been a petty thief. Then Joe needed help, a muscle man to do the hard labor while he played the front man and kept the customers happy."

Sophy pulled out her lipstick mirror and held it out at an angle, catching a glimpse of Claire's legs.

The girl was squatting behind the tailgate, facing Sophy's direction. Blood trailed down the side of Claire's bare calf.

Sophy smiled. She hadn't missed after all.

"Were you married to Joe when he began fencing goods?"

"Huh-uh," Sophy said, shutting the mirror and stuffing it back in her shirt pocket. "I was wiping down tables again by then. When he came back to Jackrabbit Junction, he'd had his hands dipped in illegal shit for about a decade."

"Did Arnie move back here with Joe?"

"No. He'd just stay for a few weeks when he'd come. Back then, Arnie did a lot of traveling. He'd drive in at night with the goods from L.A. and head straight up to the mine to unload."

"How do you know all of this? Were you in on it?"

"I kept my eyes open. When Joe came back home, flashing his money clip around, I suspected he was doing something dirty to have that much cash. A degree in Business Administration doesn't buy you a diamond-studded, gold Rolex. When Arnie started showing his ugly face around town, I knew Joe was up to no good."

"Because Arnie had been a thief?"

"Because Arnie offered me five hundred bucks cash to fuck him, and Arnie never could keep more than twenty bucks in his pocket at a time in his life."

"Oh."

"You see, anything Joe had, Arnie wanted. Ever since we'd first met, back when I was hell bent on marrying Joe, Arnie'd wanted me." Sophy neared the back wheel well.

"So you slept with him?"

"Not until he finally gave me what I wanted—the truth about Joe's doin's."

"Did Joe ever find out?"

"Not at first. Arnie was dumb, but not a complete idiot. He knew Joe would kill him for leaking information to me."

"How'd you end up with a room full of pricey antiques?"

The realization that the bitch had been in her house made Sophy burn from head to toe.

She trailed her fingers over the smooth hickory stock. The idea of blowing a hole in Claire's skull made her pulse pound. "Nobody gets sex from me for free, sugar," Sophy said, careful to keep the anger out of her tone. She didn't want to alarm Claire. "By then, Arnie had figured out a way to skim from the big shipments without getting caught, and I wanted what he had."

"So why did you kill him?"

"He stopped sharing. When I threatened to tell secrets to a certain Mafia man who'd come to town looking for some expensive goods Arnie had stolen, Arnie panicked. He went and told Joe I was blackmailing him."

"You killed him for ratting you out to Joe?"

"Nope. Joe and Arnie cooked up an idea to link me with those expensive goods. Arnie broke into my house and stole some of my stuff, thinking he'd lead the Mafia right to me. But the idiot drank too much that night. When I ran into him at The Shaft, he bragged enough to make me realize I had to act quick or I'd be left for the vultures."

"My 9mm was enough motivation for him to join me on a trip up to Rattlesnake Ridge, and vice grips loosened his tongue. I found out he'd told Joe about us and they were going to set me up to take the heat for Arnie's stupidity. I had a better idea—if Arnie disappeared, so would the heat. Especially if I made it look like the breadcrumbs went with him."

"What did you do with the body?"

"You should know. You've already dug up something that belongs to him out in that valley."

"You mean the lighter?"

"Yeah, that's one thing. But I'm talking about something else."

"But that's the only thing I found out there."

"What about your grandpa's dog?"

"Henry? What about ... oh, my God! You mean the leg bone."

"Exactly."

There was a long pause filled only with the sound of their breathing.

Then, "You buried him alive?"

"Hell, no." She lifted the gun. "I put a bullet through his skull and then dug his grave in the sandy wash out by that big old cottonwood. But I didn't dig deep enough, I guess."

"Oh." Claire's voice sounded quiet, shaky. Like talking too loud might break something.

She could practically smell the girl's fear. Now was the time. Claire probably had that frozen, deer-in-the-headlights glazed look.

Sophy skirted the back bumper, her finger on the trigger.

But Claire wasn't there.

Instead, a little black box sat on the floor, the lid unlatched and flipped open. Inside, nestled in the red velvet lining, was a handful of sparkling stones.

Sophy's breath caught in her throat—diamonds! As she bent down to pick up one of the polished gems, two hands reached out from under the car, wrapped around her ankles, and yanked.

⟶⟶✦⟵⟵

Mac slowed to a stop on the shoulder of the road, letting the engine idle as he stared at the closed gate blocking Sophy's drive.

The gate had been wide open the last time he and Claire had come merrily trespassing along. It wasn't locked, but maybe it had been earlier. Claire might have cut through it and was up there sniffing around.

On the other hand, Sophy could be up there with that 9mm, just waiting for unwanted visitors.

He rubbed his jaw, scraping his fingers over the stubble growth.

Then again, maybe Claire wasn't up there looking for trouble. Maybe she really was just running errands, and there was a logical explanation for her packing the bolt cutters in the pickup. Maybe stress and Sophy's attacks over the last few weeks were making him paranoid. After all, Claire was a smart woman. She would know better than to ...

A movement up near the top of the hill caught his attention.

He shielded his eyes from the sun and squinted.

Something white was racing down the steep slope of Sophy's drive, heading directly toward him. Something that looked a lot like a certain beagle he knew.

"Damn it!" When was that woman going to learn how dangerous it was to go around poking rattlers with short sticks?

He stepped out of his truck. Henry hit him at chest level, slamming Mac backward a step. He'd managed to lather Mac's face with dog breath and slobber before Mac could get a solid grip on his collar and pull him away. "Whoa, boy, calm down."

A gun blast echoed down through the valley.

Mac stared wide-eyed up the drive. Icy fingers of dread poked at his spine.

"Claire?" he whispered.

With a sharp whine, Henry buried his snout in Mac's armpit.

Adrenaline kicked Mac in the ass. He tossed the dog in the pickup cab and jumped in after him.

"Hold on, Henry," he warned as he shifted into gear and floored the gas pedal. "We're going in."

⟶·◆·⟶

With her ears clanging from the second shotgun blast that had gone off as Sophy fell, Claire scrambled out from under the El Camino and lunged for the gun lying inches from Sophy's hand.

The sharp-clawed bitch was still flat on her back, gasping for oxygen, right where she'd landed when Claire had pulled her feet out from under her.

Claire latched onto the wood stock at the same time Sophy rolled to her side and gripped the double barrels. They both jerked in a frantic game of tug-a-war, neither winning.

"Let go!" Sophy yelled, bracing a boot against Claire's bare thigh.

Claire winced as a boot heel dug into her leg muscle, but held on tight. If she lost this battle, there'd be no others.

Dust filled her lungs as they writhed around, grunting and kicking.

Sophy pushed to her knees, pulling Claire up with her.

Before Claire could get her balance, Sophy lashed out, claws extended towards Claire's eyes.

Claire turned her head just in time to save her eye, but sacrificed her cheek in the process.

"Ouch! You bitch!" She tugged the gun hard enough to lurch Sophy closer. Without releasing her hold on the stock end of the gun, Claire swung her elbow, nailing Sophy's cheek with a dull whack.

The damned woman held tight.

Sophy hauled the shotgun toward her, pulling Claire within range, and slammed the crown of her head into Claire's jaw.

Claire's teeth jarred. Had her tongue been between them, she'd have bitten it in half. The taste of blood tainted her mouth. Pain shot up through the side of her face, but Claire clung to the gun, refusing to be shaken loose.

By the time she stopped seeing starbursts, Sophy was on her feet, dragging Claire on her knees along the dirt toward the rock-filled oil drums.

Claire shook the haze from her head and stumbled to her feet, using momentum to ram Sophy into the wall.

Sophy grunted in pain, but shoved back, using the wall to brace herself.

Claire's heel caught on one of the large pieces of quartz sitting on the floor next to an oil drum and she reeled backwards, her grip slipping from the shotgun. She managed to grab the top of a drum to stop from falling.

But by then, Sophy had the shotgun aimed at Claire's face.

"Now," Sophy panted, blood running down her cheek, "I'm going to put a hole in your fucking skull."

Claire clutched the top of the drum, realizing the lid was loose. She was just three feet from the shotgun's barrel.

Sophy's finger reached for the trigger, but the rumble of a engine and tires skidding in the gravel made her hesitate. Her gaze slid behind Claire.

With all the strength she could muster, Claire swung the lid up at the shotgun.

Sophy pulled the trigger as the lid collided with the long barrel. Shotgun pellets sprayed the shed's support beams, missing Claire's head by mere inches.

Claire didn't wait to see Sophy's reaction. She swung the lid down on the top of the bitch's head.

A loud clang rang throughout the shed and the lid vibrated in her hands. Sophy's eyes rolled toward the heavens, then she slumped to the ground in a rumpled heap.

Before Claire could celebrate her victory, a two-by-four rained down from overhead and smacked Claire on the shoulder, slamming her into the rear of the El Camino. Her forehead kissed the shiny chrome bumper on her trip to the ground.

Silence followed, filled with dust fairies floating in the air.

Claire blinked, her view of the shed floor perpendicular, watching to make sure Sophy didn't wake up ready for round two. Her calf burned as dust settled into her wound.

"Claire?"

She heard Mac's voice from far away and groaned in reply. Two furry white legs blocked her view of Sophy. A warm tongue lapped at her cheek.

Henry had called in the cavalry. Maybe she'd let him remain a boy dog after all.

"Claire." A pair of jean-clad legs took the place of Henry's. Mac cradled her face in his hands and brushed her hair back.

He smelled good, like desert sunshine on line-dried sheets. How come he always smelled so good?

"Claire, talk to me. Are you shot?"

"Mac," she mumbled through lips caked with dirt.

"What, sweetheart?"

"You were right."

"About what?"

"Sophy's dangerous."

Chapter Twenty-Four

Wednesday, April 28th

Claire woke up feeling like she'd been scraped off the bottom of somebody's shoe.
Sunlight peeked through the cracks of Gramps's faded curtains, burning pink lines on the inside of her eyelids. The pillow that cradled her face smelled like Gramps's favorite aftershave: Ice Blue Aqua Velva—so sharply metallic it chafed her sinuses.

What in the hell was she doing in Gramps's room?

Blinking the sleep from her eyes, she sat up, her spine cracking in popcorn-popper style, and stared at the bandage strapped around her bare calf.

Like a spring flood, memories washed over her ... Deputy Sheriff Droopy with his permanently sunburned cheeks asking her questions, scribbling in a notepad, and sliding the box of diamonds into a Ziplock bag marked "Evidence;" Sophy riding away in the back of Sheriff Harrison's Bronco as she beat on the window and screamed fogged obscenities onto the glass; Mac carrying Claire into the Emergency Room at Cholla County General; a starched white hospital room buzzing with candy-striped old ladies; and two tiny blue pills that made Sophy's shotgun fade away.

How long had she slept? Claire checked the bedside clock. Two-oh-nine.

She blinked at the date. *Holy shit!* She'd been out for

almost twenty-four hours. Those pills could drop a horse.

As Claire limped toward the bathroom, grunting with each footfall, she listened for the rumbling of voices outside, but the only rumbling she heard came from her stomach.

Fudge marble cake sounded positively orgasmic. Top it off with a chili-bean burrito and she'd never need a man again.

She winced at the mirror's reflection. Frankenstein's twin sister stared back at her, complete with greenish-purple bruises and steri-strips. She'd have to wear a ski mask for a week.

Showering stung more than soothed, but at least she didn't stink like an ape's armpit.

Tennis shoes were too much work after her jean shorts and Yosemite Sam T-shirt, so she slipped on Gramps's brown leather slippers and stepped into the heat-rippling air.

A Steller's Jay shrilled from the canopy of one of the cottonwoods overlooking Jackrabbit Creek.

"Stuff a cork in it!" Claire yelled back and scowled at a passing grasshopper.

Limping toward the General Store, she tried to pinpoint the source of unease making her antsy as a turkey on Thanksgiving morning.

With Sophy locked away in a Yuccaville jail cell waiting for an all-expense paid vacation to the big house, Claire should have been picking daisies and whistling "Zip-A-Dee-Doo-Dah." Instead, here she was snapping at Jays, cursing the sun.

Oh, who was she trying to fool? She knew the source of her angst.

His long legs and hazel eyes were always hovering in the shadows of her thoughts lately. The desert-fresh scent of his skin had been branded into her memory.

She kicked at a large pebble.

This whole head-over-heels-for-one-man business left her reeling, like she'd stepped off the Tilt-O-Whirl after spinning for an hour. But the way her heart flipped and flopped at just the thought of seeing Mac made it clear there was no coming back down to Earth now. She was totally screwed.

If only she could block out those nagging fears whispering in her ears, demanding she stomp out the fires he'd started and ride like hell for the hills—the Black Hills, that was. With or without Gramps.

At the sound of a rattling engine approaching from behind, she shuffled to the shoulder.

A pink Fleetwood Mini Motor Home rolled up beside her. Chester's sparkly playmate, Fanny Derriere, sat behind the steering wheel. Her rhinestone-studded cowboy hat blinded Claire with dazzles of reflected sunlight. Black puffs of exhaust filled the air as the Miss Piggy-mobile passed her and crept out of the R.V. park.

It looked like the boys' babe-hunting season was coming to an end, and none too soon for Claire. If she never saw another sixty-five year-old woman in a thong bikini and cowboy boots, it'd be too soon.

As she neared Ruby's store, she slowed at the sight of Gramps standing on the porch. Rosy Linstad was with him, smiling and laughing as she talked, her words drowned by the guttural growl of her red Chevy Dually idling in the drive with a Coachmen Fifth Wheel hooked on back.

Claire slipped behind the drooping willow branches, peeking through the leaves in time to see Rosy drop a kiss on Gramps's cheek, then crawl into her Chevy and cruise toward town.

She hid until Gramps disappeared into the store. With Rosy gone, the Internet Floozy Alert level dropped from orange to yellow. The sky seemed bluer all of a sudden, despite the fact that Mac's pickup was nowhere in sight.

She patted Mabel's hot roof as she passed and climbed the front steps. Jess sat behind the counter, smiling instead of shooting surly glares for once.

"Hey, kiddo." Claire grabbed a cherry Hostess fruit pie from the shelf. From the backroom, the King of rock-n-roll crooned about being all shook up. Join the club, Elvis, Claire thought with a wry grin. "Are Gramps and your mom back there?" she asked, nudging her head toward the curtain as she tossed a five-dollar bill on the counter.

Jess nodded and handed Claire her change. "Along with the other old dudes and Henry."

Chester's wheezy laugh blocked out Elvis for several seconds, confirming Jess's story.

"Mac around?"

"Nope."

The definitive tone in Jess's voice made Claire pause, her hand still buried in her front pocket with the change.

The kid hopped on the stool and lifted her bare foot up next to the cash register. Her face scrunched in concentration, she carefully dabbed neon orange paint on her big toenail.

"He over in Yuccaville?" Claire pressed.

"Nuh, uh."

"Up at the mines?"

"Nope."

Claire frowned, her heart hopping up into her throat like a bullfrog on PCP. "Where is he?"

"Tucson." Jess moved to her next toe. "Left yesterday afternoon. Said he needed to get back to work."

"Oh." Claire swallowed her heart back down to her chest. "I see. Did he, uh, mention when he'd be back?"

Jess shook her head, working her way to her smallest piggy. "But he left something for you." She dropped the nailbrush in the bottle and reached under the counter.

Maybe it was a note explaining why he'd up and left without saying good-bye to her. Maybe a phone number or address where she could reach him. Maybe a ...

"Here ya go." Jess held out a sealed manila envelope.

"Thanks." Claire took the envelope.

It was light, but slightly bulky, soft when squeezed. Maybe he'd bought her some lingerie.

She walked toward the curtain, taking a bite out of her fruit pie. The cherries tasted bland, picked too early; the crust dry and flaky, the glaze sugar-free.

Laughter greeted her as she slipped through the curtain. Wispy whirls of cigar smoke danced in the air, twirling about with the help of the air conditioner.

Her fingers itched to tear open the envelope, but four pairs of eyes kept her in check.

"Hot damn!" Chester said, his mouth open wide enough to catch flies. "You need to learn how to duck and weave, girl."

Claire slipped the envelope behind her back and walked over to the card table. They were playing with pennies, and judging from the stacks in front of Ruby, she wasn't taking any prisoners.

Henry barked once at Claire from the couch, then

returned to chewing on a rawhide bone twice the diameter of his head. Somebody had replaced his old leg bone—actually Arnie's leg bone—with a new one. The memory of Mac telling Sheriff Harrison about the bone Henry had found flittered through her thoughts.

"*Ay yi yi*," Manny said, tugging her arm to turn her in his direction. "Look at that shiner." He grinned at Gramps. "Please tell me there was mud involved. And bikinis."

"String bikinis," Chester muttered around his cigar while looking at his cards.

"No, thongs—with tops made from little triangles tied with dental floss." Manny showed an example with his fingers.

"Stop thinking about my granddaughter in a bikini, Carerra, and throw down a damned card." Gramps shuffled the cards in his hand.

Manny winked at Claire—the conspiratorial kind rather than the make-a-girl's-skin-crawl type. "Well, now that Kat kicked me out of her bed and left me limp and dry, I have to focus on the females left. Since you're busy being Mighty Mouse with Ruby, saving her day and all, that leaves Claire."

Claire looked at Ruby. "What does Manny mean by saving your day?" What had happened while she was playing Rip Van Winkle?

Ruby opened her mouth, but Gramps cut her off. "Never mind."

"But—" Claire started.

Pale blue eyes shot her a warning glare. "Remember rule number seven."

"What's rule number seven?" Ruby asked Claire.

"That's not fair," Claire argued. "This is different."

"How?"

"Harley, honey, what's rule number seven?"

"I'll tell you later, when we're alone," Gramps said to Ruby, his smile warming a blush onto Ruby's cheeks.

Claire crossed her arms over her chest; the envelope bumped against her stomach. What in the hell was going on? "Gramps, she's my boss. If you screw this up, I could be fired."

"I'd never fire you, Claire." Ruby patted her arm.

Gramps's eyes twinkled. The old buzzard had won this round.

"What's in the envelope?" Chester asked and snatched it from Claire's fingers.

"Hey! Give it back." She reached for the envelope, but Chester tossed it to Manny.

"Looks like a man's handwriting," Manny said, inspecting the penmanship on the front. He shook the package. "Sounds silky, like lingerie." He would know.

The boys chuckled. Ruby frowned at them over her cards.

Claire moved closer to Manny and reached for the envelope. He tossed it back across the table to Chester.

"Not funny, Manny," Claire said and poked his arm hard enough to make him jump before walking back around the table toward Chester. "Give it to me, Chester."

He held it away from her. "What's the magic word?"

"It's *black-eye*," Gramps said and threw down a card. "You'd better give her the package, Chester, before she gives you one."

Claire grabbed for the package and managed to get a grip on the sealed end of it. She yanked hard, but Chester still had a secure hold. With a rip, the envelope tore in half and her butterfly panties dropped onto the table.

Her first impulse was to keel over dead with mortification. Instead, she snatched up her underwear and stuffed them in her pocket.

"Cute panties," Manny said, laughter thick on his tongue. "I prefer lace and bows, but Mac seems like a butterfly-type of *hombre*."

Claire was having trouble ungluing her tongue from the top of her mouth. Overriding her humiliation, white-hot fury tore through her veins. Flames of anger seared her neck and her cheeks. That rotten, no-good son of a bitch! How dare he leave her there in Jackrabbit Junction without even a good-bye?

"Sorry, Claire," Chester said, handing her the other half of the envelope. "I didn't mean for that to happen." The solemn look in Chester's eyes spoke of true remorse—something Chester probably rarely felt.

She should have felt flattered.

"Don't worry about it," she said in a voice stronger and lighter than she felt at the moment, what with the hundred pound weight of rejection crushing her chest. "They're just undies. It's not like I haven't seen yours."

"*Dios mio*, who hasn't?" Manny asked, chuckling at the glare Chester gave him. "What, *mi amigo*? Just two nights ago, you circled the park in nothing but your rainbow sock suspenders and skivvies—the ones with the pink hearts."

"I did not!"

"Yes, you did." Gramps joined in the mirth. "You were at least three sheets to the wind at the time and pissed as a newly castrated steer because Nasty Nurse Nancy walked out on you after she saw Chester Jr. in his pre-Viagra state."

"Oh, yeah." Chester cracked open a beer and gulped down half of it. His skin looked a tad bit pinker under the bristle of gray whiskers. "I should have popped some pills earlier for her. She's a double-your-pleasure kind of woman, if you know what I mean." He waggled his eyebrows at Manny.

"I can't believe you use that crap," Manny said.

"Better than that Swiss pump you use." Chester grinned at him around his cigar.

Claire recognized an exit opportunity when she saw one. She backed out through the curtain.

Jess was adding a second layer to her toenails, singing some hip-hop song under her breath.

"See ya later, Jess." Claire passed the counter, not waiting for a reply, and stormed out through the screen door.

Racing down the steps, she limped as fast as possible back to Gramps's Winnebago. Fury drove her forward; embarrassment nipped her heels.

If she ever saw Mac Garner again, she was going to cram her underwear down his throat until he choked on them.

—————◆—————

Jess, Ruby, and Harley were all sitting on the front porch when Mac parked in front of the store.

The evening sun had lost its strength and was fading below the western skyline in a purple-shrouded death. Venus was out already, showing off with luminous splendor.

The air smelled clean, fresh, untouched by humans, unlike the man-made smog he'd waded through on his way out of Tucson in the rush hour traffic. Crickets were warming up for their evening serenade.

"Hi, Mac!" Jess said, a big smile warming her face. She scooted over on the bench to make room for him.

He nodded at each of them as he climbed the steps and asked the question that had been on his mind all day. "How's Claire?"

Ruby chuckled and touched Harley's arm. "You owe Jess five bucks. He couldn't even make it up the steps before asking about her."

"Have you no pride, son?" Harley shook his head in disgust, but the warmth in his eyes told a different story.

He dug in his pocket and tossed a wadded bill in Jess's

direction.

Jess caught it with a grin of triumph.

Mac dropped on the bench next to Jess, hitting her in the shoulder with a mock punch. "What did you think of the school?"

"It looks like any other high school—maybe a little smaller. Couldn't Yuccaville have chosen a different mascot? I mean a wild pig, how silly is that?" But Jess's words didn't hold much fervor.

Mac could see her happiness in the way she was swinging her legs and chomping on her gum. "As silly as you," he said, earning a light pinch in return. He turned to Harley. "Did all of the paperwork come in today?"

Harley nodded and draped his arm around Ruby's shoulders. "We're going to the bank tomorrow to sign everything."

Mac stared at his aunt, trying to read something behind her smile. "You sure you're okay with this? I can still call my—"

"This is better," Ruby said. "I'm one hundred percent okay with it." She dropped a kiss on Harley's cheek and snuggled into his side.

Looking away, Mac tried to hide his concern for his aunt. When it came down to it, it was her business, her choice. He'd made his feelings about it clear before heading for Tucson and Ruby had listened, but the stubborn look in her eyes told him she'd already made up her mind.

"Claire was looking for you earlier," Jess said.

Just what he wanted to hear. Mac looked at his cousin. "She was?"

"Yeah, I gave her the envelope."

"Unopened?"

"Of course." Two words, spoken indignantly.

"Good. Where is she?"

"Back at the Winnebago." Gramps answered.

Then off to the Winnebago he would go. Hey-hey, ho-ho.

"But you'd better be careful when you open that door," Gramps added. "She's ballistic as a badger with a burr up its ass and doesn't want any company."

"Why?" Mac asked as he stood.

"I don't know, but Manny has a bruise the size of my clock radio on his arm because he wouldn't listen to me and tried to go in and calm her down. You might want to wear your hard hat."

Minutes later, Mac rapped on the Winnebago door.

"Go away, Manny!" Claire shouted. Something hit the other side of the door with a loud thud. A metallic clang followed.

Mac waited for several seconds to make sure no other projectiles were going to be launched, then slowly turned the doorknob and opened the door a crack. He could hear Claire in the back of the Winnebago, the floor creaking under her feet as she tromped around, muttering under her breath.

Quietly, he slipped inside. A dented toaster lay on its side next to the doorway. He grimaced. The woman meant business.

Then he noticed the suitcase, stuffed so full it bulged.

His gut hit the floor. She was leaving him. Harley had warned him about her, but Mac had been stupid enough to believe he was different. To trust that look in her eyes the other night.

A ball of anger formed in his chest, burning.

He had two options now: turn and leave with his pride intact, or stay and fight.

He closed the door and locked it.

⸺⸺◆⸺⸺

Claire zipped closed her duffle bag. "There. Done."

Now all that was left was convincing Gramps to drive her to the airport in Tucson tonight where a one-way ticket awaited her.

She hoisted her bag on her shoulder and turned toward the doorway.

All thoughts screeched to a stop.

Mac stood not four feet away, his shoulders filling the doorframe, his eyes hard in the soft lamplight.

A pulse ticked in his jaw. "Where are you running off to?"

The anger and pain that had been simmering inside her for the last few hours raged up through her core like a volcano. "Where am I running off to?" She threw her duffel on the bed behind her. She needed both hands free to fight. "You're one to talk. You can't even wait until I wake up before scampering back to Tucson."

"I didn't 'scamper' anywhere."

"Oh, bullshit! You raced out of here like your hair was on fire. If you're going to dump me, you could at least tell me to my face rather than sneak off without saying goodbye."

Okay, so that was a bit hypocritical to say in light of her own past relationship termination techniques, which included faking her own death. But now was not the time to get nitpicky.

She took another breath and lashed out some more. "And then you have the nerve to give me back my underwear!"

The perplexed frown on his face didn't stop her.

No way, she'd been steaming too long to cap the vent now.

Her heart pounded through her fingertips. "What kind of guy doesn't even keep a pair of panties as a memento? Didn't you ever see *Sixteen Candles*? You could sell those things on Ebay!"

"Jesus, Claire!" Mac's lips twitched. "Would you just shut up for a moment and listen to—"

"Talk about kicking someone while they're down. Next time why don't you just broadcast over the damned radio that you're rejecting me. Better yet, buy ad space on the front page of the *Yuccaville Yodeler.*"

Mac started laughing, his chest shaking, which made her want to dump all of his expensive toys down the nearest shaft.

She grabbed the only thing she could find—a dirty pair of Gramps's socks—and threw them at him one at a time.

He blocked her missiles and grabbed her by the shoulders. "Claire, listen to me."

She jabbed him one last time in the ribs with her knuckles, finding a little satisfaction from his grunt of pain, before looking up at him. The intensity burning in his eyes made her kneecaps melt. "Don't look at me like that. You're not playing fair."

His gaze grew even more devilish. "I didn't run off to get away from you."

He smelled like sage and sunshine. "How do you always manage to smell so damned good?"

He ignored her question. "I had to go take care of a work emergency that cropped up."

"Oh." The fire left her core and seeped to her cheeks. Well, crud. Wasn't she the foolish one? There was nothing like ranting and raving at a guy about being rejected to show just how desperate she was for him.

"Plus, Steve called while I was home. He got the report back on the bone sample. Based on what he called 'growth plates,' the bone belonged to someone over the age of twenty-five."

Claire nodded. Arnie must have been in his 40s or 50s.

"His ex-girlfriend also measured the level of nitrogen

and the amount of amino acids in the sample. Judging from the results, we're betting the bone was Arnie's, but the only way to be certain would be to find the rest of him. You interested in joining Sheriff Harrison's search party?"

"No way."

"I'd hoped you'd say that." Mac pulled her closer. "Now that I'm back here, I'm not leaving until I convince you to come with me."

How fast could one's heart beat before it exploded? She licked her lips. "Come with you where?" If he meant go with him to get a beer at The Shaft, she was going to knee him in the 'nads. This falling for a guy business was for the birds.

"Home," he said, kissing the bruise on her forehead. "With me." He breathed another kiss onto her cheek bruise. "To Tucson." His teeth nipped her lower lip.

If he didn't kiss her properly soon, her lungs were going to collapse from a lack of air intake. Her toes tingled, ready to jump. But before she took a leap of faith based on his words, she needed to clarify one more thing. She'd sprung to the wrong conclusion too often lately. "You mean for a visit? Like a sleepover?"

"Like an unending sleepover." He grinned, but uncertainty wavered in his voice, his eyes. "Or however many you want."

Her heart swelled, just like the Grinch's on Christmas Day, until it rattled against her rib cage. "You like me that much?"

He pulled her tight against him. "Yeah, can't you tell?"

She nodded, smiling away the jet streams of anxiety streaking through her mind. "I'm kind of stuck on you, too," she said, slipping her hands under his T-shirt.

"Claire," he warned, backing her up until her thighs butted up against the bed, "I want an answer first."

"I'll think about it." She pushed onto her tiptoes and

nibbled on his earlobe. "You might need to work on convincing me a little. This time without the tool belt."

Her T-shirt was over her head and on the floor before she could take another breath. Shit. "How do you do that so damned quick?"

Mac pushed her onto the bed. "You want convincing, I'll give you some." His shirt followed hers.

"As Manny is fond of saying, '*Ay yi yi.*'" She trilled her tongue and wiggled up the bed.

His gaze raked over her from head to toe and back again. "You tempt me, Siren."

Someone pounded on the front door. Mac hesitated, his hand reaching toward her.

"Ignore it." Claire sat up and grabbed his wrist.

The pounding came again, harder this time. "Claire, open the damned door!" Gramps hollered. "I need Mabel's spare keys."

"Go away," she yelled back. "We're busy."

Mac closed his eyes and shook his head. "I'll never hear the end of it now."

There was a long, silent pause from outside. Then, "You got an hour, then I'm coming in, even if I have to pry the damned door open."

"Such a crusty old buzzard," Claire said, unbuttoning Mac's fly. "I don't know what your aunt sees in him."

Mac glanced over his shoulder. "I'm afraid she sees a way out of this mess that doesn't cost me any money."

"What are you talking about?" She paused, her fingers clutching the waist of his jeans.

"The mines."

"What about them?"

"Your grandfather is buying them. Didn't he tell you?"

Claire blinked, repeating Mac's words in her head a couple of times. "You mean Ruby's mines?"

Mac nodded.

"He failed to mention that small detail." Claire covered her face with her hands and flopped back onto the bed. "God! Mom's going to kill me."

"What business is it of hers?"

"None, but she won't listen when I tell her that."

"Maybe it's time for Harley to spell it out for her." Mac straddled Claire and pulled her hands away from her face. "Harley is a big boy. I have a feeling nobody is going to push him around any time soon, not even Ruby—although she may be able to sway his opinion every now and then."

Mac kissed the tip of her nose.

"I wonder if Gramps plans on staying down here."

Mac's mouth moved to her neck. "Ruby seems to think so. He wants her to get the bank off her back so she can fix the things around here that have been broken for too long."

Claire squirmed under Mac's lips. "Grandma would be happy to hear Gramps saved her favorite valley." *And grave.*

She raked her nails down his back.

"Mmmmmmm." He buried his face in her cleavage. "You smell like chocolate." He unclasped her bra.

"I had a Ho-Ho earlier." She shrugged off the flimsy bit of pink fabric. "Some of the frosting dropped down the neck of my shirt."

Mac stared at her chest for several seconds. Then he met her gaze, and her world tipped on its side. "Come live with me in Tucson, Claire. My life sucks without you."

Under the smoke and fire burning in his eyes, something smoldered that warmed her clear through to her split ends. "Well, when you look at me like that, how can I refuse?"

His grin sat crooked on his lips. "I promise to keep the cupboards stocked with Moon Pies."

"Do that and you'll never be able to get me out of the house."

"It's all part of my evil plan."

She pulled him down on top of her. "Shut up and have your wicked way with me."

And he did.

But for only an hour—this time.

Chapter Twenty-Five

(Four Days Later) Sunday, May 2nd

So, are Mac and you going to get married this summer?" Jess asked Claire, blinking those long red lashes innocently.

But Claire hadn't just climbed off the train from Naïveville yesterday. She dropped a dollar in Jess's hand and tore open the pack of Twinkies.

Ruby, who was busy stocking bags of sour cream and onion potato chips on the store shelf, laughed under her breath.

Claire shot her a knock-it-off glare, but Ruby ignored her.

"Who wants to know?" she asked Jess. Ten dollars said Gramps put the girl up to this.

"Nobody. You know us teenagers, we're just full of curiosity." Jess's dimples were showing, her giggle forced.

She was definitely full of shit.

"Well, you tell Mr. Nobody that all bets are off when it comes to that subject, so he should focus on what he's going to tell his daughter when she calls tonight."

"When are you and Mac heading for Tucson?" Ruby asked.

Claire leaned against the counter. "As soon as he's ready."

"You don't want to talk to your mom?"

"I'd prefer to be in Antarctica when the phone rings."

"You think it will be that bad?"

The worry lines on Ruby's brow spurred Claire into a lie. "Nah. She'll just talk loud and interrupt Gramps a lot. If he's smart, he'll hang up and you'll change your phone number."

"I haven't had to deal with adult children before."

"Hey! I'm an adult," Jess said. Claire and Ruby both shot her a *yeah-right* smirk. "Almost! In two years, I'll be legit."

"Lord help us then," Ruby said, a twinkle in her eye when she glanced at her daughter.

"Where's Gramps?" Claire asked around a mouthful of Twinkie. She needed to talk to him about the flight she and Mac were going to make to South Dakota next weekend. Find out what he wanted boxed and shipped sooner rather than later.

"He's in the back fixin' to wash up the breakfast dishes. Manny is yakking his ear off about his hot date last night."

Claire rolled her eyes. For Manny, every date was hot. He made sure of it by wearing his infamous homemade Chili Pepper cologne—it'd burn a hole through anyone's sinuses.

Slipping through the curtain, Claire paused on the kitchen threshold at the sight of Gramps in a blue-checkered apron. A laugh escaped her lips. She needed a camera.

"*Buenos dias, mi amor.*" Manny leered at her as usual. "Mac wanted me to tell you he changed his mind and has left without you."

Claire clutched her heart with soap-opera like drama. "Really?"

"*Sí.* He said you were to come stay with me and take care of me for the rest of my golden years."

"Mac?" She turned to the man sitting opposite Manny, his face buried in the *Arizona Daily Star* newspaper. "Is this true?"

Mac lowered the paper to the table, his gaze traveling over her shorts and Jessica Rabbit tank top very slowly. He shrugged. "A life with Manny would be spicy, to say the least."

Claire grinned.

Mac winked at her, then returned to his paper.

"Did Chester make it out of here alone?" she asked Gramps.

"Nope. He's following Candy home. Says he's going to stay with her for awhile and let her sweeten him up."

"She'll kill him first—he's diabetic."

"Ahhhh, what a way to go," Manny said, sipping his coffee.

There was a loud clunk from the rec room, then a squeal. The air conditioner rattled like a penny in a tin can.

"That's it. I've had it with that piece of shit." Claire marched over to the brown beast and gave it several Fonzy-punches on the side, but the thing just rattled louder.

"Claire," Ruby said from behind her. "Don't worry about it. I'll just go buy a new one in Yuccaville tomorrow."

That would be admitting defeat. Besides, Ruby might not have the bank biting at her heels, but she wasn't exactly floating in riches, either. "No way am I giving up that easy. This is personal now."

Manny came in from the kitchen, Gramps followed with the dishtowel still in his hands.

"Where's my tool belt?" she asked.

"In my bedroom," Mac said, leaning against the kitchen doorway.

Claire's shoulders tightened at Manny's bark of laughter. She could have done without everyone knowing that intimate detail.

Ruby lifted a toolbox from behind the bar and set it on the counter. "Here." She handed Claire a hammer and screwdriver.

Minutes later, the plastic face grate lay in pieces on the floor. It hadn't been very cooperative.

Mac held the flashlight as she reached past the blower wheel for the clamp holding it on. The clamp was loose, easy to wiggle. Her fingers brushed something cold and hard loosely duct-taped next to the clamp. "What's this?"

"What's what?" Mac asked.

"This?" She pulled her hand out and opened her palm to show him what she'd found.

"A skeleton key," Ruby said, picking it up.

"That's what was rattling all this time," Claire said.

"I thought Joe bought this air conditioner new. I have a user manual for it down in his filing—"

"Wait a second!" A light blazed in Claire's head. She plucked the key from Ruby's hands and raced down the basement stairs two at a time. Mac and the rest of them followed.

Joe's office smelled the same as usual—like old paper and cured leather.

Claire hit the lights. She grabbed the antique writing box from the floor and placed the square box on Joe's desk. The group circled her, watching.

The key slipped into the keyhole without a hitch. Claire turned it, heard a clink, and flipped open the top.

The underside of the lid had what looked like a chalkboard on it. Claire lifted the inkwell, pounce pot, and pen from the rectangular tray in back. The flat wood surface that angled down from the inkwell tray was split across the middle. Under it were two secret cubby holes.

She opened the first cubby hole, and nearly choked on her tongue.

Bound stacks of crisp one hundred dollar bills filled the compartment.

"Holy *frijoles!*" Manny whispered.

Claire opened the other cubby hole to reveal more hundred dollar stacks packed sardine-tight.

"Oh, my," Ruby said, her hand on her forehead.

Claire looked up at Mac. He was frowning down at the money, his lips moving. Calculating, she guessed. She turned to Ruby. "Looks like Joe was saving for your future after all."

Gramps scowled.

"If those are really bundles of hundreds like the wrappers say," Mac said, his eyes still on the money, "there's close to a quarter million dollars sitting here."

Ruby plopped down into the leather chair, her face full-moon pale. "Oh, my," she said again, more breathlessly.

Manny let out a long, slow whistle.

A grin surfaced on Claire's lips. She couldn't help it. Finally, Ruby would be able to sleep at night. "You told me Joe used to ramble about having money somewhere, but couldn't remember where he'd put it."

"I did," Ruby fanned herself with her hand. "But I never believed him. I thought it was just a side-effect of the stroke."

Mac shook his head. "Damn. That's a lot of cash."

"Guess you won't be needing me much around here after all," Gramps said, still scowling.

Claire frowned at the old buzzard. Typical man. If a woman didn't *need* him, why would she want him?

"Don't be silly, honey." Ruby smacked Gramps's forearm. "I'd need you even if that there box was full of gold bars."

Gramps grunted, but the scowl faded.

Mac rounded the desk and wrapped his arms around Claire, pulling her back against his chest. "Let's go. They don't need us here anymore."

He towed her towards the door.

"Where are we going?" she asked as he led her up the

stairs.

"Tucson." Dropping his arm around her shoulders, he directed her toward the backdoor. "There's a new four-poster bed there to break in."

She stopped in her tracks just outside the door. The warmth radiating through her had nothing to do with the Arizona sunshine.

"MacDonald Abraham Garner, I'm not an easy woman."

He planted a hard kiss on her lips. "I'm counting on that, slugger."

The End ... for now

Connect with Me Online

Facebook (Personal Page):
http://www.facebook.com/ann.charles.author

Facebook (Author Page):
http://www.facebook.com/pages/Ann-Charles/37302789804?ref=share

Twitter (as Ann W. Charles):
http://twitter.com/AnnWCharles

Ann Charles Website:
http://www.anncharles.com

About Ann Charles

Ann Charles is an award-winning author who writes romantic mysteries that are splashed with humor and whatever else she feels like throwing into the mix. When she is not dabbling in fiction, arm-wrestling with her children, attempting to seduce her husband, or arguing with her sassy cat, she is daydreaming of lounging poolside at a fancy resort with a blended margarita in one hand and a great book in the other.

Five Fun Facts about Ann Charles

I lived in a small town just south of Flagstaff, Arizona for one year, working for Northern Arizona University while attending college there (majoring in Spanish). I loved every minute of living in Arizona and plan to someday return in my own R.V. for several months of the year. I have a LOT more exploring to do.

One of the things on my bucket list is to float around Lake Powell for a week in one of those sweet houseboats— just like how my Fischer Price people used to float around on their cool little houseboat in my dad's pool when I was still wearing floaters and a pair of nose plugs.

When I was a kid, my mom took my siblings and me to a mission on the Navajo Reservation for the summer. Playing tag in the high desert, eating fresh Navajo fry bread, exploring a horse graveyard, trying to climb a greased pole, and screaming and flailing as fire ants bit my legs after I stumbled into their mound are some of my most treasured memories.

One warm summer day, I was invited by a friend of mine from Northern Arizona University to join her and her family on the Hopi Reservation for one of their ceremonies. With the Little Colorado River in the background, I ate hominy and fresh fruit, laughed with her friends and family, and watched in awe as the dancers moved with grace and skill. I will never forget that day—the music, the scenery, the people—and will always appreciate the kindness shown to me, a stranger to most everyone there.

———◆———

I climbed to the top of the San Francisco Peaks (I believe it was Humphreys Peak at 12,633 feet) once with my half-wolf, half-malamute dog. At the top, as we panted while staring down at the world way below, we both agreed that climbing to 12,000 feet was for the birds, and we never hiked that high again.

Sneak Peek!

Want a sneak peek at Ann Charles' second book, *Jackrabbit Junction Jitters**, in the Jackrabbit Junction Mystery series? Read on ...

Jackrabbit Junction Jitters is available now.

JACKRABBIT JUNCTION JITTERS

Chapter One

Jackrabbit Junction, Arizona
Wednesday, August 11th

W hat do you mean we have to hoof it?" Claire Morgan slid out of the passenger side of the old Ford pickup and joined her grandfather. Gramps stood grimacing at a front tire that appeared to have melted under the setting sun. "Can't you just throw on the spare so we can get out of here before the storm hits?"

"There is no spare," Harley Ford grumbled. He reached for the grocery bags in the pickup bed.

Claire fanned her T-shirt and squinted through her sunglasses at the cumulus cloud puffing like a microwaved marshmallow as it raced toward her. Lightning lit the inside of the massive cloud paparazzi-style.

Across the valley, just past the dusty pit-stop of Jackrabbit Junction, a towering vortex of dirt churned devilishly. Gusts of sun-baked air whooshed past her, pelting her cheeks with invisible grains of sand, garnishing the roadside barbed-wire fence with plastic bags and tumbleweeds.

She swiped at the sweat dripping down the side of her face. The August sun and gravy-thick humidity had liquefied her makeup hours ago. She couldn't wait for the storm's cool rain to take the sizzle out of the evening air. "Maybe we should just wait this out. Sit in the cab and watch the storm pass."

Monsoon season in southeastern Arizona offered trial and tribulation in biblical fashion: floods, sandstorms, and lightning. Throw some locusts into the mix, and it would be the plagues of Moses tailgate party.

Gramps passed her one of the grocery bags. "Next you'll want to hold hands and sing campfire songs."

"Is that how you wooed Ruby?" Claire grinned, referring to her soon-to-be step-grandmother. "Serenaded her with Koombyah and Do Your Ears Hang Low until she agreed to marry you?"

Thunder rumbled across the valley, sounding an early warning. A violet curtain of rain draped from the colossal cloud, veiling the mayhem behind it.

"My love life is off limits to you this visit, wiseass. Don't forget it. Now quit wasting time whining and grab your stuff. It's not even a mile to the R.V. park. Besides, I have something to tell you, and I'd rather not be within arm's-length when you hear it." He raced toward the Dancing Winnebagos R.V. Park as fast as a seventy-year-old with a trick-hip could giddy-up.

Claire frowned after the ornery goat. The last time he'd spread some joy with one of his announcements, she'd needed a six-pack of Dos Equis and a box of MoonPies to find her happy place. This called for an emergency fix. She leaned into the cab and popped open the glove box. Scrounging through the nest of ink pens and fast-food napkins, she grunted in satisfaction when her fingers touched the pack of menthols she'd stashed.

Her flip-flops slapped the asphalt as she followed him, the back of his green shirt patchy with sweat by the time she caught up. "All right, Gramps. Let me have it."

His forehead wrinkled in a disapproving scowl at the lit cigarette dangling from her lips. "I thought you'd quit."

"I did." But that was before her love life had taken a Tasmanian-Devil-inspired spiral. "This is just a figment of your imagination, so stop stalling and spill."

"Remember I told you somebody broke into Ruby's

place through the office window last month?"

"What?" She stopped in the middle of the road, momentarily forgetting about the thunder, the wind, and the sore spot between her toes where her plastic thongs rubbed.

Ruby's office was practically a museum, full of expensive antiques collected not-so-legally by her first husband, Joe, who'd overdosed on potato chips, Marlboro cigarettes, and stress years ago and had been taking a dirt nap ever since. To Claire's knowledge, only three people had any inkling of the treasures hidden in Ruby's basement, and two of them were about to be drenched with Mother Nature's dirty bathwater.

"I remember you mailed me a new key, no explanation included." She couldn't believe he was just now telling her this.

Gramps glanced over his shoulder. "You'd better move your ass before a bolt of lightning zaps it."

She jogged up next to him. The wind whistled around them. "What got stolen?" She would've grabbed the first edition copy of Moby Dick. No, Treasure Island.

"Nothing."

That made no sense. "Anything get destroyed?"

"Nope."

"Then why did they break in?"

"We've been wondering that ever since it happened."

She took a drag from her cigarette, savoring the slight cough-drop taste before blowing smoke into the wind. "What makes you so certain it was a break in?"

"Crowbar dents in the window sill and a busted lock."

"Did you call Deputy Sheriff Droopy?"

"Yep. Ruby insisted since Jess lives there too."

On the threshold of her sixteenth birthday, Ruby's daughter, Jess, was at that know-it-all, boy-crazy age that

caused her mother to swing between loving her
unconditionally and wanting to duct-tape her mouth shut
and send her to a convent.

"But since nothing's missing," Gramps continued, "the
deputy's hands are tied."

"His hands aren't tied. They're super-glued to a
cheeseburger."

"Don't start again, Claire."

She had trouble biting her tongue when it came to the
sheriff's pathetic choice for a second in command. "You
think the burglar was after the money?" A few months ago,
Claire had found a wad of cash in Ruby's office, stuffed in
an antique desk—a goodbye gift from Joe.

"Ruby doesn't, but I do. Jess doesn't keep secrets
well."

The National Enquirer kept secrets better than Jess.
Ruby needed to deposit the cash somewhere safe, but her
hatred of banks and bank vice-presidents, especially
Yuccaville's one and only, rivaled Willy Nelson's sentiment
about the IRS.

Lightning flashed to their left. A resounding crack of
sky-splitting thunder followed much too quickly. Claire
winced and flipped-flopped faster. The smell of rain and
wet earth hung heavy in the air.

"So, what's Plan A? Track down the burglar? There has
to be some clue left." Something someone experienced at
sleuthing, like Claire herself, could find.

Gramps groaned. "That's why I didn't want to tell
you."

"Did Droopy check for fingerprints?"

"I knew you'd go off half-cocked—"

"All you need is one hair for a DNA test."

"—and end up getting into trouble, as usual."

"I've been suspicious for months about that guy with

the mullet and Care Bear tattoo who works thirds at Biddy's Gas and Carryout."

"But Ruby wanted you to know—"

"You should have told me before the trail cooled."

"—since you and Mac are going to be running the R.V. park while we're on our honeymoon. When is Mac getting here, anyway?"

Thunder boomed again, a closer teeth-rattling forewarning. Claire leaned into the wind, protecting her cigarette with her body as she took another drag. Now was not the time to mention that her relationship with Mac, Ruby's nephew, was on the rocks—well, more like on the pebbles, but there were some definite rocks ahead. Maybe even boulders.

"Friday night." Mac had been working four-tens at his engineering firm, Tuesday through Friday, for the last month.

"We've set you two up in my Winnebago."

"What's wrong with the spare bedroom?"

"It's occupied." Gramps's face looked pinched, like he was sucking on an unripe grapefruit.

"Ruby has family coming for the wedding?"

"No."

Was it Claire's imagination or was Gramps walking even faster. "Then who's staying in the spare room?" Gramps and Ruby had been sharing a bed since day one, so unless they decided to spend a little time apart before the big day, the spare should be available.

"That's the thing I needed to tell you about."

"I thought the break-in was the bad news."

Gramps shook his head. "Katie is coming for a few weeks."

Claire chuckled. "Come on, Gramps. Kate isn't that bad."

As far as younger sisters went, Kate was the typical spoiled favorite who never seemed to do anything wrong and whose ability to lie made used car salesmen drool.

Lightning cracked and sizzled.

"I agree. Katie is an angel."

He would say that. Kate was taller, thinner, smarter, and never mouthed off to Gramps.

"But she's not coming alone." Gramps was practically running now. "She's bringing your mother."

"What?!" Claire skidded to a stop on the asphalt. The cigarette slipped from her fingers.

Thunder crashed and the sky fell.